TO: CRYSSTAL

FR: Chiss

Rm w/a Vu

a novel by

A.D. RYAN

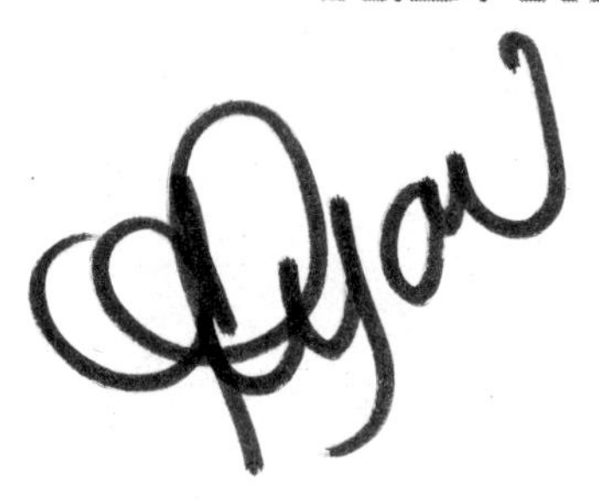

Ryan, A.D.
Rm w/a Vu / A.D. Ryan

ISBN 978-1523496914

Text and Cover design by Angela Schmuhl
Cover Image: Shutterstock, © Stokkete
Back Cover Image: istock, © mocker_bat

CONTENTS

Acknowledgements

Here we are again. Book six. Can you even believe it? I can't. These last two years have been quite a journey, and there are so many people to thank.

First, to my incredible husband and my amazing littles. You guys inspire me each and every day. The support I feel from all of you is immeasurable and will forever be appreciated. You all deal with my special brand of crazy, even joining in whenever a new book is finished and arrives in the mail. I couldn't ask for a better family. Thank you for being awesome humans.

My parents and siblings, who are always asking questions about what I'm working on—this often leads to awkward pauses between my parents and me as I find a way to skirt the naughty storylines. I appreciate all you guys do from silent support, to sharing my work with others, and even the brutal honesty.

Speaking of that honesty; Marny, you've inspired me since the early days of my writing "career." You were always straight with me on when my story direction sucked, and I've always valued that. I love you, and I miss hanging out with you. We really need to stop having lives so we can, like, do nothing with our chother, mkay?

Tiff and Lynda, who saw this story before anyone else, you've given me so much guidance over the years, and while life has gotten in the way of us talking as often as we used to, your help has been invaluable. This was the story that brought us together, and I'm so grateful that you've both stayed with me all this time.

My pre-readers and street team; you guys ate this story up and had such lovely things to say. I can't lie and say I never doubt my writing, and this book is so quirky and goofy that there were a lot of doubts along the way. It was your constant support that kept me from working on something else entirely.

And finally, to the ones who've been anxiously awaiting the phoenix that has been born from the ashes: my fandom friends. I hope you love the changes this story has gone through since I first wrote it several years ago.

Thank you all for standing by me and supporting this crazy dream I had.

chapter 1

U*gh*. My neck is positively aching, and I let my heavy, book-filled backpack fall from my shoulder to relieve it as I prepare to exit my last class of the day. Why I chose to take on such an intense course-load is beyond me—I guess my anxiousness to finish college and start my career as soon as possible could have factored in at some point.

Regardless of my reasoning, it's what I chose, and I am suffering the repercussions now in my sophomore year at Arizona State.

As I stumble down the last few steps, my English prof, Professor Drayke, calls me over to his desk and hands me my latest paper. I groan when I see the giant red "B–" that's written at the top of the page as well as all the little notes and comments. Considering I want to get a job in publishing, I can't exactly afford my grades to keep declining the way they have been. I already know I'm going to have to study my ass off for midterms coming up right away, which is going to piss Ben off since I'll be locking myself away more than I already have been.

"Not your best work, Miss Foster," Drayke tells me, pushing his thick-rimmed glasses up his nose. He's looking at me, his dark eyes boring into me, waiting for some kind of explanation.

I refrain from rolling my eyes at him, nodding solemnly instead. "I know."

"What happened?"

It's clear that he doesn't really care, but I decide to answer him anyway. "I guess I'm just feeling overwhelmed by my courses this semester. I'll work harder, I promise."

Drayke acknowledges me with a nod, a few strands of his greying hair flopping over his forehead, and then waves me away dismissively.

Shoving the paper into my bag and throwing it over my other shoulder, I think about what I'm going to tell Ben. He isn't going to be happy that I'm cancelling our movie date tonight—especially since it will be our first one in weeks, and I took the night off from my job at the coffee house so we could spend some time together.

His patience with my additional studying is starting to wear thin, and it'll only be a matter of time before we have a huge fight about it. On the plus side, this also means I won't have to put out. It's not that I hate sex; I just don't get what the big deal is. It isn't all fireworks and revelations like the movies lead you to believe. I often wonder why we're even together. I really should just end things. Set him free to do whatever he wants. Maybe after finals, when I have time to actually sit down with him.

After the inevitable fight, Ben will come crawling back—he always does—and he'll have with him flowers or a gift of some sort. Instead of just acknowledging the argument, Ben always throws money at the problem in hopes it'll go away, but it really only insults me. Then we wind up in bed together. That sex isn't usually so bad. He's usually a little more tender and giving. Not always, but on occasion.

As I make my way, I pull my cell phone out of my pocket and dial Ben's number. There's no answer, leading me to believe he's probably on his way over and I'll have to cancel our date face-to-face. With a sigh, I enter the building that my room is in and trudge down the hall. The closer I get, the more clearly I make out what sounds like breathless moans coming from this year's roomie, Delilah, inside. This isn't new; Delilah has a reputation, and apparently she feels the need to uphold it.

A flare of annoyance rises in me because I can't just walk into the room. Well, I suppose I could, but walking in on someone having sex isn't something I particularly enjoy doing. I'm pretty sure I still suffer from a mild case of Post Traumatic Stress Disorder after seeing my mom and dad on the kitchen counter the last time I dropped by the house to say hi.

You can bet your ass I called from that point on.

Dropping my book bag to the floor with a heavy thud, I lean against the wall. I slide down until I'm sitting on the hard tile with my elbows on my knees and my hands in my hair. Other students walk by, going to and from their rooms and the washrooms, and every time one of them looks down at me, I feel like an animal on display at the zoo. They probably think I've locked myself out. Of course, if they know my roommate—which most of the male population does—they know what's really going on.

The sounds coming from behind the thin door are escalating. People are staring, not just at me now, but at the door too. I blush, offering each and every one of them a shrug, only to be met with sympathetic eyes. If I could afford private housing, I would be there in a second.

"Oh, yes!" I clench my eyes shut, hearing Delilah's mounting cries. *"Fuck me harder! Oh, you like it dirty, big boy?"*

Good grief. I know Delilah is a little freaky, but I didn't think she was into reenacting bad porn.

As if hearing her cry out in the throes of whatever-the-hell it is she's doing isn't enough, I'm now being subjected to the low, guttural grunts of her male partner. I bury my face in my hands, gripping my hair at the roots and tapping my foot against the crappy tile rapidly, trying to think of more pleasant things than what's really going on in there.

"Oh…oh…OOOOOOOH!"

Aaaaaaaand, she's done. Lifting my face from my knees, I smooth down the front of my hair because I know it's probably standing up from the rough tugging. This won't be the last time something like this will happen, and I know I should look into moving rooms. I wait a few minutes, really enjoying the silence coming from our room as I assume they're getting dressed. I'm confident in this assumption because Delilah seems about as cuddly as a porcupine.

Finally, Delilah's laugh is heard from behind the door, and it sounds like she's getting ready to kick her latest tryst out. *"That was great. I don't know why we don't do this more often."*

Not wanting her to think that I've been out here eavesdropping like some kind of pervert, I stand up and try to make it look like I've just got impeccable timing. I grab the shoulder strap to my book bag, lifting it at the exact moment that the door swings open. What I see on the other side stuns me. Or should I say *whom*...?

chapter 2

"B—Ben?" I blink because I must be seeing things, but when I open my eyes again…and then again, I'm staring directly into the faces of my *bitch* of a roommate and my lying, sack of shit boyfriend. "What the hell?"

"Hey, Jules," he says, smiling suddenly. His eyes still show just how shocked he is to find me here. Outside *my* room. "I came by to see you. Delilah and I got to talking."

"I was in class. You knew that." I don't think I've blinked again, and my eyes are drying out.

Ben scratches the back of his neck, dropping his gaze from me. "Oh, yeah. Well, I thought you'd be do—"

"What the hell?" I shout, cutting him off before he can feed me some lame-ass excuse.

"Uh…uh," he stammers, looking back at Delilah and then me again.

Annoyance and notes of anger course through my veins. I'm actually surprised I'm not angrier about uncovering his unfaithfulness, actually. Weird. I let my bag fall from my shoulder, catching the strap in my hand and swinging it at him. It connects with his shoulder even though he tries to shield himself from it. "You lying, cheating sack of *shit*!" I look at Delilah and point, my eyes narrowing and my nose scrunching up as my lips curl up into a snarl. "And you. You fucking bitch."

"Juliette," she says, holding her hands up because I'm sure she thinks I'm going to assault her with my heavy book bag next. The thought never crosses my mind, though. Strangling her? Well, that's another story… "It's not what you think."

I laugh dryly, just once. "Oh, it's not? Well, I feel pretty damn foolish, then," I say, stepping into the room and flinging my bag on my bed. Ben seems almost relieved, like Delilah's really been able to convince me that damn quickly. I'm sure to nip that shit in the bud immediately.

Crossing my arms, I turn to them and sneer. "So," I say, "you like it dirty…*big boy*?" I can see Ben swallow thickly. "Yeah. *That's* what I thought. And to think I was going to offer to…" I can't even finish the sentence without my stomach rolling.

"Juliette…" His tone is soft, like he's trying to appeal to some part of me that's sympathetic. Won't he be surprised to find that no such part exists.

Shaking my head, I walk to my dresser to grab a few things. "Save it. Honestly, I don't even care that the two of you are…whatever you are. You made this really easy on me. You two are perfect for each other. I'm out of here. Delilah, the room's yours. Have a nice fucking life." The double entendre isn't intended, but it's more than fitting. "I'll be back for the rest of my stuff as soon as I've made other arrangements. Touch any of it, and you'll wish you hadn't. You've already taken something of mine; I'd say I've been more than generous."

I throw my bag back over my shoulder and stalk toward the still-open door. People are no longer walking by; they're standing in the doorway, blocking my escape. I'm still receiving sympathetic stares, but I don't want their sympathy; I just want to get the hell out before I break down. Though, if I'm being honest, I'm too angry to cry; I don't even feel the sting of tears in my eyes.

Pushing my way past the gawkers in the dorm hall, I proceed to our R.A.'s room. I really hope she can move me into another room as soon as possible. It's the middle of the semester, and I know it'll be tough, but I'm not above hoping for a miracle.

My knuckles barely touch the wooden door before it's yanked open. It's almost as if she was expecting me. "Juliette, what can I do for you?" Daphne asks with a smile that brightens her green eyes.

"Daph, you have to help me out. I need to move out of my dorm. Please tell me you've got another room or bed available somewhere." I flop down on her bed and let my heavy bag fall to the floor with a heavy thud.

Daphne leans against her desk, pulling her shoulder-length strawberry blonde hair into a ponytail. She looks at me, but she doesn't speak for a minute. She's trying to figure out what's happened. Yes, she's my R.A., but Daphne Robicheaux is also one of my closest friends. We met last year and started hanging out whenever we weren't busy with our studies.

"Is Delilah's revolving door of men still active?" she asks carefully.

I laugh, turning my head to her. "Something like that." Daphne's eyebrows rise, waiting for me to continue. "Her latest customer was Ben. *My* Ben." Her eyebrows stay up, but her mouth falls open. "Yeah. That was my reaction too."

A loud, repetitive knock on Daphne's door fills the room. She shakes her head and pushes off the desk to answer it. It shouldn't surprise me to hear Ben's voice, and I refuse to get up to go talk to him when he *commands* Daphne to send me out.

"She doesn't want to talk to you, Connely," Daphne tells him fiercely. I can almost visualize her feral stare as she looks two feet up into his eyes, and it makes me smile.

"Don't start with me. I want to talk to her now." He sounds angry, which is laughable.

I push myself off the bed, walk to the door, and touch Daphne's shoulder. Slowly, she turns and looks at me. "I'm going to go and stay with my parents. You'll call me if something opens up?" While I know that Daphne would gladly let me crash in her dorm for a few days, I don't want to run the risk of another run-in with Ben or Delilah. What better way to avoid that than to stay with my over-protective father?

"Juliette..." I ignore Ben as I squeeze through the very narrow space he's left between him and the doorframe.

People are still staring, and it doesn't help that Ben is following me through the dorm and out to my car, yelling my name the entire time. There's a part of me that wants to turn around and tell him to screw off, but I know it will only open the lines of communication. And talking to him isn't something I ever want to do again.

"God damn it, Juliette!"

I stop dead in my tracks, right next to my car, and turn on my heel to glare at him. "Don't you *dare* talk to me like that, Ben. I didn't do anything wrong. You'd do well to remember that."

"You were never around!" he shouts, waving his arms in the air like a maniac. Our audience has followed us outside and is now watching our little soap opera play out. "You were always off doing something, and were so pre-occupied whenever we were together."

My eyes widen, and I stare at him dumbly before I find my words. "So this is my fault? No. I don't think so." Shaking my head almost violently, I turn and unlock my old, green Civic before throwing my bag in. Instead of staying on the white leather seat, it falls to the floor after hitting the passenger side door. "And for your information, it's not like I was off doing some*one*. I was studying. We are in college, you know. It's what we do."

Ben doesn't seem to think he was wrong. At all. "Yeah, well, I have needs, Juliette."

"Yup, I know." I nod, pressing my lips together. "And it's no longer up to me to meet them. Don't come by my parents' house either. My dad doesn't take too kindly to people who cheat on his daughter."

I hop into my car and start it up. My heart is pounding so hard I can feel the blood pulsing through my veins, can hear it in my ears. I sit there for a minute, trying to stop the shaking in my hands before I put the vehicle into drive. Driving all the way to my parents' place isn't something I want to do, as it's a longer commute than I would like, but I really have no other options at this point.

Once I feel a little more in control, I put the car in gear and am just pulling away when a very large hand flattens against my window with a *BANG!* "JULIETTE!" I pretend not to hear him, pretend not to see him, and I press my foot down on the accelerator, my tires squealing against the hot pavement.

As soon as I'm out of the parking lot, I grab my phone from my pocket and dial my mom. I'm really hoping they won't mind me intruding for a while until Daphne can find me a new dorm room.

There's no answer, so I decide to try my luck. Mom's probably at the bakery doing payroll or something, so I probably have a couple of hours of quiet before I'll have to explain anything to her. I toss my phone on the seat next to me. It starts ringing, and one glance shows me that it's Ben. It shocks me that he's still trying to get me to understand his motivation for banging my roommate. Resisting the urge to toss it out the window, I pick the phone up and turn it off completely because I know now that he's not going to stop. He's always been a persistent bastard.

As I navigate the streets of Phoenix, I think about how we even got to this point. A year ago, I had been a freshman at the West campus of ASU. I hadn't known many people because most of my friends decided to go to various colleges around the country—some even in England. I stayed close to home mainly because I loved Phoenix.

It was on my first day that my roommate, Tanis, introduced me to her older brother Ben. He was charming and always cooking up excuses to stop by our room to "check on his baby sister." Of course, I would later find out that he knew she was in class, and it was just his excuse to come talk to me.

I hadn't dated anyone before—not really. There was a boy in high school that was nice to me. We went out on a couple of movie dates with friends and held hands. But it was never really serious. We never even got to second. I found out after graduation that he was gay.

Talk about a blow to one's ego; I questioned my femininity for a while after that.

When Ben and I started dating, it was obvious that he wanted a more physical relationship, but I wasn't really interested in sex at first. My mom had me straight out of high school, and that wasn't a life I would have chosen for myself. So I waited.

I placated Ben for a while, nervous to go further than I

was ready for. I'd let him feel me up, get his hand in my pants, and eventually, when I thought I was ready, we had sex. It was all right. Like I said before, there weren't stars or fireworks that went off like I was led to believe there would be, and, honestly? I thought it was supposed to last longer. Of course, I really had nothing to base it on; Ben seemed to enjoy himself, so I figured maybe it was just me.

We had fun in the beginning; he'd take me to all the parties, introduce me to all of his friends, and then we'd go back to his dorm and fool around. My freshman year was my party year, but when my sophomore year came around the corner, I knew I had to buckle down. So, I increased my courseload, and Ben seemed really supportive. He didn't stop his partying ways, but he supported me and led me to believe that it was okay that I was focusing more on my studies than him.

Well, now I know it's because Delilah was busy diddling him.

Releasing a deep sigh, I round the corner onto my parents' street and park my car along the curb. Dad's cruiser is in the driveway next to mom's SUV, and I look at the clock on my newly installed CD player to see that it's nearly dinnertime. I don't relish telling my mom what happened, and I look even less forward to Dad hearing about it too. But I know it's going to happen, so I take a deep breath, grab my phone and backpack, and climb out of my vehicle.

I fiddle with my keys as I ascend the steps of the front porch, trying to locate the key to the house. When I find it, I slide it into the deadbolt and turn it, pushing the door open and stepping over the threshold.

"Oh, Cam. That's it. Oh yeah...right there."

"OHMYGOD!" I scream, completely horrified at having walked in on them...*again.* My timing really is horrible. I'm starting to wonder if I should wear a bell or announce my presence to the world. I'll bet my dad even has a bullhorn I can borrow for such things.

Through my periphery, I can barely see my mother fall off the couch—where I unfortunately assume my father is laying—and I slap my hand up to act as a blinder between them and me.

"What the hell is wrong with the two of you?! Jesus!" Naturally, I don't wait around for an answer before I bolt up the stairs and slam my bedroom door.

Nothing in my room has changed since the day I moved out—just as my parents promised. My twin bed remains dressed in deep blue linens; my desk sits near the window, empty because I took my laptop with me to school; and my dresser is in the corner, topped with a mirror and various candles. I don't give myself the opportunity to soak up the familiarity of the room before I flop down on my bed and pull my pillow over my head. There's a brief moment of time where I wonder if I can asphyxiate myself until I pass out. Maybe the lack of oxygen to my brain will trigger amnesia.

There's a light knock on my door, and I recognize it instantly as my mother's.

"Go away!" I cry into the pillow. I'm sure she doesn't hear me, because the door creaks as she opens it and my bed dips at my knees beneath her weight.

"I didn't realize you were coming home," she says as if it's an excuse to act like a teenager. "Your father came home for—"

I yank my pillow away from my face and gawk at her. "Oh, I know what he came home for."

Mom shakes her head with a sly smirk, her dark hair flowing freely around her face. "*Dinner*. Your father came home for dinner. He's working the graveyard tonight."

"And you decided that dessert should come first." The minute the sentence leaves my mouth, a queasy feeling rolls through my stomach, and I bring the pillow back up to my face, pressing harder than before.

Before I can successfully suffocate myself, the pillow is torn from my grasp, and my mother stares deep into my eyes. "What's going on?"

It's hard not to spill my guts to her because she's just so damn easy to talk to. So I sit up, cross my legs like a pretzel in front of me, and begin to tell her what happened with Ben. She pushes my long brown hair behind my shoulders as I speak, and I'm shocked when she doesn't seem too surprised. I really thought she'd liked him when I had introduced them. Apparently, I was wrong.

"He's an idiot. I always knew you could do better." This is just one of the many things she tells me. Oddly, it comforts me.

"Honestly, I haven't even cried. Is that weird? I mean, I thought when someone you loved did something like that, you cried..."

Mom laughs heartily, placing her hand on my knee. "Oh, honey. I'd be willing to bet you never really loved that boy. Trust me, when you fall in love, you'll know it." I'm confused, so all I do is stare as she gets this wistful look in her blue eyes. "He will be your entire world. Just being away from him will feel like the end of your world, and when you're reunited, you'll feel a sense of total completion."

"Sounds a little *Jerry Maguire* to me," I mumble.

With a one-shouldered shrug, she stands from the bed. "Maybe. But you'll understand one of these days."

I am quick to disagree as she pulls me to my feet and from my room for dinner. "Nope. I'm giving up on relationships. I'm going to focus on school and my career. I don't need a man."

"Oh, sweetie." She wraps her arm around me securely as we descend the stairs. "You can't control these things from happening. You'll see."

I find it hard to believe that I'll ever be able to trust any man again, but I force a smile to my face to placate her. She's always been a bit of a romantic soul, and I hate to take that away from her just because it decided to skip a generation.

So, instead of arguing, I smile and rest my head against her shoulder. We enter the kitchen to find my father at the table, his red face buried in the paper—as it should be. "Whatever you say, Mom."

chapter 3

Hearing my mother giggle across the hall as my father does…whatever the hell he does, is starting to drive me crazy. I've been here almost two weeks. Not only is the drive to school more than I want to deal with, hearing them night after night after night…well, it's not something one should ever have to go through. Is this some sort of mid-life crisis? It's not like they're even that old…

Neither of them seemed put-out with me staying here; in fact, they both seemed to enjoy catching up with me. However, when Mom told Dad *why* I was staying, well, it took a lot for us to convince him that the jail time wouldn't be worth it. His face turned an even deeper shade of red as his rage suppressed his earlier embarrassment from having been caught on the couch with my mother. He even tried telling us that, as a cop, he was certain he'd be able to hide his involvement. While I admit the offer was morbidly considerate, it was wrong, so Mom and I talked him off the ledge.

When he finally calmed down, he assured me that I was welcome to stay as long as I needed. He even told me that the house just hadn't been the same since I'd gone. I had to bite my tongue so as not to point out the more obvious changes, not really feeling the need to embarrass him further—or remember the sounds and brief glimpse I caught myself.

"Cam, stop it!" my mother squeals, and then I hear the deep tenor of my father saying something in return. His voice is muffled, which can only mean one of a few things I really don't want to wrap my head around for fear of needing industrial-strength brain bleach. Honestly, I'm glad I can't make out what he's saying, because I know I'll run to my desk and drive sharp pencils into my ears. I might even attempt to lobotomize myself; I'm sure there's a Google or Wiki article about "Do-It-Yourself Lobotomies" out there somewhere. Though I can't imagine they're entirely safe.

She giggles again, and having heard more than enough for the day, I throw on my work uniform—a pleated black skirt and a green polo shirt—grab my bag, and hit the stairs before I hear things I can't *un*hear. I'm moving so fast that I think I might have even jumped from the top step and landed safely on the main floor.

I'm just opening the door when I hear the creak of my parents' door at the top of the staircase. "Juliette?" my mother calls down. "Are you going somewhere? I was going to make breakfast."

Oh, right. I forgot to mention that it's nine o'clock in the morning. They like to get an early start on their day.

"I'm heading into work," I reply, yanking the door open. "I wanted to get a little studying in before my shift, and the cafe is typically pretty quiet this early."

Her footsteps are heard as she heads for the stairs. "Are you sure? I was going to make waffles." She descends the steps barefoot and dressed in her bathrobe, her cheeks lightly flushed, and her lips plump and red.

I clear my throat, trying not to think of why she looks this way. "Yeah," I tell her as she sits on the bottom step and looks up at me. I know she can read the look on my face; the way my nose is scrunched up because of what I heard is a dead giveaway. "As tempting as it is, I think it's best I go…study."

"Juliette…" I know that tone. She's about to tell me she and Dad are adults—like me—and that adults have sex. I'm no stranger to this talk.

I have to interrupt her before she says the words *"your father and I"* in the same sentence as *"have sex."* "Save me some of those waffles, though. I'll throw them in the toaster for breakfast tomorrow. Thanks!" And I'm out the door.

The drive to the cafe I work at could be faster, but my

poor car is on its last leg. With school and my low pay, I am unable to rectify that, though. The more distance I put between me and the house, the more able I am to focus on anything but the awkwardness I've been enduring the last few days.

One would think that they could control themselves with their daughter around. They're animals, though. Plain and simple. At least they're keeping it in the bedroom while I'm staying there; I do have that to be thankful for.

"Hey, Juliette!" Katie greets excitedly as I enter the cafe. She's busy wiping down the counter as I toss my bag onto an empty chair and make my way to her. "I thought you weren't supposed to work until later?"

Katie and I went to high school together. We weren't best friends by any means, but we hung out on occasion. She was a sweet girl and fun to work with. She chose to go to Paradise Valley Community College here in Phoenix and still lives with her mom, so unfortunately she isn't an option to bunk with. I would gladly room with her if I could.

"I had to get out of that house," I confess, popping behind the counter to pour myself a coffee and grab a muffin.

Katie looks at me with empathy because she's been listening to me gripe about my parents' lapin-esque activities. "Still no news on a new dorm, huh?" Thankfully, she's not one to talk about my reason for escaping my parents almost daily.

I shake my head. "Nah. Daphne tells me that because it's so late in the year, the chance of something opening up is unlikely. And people in private dorms aren't usually looking to take on a dorm mate."

I'm putting cream and sugar into my coffee when Katie turns to me, leaning her hip against the low counter that our espresso machine is on. "Ben stopped by last night."

"I hope you spit in whatever froufrou drink he ordered."

"Thought about it," Katie tells me with an impish smirk. "Instead, I told him you were out on a date."

I sputter on the sip of coffee I've just taken, coughing as the piping hot beverage burns my trachea. "You did what?"

Katie looks pretty damn proud of herself. "He looked

pretty pissed too. He kept asking who it was and where you'd gone."

Wiping at my chin with a napkin, I ask, "And what did you say?"

"That it was just some guy you met. That pissed him off even more." I didn't think her smile could get any wider, but it does.

"While I'm not sure angering him is a wise decision," I say, "I have to admit, the idea of him being jealous is quite appealing."

The chimes above the door ring, and I turn quickly, thinking that maybe Ben has decided to stop by again. I'm happy to see it's not him, just a group of students coming in early on a Saturday morning for coffee and breakfast. Picking up my own muffin and coffee mug, I leave Katie to her work while I go to the table I've claimed and pull out my laptop to start that paper I told Mom I needed to do.

As always, I become so immersed in my schoolwork that nothing else seems to register. Katie is awesome about making sure I'm not interrupted and keeps my coffee cup full. She brings me a ham sandwich, even though I haven't asked for it, because she knows I'll need to eat before I start my shift.

I acknowledge her with a smile before pulling the plate toward me. "Thanks." I take a bite and then notice the folded paper under her arm. I chew slower as I stare at the mangled paper, and I suddenly realize that my parents' place *isn't* a last resort. "Hey, you mind if I take that?"

Katie looks down at it and shrugs. "Knock yourself out. Mind if I ask why?"

I set my sandwich back down and brush the crumbs from my fingertips before taking the outstretched paper and opening it to the last page. "Because I'm going to find a place where people aren't having sex all the time."

"The classifieds?" Katie seems a little apprehensive about my plan. She wouldn't be if she had to live with what I currently am.

Wishing me luck, Katie heads back to work, and I peruse the multiple ads. I don't get to look them over very long, just long enough to circle the first three that catch my eye, before I note the time and pack everything up into my bag so I can start my shift. As soon as I clock in, Katie takes her break, leaving me with three customers in line.

The routine is the same, save for the order the drinks come in, and in the first hour I've probably made five frappuccinos, ten espressos (three of which were doubles), six cappuccinos, and twelve lattes. All different flavors, so that keeps me on my toes.

Katie comes back from her break as soon as the crowd thins, because that's how it always happens, so we spend the next little bit cleaning up the back counter and stocking everything we'll need for the dinner rush. As we do, Katie starts talking about her boyfriend and how they are planning to take a trip to Jamaica as soon as school lets out.

Hearing her talk about her rock solid relationship only serves to remind me of my failed one. I'm happy for her, sure, but it does little to offer me any solace. While I'm in no way ready to date, just knowing that it is possible to be in a happy, *committed* relationship kind of bums me out. I mean, even my parents are in that mid-life, 24/7, I-can't-keep-my-hands-off-you stage. How depressing is *that*? I'm in college. Shouldn't I be going to parties and hooking up with guys at random?

Katie leaves at four, having finished her shift, and the closing server, Mel, comes in to take her place since I'm off in just two hours myself. Mel tells me she can hold down the fort if I want to take a break, so I grab a muffin and a bottle of water before grabbing my paper and a pen. Sitting at one of the tables by the window, I draw my knee to my chest, my foot flat on the seat of the chair, and I chew on the cap of the red pen while I scan the advertisements.

There's one that sounds promising…right up until the douchebag mentions that *"hot chicks welcome to inquire."* I immediately cross it off; there's no way in hell I'll even entertain the idea. There's another one, but this time the woman is all business and isn't *"looking for a BFF."* While I'm not either, I am completely turned off by what comes across as PBS: Potential Bitch Syndrome. Seriously, where did people learn to write ads these days?

Another one catches my eye, and I circle it before moving on. There are less than a handful of decent ads in the paper, and it's a little disheartening. It doesn't bode well for my odds. Then I realize that I don't have to limit myself to the paper; Craigslist, while a little scary, is usually swimming in ads seeking a roommate.

By the end of my break, I've found well over ten between the paper and Craigslist. I feel like it's a pretty decent start to getting out of my parents' house.

The rest of my shift is a breeze, and I clock out ten minutes after my shift was supposed to end, having helped Mel with the last few customers before leaving her and Rick for the night.

"Night, guys!" I call after me as I push the door open and walk out into the dry, desert air.

"Good luck on your apartment hunt," Mel says with a wave.

It's pretty warm outside for late fall, and I can already feel the heat permeate my clothes and skin. Once I'm inside my car, I roll both of the windows down so I don't melt. Knowing that my dad's shift at the department starts in a half hour, I drive slowly; I really don't want to chance walking in on anything else. I still plan to call, because I've definitely learned my lesson.

When I'm a block away, I call the house. With a laugh, my mom assures me that Dad has left, and she deems it safe for me to come in without knocking. I put the car in park and grab my things before trudging up the driveway and through the front door.

"Hey, Mom! I'm home," I announce before hiking up the stairs and putting my bag in my room. I toss the paper and my laptop onto the bed and am just slipping out of my coffee-stained work shirt and into a light tank and jeans when my mom comes in and flops down on my bed.

"How was work?"

"Good."

"Did you get your paper done?" she asks, lying on her side as I affix my loose ponytail into a bun to keep the hair off my neck before it sticks, and I turn my fan on the highest setting.

I shake my head. "Nah. I got a good start on it, though, so I should be able to finish it in plenty of time."

"That's good." Behind me, I hear the crinkle of paper and

turn around to see her picking up my ads. "What's this?"

Scrunching my nose, I cross my arms in front of me. "I was looking through the classifieds for a place. Daphne can't get me into a new dorm room so late in the year, so I figured I would look into renting a place."

"Sweetheart, you're more than welcome to stay here for as long as you need."

I don't want to hurt her feelings, but I have to be honest with her; she knows when I'm not. "Mom, you and Dad are clearly enjoying having the house to yourselves. I really don't want to intrude on that...and not just because it's absolutely horrifying." She gives me the "Mom-look," and I roll my eyes in response. "Let me put it in a way that you can understand: could you go back to living with Grandma and Grandpa if—"

Mom's hands quickly fly up to cover her ears, and she clenches her eyes shut. "Okay! I get your point!"

Satisfied, I smile. "Then I rest my case. Come on, I'll make us some dinner." I take one of her hands and pull her to her feet. She snatches the paper up and brings it with her.

While I cook dinner for the two of us, Mom sits at the table and looks at all the ads I've circled and laughs at the ones I've eliminated. "You know, this one guy might not be so bad."

I shoot a glance at her with an arched brow. "You mean the hot chicks guy?" Mom nods. "Mmm, no thanks. I've had my fill of self-righteous assholes to last me a lifetime."

Bypassing the fact that I just swore—something I don't do much of at all, let alone in front of my parents—my mother continues. "I bet he's cute..."

I laugh dryly. "There isn't a doubt in my mind," I tell her as I cook the chicken for our salads.

"Juliette?" I turn my head to see she's now leaning over the counter that separates the dining area from the kitchen. "I know that living off-campus, even with a roommate, can be quite expensive." She's not kidding; I've already decided to take on more shifts at work so I'll be able to afford it *and* food. "Your father and I are going to help. If you find a place, you let us know how much it is and we'll pay half."

I shake my head; it's far too generous an offer. "Mom—"

She doesn't let me finish. "You still have to keep your

grades up, but I don't want you to have to work even more just because you can't afford to live. That's how people wind up quitting their education. We want what's best for you, and we're just so proud."

I rush around the counter and wrap my mom in my arms. "Thanks, Mom. This really means a lot. I'll try to find a place that's reasonably priced."

She laughs, rubbing my back lightly as she embraces me back. "That's all we ask, dear."

After dinner, I tell Mom I need to work on my paper, but as soon as I'm on my bed, my laptop open in front of me, I can't seem to focus on it. So, deciding I need to take a break already, I grab the paper and my phone and start to make a few phone calls.

The first place I call sounded great when I found it earlier, but as soon as I start talking to the woman, I realize it isn't for me. While the idea of a house with three appliances and access to a personal laundry room sounds great, the fact that the woman was charging close to fifteen hundred dollars a month did *not*. That is more than my entire month's salary. There's no way I can afford that, even with help from my parents.

I call a couple more, and either they're taken or the person renting it sounds like a total crack addict. Honestly, I don't fancy taking care of some junkie's screaming children while they cook meth in the shared basement and blow us all sky-high. Nah, I'm good.

I blow through all the ads on Craigslist and most of the ones in the paper. I'm starting to lose all hope that I'll find a place and contemplate not calling the one ad I have left for fear of being disappointed, yet again. I look at the ad left in the paper and read it again:

Rm w/ a Vu

Looking for roommate
to share 3 bdrm house in
Phoenix.
Must be tidy. No pets.
If this is you, please call (480) 555-1367

I don't know why I do it—habit at this point, maybe?—but I dial the number and hold the phone to my ear as it rings. The fact that it goes on ringing leads me to believe that no one will answer, but just as I am about to remove the phone from my ear, I hear a light click.

"Hello?" The voice shocks me at first, mostly because it belongs to a guy. So far, all the ads I've responded to have been females. I'm not sure how a male/female roommate situation is supposed to work, and I'm also not sure I'm entirely comfortable with the idea either.

"Damn it." The irritation is clear in his voice, and I realize that I haven't spoken.

Before he can hang up, I jump off my bed and begin to pace the floor before I speak up. "Wait. Sorry... Hi." I run the fingers of my free hand through my hair and take a deep breath.

There's a light chuckle from his end of the phone, and there's something about it that forces me to sit back down on my bed, the hand in my hair dropping into my lap. "Hello. Sorry, I thought you'd hung up."

The corners of my lips turn up into a smile, and I exhale a relieved half-sigh-half-laugh. "Oh. No...uh, I'm still here." I can't help but let the smooth sound of his voice envelope me like a warm blanket. I find myself feeling kind of dazed.

"Can I help you with something, Miss...?"

"Oh! Yeah, sorry," I say, slapping my hand to my forehead. "My name is Juliette, and I was calling about your ad? For the room? You know, the one with the view?" He laughs again, this time it's a much heartier sound, and I imagine him as some blue-eyed man with thick hair, sitting on his couch watching some kind of sporting event while he's listening to me ramble on like an idiot.

"I'm sorry," I say again.

"No need to be. The room is still available," he tells me softly, and I'm pulled right back into the velvety sound of his voice. "Would you like to come take a look at it?"

"Uh huh," I reply before shaking my head clear of the weird fog that rolls in. "I mean, yes. That would be great. Are you free tomorrow?"

"Tomorrow would be perfect. Do you have a pen? I'll

give you the address and directions, as it's in one of the newer areas of Phoenix."

After jotting down the address and directions, I hang up the phone and hold the paper in my hands like it's my lifeline to…something. I'm not sure what it is, but there was something about his voice—his energy, even over the phone—that appealed to me. I laugh at myself, because it's clearly ridiculous; for all I know, he could be some sixty-seven-year-old bald dude who walks around in his boxers and a sweat-stained tank top…

"Ewwww," I groan to myself as the possibility of that being a reality actually sets in. "He could be some sixty-seven-year-old bald dude who walks around in his boxers and a sweat-stained tank top."

I'm just about to call back and tell him that something came up and I'll reschedule later if the room is still available, when the front door opens and my dad calls out, "Honey, I'm home for dinner!"

While I hope to *God* that there's no sexual innuendo haloing his statement, I'm finding it hard to believe. It's when I hear my mom's giggle from the kitchen just beneath my room that I toss my phone back on my mattress and declare aloud, "I'll take my chances with the old guy."

chapter 4

"So, how much is it?" Mom asks as she watches me rifle through the few clothes I had been able to stuff into my bag when leaving the dorm last week.

My hands stop moving over the hangers in my closet. "I kind of forgot to ask, actually."

Mom laughs. "Shouldn't that be the first thing you find out?" she teases lightly.

She's right, of course, and I try to remember why I hadn't even thought to ask. The sound of his voice suddenly invades my head, and I find myself feeling funny again. I have to tell myself that I'm acting ridiculous, because I've never even met the man. I easily chalk it up to a lack of sleep and my excitement over the prospect of moving out. Shockingly, it wasn't because of my parents' "carnal interludes" for once.

While I had briefly thought that the man could be an old bald guy, the more I lay in bed thinking about it, the more my mind imagined him the opposite. I like it better that way; it's way less creepy.

Don't get me wrong; I still gave my mom the address when telling her about the place because no matter how pretty this guy might be, people are still kind of crazy nowadays. I watch the news and am the daughter of a Phoenix police officer...I know things.

"And the woman you'll be renting from? She seemed nice?" I freeze as I reach for my brown v-neck shirt, unable to meet her gaze. It's true; I may have withheld a thing or two.

"Juliette?" She drags out my name, using the tone that mothers use when they know you're keeping something from them. It's like a superpower.

"The, uh…landlord seems great," I tell her quickly. I'm a little terrified to tell her that this person is a guy. While my mother is a pretty open-minded person, she's also very loose-lipped. If she were to tell my dad, well, he'd activate the GPS I know is in the cell phone they bought me for my last birthday and have me followed. Cop, remember?

I know it's stupid and irresponsible to keep this from them, but I still don't even know if I'm taking the place. Why upset them—well, mostly Dad—if it doesn't work out?

With a laugh, I pull my shirt down over my face and turn to Mom. "Definitely not someone in the boyfriend-stealing market…not that it's really a concern since I don't plan on having one for quite a while."

Mom rolls her eyes, probably because she doesn't believe I can refrain from having a boyfriend. Well, I've got news for her; I went without almost all the way through high school…I could so do it again. I'll show her.

"Do you want me to come with you? Your father is working all day, so I would be happy to tag along," she offers.

I admit, it's probably not a bad idea, but that whole "her telling dad I went to look at a place that some guy was renting through the classifieds" thing keeps me from accepting. Not wanting to hurt her feelings, I try to quickly work out how to let her down easily; I know she likely just wants us to spend the day together.

I meet her eyes through the mirror to find her perched on the edge of my desk while I go about brushing my hair. After securing a ponytail at the back of my head, I set the brush on my dresser in front of the mirror and turn to her. "Thanks, but I'll be okay. You should stay home in case Dad stops by for lunch. You guys haven't had much alone time since I've been back." Not that this has stopped them, and I'm pretty pleased with myself for not cringing or gagging when my brain is suddenly plagued with the horrific sounds.

Once I'm ready, we head downstairs where we eat a small breakfast of eggs and toast. After I do the dishes, I kiss

Mom on the cheek and grab my keys so I can take the first step toward moving back out. I'm sure to promise that I will text her when I get to the house and again when I am heading home.

"Good luck!" Mom calls after me as I bound down the three porch steps and into the sun. It isn't terribly hot, definitely a little more seasonable than it had been yesterday, and I am glad I had chosen longer sleeves as opposed to the tee I'd been contemplating.

My beast of a car seems to take a little more effort to start, which only worries me that it's going to conk out on me sooner than I'm ready for. There's a very good chance I'll be bussing to and from school in the days to come. Awesome.

Having watched Dad fiddle with all the little gadgets and whats-its under the hood, I want to assume it's the alternator causing me grief. Or maybe the starter? Okay, I really have no clue. I should have paid more attention.

"Come on, come on, *come on*," I whine, turning the key once more, pumping the clutch a little more forcefully before something clicks and my car roars to life. As I pull out onto the street, I make a mental reminder to tell Dad to have a look at the engine when he gets home.

I grab my phone from the seat next to me and search for directions. The address is in one of the newer areas of town that I've never been to. I start to imagine the style of house, and if there's a yard—not that I need one; it's just a passing thought. The ad also said that it was a three-bedroom home; did that mean it's just a basic one-story house? Honestly, I'm not quite sure what to expect.

Throughout all my musing, I almost don't realize when I've come to the street I need. Or at least, I think it is; I have to look at the address on my phone several times to be sure. It doesn't matter how long I've lived in Phoenix, I always seem to get lost whenever navigating one of the newer areas. And I can tell you, with absolute certainty, that *this* is not one of the areas I've ever been to; I'm pretty sure there's some kind of cover charge just to look at these houses.

Of course, the minute the street sign I'm looking for comes into view, I catch a glimpse of a few of the homes along the block, and my jaw drops. These houses are stunning, multi-level homes with balconies above large front porches.

"This can't be right," I mutter to myself as I pull onto the street. Slowing my vehicle down to a loud, rattling crawl, I pick up my iPhone and double check the address of the house I'm looking for.

There has to be some mistake, I think to myself as I pull up to a house that isn't my idea of an average house. It's not overly huge, but it couldn't have been cheap. It's two stories high with two thick columns that hold up an eave—which doubles as a balcony—over the double front doors. I look at the gold numbers on the side of the house and then my cell phone screen. They match. How can that be? I know I'm going to feel like an ass the minute I get to the door and the person answers, telling me I have the wrong house, but something pulls me from my seat and propels me up the front steps anyway. Probably my desire to leave my parents' house.

After sending my mom a quick text to let her know I'm here, I ring the bell, pulling my hands back and clasping them in front of me nervously. Through the glass on the door, I can see someone approaching, and I suck in a breath, preparing myself to be shooed away like some door-to-door solicitor who probably knows better than to show up here.

The minute the door opens, I release the breath I'm holding and stare like I've never stared before. The man standing before me is...well, he's absolutely gorgeous. His hair is a disheveled brown mess atop his head, his jawline sharp and covered in short stubble. I find myself wondering how it would feel against my skin, and a blush warms my cheeks. Then...oh god, *then* I find his eyes. His piercing, dark blue eyes. They're only made more stunning when he smiles and the corners of his eyes crinkle slightly.

"You must be Juliette." I think my head moves up and down, but if it is, it feels disconnected from the rest of me. There's an awkward pause between us when his eyes lock with mine.

He's nothing like I imagined him to be. First, he's certainly not a 60-something-year-old bald guy in boxers and a sweat-stained tee. While I am thankful for this, it also worries me because how can I possibly live with a guy this good-looking? Standing within a foot of him makes my knees feel weak...not to mention the deep tickle that starts in my belly and works its way south of the border.

What the hell is *that?* It's a rhetorical question, because I know what is happening with my body...but to be feeling this over a complete stranger? It's unlike anything I've ever experienced—even with Ben—and my cheeks burn like they're on fire.

We're still staring at one another, and I honestly don't know how much time has passed. I know I'm supposed to say something, but my brain and my mouth aren't cooperating with each other right now.

The man must be confused, because his eyebrows pull together. "Are you not?"

My lips part, but the only sound that escapes is a breathless, "Huh?"

He chuckles. I enjoy the sound even more in person than over the phone. "Are you Juliette?"

"Yes," I manage to squeak out. "Sorry, yes. I called last night about—"

"The room," he finishes for me. "I remember. I'm Greyston Masters." After introducing himself, he offers me his hand, and I take it. The way his warm hand closes securely around my own makes me sigh.

Get a grip! I inwardly scold myself, yanking my arm back and hugging it to my chest while my cheeks continue to flame. He regards me with one raised eyebrow. Clearly he thinks I'm insane and won't want to take me on as a tenant. I should probably just g—

"Please, come in. I'll show you the house and the available room for rent," he offers, gallantly stepping off to the side to invite me in.

"Oh," I say, somewhat shocked that he hasn't slammed the door in my face with such force that I stumble backward. "Great."

Once I'm inside, he closes the door. "Follow me."

I listen, because I feel somewhat compelled to. It's strange, this feeling I'm experiencing, but I shake it off because deep down I know I don't believe in any of it. I even start to consider the possibility that I'm just seeking some kind of rebound.

I bet Greyston would be a great reboun–

I derail that train of thought before things inside my head get inappropriate–*er.*

We make our way slowly through the main level, and I can't stop ogling the man. I do hear him; it's just my eyes that aren't paying attention. He shows me the living room first, and I'm proud of myself for being able to tear my eyes away from him long enough to admire his ability to decorate his home without it looking like a total bachelor pad.

He laughs, and I feel my heart quicken as I take in the way his eyes sparkle and how the outer corners crease when his smile reaches them. "My mother may have influenced a few of my decisions."

"Meaning she made them for you," I quip playfully, a wide smile forming.

"Essentially, yes."

As we make our way through the rest of the main floor, my eyes continually find their way back to Greyston. His messy hair, the cut of his jaw...but mostly his ass. I can't help it. I blame whoever designed the jeans he's wearing. In fact, I am currently trying to devise a way to check out the tag on his pants so I can send an angry note...or a thank you letter; I'm still not entirely sure.

I have to get myself back under control, because if I do decide to live here, things could get awkward. I don't want awkward. I *have* awkward at my parents' house.

"The basement is just through this door. It's finished, and the laundry room is down there." He pauses briefly, seemingly nervous. "I'd show it to you, but I can imagine that leading a girl that responded to an ad I placed in the paper down into my basement might seem a little daunting."

While I feel like I can trust him, my logical inner voice does kick in...and it sounds an awful lot like my father. "Not a problem. I'm okay. Thanks, though. It's always good to know."

The kitchen is open with a small dining set near the patio door. Through the glass, I see a sleek stone deck that looks out toward the desert. It's absolutely stunning, and I'm suddenly very aware that there's no way I am going to be able to afford this place. Yes, it probably shouldn't have taken me this long to figure that out, but it did.

I'm just about to say something when Greyston speaks up. "Come on. I'll show you the upstairs."

"O-okay," I stammer.

Leading the way back through the kitchen and to the main entry, we turn left toward the stairs and begin our ascent. We walk down the hall, peer first into the study and then the washroom before Greyston shows me which room is his. He's got his own bathroom, which means I won't have to worry about sharing…

Apparently, I've fallen back into thinking I'm moving in here, regardless of obviously not being able to afford it.

"And this is the available room," Greyston says, opening the door across the hall from his and next to the study. He doesn't enter, instead standing in the hall while I step through and then following me inside. There is a queen-sized bed, which beats the single in my room at Mom and Dad's as well as the one at my old dorm room, and it's dressed in basic white linens, probably to showcase the pale Caribbean blue color of the walls. There is also a tall white dresser against the wall next to the door, and a shorter, longer dresser on the opposite side of the room.

"There's an ensuite bathroom here too, so you'd have complete privacy," Greyston says softly from behind me. "And here"—Greyston goes to one of the two doors in my room and opens it—"is the closet."

Curious, I poke my head in, only to inhale a breath when I see it's quite possibly larger than my current bedroom. "This is incredible," I say quietly, taking a step back and away from the closet. It's then that I notice the floor-to-ceiling drapes that must be hiding the window. Turning to Greyston, I point at them. "May I?"

In response, Greyston crosses his arms and leans against the wall, smiling brightly. "Be my guest."

The size of the closet shocked me, but what I find behind the curtains quite literally takes my breath away. I push the white drapes back, but instead of finding a basic window, I find French doors that lead to a balcony. The fact that I can see the desert means we're right above the kitchen.

The ad isn't wrong; this room has a view, and it's unbelievable. I open the doors and step out onto the balcony. Not only can I see the desert, but when I look down I see there's a pool too. Living here would be incredible.

"So," Greyston says, stepping into my peripheral view, "what do you think?"

"It's amazing," I reply breathlessly. "But, I'm afraid to ask how much it is."

"Why don't we head back down to the kitchen, and we can discuss that there," he suggests.

Sadly, I know that no matter how much we discuss it, there is absolutely no way I'll be able to afford it. I really should just tell him, but for some reason when I try to speak nothing comes out.

When we reach the stairs, I notice a closed door at the end of the hall. Of course, I'm curious, but when I look to Greyston, he's halfway down the stairs. Realizing it's not my place, nor is it likely my business, I push the curiosity to the backburner and follow Greyston to the kitchen.

"Can I offer you something to drink? I could put on some water for tea, or I've got fresh lemonade in the fridge," Greyston offers, pulling out one of the chairs at the table for me.

This chivalrous act catches me off guard, but I recover quickly, smiling. "Thanks. Um, lemonade sounds lovely."

"Coming right up."

Greyston returns moments later with two glasses and sits in the seat across from me. "So, Juliette," he begins, "tell me a bit about yourself."

"Well, I'm an only child and a student in my sophomore year at Arizona State. I work at Mama Java's Coffeehouse... Um, what else do you want to know?" I ask.

He seems to be perplexed about something, but before I can ask, he voices whatever is on his mind. "I apologize if this comes across as rude, but if you're a student, why aren't you staying in on-campus housing? I mean, that would seem to make the most sense."

I smile, though it's not an overly happy one. "I was staying in a dorm, but the girl I bunked with had...less than desirable traits that one might look for in a roommate."

It seems like Greyston understands without my having to say much more. "Ah. She couldn't respect boundaries."

I laugh and take a sip of my drink. "Something like that," I tell him. "And now I'm back at home with my parents."

"And that doesn't work for you either?" he inquires.

"Mmm," I hum, somewhat uncomfortably. "Not so much." It's time to admit that I can't afford this place, so I inhale a deep breath and say, "Look. The house is great, and the room is unbelievably beautiful...but the truth of the matter is, I just don't think I can afford it. I want to—believe me, I do—but with my being a full-time student and working whenever I'm not busy studying...well, it's just not feasible."

Greyston chuckles again, and I begin to wonder if it's possible to miss something you've only been briefly exposed to.

My guess would be yes.

"Juliette, I haven't even told you how much the rent is."

Wrapping both hands around my lemonade glass and feeling the cold beads of condensation on my palms, I shake my head. "I can't imagine it to be cheap. I mean, the mortgage alone on a home like this has to be—"

"Surprisingly lower than one might expect with a large enough down payment," Greyston says, cutting me off before I can completely turn him down. If it had been anyone else interrupting me, I probably would have gotten annoyed, but not him. Not in this moment, anyway.

"Listen, Juliette," he continues, "I'm constantly on the road for work—sometimes for weeks at a time—and am in need of someone to watch over the place while I'm away."

"Still—"

Again, he doesn't let me finish. "You'd really be doing me a favor," he says as I bring my glass to my lips. "Five hundred a month."

The number shocks me, causing me to choke and sputter on the drink I've just taken. "What? You can't be serious...Are you saying that because I basically just told you that I'm poor?"

Greyston's laughter fills the kitchen. "Not at all. I just figured that since I was basically asking you to house-sit whenever I'm away that it would be unfair of me to ask an unreasonable amount for rent."

I don't know what to say—a first, to be sure. Here I am, sitting in a gorgeous home in a beautiful new community—which is coincidentally not too far from school—and it's actually affordable *without* my parents' help? It's all just too good to be true. The fact that my potential landlord is easy on the eyes doesn't hurt, either.

The kitchen is silent, save for the soft *tick, tick, tick* of the clock over the doorway. Greyston is watching me, waiting for my answer. He doesn't look annoyed that I'm taking my time—and I'm honestly not sure why I am, because I basically want to say yes to anything he might suggest…and I do mean *anything*.

Finally, I find my voice. "I only have one more question."

Greyston nods once, slowly and carefully, as though he's afraid of what my question might be. It's really pretty adorable.

"When can I move in?"

chapter 5

I don't regret the question, but the minute it leaves my mouth, I realize I should probably know more about the man sitting in front of me. Besides how gorgeous he and his home are.

Before I find the opportunity to back-pedal and ask about him, Greyston smiles and responds to my question. "Whenever is good for you. I know we're just over three weeks into November, but feel free to bring your stuff by any time. Perhaps over the Thanksgiving long weekend, but after the actual holiday?"

"Really?" Greyston nods and takes a sip of his lemonade. When he licks his lips afterward, I find it hard to focus on anything else. The way I'm feeling really is ridiculous, and I momentarily question my sanity.

When I realize that Greyston is staring at me as I continue to gape—probably slack-jawed—I try to recover. "Okay, well I can probably stop by the dorm and start bringing some things over a bit at a time... You're sure it's not too soon? I'd hate to be an imposition in any way. I mean, if you're busy..."

"Juliette, relax. It's fine," he says with a smile, pushing his chair back from the table and standing up before walking around to the other side of the island counter. After rifling through a drawer, he returns to his seat and holds out his hand, palm up. In it is a small silver house key.

I still can't believe this is happening. There's no way I

should be able to afford a place like this, but it seems I've hit the jackpot—and I'm not just talking about the house.

"Thanks," I say, taking the key from him. The warmth of his skin causes my breath to hitch and my stomach to flip-flop. I even think my eyes flutter. "So, is there, like, a lease or something you want me to sign?" I ask, trying really hard to control the light waver of excitement in my voice.

Greyston laughs almost nervously, running his hand through his soft-looking hair, and I expel a soft breath. "Actually, I haven't had time to draw one up. I only just got back into town yesterday, and I was just walking through the front door when you called. Give me a few days?"

"Oh, yeah…sure. I can sign it when I start bringing my things over." I find myself feeling more and more giddy each and every time I make mention of the fact that I'll be living here.

"Perfect."

I can't agree more.

As we sit here in a brief moment of silence, I start to obsess about just how little I know about the man I just agreed to move in with. While I don't need to know every little detail about his life up until he opened the door for me, the basics would probably be a good idea. Especially since I'll have to be able to assure my dad this guy isn't a psychopath.

"So," I say, breaking up the quiet in the room, "you said you travel a lot…for work?" Greyston nods, so I continue. "What is it that you do?"

"I'm a sports agent, actually," he explains with an air of pride lacing his voice. "It's why I'm out of town so much. I'm often away signing and recruiting new talent."

My dad is going to love this guy. Possibly more than me… *Wait…um…*

"That sounds really cool. Have you been doing it long?" Yes, I am aware how the question sounds, but it's too late to take it back. Maybe he won't notice. I'm sure it's just me because my mind has been in the gutter since I first got here, and my mentality is now mirroring that of a twelve-year-old boy.

"About five years now," he tells me coolly. Apparently it

is all me.

"Did you always know that's what you wanted to do with your life?" I ask, trying to keep the conversation rolling because I don't think I'll ever tire of hearing his voice. Yup, I've definitely gone crazy. There's no longer a doubt in my mind. It's okay, though; I think I can make peace with it.

"Yes and no." Greyston laughs and takes another drink. "I was pretty into sports in high school, and even went to college on a football scholarship."

I never much cared for football...until now.

"It was in my senior year of college that I was approached by an agency. It wasn't to sign me, though." I half-expect this to be upsetting for him, but he sounds surprisingly happy about it all. "They wanted to recruit me to work *for* them.

"My college team was good...and I mean we were *good.*" I'm not sure why—because normally I would be repulsed—but the cocky tone in Greyston's voice sends a shiver down my spine. I'm basically fighting the urge to launch myself across the table and straddle his thick, football-playing thighs.

While I inwardly struggle with this, he continues speaking...not that this helps my situation any. "The agency had heard that I'd played a big part in scouting the players, and they thought I'd be an asset. So I looked over what they wanted to offer me, and I couldn't pass it up," he finishes explaining. "It's been pretty great."

I laugh, absent-mindedly playing with the rim of my empty glass. "You know, I was worried about what my dad was going to think of all of this—my shacking up with a guy I just met..." My eyes snap up to his, widening because I *so* didn't mean it the way it sounded. "N-not that we're 'shacking up'," I amend.

Thankfully, he doesn't dwell on that part of what I've said. "And you think he'll be okay with it now? Knowing I'm a ruthless head-hunter for up-and-coming athletic talent?"

I lock eyes with him and lean onto the table. "I don't think you understand; my dad is insane about sports. Like 'teenage-girl-obsessed-with-vampires' insane," I explain, gaining another deep chuckle from him. Even though this newly-learned information about Greyston might help me soften the blow, I'm not naïve enough to think my father won't still be initially upset about everything.

"So, I realize that it's kind of personal, but the more information I can give to my parents, the better my chances are of *not* being put into solitary confinement," I half-kid. Greyston laughs, but I don't think he really gets that my dad would probably go to such lengths to keep me safe—not that Greyston is really a threat to my safety.

Getting up, Greyston heads back to the fridge and grabs the pitcher of lemonade, topping up both of our glasses before setting it on the table and sitting again. "Well, my full name is Greyston Evan Masters. I'll be twenty-eight on January twentieth. My parents, Daniel and Jocelyn, live here in Phoenix. My father is a financial analyst. They live pretty comfortably, so my mom was fortunate enough to get to stay home while I grew up, and we wanted for nothing. Once I went off to college, she took an interest in interior design as a hobby."

"Any siblings?" I ask.

Greyston shakes his head. "Nope. Like you, I'm an only child."

Greyston and I talk a little bit more about his upbringing in a small town just south of Phoenix before my phone vibrates in my pocket. I notice the time first and realize I've been here for more than two hours. It seems only right that my mom is calling.

"Sorry," I apologize to Greyston before pointing to the patio door. "Do you mind?"

Greyston winks, and I damn-near fall out of my chair. "Hey, it's your house now too."

Yeah, I think I'm about to die and go to Heaven.

Trying to calm my now-thundering heart, I stand up and answer my phone, sliding the door open and stepping out onto the deck. "Hey, Mom."

"Hi, baby. How did it go? Did you find the place okay?"

"Yeah, I did. It's amazing, Mom. You'll love it." I look back over my shoulder to see Greyston cleaning off the table.

Naturally, my eyes fall back to his ass as he leans over to wipe the wooden surface. I apparently have no sense of morality left. "I'm actually just finishing up, I think. I'll be on my way home soon, okay?"

I stay outside for a minute after hanging up, looking out toward the desert from the back porch. A breeze picks up, and I inhale the fresh air as the sun peeks out from behind the clouds and warms my face.

"Everything go okay?"

I turn toward the voice and smile when I see Greyston leaning against the doorframe. "Yeah. I didn't realize how much time had gone by. I'm surprised she didn't have my dad dispatch a search unit." Greyston eyes me curiously. "Oh, he's a cop."

"Impressive."

"It kept me from getting into any real trouble as a teenager, I suppose," I joke, slipping my phone back into my pocket. "I should probably get going, though."

Backing up into the kitchen and making room for me to pass through the threshold, Greyston nods. "Of course."

"I'll call and let you know when I plan to start bringing my things over, if that's okay?"

Smiling, Greyston walks me to the door. "I look forward to it."

I let the words repeat over and over in my head, wondering if he's flirting with me. The idea that he might be is appealing, but the possibility that he's not is more likely.

"Thanks again for everything, Greyston. It was nice meeting you," I tell him, holding out my hand for him to shake. Truthfully, I want to hug him, but it's probably inappropriate—especially since I'm not sure I could control myself enough to eventually let go. Even from a foot away, his scent is intoxicating. I wonder what cologne he wears…

"And you, as well, Juliette." Before I am able to, Greyston reaches out and opens the door for me. It's sweet, just like when he pulled my chair out for me in the kitchen. "Feel free to call me if you need anything in the meantime, okay?"

My heart skips a beat, and I can't seem to stop my smile

from widening almost painfully. "Yeah, okay. Um, bye."

"Bye."

Walking down the stairs feels weird, almost like it's not right. Was this what my mom was talking about last week? I laugh at myself as I approach my car because the idea that I could feel this way after only a couple of hours is silly. It's just not logical. Maybe I feel like this because Greyston has offered me an incredible opportunity, and I'm seeing him as some kind of white knight.

Okay, that just invites a whole new rush of fantasies that are bound to get me in trouble.

Shaking them off, I tell myself that I'm probably just reading too much into it—seeing signs where there are none—but when I see Greyston standing on the porch as I climb into my car, I start to wonder if maybe Mom is onto something. He waves, and I return the gesture, pulling away from the curb and heading for home.

Dad's cruiser is in its spot next to Mom's SUV when I arrive. He's home early, and I feel dread knotting in the pit of my stomach. There's no way I'll walk away sane if I have to see them going at it a third time. Even though I don't actually want to acknowledge that it's a possibility, I grab my phone and text my mom to let her know I'm right outside.

She responds almost immediately. A good sign, for sure.

Juliette, get in the house.
We're not animals ;)

Yeah…right. She thinks she's so funny with that little winky-face.

Knowing that she probably wants to be caught just as much as I want to catch them—which is not at all—I head for the house. I'm happy to see that they're sitting in the living room, Dad in his recliner and Mom on the end of the couch closest to him.

"Hey, honey," Dad says as I lean down and kiss his cheek first, then Mom's. "Your mother tells me you went to look at a place today?"

I take a seat next to Mom, nestling up against her as she wraps her arm around me and hugs me close. "I did. It was beyond perfect...and the price was more than reasonable. I probably won't even need you guys to help out," I tell them excitedly.

"Oh?" Mom inquires.

"Yeah, it's only five hundred a month. For a *house*. It even has a pool...and my room has a balcony that looks out toward the desert. It's stunning."

Dad's inner-cop suddenly shows. "Sounds a little too good to be true, don't you think?"

What *I* think is he just likes having his baby girl home again. "That's what I thought, but that's what the guy said he wanted," I tell him, shrugging slightly.

Mom squeezes me supportively. "Well, that's great, sweethear—"

"Wait a minute," Dad interrupts, his voice low and interrogating. "*He?*"

Shit.

Mom must not have caught it until he repeated my slip-up. Slowly, she loosens her grip and sits up. "You told me this person was a woman," she says, her eyebrows rising. The look in her eyes is the same one I had seen when I was sixteen and lied about sleeping over at Katie's house so I could go to a party.

"*Technically,*" I say, going back to our conversation earlier in the day, "you *assumed* the landlord was a female, I just failed to correct you."

Before she can say anything else, my father launches himself out of his La-Z-Boy and booms, "Absolutely not! It's out of the question!"

"Dad, he's a really great g—"

"I don't care if he's the King of England; you're not moving in with some guy you found through a classified ad," he orders. "I raised you better than that, Juliette."

I hate when he talks to me like this. There used to be a time when I'd roll over and just submit to whatever he demanded because I knew he loved me and was just looking out for me. But now? Well, I know he still loves me, and that's where his little outburst is coming from, but I like to think that he's raised me to be a pretty good judge of character.

"You're right," I tell him, forcing him to stop pacing the floor in front of the flat screen and look at me. I stand up so I don't feel about three inches tall while I try to tell him how I feel. "You raised me to know better than to just move in with a stranger. But, isn't that essentially what one does in college when they get a new dorm mate? I didn't know Delilah from Eve, and she wasn't cra—" I stop myself mid-sentence when my father crosses his arms and raises his eyebrows in challenge. "Okay," I continue, "bad example.

"My point is, I asked this guy all sorts of probing questions. I think I know more about him than I even knew about Ben, for crying out loud." My dad still doesn't look convinced, so I cross over to him and look up into his stern brown eyes. "Daddy," I say softly, and I can see his resolve beginning to break. "I'm twenty now. A grown up. I need to do this. I don't know how everything will turn out, but isn't that kind of the point of life? We wouldn't learn anything if we knew what was going to happen next."

"I just… Juliette, if anything ever happened to you because I failed to protect you…" The poor guy looks absolutely terrified. Will he stay up nights worrying that my new living situation is dangerous? I don't want that, and I start to wonder if my moving in with Greyston is something he can even handle.

"Cam," Mom says, interrupting my thoughts before I start to seriously consider calling Greyston and telling him I can't move in with him. "Maybe we should trust that she knows what she's doing. You did educate her on everything she needs to know to keep herself safe."

She does it. She breaks his resolve.

With a sigh, he flops back down into his chair, propping his arms on his knees as he looks up at me. "I'm going to want to meet him. If I am going to be able to trust that he's providing a safe place for you to live, I'm going to want to get to know this guy."

My head bobs up and down quickly. "Yeah. Obviously. I'll give him a call and set it up." Relieved, I look between my mom and dad. "Thank you for being so cool about this...eventually."

Dad laughs, making me feel a little more at ease. "That's me. Cool."

Since the situation has been diffused, Mom suggests ordering a pizza for dinner to celebrate. I'm not sure if we're celebrating my new digs, the fact that I came home for once and didn't catch them getting coital on a new piece of furniture, or that Dad's head didn't explode when he found out about my new roommate. Maybe all three.

Pizza night also means we eat in the living room and watch a movie. It's been a tradition ever since I can remember, and one of my favorites. After we all finish eating and our movie ends, I clean up before excusing myself to go and do my homework. I still have to finish up my paper before class tomorrow, and I am not going to let Drayke down again after my last grade.

Just as I am putting the finishing touches on my paper, Daphne calls. I tell her I've found a place, and she has a hard time containing her excitement. Her enthusiasm is contagious as I tell her about the place. She's sweet to offer to help me pack up when I ask if she's seen Ben loitering around my room. It annoys me that he's apparently been hanging around almost every day; I may have to take her up on her offer, even if just to utilize her as some sort of buffer.

After saying goodbye, I set my phone on my nightstand, move my laptop over to my desk, and get dressed for bed. Opening my door, I pad into the hall, sure to walk heavily—just in case—and stop at the top of the stairs. It's been pretty quiet down there, so I'm confident I'm not interrupting anything as I call down—because I'm not dumb enough to risk *going* downstairs. "Mom? Dad? I'm turning in now. Goodnight."

"Goodnight, sweetheart," Mom says back.

"Sleep well, Jules."

I turn off my light, slip back into my room, and slide beneath my thin comforter, nestling in for a solid night's sleep. It's still early, but the previous night's lack of sleep finally catches up with me.

I'm in such a deep sleep that I miss my alarm and start the morning late. The morning is a blur as I run around my room, dressing and gathering up my things. Thankfully, Mom has been up for the last two hours and has prepared me a breakfast sandwich to take with me on the way. I make it to school with just enough time to slip into my first class without the professor noticing.

At lunch, I call Greyston and let him know that I'd like to bring a few things by. He doesn't answer, but I leave a message, assuming he must be working. I tell him to give me a call by the end of the day if that poses a problem; he doesn't, so I suspect he probably won't mind. Plus, he did give me a key and tell me to start moving my stuff over whenever was convenient.

When my classes are over for the day, I decide to head down to the dorm. I know Ben should be in his pop culture class, so I should be able to get in and out without seeing or hearing from him. Walking through the quad, I decide that I don't feel like lugging my backpack around as well as tote boxes to and from my vehicle, so I toss it onto the front seat before I go off to pack.

As I make my way through the lot, I start to feel really good about the new direction my life has taken. I never thought that Ben's cheating on me would turn out to be a good thing.

Nobody really pays attention to me as I make my way through the hall; it would seem that steering clear of this place for the last two weeks has made everyone forget the drama that had unfolded here. I was definitely a little nervous that people would remember everything and stare while pointing and gossiping about me. Needless to say, it's a relief when they all let me walk by without so much as a glance.

I round the last corner to go to my old room and stop dead in my tracks, slowly backing up out of view and pressing my back against the wall.

Even though I am certain he should be in class, Ben is

pacing the hall in front of my door. I thought I would be able to face him, but seeing him makes me realize I can't. It's not that I think I still have feelings for him—I don't. I honestly just that I don't really enjoy confrontation, and I definitely don't want to get into it with him when there are students milling around in the halls. And there's no way in hell I'm going to close myself in a room with him.

Without thinking, I grab my phone from my pocket and blindly select a recent contact.

"Hello?"

Relaxing a little, I exhale softly. "Hey, I need a favor."

chapter 6

I know I shouldn't have made that call, and honestly, I didn't even realize what I was doing until it was already done. Sure, there were several other people I could have asked for help, but none of them came to mind in that moment.

For some reason, all I wanted was *him*.

"Juliette?" I turn toward the main doors and see a familiar head of brown hair. Just the sight of him relaxes me a little, and I smile.

He's making his way toward me, and I don't fail to notice how every pair of female eyes is on him as he passes by. He doesn't seem aware of any of them, though; his eyes are locked with mine.

"Hey," I say to him when he stops in front of me. He looks good in another pair of jeans and a light grey sweater, and I'm finding it hard to focus for a split second, suddenly caught up in the same fog as yesterday. Finally, I find my voice. "Thank you so much for coming. I'm sorry if I pulled you away from something important."

Grinning, Greyston shakes his head. "Don't worry about it. I'm glad you felt you were able to take me up on my offer to call if you needed anything. Packing a few boxes seemed much more appealing than paperwork anyway," he jokes, making me laugh. "So, which room is yours?"

All I do is look at him for a moment, still kicking myself for not being completely forthright with him over the phone.

"Um, before I take you there, I should probably tell you something."

Even though it probably shouldn't be possible, Greyston's smile widens, his blue eyes sparkling. "Don't tell me you have a cat."

I'm momentarily confused until I remember the "no pets" stipulation in the ad. "Oh, no. It's nothing like that. It's just… I, um…" I can't seem to say what I have to.

This seems to concern Greyston. "Juliette, what is it?"

"My boyfriend," I blurt out, causing his brow to furrow in confusion. "Well, more accurately, my *ex*."

"Oh."

It's obvious he doesn't know what else to say, so I continue. "We broke up last week, and he's been trying to find a way to talk to me ever since. But I really have no interest in hearing anything he has to say." I take a deep breath, because I'm starting to ramble. "Well, he's supposed to be in class, but he's not. He's right outside my room."

Realization shines in Greyston's bright eyes. "Ohhhh. So you wanted me to tag along because—"

"Because I'm hoping he won't air our dirty laundry in front of others. Especially not a stranger," I admit, ashamed that I'm basically using him. I'm a terrible person. "God, I'm sorry. That sounds pretty crappy, huh?"

Greyston shakes his head like he understands. "Nah. It just sounds like you want to put this part of your life behind you without any drama. I get that." He's possibly even more attractive to me now; I'm so screwed.

"So, which room is yours?"

After taking a few deep breaths, I lead him back around the corner. Ben is still there, even though at least a half hour has passed since I called Greyston. My step falters when he turns and sees me. It isn't until I feel a warm hand press against the small of my back that I proceed. I try to breathe normally while Greyston's hand remains on me, but butterflies have taken up residence in my stomach, and my entire body feels like a crackling live wire.

Ben notices the innocent touch, and his eyes leave mine to find Greyston. I'm barely able to contain an arrogant smirk when Ben's stare hardens angrily, and his hands ball into fists at his sides. He looks like he's about ready to punch something…or some*one*.

"Where have you been?" Ben demands, still staring at Greyston but clearly talking to me. "I've been calling you and calling you… I even stopped by the coffee shop."

"I know. Katie told me," I tell him, surprised by how icy cold my voice sounds as I push past him and slip through the door with Greyston hot on my tail. "I was out. I thought she told you."

Ben laughs dryly. "You don't go *out*," he states like he knows me so well. "You're too busy studying these days." Okay, so maybe he does.

The ridiculous accusation of his cheating being my fault haloes his statement, but I refuse to give him the satisfaction of seeing just how much it stings. "Maybe that's just what I told you."

"Juliette?" Greyston interrupts softly, drawing my eyes to his. A wave of calm passes through me, casting the nerves aside as I get lost in a sea of blue. "Where do you want me to start?"

"Um, that's my stuff there. I think I still have a few boxes in the closet from when I moved in," I tell him, my voice smooth and controlled, and point to my side of the room. "I should be able to fit most of it in my car."

While Greyston puts together one of my broken-down boxes, I start stripping the bedding off the single bed. Greyston and I are working together to fill a couple of boxes with my belongings, and I'm trying really hard to ignore Ben, but I can feel him standing right behind me.

"Look, Ben," I say without turning to face him, "I have nothing left to say. Honestly, I don't even care anymore."

"What is that supposed to mean?" he snarls, grabbing my arm lightly and forcing me to turn around.

Before I even know what's happening, Greyston has pushed his way between us, forcing Ben to break his hold on me. He stares directly into Ben's eyes. "I believe she told you she had nothing to say. Why don't you run along to class now, *boy*, and leave us to pack up her things?"

Something goes through me when Greyston stands up for me. I don't know what it is as I've never experienced anything like it before. My entire body tingles, my knees feel weak, and my breathing deepens as he stares Ben down.

"And just who the hell are you?" Ben demands. He doesn't give Greyston a chance to respond before looking behind him at me. "Is this the clown you went out with the other night?"

"So what if it is?" I ask snidely. I know it's wrong to lie about something like this, but I can't help but let Ben believe that Greyston and I were together in some way.

He sneers at Greyston and then me. "Didn't take you long to move on."

I can't control the maniacal laughter that suddenly fills the room. "You're joking, right? You're accusing *me* of moving on too soon? You've decided to play the pot today, then?"

Ben's nostrils flare, and he focuses solely on me. Whatever he's about to say won't be pretty, but I'm ready for it.

Greyston doesn't let him get a word in edgewise, though, turning to me and holding my upper arms lightly. Slowly, he runs his hands over the length of my arms, and I sigh when they clasp mine. "Why don't you take the first box out to the car while I finish up here, then we can head home."

"Home?" Ben repeats. "You're living together?"

I narrow my eyes angrily at him. "Not that it's any of your business, but—" Before I'm able to finish telling him that I'm just Greyston's tenant, Greyston shakes his head, silently telling me I don't have to say anything. Why?

"I'll meet you out by the car after I'm done here, okay?" he says, tilting his head toward the door.

Glancing once more at Ben, I nod before grabbing the box on my bed, and heading for the door. "I'll see you outside," I say to Greyston.

"Juliette," Ben calls after me, but I don't turn around. "Juliette!"

I keep ignoring him and continue down the hall. People are looking at me again, and I try to pretend not to notice. Instead, I focus all of my energy on not dropping the box or having the bottom of it break apart, spilling its contents in the hall.

After making it to my car, I put the box in the back seat, moving around and leaning on the trunk while I wait for Greyston. I check my phone periodically and realize that almost twenty minutes have gone by since I left my old room. Worry starts to set in, and I'm about to go check if everything is okay when I see Greyston emerge with another two boxes stacked in his arms.

I push myself to my feet and meet him halfway, taking the top box from him and leading him back to my car. "So, did he leave after I did?"

"More or less," Greyston vaguely replies.

I push the box into the back of my car and turn to him. "What does that mean?"

Greyston closes the back door and smiles at me. The way the right side of his mouth curls up a little crookedly, flashing his brilliant white teeth, makes my stomach flip; I wonder if he knows that's a pretty deadly weapon. "He tried to start something, and I finished it. I don't think he'll be bothering you for a while."

I'm curious to know what he said to Ben, but the look in Greyston's eyes tells me more than I need to know. That and the fact that the backs of his knuckles are red and slightly swollen.

He sees me eyeing his knuckles and shakes his head. "I regretted it the instant it happened…well, kind of." Greyston runs a hand through his hair, tugging on it once he reaches the back of his head. "Shit. You must think I'm some kind of barbarian."

"What?" I ask incredulously. "Not at all. I'm just…confused." I laugh, scooting a little closer to him.

"After you left, I tried to go back to gathering your things," Greyston begins. "The minute my back was turned, he started in on me about you. About *us*. I had no interest in speaking with him—he's a twit." My lips twist up into a smirk, and I fight a snicker. "I'm sorry, but he is."

Shaking my head, I hold my hands up in surrender. "No. No need to apologize. I can clearly see that now. But, obviously you didn't hit him *just* because he's an idiot?"

Greyston chuckles, relaxing a little. "No, that's not why I hit him." He pauses and looks me in the eye, likely gauging my reaction to everything so far. "He cheated on you," he says quietly, resting his left hand against the top of my car.

With a sigh, I lean my back against the side of the car. "He did."

"With your roommate." It isn't a question; he's telling me that he knows without a doubt.

Swallowing thickly, I glance at him through the corner of my eye. "Did he...did he tell you that?"

Greyston shakes his head. "No, I gathered as much from the way the two of you were arguing." He pauses for a minute, letting out a quiet snort-like sound. "Well, that, and your ex-roommate showed up. She has issues taking no for an answer, doesn't she?"

"Ew," I say, feeling a little nauseous that Delilah tried to sink her teeth into someone as sweet and caring as Greyston. "I'm so sorry."

"Don't worry about it." Another pause. "I had already deduced that he'd been unfaithful, so when he started calling you out for being *unladylike...*" Based on his brief moment of silence, I have a feeling that Greyston is trying to sugarcoat whatever crass name Ben called me. "I know we've only just met, Juliette, but to hear him talk about you like that? Well, forgive me, but it pissed me off. You're a sweet girl. You don't deserve that."

I swallow thickly and try to control the impulse to pull his face to mine and kiss him senseless. It's really the most self-restraint I've ever shown *in my life*. "So you hit him," I say in a raspy voice, knowing already that it happened.

"Well," Greyston responds, his nose scrunching adorably and his eyes narrowing. "Would it be terribly juvenile to say he started it?"

I can no longer hold back my laughter. "While I think that defense only works in six-year-old court, I can totally relate."

"He's jealous, you know." I draw my eyes to his, confused by what he's said. He must see this and decides to clarify further. "Of what he thinks you and I are." Chuckling,

Greyston shifts and bumps his shoulder against mine playfully. "I say make him stew in it. Let him think what he wants."

I can't help but laugh and actually feel a little better about asking for Greyston's help. When I originally called him, it was only to ask him to act as a buffer between Ben and me; it never once occurred to me to ask him to pretend to be my new boyfriend.

The metal of my car groans as Greyston pushes off it, my eyes, naturally, following him. "Come on," he says. "Let's take your stuff back to the house."

My cheeks warm, and I bite my lip as I place my hand in his. "That sounds like a good idea." I'm just about to hop into my car when I turn back to him. "Hey, thanks again for helping me out. I didn't mean to use you like that. I just... Everyone else I know is aware of what Ben did, and I didn't want to talk about it. To me, you were, I don't know, safe?"

"It's really not a problem. I was happy to help in whatever capacity I could. Come on, let's go home."

My heart starts fluttering, and I feel like I'm going to pass out. I realize that hearing Greyston call his own house "home" shouldn't make my stomach flip, but it does. It's been a pretty stellar couple of days.

Well, minus the Ben part.

When we arrive at the house, Greyston hops out of his sporty little black Lexus, rushing to help me bring my boxes inside. After we haul the boxes up to my new room, Greyston excuses himself to take care of a business call while I begin to unpack a few things.

I'm just setting the time on my alarm clock when I realize I should call my parents and let them know where I am. I don't want them to worry.

Sitting on the edge of my bed, I dial the house phone. Mom picks up on the second ring. "Hello?"

"Hey, Mom," I respond.

"Hi, sweetie. Where are you? Your father and I were expecting you a half hour ago."

I look around, a big smile forming as I take in the soft blue of the walls of *my* room. "Sorry. I meant to call. I finally stopped by the dorm and packed my stuff. I just wanted to bring it by Greyston's place before I came home."

"Oh, well that makes sense. How did it go?" Something in her voice tells me that she's wondering if I ran into any unwanted drama.

"Fine," I tell her, but I sense she knows I'm leaving something out. I sigh heavily. "I'll tell you everything when I get home. I should finish up here, though. I'll see you in a bit?"

"Sounds good, baby. I'll save you some dinner."

After putting my few belongings away, I break down my boxes and leave them in my closet until I can ask Greyston what I should do with them. I stand in the middle of my room and look around at the few little odds and ends that I've put out. It's weird how they all seem to just belong.

Knowing I should probably get home, I pull myself away from the amazing view and lock my balcony doors. Still in a state of disbelief, I run my hand over the smooth bedspread on my way to the door. Living in a house like this while still in college shouldn't be possible, but Greyston made it so.

I wander down the hall, noticing for the first time the photos that hang on the walls. I stop at one of Greyston and two people I assume to be his parents. They look nice. Loving. It's no surprise that Greyston grew up to be such a great man.

Tearing myself away from the happy faces in the pictures, I wander closer to the stairs, stopping immediately when I see that door on the opposite side of the staircase. My curiosity returns.

My hand rests on the doorknob, and just as I'm about to turn it, I realize what I'm doing. I yank my hand back, fully aware that I've almost invaded Greyston's privacy. I decide to ask him about it...once I'm a little more comfortable here, that is.

Greyston is in the kitchen preparing something to eat when I finally make my way downstairs. He hears me enter the room, turning to me with a smile. "Hey. Get everything squared away?"

"Yup," I tell him. "I broke down the boxes and left them in my closet, though."

With an arched brow, Greyston turns his head toward

me as I sit at the island. "Planning a midnight move already?"

I laugh, and a blush ravages my cheeks. "No. I just didn't want to leave them lying about."

He turns back to the stove and chuckles. "Not a problem. It's recycling day on Thursday. I'll grab them and put them out for pick up."

"Thanks." I push my stool back from the island and prepare to stand when Greyston turns around with two plates in his hands.

His eyebrows furrow slightly. "You're not leaving already, are you?"

"Oh…"

Greyston sets both plates down on the island, one in front of me and the other next to it. "It's just, I haven't cooked for myself in so long, and I wound up making too much. I was thinking maybe you'd like to join me?"

Because it's all I seem to be able to do in Greyston's presence, I smile as wide as that creepy cat in the *Alice in Wonderland* reboot. "Yeah, I can stay," I say, sitting back down and looking at the amazing-smelling pasta dish he's prepared. "Just let me text my mom to let her know I'll be a little longer."

"So," Greyston says when I set my phone back down. "I realized yesterday after you left that we didn't really talk about how this cohabitation thing was going to work."

He's absolutely right. It never even occurred to me in between all of the inappropriateness. I'm not sure if there are questions I should ask, mainly because it's just as rampant as it was yesterday. Good thing Greyston knows how to keep a conversation rolling, because I can't.

"Obviously, I want you to feel at home here. There's a lot of shared space, and I don't want you to feel that if I'm in a room, you can't come in."

I'm just swallowing a bite of pasta when he says that, and I begin to cough after inhaling a string of linguine. Immediately, thoughts of him in the shower and me walking into the steamy bathroom fill my brain… And now I'm imagining him in his bedroom—naked—and I just come on in, because he said I should feel at home, and that's what I do at home—walk in on people at the worst possible times.

With my coughing fit under control, I look over at Greyston, who is a very serious shade of red. It's good to know I'm not the only one with a terminal case of foot-in-mouth disease.

"I'm sorry. That didn't quite come out right. What I meant to say was—"

I wave my hand dismissively, because if he goes into clarifying, I'm still going to transform it into something filthy. "That's okay," I tell him, my voice dry and raspy.

Greyston hops up and grabs me a glass of water, watching me, concerned, as I chug it. "Are you all right?"

I nod, setting the glass down. "Yes. Fine, thank you."

"I guess I just don't want you to feel like you have to tiptoe around here. If you're hungry at two a.m. for whatever reason, feel free to raid the fridge or pantry. If you want to have guests over, that's fine. All I ask is no outrageous parties."

"Oh, yeah, of course. I'm not really one for parties anyway. I'm way too involved with my studies," I tell him.

Nodding, Greyston pushes his food around his plate. "We'll have to figure out some sort of laundry schedule...for obvious reasons."

Great. Now I'm wondering if Greyston prefers boxers or briefs.

We continue to discuss how we see this living together thing working out. Turns out it shouldn't be too much of an adjustment, especially when he reminds me about his work schedule from time to time.

"I don't have any trips lined up as of yet, but sometimes they're very spur of the moment," he explains. "I'm not your parent, Juliette"—*thank God for that*—"and you're not a child. If you'd feel more comfortable having someone come and stay with you while I'm away, I'd understand. Girlfriend, boyfriend... Whatever."

I laugh. "I don't think that last one will be happening."

Greyston doesn't look at me, instead seeming a little too interested in the piece of broccoli in his Alfredo sauce. "I doubt that." His voice is quiet, but I still hear him.

He sets his fork down and turns his whole body toward mine. "All I'm saying is that I don't want you to think of me as your landlord. I'd like for us to be friends. This is your home now too."

"Thank you," I respond, touched by just how much he wants me to feel like I'm at home.

We each take another bite, having ironed out a few details, before Greyston asks, "So, how did your parents take the news about you moving out?"

I giggle. "Moving out was never the issue. The issue was my living with a man." Greyston chuckles lightly. "My dad was fine after I explained things a little more rationally. He's still concerned, but I'm his only child. I get his fears."

"He just wants to keep you safe," Greyston deduces.

"Exactly," I agree. "Actually, he has one stipulation."

Greyston's eyebrows rise curiously. "Which is?"

"He wants to meet you," I tell him, kind of nervous for his reaction.

"I can do that. If it's going to set your father's mind at ease, I'd love to get together," he offers.

Beaming brightly, I lock eyes with him. "Great! I'll set it up."

When we've both finished dinner, I offer to clean up before I have to go. I'm just rinsing the last dish and putting it in the dishwasher when Greyston's phone rings.

Apologizing to me first, Greyston picks up his phone. "Hey, Callie," he answers, looking at me briefly before standing up and heading for the patio. "No, no. Now's fine. How was your day?"

Once he's outside, he closes the door, and I'm left standing by the sink, watching him through the window as he laughs into the phone with some woman named "Callie."

chapter 7

"Of course he has a girlfriend," I mumble to myself as jealousy needles its way under my skin, my eyes never leaving him through the window above the sink.

I imagine her to be a total knockout. I mean, there's no way someone who looks and acts the way Greyston does could possibly be with anyone less than gorgeous. My vision of this Callie person is ethereal.

She's tall, because Greyston is, and she's got curves that a woman should be proud of. And while my body isn't terrible, I know it's not nearly as voluptuous as I imagine hers to be. Because of her terrific body, there isn't a doubt in my mind that she's a rock star in bed. And me? Well, I drove away the only sexual partner I've ever had because I didn't like it enough to want it. Add being the last female a gay guy dated before coming out of the closet, and my track record is pretty friggin' stellar. She'll be really nice too, not some cold as ice bitch who thinks she walks on water, because I don't think Greyston would put up with that. Not even for rock star sex.

The more I think about Greyston's perfect girlfriend, the more frustrated and stupid I feel for ever thinking he was flirting with me. The way he stuck up for me with Ben, the winking... Clearly, I was reading way too much into what were obviously very innocent and *friendly* gestures. As usual.

Grumbling some more, I wipe my damp hands roughly on the dishtowel I'm holding when the door slides open and

Greyston walks in.

"Sorry about that." He takes in my agitated state and frowns. "Are you all right?"

Blushing, I drop my gaze from him and tuck my hair behind my ear with my free hand. "Yeah, I should really just get going. Let you get on with your night and all that," I tell him, tossing the towel onto the counter and snatching up my phone. I wouldn't be surprised if he can hear notes of jealousy in my voice. I sure as hell do.

He follows me from the kitchen, his long stride allowing him to beat me to the door. "You don't have to, you know. I actually don't have any plans for the night. Feel free to stay and make yourself at home." I'm right back to feeling confused.

"Thanks, but my parents are expecting me," I say, offering him an uncertain smile. "I'll bring the rest of my things by...if that's okay?"

Greyston smiles, eyes glimmering. "Don't be silly. Of course it's all right. You'll call if you need any help?"

I nod. "I'll talk to you soon. Thanks again for everything this afternoon. It really meant a lot."

Still grinning, Greyston opens the door for me. "I'm just glad I could help. You'll drive safe?"

"Always do," I assure him before waving and making my way down the steps.

Like last time, he stands in the doorway until I drive away—and who knows, maybe he stays there for a while after I'm out of sight. *Unlikely,* I deduce.

I arrive home without dwelling too much on the new information I've learned about Greyston's availability, only to find my dad in the kitchen, cleaning his guns. He's got the table covered in canvas, and his various guns and cleaning supplies are spread out in front of him.

"Hey, Daddy," I greet, walking to the fridge and grabbing myself a bottle of water and a beer for him. "Where's Mom?"

"Thanks, kid," he says when I set the beer on the table and pull up a chair beside him. "She went to meet your aunt for coffee. How was dinner with your new landlord?" I can hear the tension in his voice just mentioning Greyston—even if it isn't by name.

"It was good. He said he's more than willing to meet with you. Told me I should set it up," I inform him.

"He know I'm a cop?" He stops cleaning his shotgun just long enough to glance up at me without moving his head, one of his eyebrows arching menacingly.

"He does, so your scare tactics won't work on him," I'm sure to point out.

Smirking wickedly, Dad stares down the barrel of his unloaded weapon. "We'll see about that."

Having seen this over-protective side of my father before, I just laugh and shake my head. "Besides," I continue, ceasing my laughter, "it's not like I'm dating him, or even plan to."

Dad remains silent, setting his gun aside and reaching for his Glock. There's something in his eyes that tells me he's still afraid of not being able to keep me safe. It's silly, considering I lived in the dorms all last year and nothing bad happened. This won't be much different.

Except for the being alone in a big house with just one person and no one around to hear me scream...

Okay, so maybe I can see where he's coming from.

Instead of freaking myself out entirely, I decide that I need to remind him that he taught how to take care of myself. I set my water down and wipe my hands on the thighs of my jeans. "Do you need a hand?"

Smiling, my father hands me the still-assembled gun, hand grip first, and grabs another for himself.

As though it's second nature—which, it kind of is—I keep my finger off the trigger and eject the magazine before I pull the slide back and check the chamber and magazine well for any cartridges. I do this several times because with this particular type of Glock I'll need to engage the trigger to dismantle it. And I can't be blowing holes in the walls or floors all willy-nilly. To be doubly safe, I remove all ammunition from the room and put it with all the rest on the also-canvas-covered dining room table.

With Dad watching on, I dismantle the gun. First, I decock the striker, pull the take down tabs, and then pull back toward the rear of the frame. The slide then moves freely off the front of the handgun.

I do this all in under twenty seconds, and Dad chuckles proudly. "Glad to see you remember all of this."

"Of course I do. Gun safety is important," I tell him, parroting words he's spoken my entire life.

While I set the broken-down firearm out in front of me, I think back to a time when I was little. Fresh home from work, my dad would always, *always* unload his guns, being sure to put the ammo out of reach. It was ingrained into me from the minute I could understand that we were to respect the rules of gun safety.

Every time he would set up to clean them, I would sit at the table and watch him, propping my face in my tiny hands. It was fascinating to me as a child, especially when he would explain what he was doing as he did it and why. I learned a lot just watching him.

I was sixteen when he and my mother felt I was old enough to let me learn how to disassemble a gun. Always a responsible gun owner, he had checked to make sure it wasn't loaded and the safety was on before handing it over and tutoring me.

It was later that day that he took me to the shooting range and taught me how to use it. I won't lie; I thought it was going to be easy. I mean, I had shot a bow and arrow in archery class for gym before and had to wonder how much harder aiming a gun could be. Well, bows don't have a kickback, and I missed the targets time and time again.

Eventually, I got the hang of it, and I very rarely miss my intended target these days.

I've got the gun's parts laid out in front of me in the order I'll be cleaning them: frame, slide, barrel, and, finally, the guide rod and recoil spring. I look up to see that Dad is already wiping the parts to his backup firearm—a Smith and Wesson Airweight Revolver—down, and I reach for an extra rag.

Since Dad doesn't fire his gun often—a blessing, to be sure—there's not a lot of carbon build up to be removed. After wiping all of the parts down, I apply the solvent and let it sit for a few minutes before scrubbing the whole gun and wiping it clean with a lint-free cloth—inside and out.

Finally, I oil the inside of the barrel and the rest of the necessary parts thoroughly. Satisfied with how clean it is, I reassemble the gun and check that all the parts slide properly before wiping it down to remove any excess oil.

"There you go," I say, handing the gun over to Dad for one final inspection.

He sets his revolver down and looks over my work. I'm not offended; I need to know that it's operational so that it doesn't misfire when he might need it most.

"You did good, Jules," he praises. "Maybe I was a little premature to think you couldn't take care of yourself."

"Well, to be fair, I only cleaned the gun." I smirk mischievously. "Though, if you'd like to take me to the range to see if my aim is still better than yours, old man..."

Just then, the door opens and Mom calls out for us.

Dad smiles. "You're lucky your mother's home."

With a scoff, I lean back in my chair and cross my arms. "You mean *you're* lucky," I correct him cockily.

"Pot*ay*to, pot*ah*to." He sets his finished revolver down and pushes away from the table to greet my mom as she enters the kitchen. "Hey, sweetheart."

Mom giggles as Dad wraps his arms around her and kisses her. It doesn't take long before they forget I'm here, and I loudly scrape my chair across the tile before standing up. "Okay, well I can see the two of you are in need of some adult time." Mom and Dad don't let go of each other, but they do acknowledge me by turning their heads.

Backing out of the kitchen, I point over my shoulder. "I'll, uh, be up in my room. Music blaring. Dad, I'll call Greyston and see if dinner tomorrow sounds good?" I don't wait for him to answer. I turn around and book it up the stairs. "Cool! Later!"

Up in my room, I close my door and turn on my stereo. It's not too loud, and I can hear the murmured voices of my parents below me. If I listen really close—not that I'm doing it on purpose, believe me—it sounds like they're on separate ends of the kitchen and not...you know...*together.*

I'm able to relax a little knowing that I'm not going to hear them in the throes of passion, and I pull my phone from my pocket, flopping down on the edge of my bed. My fingers move swiftly over the touch screen until I locate Greyston's contact info.

He picks up on the second ring. "Hey. Miss me already?" Obviously he doesn't realize who's calling him; maybe he thinks it's that girl...*Callie.*

Nervously, I bite my lip and try to hide the disappointment in my voice. "Hi, um, this is Juliette?" I don't know why I sound like I'm questioning my own identity, but I do.

"I know that..." Greyston chuckles. "But *you* sound a little unsure."

"Sorry. I just thought that maybe you thought I was...someone else."

Greyston's quiet for a minute, and I find myself wondering what it is I interrupted him doing. I start imagining him in a lot of naked at-home activities. Laundry, cooking, cleaning...

Okay, so I guess they're not really *supposed* to be naked activities, but that's apparently how my foggy brain likes to think Greyston spends a majority of his time when he's at home. Naked.

"So what's up?" Greyston asks, interrupting my perverted thoughts. Again.

I shake my head clear and try to remember why I'm calling him. "Oh, sorry. I talked to my dad, and he thinks tomorrow would be a good night for you to come over for dinner. You know, before I move in full time... Unless you have something already planned?"

"Nothing that can't be re-scheduled."

His response shocks me. He hardly knows me, and he's willing to rearrange all of his plans just to meet my parents? "You're sure? I don't want to interfere with work or anything."

"Trust me, it's fine," he assures me. "What time should I come over?"

Thinking for a minute, I try to remember what time Dad

will be home from work; I want to make sure I have enough time to prepare Greyston for some of Dad's usual interrogation techniques. "I have class until four, so maybe around five? That way we have time to talk before my father monopolizes most of your time with his nonsense."

"Juliette..." Greyston's tone sounds almost chastising. "His wanting to keep you safe isn't nonsense. Cut the guy some slack."

I laugh. "Keep that frame of mind and you'll have no problems winning him over," I tell him. "And if all else fails, you've still got that sports agent card to play."

"Yes, I suppose I do," Greyston agrees with a laugh, and I find myself remembering how his smile makes the outer corners of his eyes crinkle. "But I think your father and I will be able to find common ground on the issue of providing you with a safe place to live."

All thoughts of Callie disappear in an instant when he says that. I know I'm likely hearing something in his tone that's not really there, but I can't help but let him dazzle me just once more.

chapter 8

I'm home around four-thirty, and I rush upstairs to put my bag away and fix my hair. I know it's pointless since Greyston has no interest in me, but that doesn't mean I still can't look my absolute best, right?

By five o'clock, I'm pacing in the living room like a crazy person, running my fingers through my hair—and then fixing it because I've messed it up—before occupying my hands by biting my nails, which is a habit I thought I'd given up when I was in grade school.

Greyston is set to arrive any minute, and I'm freaking out. You'd think I was introducing them to an actual boyfriend and not my landlord. It really is ridiculous just how nervous I am about all of this.

While I wear a hole in the area rug, Mom is in the kitchen putting the finishing touches on dinner. Dad isn't due home until six, but I know I'll need the extra time to warn Greyston about his usual scare tactics.

The doorbell rings, and it startles me a little. Gathering my composure, I check my hair in the mirror above the mantle and call out, "I got it!"

When I pull the door open, I see Greyston on the front step. He's handsome, dressed in a faded pair of blue jeans, a dark blue button-up shirt, and a black blazer. In his hands is a beautiful bouquet of flowers, and my jaw drops.

"Good evening, Juliette," he says, his smooth voice pulling my eyes up to his.

"H-hi. Thanks for coming. Come in, please. Can I take your jacket?" I offer.

"These are for your mother," he says, handing me the flowers so he can slip his blazer off to give to me. It disappoints me a little, but I get over it soon enough when I realize he's just trying to make a good impression on them.

After hanging it in the closet, I lead him to the kitchen where Mom is checking on dinner in the oven. "Mom?" She looks up, smiles, and closes the oven door before straightening up. "This is Greyston Masters. Greyston, this is my mom, Anne."

Stepping around the counter, Greyston outstretches a hand, smiling wide. "Mrs. Foster. It's a pleasure to meet you. Juliette's told me so much about you."

"It's nice to meet you, Greyston." Glancing between the two of us, Mom smirks, and I know that no good can come of it. "You're even more handsome than Juliette described. Tell me, are you seeing—"

My cheeks are *blazing*, and before she can humiliate me further, I thrust the flowers in her face. "Look, Mom, Greyston brought you flowers. Pretty, huh? You should probably put them in some water." I turn to Greyston quickly and continue to ramble, not allowing my mother to get another word in edgewise. "Can I get you something to drink? Iced tea? Water? Wine? Beer?"

Greyston is chuckling through my entire spazz-attack. "Iced tea would be great. Thank you."

I pour Greyston and me each a glass of iced tea while my mother puts her flowers in a vase. "We'll be in the living room," I tell her, leading Greyston away from her probing questions.

We have a seat on opposite ends of the couch, and I tuck my legs up under me, facing him. He doesn't seem nervous at all about tonight, facing me with his left arm draped casually along the back of the couch while the other hand holds his glass.

"Your mom seems great," he says before taking a drink.

I groan. "I'm so sorry about that. She sometimes speaks without really thinking. She had no right to try to ask if you were involved. I mean, it's really no one's business."

Greyston laughs, and I'm treated to the sparkle in his eyes that tells me it's genuine. "It's not a problem."

Glancing at the clock, I decide it's time to start warning Greyston about what to expect from my dad.

"Juliette, I'm sure you're worrying over nothing."

I shake my head, knowing for a fact that I'm not. "When he comes through that door, he'll take his jacket off but leave his holster on so his gun is in plain sight," I tell him, remembering how he'd "welcomed" Ben that same way when we'd begun dating. "He's going to try to intimidate and shake you up. You can't let him."

Before I can warn him further, the front door opens. Dad's home early.

"Jules? Anne?"

"I'm in here, Cam!" Mom calls out from the kitchen. "Juliette and her friend are waiting for you in the living room."

I swallow thickly before setting my glass on the coffee table and standing up, wiping my now-sweaty palms on my jeans. "Good luck," I tell Greyston quietly, turning to see Dad in the foyer.

As promised, Dad takes his jacket off and hangs it in the closet before joining us—holster on. Quickly, Greyston stands and makes his way around the couch, holding out his hand. "Mr. Foster. It's so nice to finally meet you."

Dad accepts Greyston's handshake—but says nothing—so I decide to break the ice. "Dad, this is Greyston Masters. The man I'll be renting the room from."

"We'll see," is all he says before taking a seat in his recliner. He doesn't sit back and get comfortable, though; instead, he sits on the edge and leans on his thighs, his deep brown eyes staring hard at Greyston.

Greyston and I sit back down on the couch, but I'm far from relaxed; my back is straight, my posture rigid, and my pulse is racing.

"So, Mr. Foster," Greyston begins, his voice confident and smooth. "Juliette tells me you're on the police force."

Dad nods. "I am."

Great, I think to myself. *We're in for the short-answer re-*

plies. This is going to be like pulling teeth.

Greyston is determined, though, and continues without balking. "I can only imagine it's a very rewarding career—to know that you're out there making the city a safer place."

There seems to be some kind of staring contest going on between the two of them, and it makes me nervous. My fingers are twitching, and I have to press my hands hard into my thighs to keep from fidgeting while the silence drives me mad.

"I do what I can," he says, and I feel as though I can breathe a little easier now that the unnerving quiet has broken. "I feel that safety in the home is where it all starts."

Here it comes.

"I couldn't agree more," Greyston concurs confidently, even going as far as to smile at my dad.

Dad smirks, but it's not out of amusement. "As I'm sure Juliette's told you, I'm not too keen about this living situation." He points between the two of us, and Greyston nods, clearly not wanting to interrupt. "I've done everything in my power to keep her safe for the last twenty years, so to hear that she was planning to move in with someone—a man, no less—that she found through an advertisement... Well, let's just say I've witnessed enough in my years on the force to be a little leery."

My mouth has just opened to tell Dad that he's jumping to all the wrong conclusions, when Greyston beats me to it. "While I understand your concerns, Mr. Foster, I assure you that I mean your daughter no harm. I don't know what all Juliette has told you, but my home is located in one of the newer communities here in Phoenix, and I had a state-of-the-art alarm system installed upon moving in."

"So, no one can get in, and no one can get out."

My eyes and mouth widen in disbelief. "Dad!" I scold. "That's not what he's saying. God, chill out."

Maintaining his composure, Greyston smiles and turns to me. "No, Juliette, it's okay. I get it."

He's just turning back to my dad when I reach out and grip his bicep—his strong, hard bicep. With his eyes back on me, I inhale shakily and remember what it is I was about to say. "No. It most definitely is *not* okay," I say, glaring angrily at my father.

The cocky jerk only grins at me; he's screwing with us, and it only seems to be riling me up. "Jules, would you mind grabbing me something to drink?"

His request worries me a little, but there's something in his eyes that tells me I needn't. "Uhhhh…" I look between Dad and Greyston, and when my eyes catch Greyston's, I'm surprised by how at ease he still seems—even after my father's less-than-kind remarks. Confident, even. "Y-yeah. Sure."

As I leave the room, I hear Dad asking Greyston more about his neighborhood. While I want to duck around the corner and listen in on their conversation, I know I'll be found out one way or another. So I continue on, only hearing the first little bit of Greyston's answer before I'm in the kitchen.

"Hey, sweetie," Mom says, looking up from her cookbook. "What's up?"

"Um, Dad asked for a drink," I say with a shrug, pulling a stool from under the counter, plopping down on it, and resting my chin in my hands. "But I know he was just trying to get rid of me so he could interrogate Greyston."

"He's cute," she blurts out, and I immediately grimace.

"Oh yeah, scaring the crap out of the guy I have to live with is really freakin' adorable."

Mom laughs, shaking her head. "Not your father—well, him too, I suppose—but I was *actually* referring to Greyston."

Warmth fills my cheeks, and I find myself looking anywhere but at my mother. "Um, I suppose he's a little good-looking."

Because she's my mother, she sees right through me. "Yeah, 'a little.' Please, Juliette. You were making googly eyes at him the entire time you were standing in the kitchen."

I'm offended—and also not surprised. "I was not!" One look from her and I'm burying my face in my hands. "Okay, okay," I mumble into my palms before peeking at her through my fingers. "What am I going to do?" The left side of her mouth turns up into a sly smirk, and I grab the tea towel off the countertop and toss it at her with a laugh. "Mom!"

Abandoning her cookbook, she comes around and pulls the other stool out next to me. "Relax, I was only teasing. He seems like a very nice young man."

Suddenly, I hear Dad's laughter coming from the living room. My eyes meet Mom's, shock clearly written across my face as I launch myself off my stool. By the time I make it back to the living room, Dad is relaxed back into his chair—his holster no longer on or even in sight.

What the hell happened while I was in the kitchen? I hadn't been gone that long.

Dad looks extremely happy, his eyes shining with what I assume to be tears of laughter. I can't even put into words how shocked I am to be witnessing this. And here I thought he was going to be a hard-ass the entire evening. Clearly, I underestimated Greyston's ability to win him over.

"What's going on in here?" I ask, looking between the two of them with wide eyes.

Dad glances at me, looking somewhat perplexed. It's then that I realize I've forgotten his drink. Thankfully, Mom's right behind me to save the day.

"Juliette, honey, you forgot your father's beer in the kitchen." Mom hands Dad his beer and sits on the armrest of his chair. "Dinner should be ready right away," she announces, draping her arm over Dad's shoulders.

Settling back onto the couch—possibly closer to Greyston than before—I try to get a feel for the atmosphere in the room. Mom and Dad begin to talk quietly amongst themselves, so I decide to ask Greyston how he managed to change my dad's pre-conceived notions so quickly.

"So," I begin, "things are going well?"

Greyston chuckles quietly, shifting his body to face mine again. His knee touches mine, and a spark shoots through me. I'd blame static, but this seems to be the effect he has on me every time we're together. "Your father's not quite as terrifying as you seem to think."

"Yes," I argue. "He is."

I think Greyston is about to tell me what was said between him and my dad but is interrupted by my parents standing up, and my mom announcing that dinner is ready.

Mom and Dad lead the way to the dining room where the table is set for four: two places on one side for Mom and Dad, and two on the other for Greyston and me. Dad, Greyston, and I find our seats while Mom heads back to the kitchen to retrieve dinner.

"This smells absolutely amazing, Mrs. Foster," Greyston proclaims, pulling my chair out for me.

My parents' expressions aren't missed as I accept Greyston's chivalrous act. Their eyebrows shoot straight up, widening their eyes, and their mouths are gaping slightly. While I'm sure Greyston has already caught the looks they are giving us, I clear my throat to make them stop.

Mom's the first to speak, setting the casserole down in the middle of the table. "Thank you, Greyston. It's one of Juliette's favorites. And, please, call me Anne."

We all take a minute to dish up before Mom gets the conversation flowing. "So, Greyston, what is it that you do for a living?"

I find myself sitting up a little straighter and looking at my father while awaiting Greyston's answer. I anticipate a huge reaction because Dad's generally pretty animated when it comes to anything sports-related.

"Actually, I'm a sports agent," Greyston announces.

My dad is looking at Greyston, but there's no excitement. I have to admit, I'm a little disappointed.

"I think it's kind of cool," I say, gaining a strange look from my mom. I can understand her reaction—I'm not a sports kind of person—but I'm trying to get my dad excited about this.

Greyston shoots me that crooked smile that makes me all tingly. "Thanks. I was actually just telling your dad that it was my agency that helped sign the Cardinals' new quarterback."

Well, that would explain my dad's lack of response; he already knew. Damn, I was hoping to have been around for that.

"In fact, Cam…" I'm stunned by Greyston's use of Dad's first name, but neither one of them seems fazed. "The team's manager gave me a few extra tickets to their next game. I don't suppose you and your family would like to join me?"

Dad's eyes practically bug out of his head, and the food he's just scooped onto his fork falls back to his plate with a quiet *splat*. His astonished reaction makes me feel a little better about not having been around when Greyston told him about the sports agent thing.

"You mean the game next weekend? Against the Eagles?" Dad looks like he's about to pass out; I'm starting to get concerned.

Mom interjects, setting her fork down and placing a hand on Dad's shoulder. "Cam grew up in Philly, Greyston. The Eagles are his favorite team."

Smirking, Greyston swallows the bite he'd just taken, grabs his napkin from his lap, and wipes his mouth. "Well, that's too bad." Dad seems confused. "It's going to be hard to watch them lose, then."

Mom and Dad are staring incredulously at Greyston, and I'm not even sure how to react. Surely my dad is going to blow a gasket and throw Greyston's cocky ass out of the house. It looks like I probably won't be moving into my new place.

Goodbye, new life. I'm sure you would have been great…

"Well, that seems awfully confident," Dad retorts, shocking me completely.

Greyston shrugs, the look in his eyes goading my father on further. "What can I say? I have faith in my hometown team."

"Greyston," I whisper, gripping my fork so tightly that my knuckles turn white. There's another part of me that's fighting from poking him in the leg with it just to shut him the hell up before he ruins everything. "I don't think that this—"

Dad snorts, and it sounds as though he's amused by what Greyston has said. "And the fact that the Cardinals haven't won the last five games hasn't shaken that faith, son?"

I choke—but not on food or drink because I've been far too stunned by Greyston's comment to eat. Of course, my shock over that is *nothing* compared to hearing my father call

Greyston "son."

Did I step through some magical portal into a world where everything is ass-backward? In what universe is my dad this chummy with *any* guy I've brought home?

"Sorry," I apologize after catching my breath. "I inhaled and swallowed at the same time." The minute the words leave my mouth, I'm mortified. There's no way that all three of them don't see my face turn a shade of red that rivals the cherry-red pillared candles in the middle of the table.

Did I seriously just say that out loud?

I avoid everyone's eyes and push my food around my plate with the tines of my fork, occasionally stabbing at a broccoli floret. It feels like forever before anyone speaks again—even though it's probably only been less than a minute. This, if you ask me, is far too long to think about the double meaning behind my words…not that you really have to think to get it.

Greyston clears his throat and starts talking about sports again, easily distracting my father. I chance a look across the table to find my mother smiling sympathetically at me. "It'll be okay," she mouths, and I shake my head in disagreement.

I don't speak for the rest of the meal—even when someone directs a question my way. I'm always sure to put a forkful of food into my mouth or take a drink, limiting my responses to a headshake or a nod, and, occasionally, an agreeing hum.

With dinner finally out of the way, my mom brings out a homemade apple pie. Greyston looks like he's about to drool a little before telling my mom that apple pie is his absolute favorite.

"Oh, Greyston," she says humbly. "You're just saying that."

"No, I'm really not," he assures her, accepting the plate she's holding out to him.

She finishes serving the pie before taking her seat, and is just about to take her first bite when she looks like she's forgotten something. "Juliette, honey, would you be a dear and grab the whipped cream? I didn't have the chance to whip it myself, so just grab the can out of the fridge door."

"Yeah, sure," I agree, pushing my chair from the table and heading for the kitchen. I take the time away to give myself a stern talking-to about sticking my foot in my mouth. When I'm sure I can control myself for another hour or so, I return to the table and offer the whipping cream to Greyston first.

It would be an outright lie to say that watching him accidentally get a bit on the tip of his index finger doesn't do unspeakable things to my body. God. I'm biting the inside of my cheek to keep from making an embarrassing noise—and crossing my legs beneath the table to quell the dull tingle that has started to spread between them—when he licks his delicious-looking digit clean.

I'd have traded my soul to wrap my own lips around his finger…

"Juliette?"

Blinking, I let my eyes wander from his fingers to his eyes. It's then that I realize he's offering me the whipped cream, and I'm staring like an attention-starved puppy. Apparently, I don't need to speak to embarrass myself completely.

"Sorry. Thanks." I take the canister from him and shake it before turning it toward my plate. My hands tremble as I push on the nozzle, causing the whipped cream to spray somewhat messily. I, too, have gotten whipped cream on a couple of my fingers, so I quickly lick them clean and cut a huge bite of my pie with my fork to keep anyone from asking me a question.

To my left, Greyston's fork clangs on his plate, and I can see through my periphery that he's just picking it back up.

After dessert, I take everyone's plates and load them into the dishwasher. I'm just putting the last fork into the basket when a deep voice startles me.

"Are you sure you want to leave this behind? Your mom is a pretty amazing cook," Greyston says. "I have half a mind to ask if I can move in here."

I laugh nervously, closing the dishwasher and turning it on. "Believe me, less than a week in this house and you'll be Googling lobotomies or the best household chemical combination to make industrial-strength brain-bleach." Greyston eyes me curiously. "Just trust me. You don't want to know."

Greyston smiles, his blue eyes locking with mine. "Well, I just hope you realize I'm not nearly as good a cook as she seems to be. I'd hate to disappoint you." This time, it's his cheeks that turn a bright shade of crimson, and he chuckles nervously, tousling his hair and looking at his feet. "Anyway, I just wanted to thank you for suggesting this meeting. I had a really great time tonight."

It's hard to hide my disappointment that the night is coming to an end, so I look down at the towel as I dry my hands. "Good," I tell him, trying to mask the sadness in my voice with a forced smile. "I'm glad you had a good time. I think my parents really liked you. Thanks for agreeing to this." I hang the dishtowel on the oven handle and look up at Greyston.

Silence hangs heavy and awkward between us before he glances at his watch. "Well, I guess I should head out. I have to be up early for a few errands. If I'm late, Callie will have my head."

It doesn't seem to matter that I just met him and I'm fresh out of a relationship, my stomach clenches and my heart aches when I'm reminded that Greyston is in a serious relationship. I must be hiding it well, though. "Of course. I'll walk you to the door."

After he puts his jacket on, I open the door for him. "I'll see you this weekend?" I remind him.

He nods once. "Definitely. Remember to call if you need a hand moving…or anything else."

Anything? I wonder silently before slapping my presumptuous inner-monologue into submission. "I will. Thanks." Greyston turns and takes the first couple of steps away from me. "Greyston?" He faces me once more, curious. "Have a good night."

His smile widens. "You, too, Juliette."

After standing in the doorway and watching Greyston drive away for a change, I close and lock the door before retiring to my room for the night.

chapter 9

The sunlight streams through the windows, drawing me from a content sleep. Slowly, I open my eyes, squinting against the bright light that bathes my room. At first, I find myself confused by the pale blue walls and fluffy white duvet I'm nestled under, but then I smile and prop myself up on my elbows as I look around my new digs. Even from my bed, I can see a portion of the desert through my balcony doors, and I still can't believe this will be what I get to wake up to every morning.

Kicking my blankets off, I twist and climb out of bed, stretching tall as I make my way past the three boxes I decided not to unpack last night in favor of sleep after a long day. I open the French doors, letting the warmth of the morning sun wash over me as I step out onto the stone balcony and breathe in the fresh air. Just as it was the last time I was standing in this very spot, the desert is breathtaking.

Of course, then I look down, and I truly understand the meaning of that expression.

Greyston is swimming lengths in the pool, his sinewy muscles move with each stroke of his arms. Unable to look away, I lean on the railing and continue to ogle him from afar.

I'm not naïve enough to think that our arrangement won't be a little awkward in the beginning. Not necessarily for him, but for me. I've got a huge crush on him, and I can't do anything about it except maybe wait to see if it passes.

Until the day that happens, though, I'm going to enjoy the view my new room comes with to its fullest extent.

I straighten up quickly when he reaches the side of the pool and looks up to find me gawking. I'm hoping he can't see just how hard I was staring. However, considering the second level isn't that far up, I'm extremely doubtful.

"Hey!" he calls up, offering me a wave. "There's coffee downstairs. Why don't you grab a cup and come on out?"

I dash back into my room and pull on a pair of jeans and a fitted tee before brushing my teeth and hair and washing my face. I grab the check for first and last month's rent from my dresser and head downstairs. Down in the kitchen, I find a fresh pot of coffee and pour myself a cup while I read and sign the rental agreement Greyston had left on the counter. After placing the check on the agreement, I head outside to find Greyston.

As I wander out from beneath the shade of the eave overhanging the dark stone patio, I see Greyston standing by the edge of the pool, running a towel over his head to dry his hair. His face is blocked by the blue terrycloth, but I'm not really focused on that part of his anatomy anyway; my eyes are far too interested in his strong arms, his chiseled chest and abs, and his muscular legs.

I'm pretty sure I'm going to melt into a puddle or spontaneously combust.

He drops the towel and begins to wipe the water droplets from his lightly tanned skin. "How was your sleep? Was the bed comfortable enough?"

Drawing my eyes away from his chest, I nod and walk toward him, taking a seat on one of the poolside chairs. "It was great. Thank you." I take a sip of coffee and then look back up at him. "Yours?"

"I slept better last night than I have all week. I tend to have difficulty falling back into regular sleep patterns after returning home from a long trip," he explains.

"Well, I'm glad you slept better last night."

Greyston sits on the chair next to mine. "You work today?"

Nodding, I sit back on my chair and relax. "I do. It's only

"So, what can I get for you?" I ask, hoping that he didn't hear me implying that he was gorgeous only moments ago.

Looking at the menu above our heads, he hems and haws for a few seconds. "Two double espressos, please, and maybe a couple of blueberry muffins, too."

I ring in his order and put the cash in the till before making his coffee. While I prepare his drinks, I can overhear Katie striking up a conversation with him.

"So, Juliette says you're some kind of big-shot in the sports industry," she begins.

"Did she, now? Well, I suppose she's right; I scout up-and-coming talent to represent," he explains.

"Here you go," I announce, placing his drinks and the bag of muffins on the counter.

He flashes me that killer smile again, and my cheeks warm. "Thanks, Juliette. I'll see you back at home later."

"I'll be there," I promise.

Before exiting the café, Greyston turns back to me. "Oh, and don't worry about picking anything up for dinner. I'll figure something out."

The minute he leaves, Katie grabs my arm and whips me around to face her. "Oh. My. God! He's delicious!"

The rest of our shift flies, and by five, Paul has shown up. Before we go, we tidy up and restock all of the supplies so Paul doesn't have to, then Katie and I walk out to our vehicles together and say our goodbyes before taking off.

It's another scorcher out, so before leaving the lot, I roll down both windows. The fact that I have to practically lay across the seat and manually crank the lever to get the passenger side down is kind of annoying. I absolutely adore my little car, but I'll admit that the luxury of power windows and door locks definitely sounds appealing.

I twist my hair up, securing it with a pen from my purse, and start my car. The sweltering heat makes me happy to be living in a house with a pool, and I begin to imagine weekends relaxing on a lounge chair and swimming to beat the extreme summer heat. Not to mention, studying by the pool with the beautiful desert view would be so peaceful.

On my way home—it's still pretty amazing to be able to

say that—I start to wonder if Greyston would be opposed to my having my parents over. I'd like to show them the house, maybe further setting my father's mind at ease. If he's okay with it, I think I'll plan something for next weekend, once I'm all unpacked and settled.

After parking my car in my brand new driveway, I grab my purse and head inside. Before going in search of Greyston, I head upstairs to my room to shower quickly and change into something that doesn't smell like the café.

Stepping into my private bathroom, I turn on the shower and brush my hair out before undressing and stepping under the delightfully cool spray of water. The water streaming down over my body is so relaxing, off-setting the sizzling heat of the late-afternoon sun, that I find myself not wanting to get out.

Opening the glass door, I grab the dark blue towel from the hook and wrap it around my body. Instead of being cooler, the air is actually a bit warmer as I step out of the shower stall and head to my closet to look through my clothes I decide on a pair of cutoff jean shorts and a tank top.

I remove my towel, hanging it on my closet doorknob for a moment while I dress. My shorts are definitely that—*short*—but I'm roasting, so the fact that they barely cover my butt and show the lower bit of my front pockets doesn't concern me too much. I'll just have to refrain from bending over.

Even though my wet hair feels nice and cool against my warming back, I know I'll need to tie it up before it becomes an issue. I grab an elastic off my dresser and fasten a messy top knot on the top of my head.

Feeling refreshed, I make my way out of my room and down the stairs. When I reach the landing, I can hear Greyston's voice coming from the kitchen. I assume he's on the phone again…until I hear a melodious female laugh.

While earlier I was mostly curious to meet Callie, I'm feeling kind of bummed out now. The closer I get to the kitchen, the more I hear of their conversation. They seem to have a really solid relationship, and I start to feel like I might be intruding if I go in there and interrupt them. My stomach rudely insists I keep moving forward, though.

"No! Are you serious?" the woman says with a giggle.

As I round the corner, I catch sight of her on one of the island stools, looking at Greyston as he stirs something on the stovetop. Even though I can only see a portion of her facial profile, I can tell I was exactly right about her being gorgeous. She's got creamy white and flawless skin, and her auburn hair hangs loose down her back, grazing the waist of her jeans. Even though she's seated, I can tell she's got the perfect hourglass figure.

Greyston chuckles, not turning to look at her, and I continue to go unnoticed. "I swear on my life, Callie. It's unlike anything I've ever experienced. I really can't explain it; you'll just have to take my word for it."

She shakes her head, the ends of her soft-looking hair flowing from the movement. "Well, if that's the case, then you should go for it. You know I only want what's best for you."

That's when he turns to offer her a smile, but before he locks eyes with her, he finds me standing in the doorway. "Hey," he says, sounding surprised. "I didn't hear you come downstairs."

"I'm pretty stealthy," I quip playfully before realizing his girlfriend might misconstrue it for shameless flirting and think I'm a hussy.

Callie turns on her chair, and her blue eyes are crystal clear and shining with happiness. "Hi," she greets, hopping off the stool. "You must be Greyston's new tenant. Juliette, right?"

I nod, my face warming a little. "I am. You're Callie?"

"Ah," she says, glancing back over her shoulder at Greyston. "So, he's spoken of me."

"Highly," I reply, even though he's only just mentioned her. I figure it's probably best that she thinks he speaks of his perfect relationship whenever he can...actually, I wonder why he doesn't.

I try not to dwell on it and shake Callie's hand. "It's nice to finally put a face to the name."

"Same here."

I notice that Greyston has gone back to busily stirring the

meal he's preparing. "I actually didn't mean to interrupt the two of you; I just wanted to grab something to tide me over until dinner." I move toward the fridge and open it up, looking for some fruit or something.

I bend over and start pushing things aside in my search for food. A clang of metal, followed by Greyston's whispered curse and Callie's delicate giggle allude to something happening. Glancing up, I see him looking down into the deep pot, his brow furrowed with frustration. With a sigh, he opens the drawer next to him and grabs a spaghetti fork, dunking it into the deep pot and fishing out a long, sauce-covered spoon.

Callie laughs again, drawing my focus to her. I assume I've missed some silent communication between the two of them, but when I see her flipping through the pages of a magazine, still snickering, I realize she must have read a funny article or something. My stomach rumbles again, so I resume my search for food, opening the fruit drawer to find some strawberries. Being allergic, I decide I don't feel like getting a raging case of hives and close the fridge.

"There's…uh…some protein bars in the cupboard here," Greyston offers, his voice rough as he opens the door next to his head. "Up on the middle shelf."

"Thanks," I say, standing on the tips of my toes and stretching for the slender box.

Another clang of metal is heard, but when I look to my left, I see that Greyston still has hold of his spoon. His face looks a little flushed, though; maybe he's coming down with something.

"How was work?" Greyston asks, his voice a little more steady now as I close the cupboard.

"Busy. I'm glad I didn't have to work the evening rush," I admit. "Anyway, I'll leave you guys to talk. I can imagine being away as much as Greyston is you like to be together as much as possible."

Both of them turn to look at me, eyes wide like I was in the process of sprouting a second head. "What?"

"Uh, nothing," Greyston stammers. I don't know when he became so nervous, but, it's a nice change of pace; I can't constantly be the one tripping over my own words.

Callie closes her magazine. "No need to go anywhere. We're not that desperate to be alone with each other," she jokes…or is she joking? It's kind of hard to tell.

"I've got homework," I tell them.

Smiling, Callie rolls her beautiful green eyes. "Greyston here tells me you're, like, some kind of genius or something. Plus, it's Saturday night; don't you have a party or something to go to?"

I clear my throat. "I'm not really the party-going type," I admit.

"Well, how am I supposed to live vicariously through you, then?" Her mock-pout makes me laugh.

"Trust me; my life is nothing to be coveted."

Patting the stool next to her, Callie invites me over with a sideways nod of her head. "Come on, join us. Greyston's kind of a bore."

"You're one to talk," Greyston retorts.

Their relationship confuses me; shouldn't they be a little more snuggly and a little less like brother and sister?

I need to take my mind off of that, so I decide to learn a little more about the woman in Greyston's life. "So," I begin, "how long have you and Greyston known each other?"

Looking contemplative, Callie looks at Greyston. "Gee, what's it been? Six years?"

"Yeah, about six years. Sometimes I wonder how we've survived all this time."

What an odd thing to say.

"Keep making wise-ass comments like that, and I'll be sure to remedy it," she teases.

Something's amiss here, but I'm not quite sure what. Is it possible that after so many years together, the romance fizzles and you become a pair of bantering old hens?

Of course, if that's true, explain my horn-dog parents. I know I sure don't want to.

"Okay, you know what?" Callie proclaims, slapping her hands on the counter and standing up. "As much fun as this little visit has been, I need to head home."

My eyes snap to hers. "You're not staying?"

Callie winks at me. "And eat his cooking? I think I'll pass. Greyston?" He looks back to acknowledge her. "Don't forget to finalize your itinerary. You don't want to get caught in a room with another single. Toby won't stand for it."

Toby?

"Shit, don't remind me. He wouldn't let up that whole trip. I thought for sure he was going to ride my ass because of it the entire weekend." Greyston's eyes snap wide open, meeting my own bewildered expression. "That didn't come out right."

"Is that what Toby said?" Callie asks in a coy voice.

My cheeks are burning, and I can only imagine how red my face is. I know I should probably go, but something is keeping me here. Morbid curiosity, most likely.

"Weren't you leaving?" I can tell by the playful edge in Greyston's voice that he's not angry.

"Thankfully, yes," she replies. "Remember. Itinerary. ASAP."

"Holy hell, Callie." Greyston sounds kind of exasperated. "You keep bossing me around like that and people are going to think we're dating."

My entire body goes rigid, and my head jolts up. Looking between the two of them, my eyes wild with confusion, I let the final piece of this puzzle fall into place. "You're *not* dating?" I ask.

Both of them are quiet for a moment, acknowledging each other and then me before practically doubling over in laughter.

"N-no," Callie stammers between giggles. When she's finally got a handle on her laughter, she continues. "I'm his assistant. While Greyston is very sweet and caring, I'm not his type."

This seems odd to me, because to look at her, she's exactly the type of woman I can picture him with. In fact, I did up until thirty seconds ago. Then it hits me.

Not his type.

Toby.

Riding hard.

Holy crap.

chapter 10

No, I tell myself. If I was able to jump to the wrong conclusions regarding Greyston and Callie, then there is a very real possibility that I'm doing the same thing now.

Or…am I? He's polite, a good cook, his house is immaculate and well-decorated, and he dresses great. I suppose it wouldn't be too unbelievable.

Callie says goodbye, and I think I answer her, but I've got so many things rushing through my poor, overworked brain that I really can't be sure.

Did she say something about Greyston booking a trip?

"Juliette?"

Taking a breath, I raise my gaze from the countertop, my blurred vision clearing the minute I lock eyes with Greyston. "Hmm?"

"You all right?" Turning the burner on the stovetop off, he crosses the kitchen and leans on the counter, facing me. "You seem, I don't quite know…off?"

I smile, deciding that I don't think I know him quite well enough yet to blatantly question his sexuality. Plus, I'm probably wrong. "I'm fine."

Greyston smiles widely, pushing himself up off the counter and clapping his hands together. "You hungry?" His eyes fall to my still-wrapped protein bar, and he snickers.

"Starved, actually," I confess.

Greyston heads to the cupboard, grabs two plates, and dishes up whatever he was working on. When he sets them down on the island counter where I'm sitting, I notice he's made spaghetti.

He takes the seat next to me and hands me a fork while I look down at my dinner, inhaling deeply. "This looks amazing," I say, picking up my fork and twirling some of the pasta around the tines. After taking my first bite, I look at Greyston. "So, you're going on a trip soon?"

He nods. "There's this baseball player in Houston that the agency has had its eye on for a few months. He's young and could do well under the right representation."

I say nothing. Do nothing.

He reaches out, grazing the skin on the outside of my knee before quickly drawing back as though the contact was out of line in some way. The fire of his touch still lingers, and I find myself wanting him to do it again. "I know you're still getting settled, and I honestly didn't think I'd be leaving this soon. I was hoping this trip would wait another couple weeks, but if we don't get him now, someone else will."

"I understand." I don't, really—he may as well be speaking another language—but it's his job, and I know he has to do it to pay the bills. "Maybe I can invite Daphne over?"

"I told you that you don't have to ask, Juliette," Greyston reminds me with a grin. "This is your home now, too. Invite whomever you want."

Nodding, I turn back to my dinner. "When do you leave?"

"Tuesday," he replies, returning to his own plate. "Come on, let's eat before our dinner gets c—"

Greyston doesn't get a chance to finish when we hear the front door open, and a deep male voice calls out, "Honey, I'm here!"

I wonder if I should be reading into that statement. Do I say something? Leave it alone? Something tells me to leave it alone—that it'll work itself out, or I'll at least be given the right opening to inquire further. I know if I assume anything out loud, I run the risk of making a fool out of myself. No, it's definitely best to stay quiet.

I think.

Our company's footsteps grow louder as he approaches

the kitchen. Was this the guy Callie mentioned earlier? Toby?

"There you are!" he booms, entering the kitchen. "I thought I smelled your spag—"

I turn just in time to see him stop dead in his tracks, cutting himself off as well. He's huge—like a bear. While his size should probably intimidate me, his baby blue eyes are warm and friendly, and when he smiles, he's got the deepest dimples that give him an almost childlike innocence.

"Sorry, I didn't realize you were entertaining." He looks at Greyston, then at me, and smiles. "I'm Toby. Greyston's partner."

Partner. Interesting word choice, but it could mean more than one thing.

"Hi." I stand up and meet him halfway to offer him my hand. "I'm Juliette."

"Juliette's my new tenant," Greyston clarifies. "The one I told you about."

Realization flashes in Toby's baby blues. "Of course. It's nice to meet you." He takes my hand in his, shaking it before standing next to Greyston. "What do you think of my boy's pad?"

My eyebrow arches questioningly. *His* boy? I try to think of another meaning behind his declaration and decide they could be best friends.

Toby reaches around and rests a hand on Greyston's shoulder, sort of half-embracing him.

Or not?

"The house is great," I reply, deciding to stop worrying about something that really isn't my business or within my ability to control.

"You're early," Greyston says to Toby. "You hungry?"

"Does an ostrich fly?" He's got his hand resting on his flat stomach, giving the impression that maybe he is. Of course, this makes his statement confusing.

Both Greyston and I look at Toby, but it's me that says something. "Um, no, actually they don't."

Toby looks genuinely surprised. "Really? Are you sure?"

I don't mean to laugh at him, but the poor guy really has no idea. "Yup. Pretty sure."

He walks over to the cupboard that holds the dishes and grabs a plate. "Guess I need to think of another rhetorical question, huh?"

Scooping a generous amount of pasta on his plate, Toby asks if Greyston has booked the hotel yet. I decide to eat my own meal, not wanting to intrude.

"Not yet." Toby shoots a disapproving look over his shoulder, and Greyston laughs. "I know, I know. I liked the idea of sharing that single bed as much as you did."

That doesn't mean anything, I try to tell myself. He didn't say they *did* share it.

"So, do you guys travel together a lot?" I ask, fishing for more information without bluntly asking and appearing rude. Truthfully, I've never been particularly good at fishing for anything, but I am going to give it a shot. I refuse to let this go on as long as the Callie thing did.

Toby leans against the counter in front of the sink and begins to eat, nodding. "Yeah. Whenever we can. It just depends on just how badly we need each other."

I nod as though I understand, but the truth of the matter is, I'm still uncertain; he could mean a lot of things. "I see. Have you guys been…*together* long?"

"About four years," Greyston replies without skipping a beat. "It was actually Callie that introduced us. We quickly became friends and then just couldn't deny how great we would be together."

"Mmmhmm," I'm still a little skeptical; sure, it's dwindling—just not in the way I've been hoping.

Toby finishes his dinner first, even though he started after us and had more than double our amount, and puts his plate in the dishwasher. "Well, I'll leave the two of you to finish up. Greyston, I'll meet you upstairs?"

Upstairs…where the bedrooms are. *There's a study too,* I quickly remind myself. *And the mystery room.*

"Okay," Greyston says, finishing his dinner and heading to the sink. "I'll be right up after I clean the kitchen."

I take the last bite of my pasta and join him. "Don't be silly. Go. I'll clean up," I offer with a smile.

"Yeah?" He's got a silly grin on his face, and it's pretty

infectious.

"Yes. Go. Do whatever it is that you boys do." I'm honestly trying not to think too much about it because I still don't really have a definitive answer. "I'll be hitting the books right away anyway."

Greyston gives my upper arm a light squeeze. "Thanks. We'll try to keep it down."

Oh, so they're noisy.

After finishing the dishes, I wipe the counters off and head upstairs with a fresh-brewed cup of coffee. As I reach the top of the stairs, I hear their voices. From behind the closed door to my right. Yes, the mystery room.

Curious—as always—I step closer, being sure to balance on the tips of my toes and move softly over the glossy hardwood floor.

"What the hell are you doing?" I hear Greyston demand.

Toby laughs. *"What? I thought you'd like that... No?"*

"Hell no!"

I search the door for a keyhole or something to peep through. I am deeply aware of just how wrong this is, but I can't seem to help myself.

"Well, what about when I do this?"

My eyes widen as I imagine what "this" could possibly be. I can't even fathom it. Flashes of them caught in some kind of torrid embrace flood my mind, and tendrils of warmth spread across my skin, caressing me until my fingers and my toes tingle.

Definitely not the effect I expected from such a thought, but a welcome one, nonetheless.

"Um, it's a little better. Still doesn't amaze me."

Wow, Greyston's tough to please.

"You know," Toby says, sounding exasperated, *"you were a lot more fun last week when we did this."*

Greyston laughs loudly. *"Yeah, well, last week we didn't have to worry about disturbing anyone else with our shenanigans."*

I instantly step away from the door, finally coming to my senses enough to know I really shouldn't be so invasive. However, in my haste to retreat, I bump into the little table against the wall, sending a candle toppling over and onto the floor with a very loud—and echoey—*thud!*

Silence fills the hall. Greyston and Toby have stopped doing whatever it is they're doing; I've stopped breathing and am just waiting to be found out. Before that can happen, I snatch the candle up off the floor and put it back on the table. I can't be sure it's even in the right spot as I dash from the scene—as quickly as I can with a cup of coffee—and the door opens behind me.

"Juliette?" Greyston calls out into the hall, but I've already disappeared from sight.

Taking a deep breath, I put a smile on my face and hang my head out into the hall. "Yeah?"

"Did you…?"

I reach out and run my fingers through my hair, stepping out into the hall. "Oh," I say. "Sorry about that. I wasn't paying attention to where I was going—the hazards of reading a text while walking—and bumped into the table." I can't lie, so I figure a slight bend and an omission is probably best. "Sorry if I disturbed you."

Greyston chuckles, stepping out into the hall. I notice he's shed the button-up shirt he was wearing and is now in a thinner cotton tee. His hair might be a little more mussed than before, but I don't get the chance to properly survey the area before he runs his long fingers through it. "Trust me," he says in a teasing tone. "You can't be any more disturbing than Toby. Do you have any idea what he was doing?"

I open my mouth to put a few guesses out there, but then think better of it. "I can only imagine," I reply sweetly. "Well, I should hit the books." I point toward my room with my thumb.

"Oh, okay. You'll let me know if you need anything?" I nod. "Remember to make yourself at home. Help yourself to whatever it is you want."

"Thank you. I will."

Greyston and I go our separate ways, but before I close my door, I hear him exclaim, "Did you keep going without me?"

I stifle a laugh as I close my door. With what I suspect is going on down the hall, it's hard for me to focus on my studies, and I think I've re-read the same paragraph at least ten times. My eyes burn, and my eyelids grow heavy. I close them for a minute, just to rest them and gather a reserve of energy, but when I open them again my cheek is pressed to the pages of my text and it's pitch black outside. One quick glance at my alarm clock tells me it's four in the morning.

"Awesome," I grumble, pushing myself off my bed. I reach for my mug of coffee—which is still full and now cold—and head downstairs. I'm sure to tip-toe past Greyston's closed bedroom door.

As I step into the kitchen, I'm surprised to see the refrigerator light on and Greyston's lower half. "Oh!" I exclaim, making him stand up.

Only, it's not Greyston. And he's not wearing a shirt.

I immediately look away. "Sorry, I didn't think anyone was up," I tell Toby. "I fell asleep studying and came down to dump my cold coffee and grab a glass of water."

Toby laughs quietly, bringing a glass of orange juice to his lips. "No worries, Juliette. Can I get you anything?"

He's sweet, just like Greyston. Exactly the type of person he should be with.

"Thanks. Um, where are the glasses?"

"Cupboard to the left of the sink," Toby says, stepping off to the side.

I grab a glass and fill it with tap water. With my back turned, I sip my water and stare out the window at the night sky that overlooks the desert. I want to talk to Toby, not necessarily about his relationship, but just to get to know him. I mean, he's got to be a pretty big part of Greyston's life; it probably isn't a bad idea to become friends.

"So, how do you feel about Greyston leaving on this trip?" Toby asks before I get a chance to speak.

I turn around and see him sitting at the counter, both of his large hands wrapped around the slender glass before him. "Fine."

Toby smiles, his dimples deepening, and stares down into his glass. "He's worried you won't feel safe," he confesses. "I'm just making sure you're okay with staying here. If not, I'd be happy to make other arrangements."

Smiling genuinely at his concern, I walk around the island and sit next to him. "It's a big house," I say. "But I have a couple of friends I can invite over."

"Guys?" Why does it sound like he's fishing for my relationship status?

I shake my head. "No. Boys are so *not* on my radar at the moment."

Toby quirks an eyebrow. "Oh? None at all?"

I laugh. "No." My cheeks warm at my half-truth, and I drop my eyes from his. "Well, there was one, but he's not exactly available," I explain quietly.

"His loss," Toby says, bumping my shoulder lightly with his fist.

I look back up at him, shrugging one shoulder. "Nah. He's with someone pretty great from what I can tell," I tell him honestly, not wanting to divulge that my crush is on Greyston.

"How is it you haven't been snatched up yet?" Toby asks, leaning in. "You're adorable."

I can feel myself blushing, and I'm thankful it's dark in the kitchen so he can't see it as I drop my gaze and giggle. "Um, thanks?"

"So, you're sure you're going to be okay here alone for a few days? If not—"

"Thanks," I say, interrupting him. "I'll be fine. Even if none of my friends can stay here, I can take care of myself."

This seems to intrigue Toby. "Oh?"

"I've taken more self-defense classes than you can imagine, and I'm kind of a crack shot," I brag.

Toby's head begins to bob up and down, his smile widening even more. "Badass."

I'm just about to thank him for his concern when a gravelly voice comes from behind me. "Hey. What's going on down here?"

I turn around to see a sleepy-eyed Greyston scratching the back of his head as he eyes us, confused.

"Oh," I say, hopping up off my chair. "I fell asleep and was just bringing my cold coffee down and grabbing a glass of water when I ran into Toby, and we got to talking."

Greyston's eyes go wide, almost like he's worried about something. Then they travel to Toby, and he rolls them. "Jesus, man. Put a shirt on. There's a lady living here now."

I laugh. "That's okay. I'm actually going to head back up to bed. I'll see you guys in a few more hours."

"Actually," Toby speaks up, pushing his stool away from the counter and standing. "I'm going to head home. I didn't mean to fall asleep here as it was."

"Oh?" I stop in the doorway, looking between him and Greyston.

"Yeah, Greyston and I were just so into fucking around"—I swallow thickly, trying to keep my expression neutral—"that we lost track of time and just passed out upstairs."

"Gotcha." I nod. "Well, I'll see you soon then?"

"Probably more than you'd like," Greyston teases.

Toby smirks. "Watch it," he threatens playfully. "I won't hesitate to drop you."

"All right," I interject, faking a yawn. "I'm going to go back to bed before I'm asked to ref a wrestling match."

"Have a good sleep, Juliette," Greyston says softly, offering me a brief glimpse of his crooked smirk.

"Thanks. You, too."

The minute I leave the kitchen, I hear Greyston quietly inquire about what we were talking about.

Toby laughs quietly before telling him that he was only asking how I felt about staying here alone and that he offered to help me out if I needed it. "Did you know she can shoot?" Toby asks jovially, bringing a smile to my face.

"I…no. But it doesn't surprise me; her dad's a cop."

On that note, I continue up to bed in case they want a minute alone to say goodnight to one another. The minute my head hits the pillow, I'm out like a light.

chapter 11

After leaving Greyston and Toby in the kitchen, I hadn't gotten more than another three hours of sleep. Like the day before, the sun wakes me up, shining through the windows on my balcony doors, and I step outside to see Greyston enjoying his morning swim.

Not wanting to be caught watching him cut gracefully through the water, I retreat back into my room and decide to use my morning burst of energy on unpacking. Once everything is put away, I decide it's time to change out of my pajamas and do a load of laundry. Having just heard on the radio that we're in store for a record-breaking heat wave, I pull on my shorts from yesterday and a fresh tank top.

Laundry-wise, I don't have much, but I've got enough for a small load of colors and an even smaller load of whites. I grab my basket and head down to the basement. I find the laundry room down the hall from a large and well-equipped home gym and turn on the machine while I separate my clothes, throwing my whites in first.

While my laundry cycles, I head outside to see Greyston still swimming. I walk barefoot to the edge of the pool and dip my toes in as Greyston swims by obliviously. Playfully, I kick out, forcing huge droplets of water to rain down on his partially exposed back. He stops in the middle of the pool, looking around until he sees me.

With a bright, toothy smile, he pushes his hair off his forehead. "Hey. Been up long?"

I shake my head and sit down so I can stick my legs in the water. "Not really. I actually just finished unpacking and throwing a load of laundry in."

The lower half of Greyston's face disappears beneath the surface of the water and he swims toward me. Once he's next to me, he rests his arms on the cement pool deck and looks up at me. He's so close to me that there's not much water between his ribs and my calf. In fact, if I moved a fraction of an inch, my toes would probably graze the hem of his trunks...

I clear my throat, trying to refocus my attention on what I originally came out here to do. "I was going to make breakfast. Have you eaten?" I ask.

"Nope. I'll finish up my lengths, and I'll meet you inside in fifteen?"

Smiling, I pull my legs from the water, accidentally grazing the side of his thigh with my foot. His lips twitch before forming a smile, and he quickly pushes himself away from the edge of the pool. Away from me. I don't take it personally; I shouldn't have done what I did. I blame it on my apparent lack of self-control today.

"Cool. I'll see you inside."

Inside, I head to the fridge to search for something to make, eventually deciding on French toast. I grab everything I'll need and begin my preparation. I'm just putting the last of six slices on when I hear the patio door slide open and Greyston's bare feet pad across the slick tile. He's right behind me—I can feel the waves of heat rolling off of his bare chest and across my back and shoulders. I take a shaky breath at the same time he inhales.

"Do you know how long it's been since I had French toast?" he asks, his breath tickling my exposed neck and ear.

I open my mouth to speak, but I can't; my voice is completely gone. It would appear that having him so close to me has forced me into a temporary state of muteness. So, instead of speaking, I shake my head, tightening my hold on the spatula to keep the tremble in my hands from being too noticeable.

He takes a few steps back, and I exhale through my lips quietly. "I'm going to go have a quick shower," he announces. "I'll be right down."

"Y-yeah," I reply, my voice having come back. "I'll see you in a few."

The minute he's out of sight, I drop the spatula onto the counter, bits of cinnamon-infused egg scattering across the dark marble surface. I run my fingers through my hair and look toward the empty doorway, wondering why the hell I can't seem to get my body to understand that he's unavailable in the *most extreme* way.

My brain gets it, but every time I'm around him, it's like I mentally check out, and my body just does whatever the hell it wants.

Okay, so maybe not, because if that happened, this counter would have my naked ass prints all the hell over it, and the smell of my French toast burning would be real and not in my imagination.

Wait a minute…

"Shit!" I shout, reaching out and turning the burner off before sliding the pan to an empty burner. I grab the spatula to remove the slice of bread from the pan, but it doesn't come easily; I actually have to scrape it off.

The smoke is thick, and the smell of burned toast and egg is heavy in the air. I open the kitchen window and turn on the fan above the stove. It doesn't seem to help as quickly as I'd like, so I slide the patio door open wide and begin to fan the air with the dishtowel that Greyston keeps on the oven handle.

"What happened in here?" Greyston asks, his eyes instantly finding mine as he rushes toward me. "It smells like you burned something."

I grimace. "Damn," I groan. "I was hoping you wouldn't notice. I wasn't paying attention, and the heat must have been too high. I burned it. That's all. No fires, I swear." He looks from me to the plated pieces of toast, still concerned. "The other five slices are fine. I promise." I laugh lightly. "I really am a decent cook, so don't hold this against me, okay?"

Letting his lips twist up into the smile I've come to look forward to, he grips my upper arm reassuringly. "I wouldn't dream of it." He releases me and grabs two glasses from the cupboard before offering me orange juice.

"Sounds great. Thanks."

I finish cutting up some fruit for a salad, leaving the beautiful, plump strawberries he has in the fruit drawer out of it, and we take what I've decided are our usual seats.

Greyston eyes his fruit bowl and frowns. "No strawberries?"

I shrug. "Allergic. I can grab the basket for you if you'd like," I offer.

"Oh, I didn't know. Sorry."

I giggle. "Why are you sorry? Should I be aware that this is somehow all your fault?" He chuckles, spearing a piece of cantaloupe. "It's not too bad," I tell him. "I won't die if I eat them; I just break out in this really itchy rash that covers almost my entire body. It's extremely unpleasant."

Greyston smiles. "Good to know."

After breakfast, Greyston offers to clean up since I took the liberty last night, and I take the opportunity to go and switch my laundry over. As I am pulling my clothes out of the washer and placing them in the dryer, it occurs to me that not *all* of my clothes are dryer friendly.

My bras and panties, for example.

I tell myself Greyston likely has zero interest in my underwear anyway, so I hang them on the little clothes rack he's got in the large laundry room. Once my clothes are swapped, I head back upstairs to find Greyston on the phone.

"Yes. Greyston Masters and Toby Singer... Mmm hmm... That's right." It's obvious that he's securing his and Toby's hotel room for their trip this week. "Perfect. Thank you... You have a good day, too."

He hangs up the phone and shrugs. "Hotel."

"I figured." I take a seat at the island. "You get everything figured out?"

"Yes. Toby will be more than pleased," Greyston assures me with a laugh.

"Oh good, because I'd hate to see him upset," I say playfully.

Greyston shrugs. "He's not a big grudge holder. He'd be over it within the first twelve hours." His cell rings, and I glance down to see Toby's name flash across the screen.

Wanting to give them privacy, I stand up and start to back out of the kitchen. "Okay, well I'm going to go and study for a bit." I head upstairs to my room where I toss my books on the end of my bed and lay down on my stomach. Pencil and highlighter in-hand, and notebook open to where I left off last night, I set to work.

About an hour in, there's a knock on my door. "Come in." I turn my head to see Greyston peer inside.

"The dryer's buzzing," he informs me. "I can grab your laundry and bring it up if you'd like? I'm headed down to put my whites in anyway."

"Oh, I have a load in the wash that needs to be switched over." I hop up off the bed, and Greyston is right behind me, his own laundry basket in his arms.

I unload my whites from the dryer and then work quickly to unload my colors so he can wash his clothes. I've got two bras and their matching panties that need to be hung before I head back upstairs. When I turn around, Greyston is looking down, seemingly stunned. It's when I follow his eyes that I see he's staring at my hands…at my underwear.

"Sorry," I apologize with a casual shrug, moving around him and hanging them before grabbing the few pairs of white ones and tossing them in the basket with my clean clothes. "Being a girl comes with some extra laundry."

He's facing the washer now, busily shoving his whites inside before turning the temperature back up and adding detergent. "Right. I suppose it does."

"Okay, well I'll be back up in my room. I'll come check on my last load in a bit," I tell him, heading back upstairs. He doesn't follow me right away, and I swear I hear him curse when I reach the stairs.

Just as I turn to see if something's wrong, he exits the laundry room, looking surprised to still see me. "Oh," he says roughly. "I thought you'd gone upstairs already."

"I was, but then I heard you say something… Are you okay?" I look him over, seeing nothing out of the ordinary.

Greyston lets out a single breathy laugh. "Oh, uh, I closed the washer door on my thumb. I'll be fine."

My eyes fall to his hands, and he quickly hides one of his thumbs within a fist. "You're sure?"

"Yes. I'm going to go out for a quick run," he announces out of nowhere. "Give you some quiet to get your studying done. I'll have my phone if you need me."

Greyston walks around me and dashes up the stairs. I follow, but not nearly as quickly. He goes up to his room, and when he reemerges, he's wearing a pair of shorts and a sleeveless shirt. "I'll be back in a bit."

I step into my room. "Sure. Have fun." I feel like he's acting weird, but I don't know him well enough to call him on it.

After I hear the front door close, I fold my laundry before returning to my studies...or, *try* to. I'm finding it hard to tear my mind from Greyston's behavior. I'm not sure what it was, but there had definitely been something in his eyes that I just can't pinpoint.

I check my alarm clock and see that almost an hour has passed. This means my laundry should be ready. Before heading down into the basement, I check out the front door to see if I can spot Greyston anywhere. I can't. While I know he's probably fine, I'm still feeling a bit weird about his sudden departure.

I'm probably over-thinking it; I usually do.

When I reach the basement, I realize I forgot my hamper upstairs, so I decide to just fold my small load and carry it upstairs instead of risking the laundry trail that I'll inevitably leave in my wake if I carry a rumpled pile.

I fold my pajama bottoms, then a couple of tank tops. As I pull my socks out, I toss them into a pile, always leaving them for last because then they'll all be there and I won't be searching for them as I go. It's really a huge time-saver.

Or, so I used to think.

I've got all of my laundry folded and have almost finished matching my pile of socks...all but one. With a sigh, I toss the lone red sock on the dryer and open it again, looking inside for the straggler. It's not there. I check the floor around me. Nothing. I think back to when I gathered my laundry this morning, and I specifically remember having both red socks in my hamper. They were right on top for crying out loud.

So where is it?

The washer next to me buzzes, and my eyes go wide. *Really* wide.

"Noooooooooo," I groan, reaching out and pulling the door open. What I find inside is a nightmare. There, on top of his freshly washed clothes is my missing red sock.

After removing it, I pull out one of Greyston's t-shirts. *Pink.*

A couple of his socks. *Pink and pink.*

Another shirt. *Pink.*

Then…a pair of boxer briefs. *Pink.*

"Oh God," I groan, dropping my face into my hands. I'm so upset by this huge err on my part that I haven't even dropped his underpants.

"Juliette?"

chapter 12

Frightened, I shriek, dropping his boxers back into the washer and slamming the lid back in place. "Jesus! You scared me."

Laughing, he pushes his sweat-dampened hair back off his forehead. He looks a lot more relaxed than when he left, and for a very brief moment, I'm glad.

Then I remember his new pink laundry.

"Nope, not Jesus. Just me." He places a hand flat on his chest. "Greyston." I laugh, but it's forced, and he can tell. "I, uh, just came to check my laundry." He peers around me, one of his eyebrows arched high. "What are you doing?"

"Nothing," I answer a little too quickly, even going as far as to hop up *onto* the washer to keep him from getting to it. Yes, I realize how stupid that is.

"I'm going to need to get in there."

I shake my head vehemently. "No you really don't."

"Juliette?" He's advancing slowly toward me, and I begin to panic, my heart racing.

I give him my best puppy dog eyes; my parents used to fall for it all the time when I was younger, so I'm confident it'll work now. "Please, don't."

He smiles, his blue eyes sparkling with nothing but mischief as he takes another step toward me. I'm still shaking my head, making myself somewhat dizzy, as he continues forward. I push myself farther back onto the washer, trying to make my body heavy and hanging onto the sides as he reaches out for me.

"Nonononono," I keep repeating over and over again. Of course, the minute the tips of his fingers touch the exposed sliver of skin between my tank top and shorts, I consider changing it to *yesyesyesyesyes!*

I'm no match for him; he moves me with ease, even against my struggles to remain between him and the massacre beneath me. He sets me on the top of the dryer, my face in my hands but peeking at him through my fingers.

"You weren't trying to poach my laundry, were you?" he teases before opening the lid and seeing the problem. "Oh."

My hands fall from my eyes to cover my mouth as he slowly pulls out several pink pieces of clothing. "I'm *so* sorry," I say, my voice muffled by my fingers. "I guess I was in such a rush to get my stuff out of there so you could use it that I missed a sock." He remains silent, and this scares me. "A-are you mad?"

He drops his hands immediately, his shirt collar still held tightly between his fingers, and looks at me. The minute his lips turn up into a smile, I let my hands fall to my lap, feeling slightly relieved. But only slightly. "They're just clothes, Juliette."

"Yeah," I agree. "But they're *pink*."

"True. But no one needs to know that."

I drop my eyes to my fidgeting fingers. "Yeah, but I'll know."

Greyston snickers. "You planning to start thinking about what color my underwear might be?" I inhale sharply, and he's quick to correct himself. "Sorry. That was…out of line."

"Uh, no, it's fine." Truthfully, if what he said was out of line, everything I've thought about him since the day we met has been so far over the line that I can't even see it anymore. And I am most definitely wondering about the color of the underwear he's wearing right at this moment.

Greyston starts pulling his clothes out of the washer, and I pull my legs up and crisscross them in front of me so he can load them into the dryer. He looks amused as he removes each piece of pink clothing.

"Come on," Greyston says after turning the dryer on. He looks up to me with a playful smirk and winks, offering me his hand. "I think you've had enough fun in the laundry room."

While the initial shock of destroying his clothes was almost petrifying, I have to admit that it's kind of funny to think that Greyston has more pink clothing than Daphne now. I start to laugh, and he looks stunned.

He lets go of my hand now that I'm firmly on my feet and crosses his arms over his chest. He's having trouble keeping the smile from his face; I can see it in his eyes. "You think this is funny?"

"I'm sorry. It isn't," I assure him through fits of giggles. "But it is kind of *funny*... Now."

"Oh, you think so?" There's a note of challenge in his voice, and when he narrows his eyes, my laughter dies instantly.

He takes a stalking step toward me, and I swallow thickly, taking one backward. I raise my arm and hold up a single finger. "Doooon't," I instruct, sounding like I'm scolding a puppy. I try to stifle a laugh at my own comparison, and then add, "Bad, Greyston."

And then he lunges.

I shriek, dodging him and running for the stairs, laughing the entire time. I've just grabbed onto the banister when his long fingers ensnare my hips. He pulls me backward, turning me and slinging me over one of his shoulders. I'm too busy struggling and laughing to really focus on the fact that his hands are so high up on my thigh they're grazing the frayed hemline of my shorts.

Well, I wasn't focused on it until *now*.

I continue to squirm in his grasp, but not too much because I'm quite enjoying the view of his ass in his running shorts. It never really occurs to me—not until I hear the patio door open, anyway—exactly what his plan is.

Flattening my hands on his firm lower back, I lift myself slightly and crane my upper body to confirm my suspicions. "Greyston, what are you doing?" It's a stupid question, because I know the minute we step out onto the patio that I am about to get thrown in the pool.

Of course, I don't expect to go down alone.

"I'm warning you," I tell him, curling my fingers into the thin material of his shirt and shifting my weight on his shoulder as we reach the edge of the pool.

"And *I* am terrified, Miss Foster." Sarcasm drips from every word. His hands slip from my upper thighs, forcing a ripple of goosebumps across my skin, and he grabs just above my knees in preparation of tossing me in the water.

The minute I feel him move to throw me in, I adjust my upper body, wrapping my arms around his other shoulder. I can feel it offset his balance already, and he tries to right himself, but I take the opportunity to swing one of my legs around his waist, sending us both into the pool. We break the surface with a loud splash, both of us emerging at the same time, laughing and wiping the water from our eyes; his are bright with amusement.

"You're trouble," he declares, pushing his hair back and off of his forehead.

I shrug before swimming toward the edge of the pool. "I tried to warn you," I remind him.

The water feels amazing as I move through it, passing by Greyston. I know that once I get out, I'll wish I was back in, so I stop swimming and let my body roll over until I'm floating on my back and looking up at the clear blue sky. To my right, I hear a splash, and when I turn my head, I see Greyston has hopped out of the pool and is headed for the house. It doesn't escape my notice that his shorts are riding a little low and showing off the very top of his muscular backside between them and his shirt.

"Where are you going?" I call out after him.

"To answer the phone and grab us a couple of towels. I'll be right back."

I shift my body upright and begin to tread water, watching him disappear into the house, grabbing the phone from the kitchen counter and coming right back outside, walking toward me and holding out the phone.

"It's your mom," he announces, walking toward the pool as I make my way to the ladder.

My white tank is clinging to my skin as I climb up onto the deck, shaking the excess water from my hands before reaching for the phone. Greyston stops dead in his tracks, clenching and averting his eyes quickly as he hands me the phone.

"I'm, uh..." His voice is raspy, so he stops talking to clear his throat. "I'll go grab you a towel."

Unable to figure him out as he quickly runs back to the house, I put the phone to my ear. "Hey, Mom. What's up?"

"Hey, sweetie. I'm just calling to see how everything is going," she replies.

I laugh. "Pretty good. I kind of ruined Greyston's laundry, though."

"Well that can't be good!" Mom exclaims with a snicker. "What happened?"

I cringe again just thinking about it. "Red sock. White clothes."

Through her laughter, she says, "Oh, dear. Was he upset?"

"Enough to throw me in the pool," I tell her, shaking my head.

She stops laughing, and her voice takes on a more serious note. "Oh, really?" I don't have to focus hard to get the underlying insinuations in her tone.

"Mom, stop," I command lightly. "You're insane if you think anything will *ever* happen there. Believe me when I say that there is nothing I can do to make him find me even remotely attractive."

"Who?"

I jump when I hear Greyston's voice behind me and almost drop the phone. "Uuuh, Mom, I'll talk to you later, okay?"

"Sure, call me!"

I hang up the phone and set it on one of the lounge chairs before looking up at Greyston. "Sorry, she's a talker."

Greyston is regarding me curiously. How much could he have possibly overheard? Have I made things awkward between us by outing the crush I have on my landlord? My landlord who is in a relationship...with another man.

A cool breeze picks up, ripping right through my soaking wet tank top, and I shiver. Goosebumps cover my entire body, and in a flash, Greyston is thrusting one of the two towels he's holding toward me and using the other to cover his head and dry his dripping wet hair.

This behavior of his can't be normal for him, and I'm right back to wondering what the hell is going on. Instead of wondering, I decide to just ask. "Hey," I say, dropping the towel onto the chair and reaching out for him. "Are you okay? You've been acting kind of funny."

He removes the towel from his head and looks at me. I almost think I'm seeing things when his eyes move south and then quickly find mine again. Then I remember I'm in a white tank top…a *wet* white tank top…and I'm not wearing a bra…and my nipples are…

"Oh god!" I exclaim, reaching for my towel and holding it to my chest. "I'm so sorry! I didn't even think when I got dressed this morning!" The heat in my face can only mean that I'm the deepest shade of red I've ever been in my life. "I can't even imagine what must be going through your head."

"I think it's safest if you don't even try," he says with a nervous chuckle. "I, uh, have to run into the office to do a few last minute things before my trip. I'll grab a pizza on the way home?"

I still can't even look at him. In the course of a day, this poor man has been subjected to my lacy underthings and now my may-as-well-have-been-naked boobs. These are the last things he wants to see.

"Sounds good. I have a bit more studying to do, anyway." He's just turning to head back inside when I stand up and say, "Hey. We're cool, right? I know I've royally messed things up today, but I don't want things to be weird between us."

"It's fine, Juliette. I think this will just take some getting used to." He offers me a smile, but it's not the crooked one that makes his eyes shine; this one seems reserved—maybe even slightly forced. "I'm going to go change and head to the office. I'll be back soon."

"Yeah," I say softly once he disappears into the house.

"Soon."

Back in my room, I strip out of my wet clothes and have a quick shower before dressing comfortably in a looser-fitting t-shirt (with a bra this time) and another pair of shorts. These ones aren't nearly as scandalous, having decided that Greyston has seen enough of the female body to last him an entire lifetime.

According to my alarm clock, Greyston's been gone for a few hours by the time the front door opens and he calls my name. I launch myself through my bedroom door, dash down the hall, and look down over the banister to see Greyston coming in with a pizza box in one hand.

His eyes find me in an instant and he smiles *my* smile. "Sorry I'm late. Callie had a stack of paperwork on my desk that had to be signed before I leave." He holds up the pizza. "I brought dinner."

I bound down the stairs to take it from him, happy that he seems to have returned to his old self. "It smells great. What kind did you get?"

"Tropical chicken," he replies, shocking me because it's not a common choice. Most people think I'm crazy, because "Alfredo sauce doesn't belong on pizza."

I freeze, looking at him inquisitively. "That's…my favorite."

He laughs, moving around me to lead the way to the kitchen. "I know. I called your mother."

"You did?"

"Yeah, after how I behaved this afternoon, I wanted to make it up to you." He shrugs, looking innocent. "I wanted to surprise you, so I gave her a call. It's a strange choice, but I'm intrigued. Alfredo sauce, chicken, pineapple, and bacon, huh?"

"I see."

He nods once before meeting my gaze, smiling. "What do you say we grab a couple slices of pizza and go watch a movie?" he suggests.

Excited to chill out in front of the TV after a day of studying and craziness, I grab the plates from the cupboard and hand one to Greyston so we can dish up our dinner. I grab two slices of pizza and a glass of milk and start toward the living room.

It was the best way to end a day that started out a little rough. I can only hope to keep from messing up anything else. While I know it's bound to happen, I want to remain as optimistic as possible that I'm through making an ass of myself.

chapter 13

There's a light knock that rouses me from my sleep. With a groan, I lift my head and see that it's barely after seven in the morning.

"Come in," I call out in my hoarse morning voice, rolling off of my stomach and pushing myself up so I'm propped up on my elbows.

The door opens and in steps an always well-groomed Greyston. His eyes widen when he finds me still in bed, his gaze travelling down to see the entire length of my naked leg is exposed before turning around and looking out my balcony door. He's clearly uncomfortable with it, so I tuck my leg back under my blanket and apologize.

"Don't worry about it," he says roughly. "I just wanted to let you know that my ride is here to take me to the airport. You're sure you're going to be okay for a few days? I can call Callie and see if she'll come check on you."

He's been like this since Saturday; overly concerned that I don't yet feel comfortable or safe enough to spend a couple of days alone. While I've really enjoyed hanging out with him and getting to know more about his job, I will admit that it's going to be a little weird to be alone in this big house.

Wanting to help alleviate the guilt I can see in his eyes, I nod. "Yes, Greyston. I'll be fine. Daphne is actually going to come over tonight."

"Oh, good. And you remember how to work the alarm system? I'd hate for your dad to come and hunt me down because I wasn't taking all of the proper precautions with his daughter."

I laugh, sitting up and hugging my blanket to my chest; the tank top I've got on isn't exactly the most modest. "Yes. I've got the code memorized. Now go, or you'll miss your flight."

He's looking at me like there's something more he wants to say, but instead, he just offers me a small smile and nods. "Okay. I'll see you Friday. Call if you have any problems, all right?"

"Will do. Tell Toby I say hi."

His smile falls slightly, though not completely, and he looks toward the door. "Yeah. I'll be sure to do that."

Greyston leaves me alone in my room, and I try to figure out what it was that made his mood sour so suddenly. As I think about it, I realize that it's every time I bring Toby up. Were he and Toby having problems? I wouldn't know because I hadn't seen Toby since that early morning conversation in the kitchen.

When I turn and see that it's now seven-thirty, I throw my blankets off so I can go and get ready for school. After a quick shower, I brush my hair and teeth before finding a pair of jeans and a green t-shirt to wear. I make my bed quickly and head downstairs to make something quick for breakfast, only to be met by the smell of bacon and eggs the minute I hit the bottom step.

I walk into the kitchen to find a covered plate in my usual spot at the island. Next to it is a piece of paper. I pick up the paper and take it with me to the coffee pot, where an empty mug waits for me to fill it.

Grabbing the pot and filling my coffee cup, I read the note.

GOOD MORNING, JULIETTE.

SORRY WE DIDN'T HAVE THE OPPORTUNITY TO HAVE BREAKFAST TOGETHER THIS MORNING, BUT I STILL WANTED TO BE SURE YOU GOT OFF TO A GOOD START.

HERE IS A SHORT LIST OF NUMBERS SHOULD YOU NOT BE ABLE TO GET A HOLD OF ME AT SOME POINT OVER THE NEXT FEW DAYS. CALLIE IS

THE CLOSEST TO THE HOUSE. BUT IF SHE'S UNREACHABLE FOR WHATEVER REASON, ONE OF MY PARENTS SHOULD BE ABLE TO HELP YOU OUT WITH WHATEVER YOU MIGHT NEED.

I scan the numbers he's listed before moving onto the rest of the note.

I'M ALSO LEAVING YOU THE KEYS TO MY CAR SHOULD YOU NEED IT.

"What?" I ask aloud.

IT MIGHT BE A TAD PRESUMPTUOUS OF ME TO ASSUME THIS, BUT YOUR CAR SOUNDS LIKE IT'S ON ITS LAST LEG. USE IT OR DON'T; THE CHOICE IS YOURS, BUT MY CAR IS HERE IF YOU NEED IT.

HAVE FUN, AND DON'T FORGET TO CALL. EVEN IF IT'S JUST TO TALK.

~GREYSTON

Coffee in-hand, I head to my seat and set the note down and read it again while admiring Greyston's penmanship. I'm still shocked over Greyston's offer to let me use his fancy little sports car. Should I accept? Even if my car still has some life left in it?

I think about it over breakfast, devouring the scrambled eggs and three strips of bacon on my plate. Once my plate is clear and in the dishwasher, I snatch Greyston's keys off the counter and head to school. I figure I'll rarely get an opportunity like this again, so I better enjoy it while I can.

The minute my ass hits the plush leather seat of Greyston's sporty black car, I sigh. While I've never been much of a car lover—they've really just been something to get me from point A to point B—I have to admit that I am *in love* with this car.

And I haven't even started it yet.

I pull the seat forward, because Greyston has at least eight inches on me, and adjust my mirrors before starting the car. It's a stick-shift, which actually isn't a problem because so is my car. Of course, this beautiful car isn't nearly as difficult to shift, and it doesn't take a majority of my lower body strength to depress the clutch.

The engine purrs like a kitten, and the car drives like a dream. It's so smooth, I don't even realize I'm driving well over the speed limit until I gain on the car in front of me. I slow down and pay more attention to the speedometer so that Greyston doesn't regret letting me use his car. The accelerator definitely seems a bit touchier than the one in my car—probably because my car borders on ancient.

I park in the university parking lot and grab my bag from the passenger seat. The minute I step out, I can sense all eyes on me. I try to ignore all the attention, but as I make my way through the lot, I spot Ben.

His face is healing, having been almost a week since Greyston decked him, but shadows of the bruises still remain. This makes me smirk, and I carry on toward the main building, setting the alarm on Greyston's car. Before I reach the doors, an arm loops through mine and walks with me.

"Nice wheels!" Daphne exclaims.

"Thanks. Greyston loaned me his car while he's away." The halls are crowded as we make our way through them to our first classes, and Daphne is asking all about the car, my new place and, naturally, Greyston. "You still coming over tonight?"

"You bet! I'm excited to prove that you're wrong about him."

I stop walking and glare down at her. "Daphne, you are *not* snooping."

We round the corner, discussing our plans, and almost run down one of my classmates. "Erik!" I cry out, startled.

He looks adorably nervous, looking between Daphne and me. "Oh, hey, Juliette."

I pick up on something in his voice, and look down at Daphne who's looking between us amusedly. It isn't until Erik stays put, focusing solely on me, that I realize he's waiting for me.

"So, listen, Juliette. I was wondering if you were going to that party at the Psi Sigma Phi house? If you were, I thought it might be fun if we went together."

While I still don't really feel like jumping back into another relationship—well, except for the one I know can never happen—there's something kind of endearing about being asked out by a guy who seems sweet and normal.

Though, I suppose Ben seemed that way in the beginning too, and look how that turned out.

I push those thoughts aside, because it's really not fair to judge the entire male species based on the actions of a complete dog like Ben Connely. Even though I still have a bit of a crush on Greyston, I know that it can never go anywhere. It's not sane or rational to sit around pining after someone who's unavailable, so I make a split decision.

"I wasn't going to," I begin to tell Erik.

His hopeful smile falls, and he shakes his head. "That's okay, I just figured I'd ask—"

"Erik!" I interrupt. "I *wasn't* going to...but maybe it would be fun."

Hope returns to his eyes, and his smile brightens again. "Yeah?"

"Yes. It's Friday, right?" I ask, and he nods to clarify, reaching into his pocket for his phone and handing it to me. "Here's my number. Call me and we'll figure out the details so you can pick me up at seven?"

"Great. I'll talk to you later then."

I turn to Daphne the minute Erik's out of sight. "Please tell me you're going to that party."

Daphne starts laughing. "You want me to be your third wheel? Juliette, if you didn't want to go with him, why did you agree?"

I roll my eyes in exasperation. "It's not that I didn't want to go—I mean, sure, there are a million other things I can imagine doing at home on a Friday night—"

"My," Daphne interrupts, "aren't we ambitious. You sure Greyston would be open to doing those things with you?"

I shove, almost sending her into an oncoming wave of students, and snicker. "Shut up. Just tell me you're going."

Daphne's eyes are filled with remorse. "I wish I could, but I have to go to my parents' place this weekend. Sorry."

"What if I can't think of anything to say?" I whine.

"Has it been that long since you've been to a frat party, Juliette?" she asks, glomming back onto my arm so as not to get lost in the masses. "People rarely talk at those things. It's all dancing and drinking and tongues down other peoples' throats."

"It's a wonder you're single," I joke.

"Hey, I'm just playing the field until Mr. Right steps up to the plate." We stop outside Daphne's class, and she lets go of my arm. "I'll see you later?"

"Definitely."

After my last class, I gather my things, dig Greyston's car keys out of the bottom of my bag, and head outside to meet up with Daphne. I open the trunk for her to put her bag inside, and she closes it.

I open my door and slide into my seat. "Did you bring your suit? We could maybe hang out by the pool for a bit tonight."

"You bet I did."

I smile. "Well then, what are we waiting for?"

When we arrive at the house, I turn off the alarm and lead Daphne up to my room so we can drop off our bags and change into our suits. I show her around upstairs, only allowing her to poke her head into Greyston's well-kept room. We reach the stairs, and I begin to descend them when Daphne grabs my arm and tugs.

"Wait. What's in there?"

I open my mouth and then close it, because I don't really know what to say. "Actually," I finally say, "I'm not entirely sure. I've never been inside."

"Well, let's take a look," Daphne suggests, moving toward the door.

Even though I would love nothing more than to do just that, I follow her and stop her before she has a chance to turn the knob and open the door. "No. There's probably a reason that Greyston hasn't shown me this room. I think it's his and Toby's special place or something." I eye the door, my curiosity growing. Would it really be so bad to take one tiny little peek?

Daphne turns the knob and pushes the door open before I can stop her—or maybe I could have, I just didn't want to. Her hands fly to her mouth and her bright eyes widen in fake shock. "Oops."

chapter 14

Once the door hits the wall behind it, I lean forward to see what it was hiding.

I'm...confused, and that confusion wraps itself around me and pulls me forward until I am standing in the center of the room. I turn in slow, calculating circles as I take in the contents of the room. "It's...it's not what I imagined," I say aloud as Daphne joins me.

"What did you think was in here?"

I blush and look at her through the corner of my eye. "Whips and chains and stuff."

Daphne's laughter fills the room, echoing off the walls and sleek furniture. There's a flat screen TV mounted on the wall, several gaming systems in the cabinet below it, and a couch several feet back. Along the other walls, various action figures and comic book memorabilia is displayed. Maybe Greyston kept this room from me because he's afraid I'll label him a nerd.

While my vision of the room may have been entirely wrong, I still know what I heard that night.

"Come on," I say, grabbing Daphne's wrist and dragging her from the room. "We shouldn't be in here. I feel weird about it."

"Juliette, it's just a game room. What's to feel weird about? Look!" Daphne exclaims, pointing toward the television. "He's got *Kinect*! Can't we please play?"

I shake my head. "No way. Not without asking permission first."

"Then call him!"

"No, he's working. Come on." I'm finally able to get her out of the room and down into the kitchen. I pour us each a glass of lemonade and prepare a little fruit tray for us to snack on while we relax outside.

As I wash the last sprig of grapes, I hear Daphne rifling through papers behind me. "Who is this incredible specimen?"

I turn to see what it is she's looking at, assuming maybe it's one of the magazines Callie was looking at on the weekend. It's not. I place the grapes on the plate and move around the island to peer over her shoulder, and I recognize the papers immediately. "Oh, Greyston must have forgotten those this morning. That's the baseball player he's trying to sign. Um…" I glance down under the photo and read his name. "Xander Richland. He's from Houston."

"Well, he's delicious!" She's not wrong. His longer wavy brown hair and golden brown eyes only add to his chiseled jawline, and his wide smile showcases shallow dimples that make him seem approachable.

It takes some doing, but I'm finally able to pull her away from Xander's profile and out to the pool. We're out there for a little over an hour, just floating on our inflatable rafts, before I hear the house phone ringing.

"I'll be right back," I say, hopping out of the pool and walking toward the house. The phone is on its cradle near the patio door, so I pick it up, smiling when I see it's Greyston.

"Hey, you."

His warm chuckle greets me before he speaks. "Good evening. How was class?"

I lean against the doorframe, looking out at Daphne lounging on one of the floatation devices. "Really good. How's Houston?"

"Warm…and kind of lonely."

"Awww. Don't say that. I'm sure Toby's keeping you all kinds of company," I say, knowing that their time away will probably be good for them if they're experiencing some kind of strain in their relationship.

"He does what he can, but he's down at the gym right now." Greyston pauses briefly before continuing on. "And I just wanted to call and check in with you. See how things are going."

"Everything's great here. Daphne and I are just out floating in the pool, having a light dinner and a glass of wine," I explain to him. "Then, I think we're going to head upstairs and do homework. All-in-all, we're a couple of party animals."

Greyston laughs, and I have to admit I miss the sound already. "Well, I'm glad you ladies are having a good night…" Greyston is distracted by something, and then I hear Toby's voice in the background. "Hey, Juliette?"

"Yeah?"

"Toby just showed up. We're going to go and grab a bite to eat. I'll give you a call tomorrow?" he offers.

It makes me feel all warm and fuzzy to hear he's going to call again. Deep down, I know he's not saying it for the reasons I want him to. I'm taking care of his house for him; he just wants to make sure everything is going okay.

"Sounds good. I'll talk to you later. You boys have fun tonight," I instruct before hanging up and rejoining Daphne.

We relax in the pool for another thirty minutes before we head inside and change into our pajamas. We both have assignments for separate classes to work on, so we hit the books. By midnight, we're both exhausted and climb under my blankets together with the intention to talk until one or both of us passes out.

The next two days go by much slower than I'd like. School seems to drag on, and work is a bit of a bore, being mid-week. Of course, then I return home alone to a big empty house, where I cook myself dinner and watch an hour or two of TV before retiring to my room and doing homework.

The only part of my day that I really look forward to is around seven-thirty at night when Greyston calls to check in. By Thursday, Greyston assures me that he's signed Xander and that he'll return on Friday as scheduled.

After hanging up with Greyston, my phone rings again. This time, it's Erik. He apologizes for not calling earlier, citing school assignments as his reason, which I totally understand. He confirms our plans for Friday night, and I tell him that everything still sounds great before giving him my address.

There are a couple of things for me to look forward to on Friday when I wake up; the first being Greyston's return home around six, and then the chance to go out and have a little fun with my peers. My excitement leads to my inability to get a good night's sleep on Thursday, and I have to rely on a lot of coffee to get me through the day.

Thankfully, I only have a couple of classes and am home just after two. The minute I curl up on the couch in front of an afternoon talk show, my eyes begin to droop, and I fall asleep.

The dreams I have are bright and cheerful. Familiar blue eyes are a prominent part of those dreams, and it seems as though we're more than just friends in this particular sequence.

We're lying in my bed, our legs intertwined and most of our clothes still on. His lips are on mine, soft at first, but soon grow hungry with need as his hands grasp at my body, wanting more, yet never pushing for it. My entire body warms as his lips begin to explore my neck, and my fingers thread themselves into the soft hairs on the back of his head to hold him in place against the hollow of my throat.

"Juliette," he whispers, his breath sending a cool tickle over the skin he's just kissed. His lips leave my neck, and he looks directly into my eyes, bringing his right hand up to softly stroke my cheek. *"Juliette."*

Something about his innocent touch feels different from all the rest in my dream, and his voice seems a little more hesitant. I try not to think about those things, pulling his face back to mine. Our lips barely touch before he speaks again. *"Juliette, I'm home."*

My eyes flutter open, and I find myself staring across the low coffee table at the TV, my brain still muddled with the fog of sleep. As I continue to breach the barrier into consciousness, I realize it's six-fifteen, and the talk show I was watching before passing out is no longer on. I'm momentarily confused. Parts of my dream still linger, but it's all fading quickly—as dreams often do. I run my fingers through my hair and turn my head toward the ceiling. My heart leaps into my throat when I notice I'm not alone.

"Holy crap!" I cry out, slapping my hand to my chest in an attempt to keep my heart from breaking through.

Greyston takes a small step back from his spot behind the couch and offers me an apologetic smile. "Sorry," he says quietly. "I didn't mean to startle you. Good dream?"

Ignoring his question, I sit up, my heart calming more and more with each passing second. "No, it's okay." Greyston moves around the sofa and sits next to me. "How was your flight?"

"Thankfully short. I couldn't wait to be home. I just hope that my next trip isn't for quite some time." With a content sigh, Greyston relaxes back onto the couch and rests his head. "So, what do you want to do tonight? Order in? We could go out if you wanted to get out of the house?"

"Oh," I say, my voice falling to barely above a whisper. "I actually have plans tonight."

Greyston seems happy to hear this. "Great. You going out to a movie with Daphne?" he guesses.

"Um, no. There's this frat party on campus. I was invited to go by a classmate. Erik."

The happy smile fades from his lips and he sits up, resting his forearms on his thighs and looking at his feet. "I see." Greyston stands up and looks down at me. "Well, I'm going to go and unpack my things. You have fun tonight."

Greyston leaves me alone in the living room, and I can't help but feel like he's upset with me. I don't like the idea, and I wonder what I might have done to upset him. Deciding to go talk to him, I make my way up the stairs. When I reach his door, I find it closed, and I can hear him talking. Even though I know I shouldn't, I press my ear to the door. His voice is far too low for me to hear, so I give up trying and head to my room to get ready for the party.

I step into my closet and look through my clothes. It's been so long since I've gone out on a date—even with Ben—that I'm kind of at a loss. I shoot Daphne a text for her advice since she knows my small wardrobe pretty well, and it's not long before I receive her reply.

denim skirt & blue halter.
you're welcome ;)

I go through my clothes, locate the items she's suggested, and pull them on. The skirt isn't so short that it gives the farm away for free, but it does show off a decent amount of leg, making them look longer than they are, and the shirt has a low back, showing off an ample amount of my sun-kissed skin. Happy with how I look, I find a pair of comfortable heels to complete my outfit and head to the washroom to do my hair and makeup. I keep it simple, playing up my eyes and the color of my shirt with a light blue shadow and adding a coat of mascara. Keeping the low back of my shirt in consideration, I pull my dark hair up into a twist and secure it with several hairpins, letting the ends fall down to brush my neck.

Just as I'm giving myself a final once-over, the doorbell rings. I find I'm nervous, but not in a butterflies-in-stomach kind of way. Taking a deep breath, I exit my bedroom to answer the door. It takes me by surprise to find that Greyston has already invited Erik in.

That's when the butterflies erupt. Not because I see Erik, I realize, but because Greyston's eyes have shifted to watch me descend the stairs. I'm not entirely sure what it is, but there's something in the way he's staring at me that confuses me. If it were anybody else, I'd swear that particular look resembled...*desire.*

I shake off the ridiculous thought and continue toward the door. When I look up at Erik, who's dressed in jeans and a black t-shirt, he's looking at me in an entirely different way than when he asked me out. I begin to wonder if Erik is expecting more than I'm willing to offer up tonight.

"Hey," Erik says, his eyes moving down the length of my body, taking a little more time than necessary on my breasts. "You look great."

"Thanks." I look between him and Greyston. "I take it the two of you have met?"

Greyston seems less than impressed; in fact, he seems

downright hostile. "Oh, we've met." I try not to read too much into it, but I think I detect a note of jealousy in his voice. This only serves to further confuse me when I pair it alongside the way he was looking at me a moment ago.

I'm about to suggest to Erik that we leave when Greyston's hand reaches out and takes mine. His hold is firm, yet gentle, and his thumb begins to move back and forth over the back of my hand. Sparks shoot up my arm, and my eyes lock on his. "Can I talk to you a minute while Erik waits for you...*outside*?"

"Uh, sure." I turn to Erik with a nervous smile. "Why don't you go wait by the car? I'll be right out."

Erik seems reluctant, but does so with one final look from Greyston. I shouldn't, but I find this odd display of his kind of sexy. The minute Erik is outside, Greyston closes the door, his palm flat against it as if holding it in case Erik tries to come back inside.

"What's up?" I ask, truly curious about what is possibly going through Greyston's mind right now.

"I don't like him," is his short reply.

I'm not sure how to reply to that. Greyston doesn't even know Erik—hell, *I* don't even know him that well yet; isn't that what dates are for? To learn about someone that you may have expressed an interest in?

"I'm sorry?" I finally say.

Greyston sighs heavily, dropping his hand from the door and running it through his hair, never breaking our stare—or his hold on my hand. "You could do so much better. I don't trust him."

I'm sure Greyston's exactly right about being able to do better. However, what he doesn't realize is that I feel as though *he* might be my "better." And he's not an option.

"Greyston," I say with a smile. "I don't think they can get much worse than Ben."

"Juliette, you don't know what he's thinking—"

"And you do?" I ask softly, smiling at him to show him I'm not upset by his need to keep me safe. He's doing this because he promised my dad; I know this to be a fact. "It's one date. I've shared a few classes with him, and he seems really nice."

"Looks can be deceiving."

There's no holding back my amusement. "*You* look like a nice guy...are you telling me you're secretly a psychopath?"

He's pinching the bridge of his nose and clenching his eyes shut. "That's different."

"Is it?" I ask. "My dad thought you were some crazy person, and he agreed to meet with you so you could prove him wrong. Shouldn't Erik be granted the same allowances?"

It's clear he's not happy that I've compared him and Erik, but it works. He opens the door, but still holds onto my hand, tethering me to him for a moment longer. There's something in the way he's holding onto me that reaches out to that small, distant part of me that's still grasping for a shred of hope that *maybe* he's interested.

Then he let's go, and it all slips away.

"Promise you'll call if you need absolutely anything. A ride, someone to talk to, anything."

I agree without a second thought, thanking him for his concern, and walk out to find Erik leaning against the passenger side door of his older Ford Focus, playing with his phone.

Upon seeing me, he slips his phone into his pocket and pushes off the car. "Well he's mighty protective, isn't he?"

He moves away from the door, and I smile expectantly, waiting for him to open it. When he doesn't, instead running around to his own door and hopping in immediately, I'm stunned. Slowly, I turn back to Greyston, who's chuckling from his place in the doorway and shaking his head.

I understand that it isn't unusual for men to make their women open their own doors or pull out their own chairs, but since meeting Greyston, I guess I had hoped that maybe Ben was the rarity.

Annoyed less than fifteen minutes into my first date, I open my door and climb in. I decide that I'm not going to hold this against Erik, and that it's just how he was taught.

The entire drive to the party, Erik is talking about the big football game on Sunday. "I'm having a few buddies over to watch the game on my new flat screen. You should stop by."

"Oh," I tell him, "I can't. I'm actually going to the game on Sunday."

Erik's eyes go wide, and he turns to me for a longer period of time than I'm entirely comfortable with since he's driving. "When did you get tickets? I've been trying for *months*."

I smile, remembering dinner with Greyston and my parents quite fondly. "Greyston, actually. He's taking my parents and me. The team's manager gave him tickets for signing the new quarterback."

Erik's mouth is now equally as wide as his eyes; it's kind of frightening. "Your landlord gave you tickets? That's... weird."

"I don't know," I tell him with a laugh. "I thought it was kind of sweet."

We arrive at the party a few minutes later, and Erik gets out of the car and starts for the door—while I'm still sitting in the passenger seat. He's docking himself points left and right, but I continue to give him the benefit of the doubt.

Walking as fast as I can in my heels, I catch up to him before we pass through the door, and he snickers. "What took you so long?"

It takes all the strength I can muster to not slam his face into the side of the doorframe. He's lucky he is able to redeem himself a little when he spots the keg and offers to get us both a drink.

"Thank you. That would be great." I watch as he crosses the room and talks to the guy manning the keg. While he's gone, I take a look around at the party to find it's already in full swing. Men and women are grinding in the large living room area as heavy dance music makes the walls and windows rattle, and there are couples making out in every corner. I haven't been to one of these things since last year, and I can clearly see that they haven't changed.

Erik returns a couple of minutes later with my beer. "Your new place looks great," Erik says, trying to start the conversation. "What made you decide to move off campus?"

I quirk my eyebrow at him, because I am more than certain the rumors surrounding my moving out of the dorms has been made public. "You're joking, right?" He says nothing.

"Well, when someone finds out their boyfriend and roommate are sleeping together, there's not really much keeping you here."

Erik doesn't seem surprised by this news, which can only tell me he did know. "That sucks," is all he says. "Can I ask if you know how he got the black eye?"

I'm just taking a sip of my drink when I laugh. "Greyston."

"Your landlord?" I nod, and Erik shakes his head in disbelief.

Erik continues to ask me questions, and I'm surprised that I'm able to contribute to the conversation here and there. However, it seems that every time I bring up Greyston, Erik becomes agitated. We talk about Erik's plans for the weekend, and when he asks what I plan to do, I remind him of the football game with Greyston and my parents. This leads Erik to ask how that was even arranged, and I explain the dinner last week where Greyston invited us all.

Naturally, I remember the whipped cream on the tip of Greyston's fingers and get that warm tingly feeling in my lower belly. I don't mention this out loud, but I imagine it over and over again before I let the memory play out to when I got whipped cream on my own clumsy digits.

And Greyston dropped his fork.

It must be the beer, because that memory shouldn't be sticking out as prominently as it is… Should it?

Erik interrupts my thoughts, asking about the car I was driving to school the past few days.

"It's Greyston's," I reply without thinking. "He wanted to be sure I had a more reliable vehicle while he was away on business."

I swear I can feel Erik's annoyance flare. "Of course. Next you're going to tell me he's the world's best cook."

"He's not bad, actually," I inform him, thinking back on all the delicious meals Greyston has prepared for us: the Alfredo dish, bacon and egg breakfasts, spaghetti…

That was when Greyston dropped his spoon into the sauce.

Something else clicks into place—even though I didn't know there was a place for it *to* click.

Hours pass, meaning I've become even more drunk. Erik and I have been doing shots in between my apparently bottomless red solo cup of beer. Sure, it's probably not the best way to avoid a hangover—or alcohol poisoning—but I'm actually having a good time. I'm not fully aware of when or why I do it, but it seems like every time Erik starts up a new topic, I bring up Greyston, always finding a way to relate it to whatever we're talking about. However, the more I talk about him, the more I seem to remember all of these little things I originally sloughed off as unimportant because I had figured there was no way Greyston would ever act that way or say certain things around me.

The way his fingers brushed my knee when he was trying to comfort me about his leaving... The smiles he's always giving me... Even just the way his eyes always lock on mine when he's talking to me.

"Greyston again, huh?" Erik says after I tell him another Greyston story. I think he's annoyed, but he could also be drunk...because I'm drunk, and I think everyone here is drunk.

"Greyston's awesome." My words are only slightly slurred as I state this as a fact. I think.

Erik seems to ignore my statement completely. "Look, can we stop talking about your landlord? How about we go and dance?"

"Uhhh..." I look behind me at the lazy dancers, leaning up against each other for balance—actually, upon closer observation they're not leaning; they're pawing at each other and on the verge of public sex. Some people have no shame.

"Juliette?" My eyes snap back to Erik's a little too fast, and I lose my balance. He catches me, but I don't like how his dry, calloused fingers feel on my arm. They itch. Greyston's, though? They're nice. Like little jolts of electricity making my heart beat faster and my stomach flip.

"What?" I ask before remembering what he just asked. "Oh, right. Um, I'm going to go to the washroom."

Unable to deny me my girl time, he lets me go, and I stumble through the large crowd to find the bathroom. I do what needs to be done, wash my hands, and fix my hair. As I glance over my reflection, I flash back to when I was coming downstairs to greet Erik back at the house. There is no denying that there was something in the way Greyston was looking at me. I smile before biting my lip, wondering what the look might have meant…

There's a knock on the door that startles me until I hear Erik's voice calling for me from the other side. When I open the door, he's holding my cup out to me. I'm suddenly not feeling like partying and just want to go home.

"What's wrong?" Erik asks, placing his hard, scratchy hand on my bare back and leading me back out into the throng of people.

"It's just getting late, and I'm feeling kind of tired," I lie. "Would you hate me if I wanted to go home?"

While he doesn't say yes, something in his eyes tells me he's not exactly pleased. "I thought we were going to dance?"

I look around at the "dancers" and cringe. "Um, I'm not a great dancer. And besides, I don't do"—I raise my hand and wave my outstretched index finger around at everybody in the room—"that."

Erik's hand moves across my back, even dipping beneath the soft fabric of my shirt slightly, and he leans in until he's whispering in my ear. It reminds me of the morning I made French toast for Greyston, only Erik's breath is nowhere near as sweet and warm as Greyston's. "Juliette, *everybody* does that."

Shaking my head, I pull away from Erik; I need his hand off me, and I suddenly feel the need to scrape my neck and ear clean with a Brillo Pad. "Mmm mmm," I disagree. "Not me. Not ever. Look, I just want to go home. Please?"

Sighing heavily, Erik gives in to my request. "Fine. Let's go."

We step outside, and Erik starts leading me to his car. I stop instantly because, even though I'm really drunk, I know that there's no way Erik is fit to drive. "Um, would you mind if we walked? I don't think you should drive."

"Juliette, I'm fine, really." I shake my head adamantly, and he concedes again. "Whatever you say."

It's about a thirty-minute walk—maybe more because I

can't seem to walk in a completely straight line. Erik keeps trying to take my hand, but I'm pretty sly and keep moving it to fiddle with my hair or adjust my shirt. He seems to be put out by my non-hand-holding, only I can't seem to care.

We finally arrive at my house, and Erik walks me up to the door. The porch light is still on, and I can see the dim light of one of the lamps in the living room. Is Greyston still up? The thought that he is excites me more than I can even say.

"I had fun tonight," Erik says in a husky voice, reminding me that he's still here. *Boo.*

I try not to giggle, but fail miserably; he sounds ridiculous. "Uh, yeah," I concur to be nice. "It was all right."

"What do you say we have a little more fun?"

Uh oh... I do not like the way that sounds. Nope. Uh uh. Not at all.

Leaning in, Erik starts to play with a tendril of my hair, his eyes moving back and forth between mine and then roving down my body. It makes me nervous. "So, you gonna invite me in?"

"No," I answer quickly with a laugh. I hate the way he keeps invading my personal bubble.

"Come on..." Erik leans in further, his hand cupping my jaw and moving back until his fingers rest on the base of my neck. His face is slowly getting closer, and he's licking his dry, cracked lips. Dread fills my body, and I grab the doorknob behind my back.

With my free hand, I reach up and grab his wrist, pulling his hand away from me, and step back. "I said *no*." I turn the knob behind me to see that it's thankfully unlocked, and I clumsily step just over the threshold, leaving Erik on the porch.

"You know what?" There's a fire in his eyes, and not that sexy, smoldery kind like Greyston's, either. Nah, he looks pissed. Rejected. "You're nothing but a tease. I put up with you going on and on and *on* about that guy all night, and I get nothing in return?"

My head feels fuzzy, and the outer edges of my vision are still cloudy from the beer. Through it all, my irritation surges. "What did you want, Erik? A medal?" He glares at me, and whatever verbal filter I have left is washed away by the alcohol in my system. I don't even know what I'm saying until I've said it. "Actually, I've got a few participation ribbons for dates who turn out to be sore losers upstairs...you want me to go grab you one, cupcake?" There's a warm, familiar chuckle off to my left, and if I really hone my peripheral vision, I can see Greyston leaning in the doorway of the living room.

Erik doesn't seem to appreciate my joke as much as Greyston does—which is because Erik's not awesome like Greyston. "Fuck you," he spits. "This was such a waste of time." Grumbling something about my being a frigid tease, he retreats down the stairs.

Annoyed that the only reason he asked me out was to get into my pants, I slam the door. "UGH!"

"Hey, take it easy, champ. What did the door ever do to you?" Greyston jokes.

Turning to face him a little too quickly, I topple over. Before I can hit the ground, though, Greyston is there to catch me. His arms are around my waist, and my shirt has risen up a couple of inches. I can feel the bare skin of his forearms against my flesh, and I exhale shakily.

"You're drunk," he points out.

I nod. "You're like a detective," I tease, poking his chest—his hard, muscley chest. As though my hand has a mind of its own, it flattens against his chest, but before I can get too out of control with my drunken groping, Greyston helps me upright, pulling my shirt back into place for me.

Killjoy.

I take in his appearance, noticing that he's dressed in a white cotton tee and a pair of grey plaid pajama pants, and he looks absolutely delicious. He clears his throat, and when I look up at him, I think I barely catch a glimpse of him checking me out, too. *Weird.*

"Why don't you go change, and I'll make you some coffee," he offers, turning me toward the stairs. "You need to sober up a little, or you'll be in a world of pain tomorrow."

For some reason, my brain turns this into something dirty, and I envision whips and chains and stuff—like I thought his fun-room upstairs held.

I stumble on the first step because I am imagining being tied up, and also because I've got no control over my legs. Sitting on the stairs, I bend over to remove my shoes—because I'm certain they're also culprits—but soon give up because it just seems like *a lot* of work.

Ever my knight-in-shining-armor, Greyston kneels before me and gently grabs my ankle, removing my right shoe and then my left. That familiar spark pulses beneath my skin and up my legs, coming to a full stop between my thighs. I wish his hands would follow that trail.

The minute I think it, his hand moves up from my ankle until it's caressing my calf muscle. I'm certain it's only been a few seconds—if that—but it feels like he's been holding onto my leg for much, *much* longer. Biting my lip, I stare at him, trying to figure out the look in his eyes. Before I can analyze further, he glances away and sets my foot back on the stair.

"Go change. I'll make coffee."

He leaves me alone and confused. As if it isn't bad enough that my mind is working over-time to wade through the alcohol, now I have to try and figure out why *he's* acting so funny?

"Ugh," I grumble, rolling over and pushing myself to my feet so I can climb the stairs. "Men suck."

Opening my bedroom door, I walk into my room and shed my clothes, dropping them to the floor as I walk to my dresser. I pull out a pair of sleep shorts, a thin tank top, and a pink button-up flannel pajama top that is covered in bright red cherries. I pull them on, leaving it unbuttoned, and giggle because the color of it reminds me of Greyston's ruined laundry.

Once I'm dressed, I brush my teeth, because the taste of beer has begun to make me feel nauseous. It's possible I'm way more drunk than I've ever been. With minty-fresh breath, I head downstairs with the intention of going to the kitchen, but Greyston has just appeared with two cups of fresh coffee and leads me to the living room.

Before he gives me my coffee, he asks me to take a seat. "Here you go. Be careful; it's hot."

I take the mug from him, blow on it before taking a sip, and then set it on the coffee table. "Thanks."

Greyston nods, smirking over the rim of his own cup as he takes a drink. "So, Erik seems *really* nice," he says, and I have this weird feeling that I've heard that before… Oh right, *I* said it before leaving with the creep.

Playfully, I lean over and shove his shoulder. "Shut up. I was wrong, okay? You happy now?"

His smile disappears, and he sets his cup next to mine before turning to me. "No. Not happy. Do you have any idea how much I wanted to punch that guy?"

"There you go again," I tease. "Always with the punching."

Greyston laughs, making me feel better because I don't like when he's so tense. "Yes, I suppose I do need to work on my impulses."

I shrug. "I don't know. I kind of wanted to punch him too. A couple of times, actually." We're both silent for a while, leaving me alone with far too many thoughts in my current state. I think back to my high school boyfriend, to Ben, and now to Erik. How is it I attract these guys? Am I emitting some kind of loser pheromone?

"I don't get it," I finally say, breaking the silence. "What's wrong with me?"

Greyston's eyes widen incredulously. "Excuse me?" I don't elaborate further, because it seems like a pretty straightforward question. "Juliette, there's nothing *wrong* with you."

"Please," I snort. "Then explain how I keep letting this happen."

Moving closer to me, Greyston rests his arm along the back of the couch and exhales heavily. "Juliette, you're the type of person who's always trying to see the good in people. It's not your fault that they fail to see just how amazing you really are."

I scoff. "Yeah, okay."

His eyes narrow, almost like he's trying to get inside my head. Not exactly the safest place to be swimming right now. "How is it you don't see just how great you are? You're warm, compassionate…stunning."

"You're insane," I tell him pointedly. "In fact, I think that's it." He opens his mouth to speak, but I reach out and rest my index finger against his mouth to silence him. "Shhh… I'm having an epiphany here. I think there's a very real possibility that all men are crazy. That has to be it." Greyston smiles against the pad of my finger, drawing my attention back to his mouth—to his perfect, soft, kissable lips.

Licking my own lips, I shift my hand slightly until it's my thumb touching his mouth, and my gaze darts between it and his penetrating stare. "You know," I say softly, "you've got the perfect Cupid's bow." My thumb moves lazily along the ridge of his upper lip, and his eyelids drop slightly.

"Juliette," he whispers against my roaming thumb, his eyes falling closed while his hand comes up to cover—but not move—mine. The minute his thumb presses into the pulse point at my wrist, I know he can feel just how fast my heart is racing.

For him.

When his eyes open again, they're a brilliant blue and filled with unmistakable want. While this confuses me, I also know without a doubt that I'm not imagining it. He continues to stare at me in a way I never expected, and when I think back over the last week, I come to realize that this isn't the first time he's looked at me…and I mean *really* looked at me.

I'm aware that my alcohol-induced state is probably forcing my brain to blow everything out of proportion, but there has to be something there; a spark that maybe, just maybe, has the potential to grow out of control.

I know it's wrong, but I can't fight it anymore. And with the amount I've had to drink tonight, I don't know if I'd be able to fight it even if I wanted to. Impulsively, I move forward on the couch until my knees touch his thigh. Butterflies flutter wildly in my stomach at what I am about to do; never in a million years have I been the one to initiate anything, and while I know there's a very real possibility that he'll reject me, something in my brain tells me to proceed.

"I want to try something," I tell him, my voice soft and raspy. I remove my thumb from his soft lips, letting my hand rub the scratchy stubble along his jaw, and I lean closer to him than I've ever been.

Our eyes are locked, our breathing is matched breath for labored breath, and he nods. I move in a little closer until the tip of my nose brushes his, and his hold on my hand tightens. My lips are so close to his I can feel the warmth of his breath. "Don't. Move," I instruct. His head bobs slightly in understanding, and I close the very small gap between us.

chapter 15

I only peck his lips at first, staring into his eyes to gauge his reaction. When he doesn't seem utterly repulsed, I kiss him again. This time, I press firmly, my bottom lip finding a home between his. With a moan, his mouth molds to mine, and his eyes close. Swept up in the moment, I allow my own eyes to flutter shut, and he drops my hand in favor of cradling my face.

In the back of my mind, I know this was only supposed to be an experiment—one I wasn't sure he would allow me to conduct—but it appears to have been successful for the most part. His fingers move up into my hair, releasing it a little from the loosening hairpins and sending a delicious jolt of pleasure down my spine.

Even though I don't want to, I stop kissing him, opening my eyes to find him staring at me, bewildered, and breathing quite heavily. I definitely see something there, something that pulls me back to him. That spark I saw only a moment ago has ignited, and my entire body feels like it's caught fire; it's all consuming, and there's only one way to extinguish the burn.

I don't think anymore; I act.

In a flash, I'm moving to straddle him, my lips seeking his out again, and I rejoice once they've made contact. It's Greyston who makes the next move, his fingers curling in my hair, and his mouth parting slightly until I feel the sensual warmth of his tongue pressing against my lower lip. Soon, my own tongue is moving languidly against his as his hands move from my hair and run down the length of my back, stopping when they reach the curve of my backside. I can feel Greyston's fingers trailing along the hemline of my sleep shorts, tickling the sensitive flesh right below my ass, while his thumbs move in firm strokes over the thin cotton fabric. The gentle movements of his fingers send shots of white-hot passion pulsing through my veins, and I can't take it anymore; I shift my hips against him to quell the intense desire I've felt for this man for weeks.

A low growl escapes Greyston when I thrust toward him again, which only makes me want to kiss him harder and deeper. So, obviously, I do. He's *more* than receptive to every single one of my impulses, pulling my hips to him again, a little rougher this time, and I gasp in surprise the minute I make contact with his own arousal.

"More," I plead breathlessly against his lips, letting my hands travel down his body, grabbing at the hem of his shirt and tugging it upward so I can feel his bare chest with my hands. It's then that his hands leave my backside and grab hold of my wrists, stopping me. He stops kissing me and just stares at me while we both pant heavily. Greyston's lips are red and swollen from our kiss, and I can see my tousled reflection in his eyes.

"Juliette," he says, holding my hands still. While his eyes still scream with desire, there's something else there too: remorse. "We can't. Not like this."

I feel sick to my stomach—and not because of the alcohol. Actually, I'm feeling slightly less drunk as reality comes crashing back down around me. I tug my wrists free and climb off of his lap, feeling pretty damn humiliated—and also like an awful human being because I basically just forced myself on Greyston with no warning.

He wanted it too, I try to tell myself, but it doesn't change the fact that I still acted without consideration for Toby. Toby, Greyston's partner. I've turned Greyston into a cheater—the same thing I've condemned Ben for.

I press my fingers to my lips because they're still hot and tingly from our kiss. "I-I'm sorry," I whisper. "I-I—" There's nothing I can think of saying that will make everything all right between us, so I rush from the living room and up the stairs.

Behind me, I hear Greyston get off the couch. "Damn it," he curses quietly. "Juliette, wait."

While I want to hear what he has to say, I also don't think I can bear it. Not right now, anyway. I hurry up the last two stairs and fly into my room, closing the door and keeping all of the lights off before flopping down on my bed and staring at the door.

I fully realize that I'm not handling this the way I should be; I should be down there right now, talking to him and clearing the air between us. I guess I'm just scared. I've been rejected, cheated on, and more recently used, and I just don't think I can handle Greyston telling me that what I was doing was wrong…that *I'm* wrong. For him. For everyone.

Basically, I'm a coward.

The light in the hall comes on, and I lift my head from my pillow the minute I see Greyston's shadow appear beneath my door. There's a gentle knock, followed by him whispering my name, but I don't respond. I let him believe I've passed out. He stays put for a few minutes before eventually retreating to his room, and I'm left alone with my guilt until I finally succumb to sleep.

When I wake the next morning, my head is pounding, and I swear I'm never drinking again. I open my eyes slowly in hopes of keeping the light of day from making the piercing pain worse. I'm pleasantly surprised to see I'm still shrouded in near-darkness. The time on my clock reads *11:00*, and since I know I arrived home closer to midnight, I know it has to be morning.

So why is it so dark?

Still lying on my stomach, I push myself up and crane my neck to look toward my balcony doors, only to find the dark shades have been drawn. I know immediately that I didn't do that, which can only mean that Greyston did.

Greyston...

I'm instantly transported to the memory of last night and how I have very likely ruined the friendship we've built. "Oooooh noooo," I groan, dropping my face back into my pillow. There's no way I'm going to be able to face him—not after that.

While the kiss was amazing, and I had experienced things that I honestly never had before in my life, it doesn't change the fact that I was out of line. I never should have kissed him. I never should have climbed onto his lap. I never should have ground myself against him like a brazen hussy.

Then I remember things a little more clearly: He *let* me kiss him. He *let* me straddle him. *He* pulled my hips against him. What I'm really having trouble understanding is *why* he let me.

Is he confused? Because, if he is, he can join my club. I'll even let him be Vice President. Maybe treasurer, too.

Thinking about this is making me crazy. What I need to do is put it all behind me and act like a grown up. Greyston will understand that I can't be held responsible for my actions while intoxicated. He has to.

Right?

An infernal buzzing sound fills the room—and my head—making my brain pulse against the inside of my skull. A pretty picture, I know; it feels about as spectacular as it sounds.

I reach for my phone on my nightstand, but it's not there. Then I remember undoing my skirt and letting it fall to the floor before pulling on my pajamas. I allow my eyes to adjust to the darkness and scour the floor for my skirt. I actually don't see my clothes anywhere at all.

My phone buzzes again, and this time, I see the screen light up on the top of my dresser. Groaning, I crawl out of bed and grab my phone to check a missed text message from my mom, wondering if I want to go for lunch with her and my dad. They're even offering to come and pick me up.

Food is really the last thing on my mind right now; I need to get rid of this headache first. Though, after that, I know I'll need hangover food, and I bet I can convince them to go to IHOP.

I quickly return my mother's text and ask if I can choose the restaurant before setting my phone down and opening my bedroom door. Across the hall, I can see that Greyston's door is wide open and his bed is made. I poke my head out into the hall and listen, not hearing anything. The silence suffocates me, and I fear he's avoiding me, which makes me feel queasy. I realize just how hypocritical that sounds since that's exactly what I did last night when he knocked on my bedroom door and I pretended to be asleep.

My phone vibrates again, and I read my mom's response; they'll be here in about an hour to pick me up for lunch. My choice of restaurant.

Knowing I don't have very long, I head into my bathroom to quickly brush my teeth so I can go downstairs to grab a cup of coffee and maybe a piece of toast to help the light stomachache I've got. I stop just inside the bright bathroom when I spot a glass of water and a bottle of Tylenol sitting next to my sink, and I smile at how thoughtful Greyston is.

Maybe I'm over-reacting about all of this.

I take two of the pills from the bottle and pick up the glass, noticing that the water is still chilled. This can only mean he'd been in my room not too long ago.

After taking them, I go about ridding my mouth of the foul after-taste of alcohol, coffee, and sleep. Looking into the mirror, I cringe at the sight of my hair; it's an absolute mess, so I take a minute to remove the hairpins and brush it, cursing at myself for not doing it the night before. Once it's looking a little less like I should be doing the walk of shame, I wash my face and button my flannel shirt before heading downstairs for coffee.

I glance into the living room to see that Greyston isn't there. I poke my head through the basement door, and I hear nothing. Finally, I enter the kitchen, and he's still nowhere to be found. The smell of fresh coffee greets me, though, and as usual, sitting next to the coffee maker is an empty mug. I pour myself some coffee, adding only a small splash of cream and sugar so as not to upset my stomach, and pop a slice of bread into the toaster.

While I wait for my toast to pop, the sliding door opens, forcing me to spin around, my heart racing wildly. He looks fantastic in a pair of slightly worn-out blue jeans and a grey long-sleeved t-shirt. He hasn't shaved, which then brings back the memory of how his stubble felt beneath my hand right before I kissed him. The memory makes me blush, and I have to avert my eyes from him.

He doesn't seem surprised to see me. "Hey," he says softly.

"Morning," I reply. "Where...? I mean, I didn't..."

His hesitance radiates off him. "I've been out on the patio," he tells me, answering the question I couldn't finish. "Thinking."

With a slight nod, I offer him a smile, knowing full well that if I open my mouth, I'll spill my guts to him, and I'm just not ready to deal with that yet. Before he can see the deepening blush that is slowly staining my cheeks, I return my gaze to the toaster.

"How are you feeling?"

I know I can't refuse to answer a direct question without coming across as rude or hostile, so I shrug, still focusing rather intently on the red elements inside the toaster. "Physically? Not as bad as I probably should," I reply.

Through the corner of my vision, I see him approach. "Juliette..."

I turn, pleading with my eyes not to bring up what happened last night. My stomach feels uneasy, and my heart continues to race when he reaches out and takes my hand in his. I glance down at the contact, watching his thumb move back and forth over the back of my hand—just like it did last night...right before I left with Erik.

"About last night," I say, speaking up before he can. "I'm so sorry. I guess I was just feeling kind of down on myself after finding out that yet another guy was able to pull the wool over my eyes. I was looking for a little...validation?" I stop talking immediately, because I know I'm not making this any better. I glance up at him through my lashes to find him smiling. I want to believe that he's harboring no ill will toward me, but somehow I'm doubtful.

"I'm not sure why you're apologizing. You didn't act alone."

There's a huge part of me that wants to take comfort in his statement. The problem is, every time I remember just how two-sided our almost-affair was, I kind of go catatonic, because the memory of just how amazing it felt when his thick, hard—

Inhaling a shaky breath, I force myself to stop thinking about it before I get myself into even more trouble. "I'm apologizing because I never should have kissed you. It was wrong. You said so yourself."

Greyston's eyebrows pull together, and he looks absolutely baffled. "Wrong? I never once said it was *wrong*."

"But it was," I tell him, running my available hand through my hair and gripping tightly at the roots until it stings. "God, on so many levels."

"Name one." The strength in his voice makes it sound like he's challenging me.

Looking him dead in the eye, I answer in an unwavering voice. "Toby. There's one."

"What? How do you figure?" I can only look at him, because how can he think Toby isn't a factor in all of this?

Greyston moves to cradle my face in his hands, looking deep into my eyes. The intensity of his stare reminds me of the night before, and I fail to answer his question in lieu of getting lost in him. My hands move mindlessly to his waist, my thumbs looping into the belt loops on his jeans and holding steady.

Greyston's eyes close, and he rests his forehead to mine. His thumbs begin to move gently along my temples, lulling my own eyes shut as I give in to the tingle that is moving through me and sigh. "Forget about him," he whispers.

There's a very brief moment of time that I *do* forget about him. I forget about him long enough to tug Greyston's body closer to mine. Long enough to stand on the tips of my toes and let my lips graze his.

Then I remember him—remember everything—and I pull away, covering my mouth with the tips of my fingers and shaking my head. "I can't. I'm sorry, but I can't, Greyston. He matters; I know he does. How can you deny that?"

It pains me to watch the expression on Greyston's face contort to one so defeated. "I guess I can't." I nod solemnly and turn to the toast that had popped a few minutes ago and is now cold.

I've just started to butter it when Greyston leans against the counter right next to me. "Can I just ask you one thing?" he asks, his voice not belying the fact that he's somewhat distraught. Not wanting to refuse him, I nod. "Why him?"

Confused by his question, I set the butter knife down and look at him. "You tell me."

I can tell he's frustrated, I just don't understand why. My head hurts again, but I'm fairly certain it's not from my hangover. I run his question over and over in my mind, but it doesn't seem to matter how I try to spin it, I can't make sense of why he's asking.

"I don't know what it is you want me to say," Greyston says. "You're the one who keeps bringing him up. Always asking about him… You do know he's not available, right?"

Dumbfounded, I stare at him. "Uh, yeah I know that. You guys made it pretty obvious the day I met him."

Silence falls between us, and we continue to stare at one another. He looks just about as perplexed as I feel, and it takes a minute, but he finally speaks again. "So, you know that he and Callie are engaged…and yet, you still—"

"Wait…what?" I interrupt, my confusion reaching an all-time high. "No…I… What do you mean he and Callie are—? I thought that…"

My hands fly to my mouth, and I stare at Greyston, absolutely horrified as all of the dots connect. Within seconds, they form a giant neon sign in my mind that reads: *GREYSTON IS NOT GAY!*

"Oh god," I whisper into my hands.

Greyston regards me with raised eyebrows as I internally kick myself for jumping to yet another wrong—and much, much worse—conclusion. "Wait, so you *didn't* know that he and Callie were together?" He doesn't wait for me to respond before he starts his own little connect-the-dot puzzle. "But you said you knew he was involved? And you said that we made it..." The instant his eyes widen, I cringe and await his outburst.

He backs away from me, and I open my mouth to begin yet another round of apologies, but no words come out. This happens several times, but it's Greyston who beats me to it, yet again.

"So, you thought...?" He's pacing on the other side of the island, looking at me, then the floor, then at me again. "That day you met Toby, you...you thought that *we* were together?"

My face kind of scrunches up, and I shrug in response. "Would you believe me if I said I was just kidding?" He stops pacing and looks at me with an unreadable expression. "No? Didn't think so. In my defense, I asked all sorts of questions, and every answer that *both* of you gave led me there. You even introduced him as your partner."

"*Business* partner," Greyston corrects. Even though I feel like he should be furious, he looks amused and somewhat relieved by this turn of events.

He moves around the island again until he's standing a few feet away, but it's me who takes that final step. Greyston reaches up to push a few strands of hair away from my face. He's handling my blunder far better than I think he should be—not that I'm complaining.

Slowly, his hands move down until they rest along my jaw and neck. The tips of his fingers tickle, and the tiny hairs all over my body prickle. I shiver.

We stand in the kitchen, silent as we try to absorb everything we'd just unearthed. The way he's looking down at me should feel odd, but for some unknown reason, this—being in his arms—just feels right.

"I've made a lot of assumptions in the past two weeks," I admit quietly, and Greyston chuckles. "So, in order to clear a few things up, I'm going to ask you one thing."

Greyston nods, leaning forward and kissing my forehead lightly. I sigh when the warmth of the gesture spreads beneath my skin. "Ask me anything," he whispers, kissing my right cheek next and making my legs tremble. "I'll tell you whatever you want to know." Then he kisses my left cheek, and my fingers curl against my thigh. Finally, he kisses the tip of my nose, and I giggle. "Ask away."

"So, just to clarify for my own personal peace of mind, you're not gay?"

Greyston breathes out a single laugh, shaking his head. "I can't believe you'd even think that, because from the minute I opened that damn door, all I seem to be able to think about is you."

My heart is pounding so hard it's all I hear behind the echo of his confession. Needing him closer, I wrap my arms around his neck. I break eye contact with him and run my lips over his stubbled jaw, stopping when I reach his mouth. "Kiss me."

I barely have a chance to take a breath before Greyston's lips collide with mine. One of his hands remains in my hair while his other arm snakes itself around my waist and picks me up so our faces are level. I thread my fingers through his soft hair, refusing to let him pull away like he did last night.

Kissing Greyston now, sober, is definitely better than it was last night. Maybe because now I know that the feelings I have for him aren't unrequited at all. The arm that's around my back shifts until he's palming my backside, and I remove one of my own hands from his hair, placing it flat on the counter behind me to hoist myself onto it.

Before setting me down completely, Greyston's hand moves down my ass, over my thigh, and his fingers hook under my knee, pulling it up and hitching it tightly around his waist before it slooooowly glides back up and slips into the leg of my sleep shorts.

Needing him closer, my other leg tightens around him, my heel resting just above the back of his knee, and I pull him forward a step until he's tucked firmly between my thighs. The fingers of his right hand curl into the soft flesh of my ass beneath my shorts, pulling me forward, and I moan into his mouth when I feel a firm bulge behind his jeans.

I'm not overly experienced in sex or anything that might go along with it; I've never initiated it, and I never really cared if I got it one way or another. Of course, if I had felt half the things I am right now—the warmth that covers my body, the toe-curling, sensual tingle that's coursing through me, the manic racing of my heart, and the deep pulsing between my legs—I might have been a little more excited by the idea.

Greyston takes his time, almost like he's trying to memorize every part of me. He's sweet and sensual, his hands soft as the glide over my body. Ben always seemed to be in a rush.

It's intense and foreign to me. Plain and simple. And I want more.

I remove my hand from his hair and slip both arms between us, curving my back so I can keep kissing him and undo the button on his jeans. He moves to pull his lips from mine, but I react instantly, one of my hands returning to his hair now that it's finished aiding and abetting the other's dastardly mission.

Thankfully, he doesn't resist, his tongue gently massaging mine. I'll be honest; I never used to like kissing like this and avoided it entirely when I could. Ben was like a wild dog, salivating all over my mouth and chin.

But Greyston? *Oh, god.* His lips are soft, the pressure alternating between gentle and firm and bringing a delightful pulse to the surface of my own. Then there's his tongue... well, it's like he's teasing me, giving me just the smallest taste of him for seconds at a time before robbing me of the sensation entirely. It's maddening, but in the best possible way.

Confident that Greyston isn't going to stop kissing me, I release my hold on his hair slightly while my other hand slowly lowers his zipper. He groans, and the hand that he's had tangled in my hair since we began kissing unweaves itself and moves down my neck. His thumb presses firm against the skin along my jaw, pushing my head back and breaking our kiss. His lips press down just below my jaw, following the hard trail his thumb is leaving down the length of my neck. The minute he reaches my collarbone, his hand leaves my body, but his mouth remains focused on the hollow of my throat—kissing, licking, nipping, and driving me crazy with desire.

I move to protest the loss of his hand, but before I can, I feel the backs of his knuckles against my ribs as he works to undo my flannel top. His agile fingers have it open in seconds, and soon his hand is hovering above my breast. I've still got my tank top on, but it's so thin that I can feel absolutely everything.

He's *barely* touching me, and yet I've never felt so much pleasure. The palm of his hand ghosts over the peak of my breast, both of my nipples hardening at the barely-there sensation, and I thrust my chest forward in hopes of forcing his touch.

He chuckles against my neck, his warm breath against my skin causing an uprising of gooseflesh. "Easy," he whispers, tightening his hold on my ass and pulling me toward him again, giving me just a small tease of what my body so desperately wants.

I whimper and plead with him, but he continues to drive me wild with whatever devilish plot he's cooked up to prolong my pleasure. He doesn't give in no matter how much I tell him to, and I decide that I'll just have to convince him another way.

I bring my feet up, hook them into the waist of his jeans, and try to work them down. He lifts his face, his gaze burning into my own, and he shakes his head. "Juliette..."

"It's okay," I tell him. "I want to."

"So do I," he assures me firmly. "But I won't have my way with you on the kitchen counter...yet."

I pull his face back to mine and kiss him harder than before. When I press my body closer to his, his hand finally makes contact with my breast, and I moan shamelessly against his busy lips when he squeezes firmly.

"Please," I plead, a tremor working through my body when his fingers curl over the top of my shirt, preparing to pull it down.

I'm lost to everything but the two of us. All I smell is Greyston's cologne. All I taste is the coffee he had to drink this morning. All I see is the blue of his eyes. All I hear is our collective moans filling the kitchen. All I feel are his soft lips, his strong hands, his hard—

"Oh my!" My mother's shrill voice burns through my perfect little bubble like a meteor, forcing Greyston and I to frantically scramble apart as we try to cover any exposed parts; thankfully we hadn't gone as far as I was hoping to, so there wasn't a lot to be seen. "I'll, uh...we'll..."

We. I don't have to turn around to know what *that* means—but I do, because apparently I'm masochistic.

I turn to find my mom pushing my wide-eyed father from the kitchen. "We knocked," she's saying, probably to me. "No one answered. The door was unlocked. We're *so* sorry."

I'm petrified. Embarrassed. *Horrified* that they saw me in a less than innocent position. With Greyston. My landlord. Who my father *used* to like.

"I'm so sorry," I say, burying my face in my hands. "I knew they were coming over to take me to lunch. I didn't think... Oh, god."

Greyston doesn't say anything, but I feel his warm hands wrap around my wrists and pull them down. "You keep doing that." I look up at him through my lashes, my eyebrows pulled together. "Apologizing," he clarifies.

I laugh dryly and drop my eyes to the floor. However, on their descent, I catch a glimpse of the top of his underwear and smirk. He must know what's caught my attention, because he reaches for his jeans and moves quickly to do them up.

"Ooooh no," I tell him, grabbing for his jeans and pulling them open again. I glance up at him once more before looping my index finger into the elastic waist of his underwear...his *pink* underwear. With a giggle, I pull him back to me before doing his pants up for him.

Smiling sheepishly, he reaches out and returns the favor, slowly buttoning my flannel top. "While I would love to come up with some clever quip about why I kept these, anything I come up with only makes me sound completely head over heels for the girl that ruined them."

I inhale a shuddering breath; I want to kiss him again, but the hushed voices of my parents in the other room keeps me from doing so. "Juliette?" my mother's voice calls out from the foyer. "Would Greyston like to join us for lunch?"

I look up at him, and his eyes widen. "I'll find out," I tell her. "Well, would you?"

He looks terribly uncertain. "You do realize that your father has guns, right?"

I laugh and back toward the doorway. "I do. But there's only a forty percent chance he's carrying. Besides, it's my mother you should be afraid of." He still hasn't given me an answer one way or the other. "You're going to have to face them sooner or later, you know. You can either do it with me, or wait until my dad shows up here one day while I'm in class."

He tries to say something—probably that my dad would never do that—but then thinks better of it, and nods. "All right, I'll tag along."

Smiling, I back out of the room. "Great. I'll let them know on my way upstairs to change."

chapter 16

"So," Mom says, turning around in the passenger seat of her SUV to look at Greyston and me. This conversation can go one of several ways, and I really hope it's headed in the direction of food.

"Where did you want to go for lunch?"

I breathe a sigh of relief and smile. "Um, IHOP?" Mom gives me a very knowing smile; there's no hiding a hangover from her. Not ever.

We've just pulled off our street, and no one says a thing. Greyston is sitting behind my mom, and I'm behind my dad, both of us sitting as close to our doors as possible to avoid any accidental—or on purpose—touching that could get any one of Greyston's appendages ripped off. I've only just begun to sample what he's got to offer, so there's no way I can risk anything bad happening now…or ever, really.

I'm about ninety-eight percent sure Greyston is safe from bullets because there were no noticeable protuberances in Dad's civilian clothes when we walked out to the car. I would have asked to frisk him, but, well that would have made an already awkward situation about five million times worse.

Every once in a while, I'll look toward the front of the vehicle and catch my dad's reflection in the mirror. Sometimes he's looking at me, other times he's looking at Greyston. While he's not angry, I can tell he's not exactly pleased—which is ridiculous if you keep in mind just how many times I've walked in on them doing way more than

Greyston and me.

Okay, so not *too* much more, but it was still more. I begin to wonder if Greyston played the football ticket-card too soon.

We arrive at the restaurant and exit the vehicle. My fingers twitch to reach out and take Greyston's hand since we're walking with less than a foot between us, but with Dad right behind us, it's probably not wise. Or safe. So, to control the urge, I tuck my hands into my jacket pockets and carry on.

I know Dad can't be too angry with us, but I know he and Mom are going to start questioning us at some point. Things like the nature of our relationship are bound to come up, as well as how long we've been together. Mom's always been pretty open-minded about a lot of things, but if Dad hears that Greyston and I hadn't even discussed becoming a couple and yet were caught getting down and dirty in the kitchen…suffice it to say he probably won't be too thrilled.

Our hostess seats us in a booth, Mom and I slide in on opposite sides of each other, and I look up at Greyston, who I fully expect to join me. However, before he can, Dad slips in next to me, forcing Greyston next to my mother.

So much for some stolen moments of hand-holding, finger-grazing, and maybe footsie under the table. Though, I suppose footsie isn't entirely out of the question, but with Greyston sitting diagonally from me, I'd probably wind up touching my mom's foot, who would think it was my dad. It would open up a whole new can of awkward that I'm not prepared to wrap my head around.

As I pick up my menu to look it over—even though I'm pretty sure I already know what I'm getting—Dad nudges me with his elbow. "Looking a little green around the gills there, Jules."

"Am I?" I look across the table at Greyston, who shakes his head subtly and offers me a reassuring smile. While I'm sure he's just placating me, it does make me feel better.

My dad hums, his tone telling me he knows more than he's letting on. "If I had to hazard a guess, I'd say you had one too many to drink last night." His eyebrow arches, and he meets my apologetic stare. "IHOP, Jules? Come on, give your old man a little credit."

"Never could fool you," I quip, picking my menu back up and shooting a quick smirk Greyston's way.

The table falls silent for a moment while we all decide what to eat before our server arrives. She's a chipper little thing, but I guarantee she makes decent tips because of it.

"Hi there," she greets. "I'm Mel, and I'll be your server today. Can I get you all something to drink?"

We all order coffee, and my parents ask for a few more minutes with the menus. Since I know what I'm having already, I put my menu down and notice that Greyston has done the same.

"You know what you're having?" I ask him, drawing over-the-menu glances from my parents.

"I do," he replies with a smile and leans on the table. "And you?"

I nod. "Same thing I always have when I feel like this." He looks at me expectantly, so I continue, blushing because the sheer amount of food I'm about to consume rivals what I saw Toby put away last week. "The International Crepe Passport." Greyston looks amused—and somewhat impressed—by my choice. Probably because it also comes with eggs, bacon, *and* sausage. "And you? What are you having?"

"The Breakfast Sampler."

The server returns then with our coffee, and Mom and Dad are ready to order. Dad and Greyston let Mom and me go first. After Mom orders her spinach and mushroom omelet, I order my meal, having decided on a banana crepe option.

"So the strawberry-banana crepe?" Mel asks, jotting our food down on her little pad of paper.

"No," Greyston and I say in unison, drawing the undivided attention of both of my parents.

I'm fairly certain my heart skips a beat when our eyes connect and he corrects the order. "Just banana. No strawberries at all."

"Oh," Mel says sweetly, looking at me. "I'm sure that won't be a problem."

Dad and Greyston order next, and I find it kind of cute

that they order the same thing.

The minute Mel leaves to put our orders in, I look across the table at my mom—who's looking mighty smug and even a little thrilled. I know immediately that Greyston speaking up about my breakfast order has brought their curiosity back to what they walked in on.

"So, things between the two of you seem to be going...well?" Mom inquires not-so-subtly.

Dad's posture noticeably shifts to Alpha-male mode, and I give him a light kick under the table. "Be nice," I tell him quietly.

"Always so quick to assume the worst, aren't you, Jules?"

I open my mouth to protest, but Greyston clears his throat, and when I glance across at him, he's got an eyebrow arched. "You can't refute that," he challenges.

"No," I grumble, glaring at him playfully. "I suppose I can't." Turning back to address my mother's original question, I smile. "Things are fine."

"Fine?" she asks, sounding almost incredulous that I haven't opened up and told her that things were so much better than fine. That, had she and Dad given me five—maybe ten—more minutes, I was pretty sure I could have convinced Greyston that the kitchen counter could have been the perfect place to finish what we started. "Seems like things are a little better than *fine*."

I pick up my coffee and take a sip. I know I can't avoid having this conversation, but I need to find a way to have it in front of my *father* without wanting the floor to open up and swallow me whole. As it is, my cheeks are on fire, and my hands are trembling.

"Mr. and Mrs. Foster?" Greyston interjects, surprising me a little because he didn't use their first names like he did at dinner. I can only assume that's because he's still feeling a little weird about this morning—and rightfully so. "I know that what you walked in on today was probably the last thing you expected, but I want to assure you both that I care very deeply for your daughter." His eyes find mine again, and I smile, wishing so badly that we weren't diagonal from each other so I could reach out and take his hand. "These last couple weeks with her have been...incredible. I would never do anything to hurt or disrespect her...or either one of you, for that matter."

"While I want to believe you," my father speaks up, "the simple fact remains that you've known each other all of two weeks. Things seem to have escalated rather quickly."

He's right. He usually is.

"I know, Dad." My agreeing with him seems to shock both Greyston and my mother. "But can you tell me that you and Mom never gave into your urges? Because based on what I've seen—"

Dad's quick to clear his throat, but not before Greyston has fully started to understand where I was headed with that comment. "I guess it just all kind of took me by surprise, is all."

Mom reaches across and pats the back of my dad's hand. "It took us both by surprise, dear. So, how long have the two of you been dating now? I mean it was just last week that you were telling me you didn't think there was anything you could do to—"

My eyebrows shoot up, and I give her a *very* pointed look. "Mom, please stop talking."

"That was me?" Greyston smirks cockily. I swear his ego's growing by the second.

"Maybe," I tell him. "And this just sort of happened, Mom. Last night...this morning? I'm not entirely sure what day we're counting here."

Dad turns his head toward me. "So, you're not even technically dating?"

"Well, we haven't labeled it yet. We haven't really gotten the chance to talk about it, you know?" I know the minute I've said it that I shouldn't have. Dad's face is turning red, and I can see that vein in the middle of his forehead beginning to pulse. "That's not...that came out wrong. It's not like we've been too busy, you know, doing *that* to talk." I'm growing more and more flustered with every attempt to fix this, so I just give up.

"Things have been pretty hectic for us," Greyston jumps

in, saving me from rambling further, should I decide to open my mouth again. "I just got back from Houston last night, Juliette had a—" He stops himself mid-sentence, probably gathering that my father will likely have a conniption if he heard I went on a date with somebody *else* last night. "Juliette had previous plans with a group of people. I had actually hoped to talk to her about all of this last night over dinner, but I didn't want her to have to cancel."

While I'm more than thankful for his stepping in to rescue me, I shoot him a look that calls him a liar; he *did* want me to cancel on Erik. And, truthfully, I really should have listened to him. You know what they say about hindsight.

Mel returns with our meals, and we stop talking while she places them in front of us. After thanking her, she turns and heads back toward the kitchen.

Deciding that this is as good a time as any to save Greyston or me having to explain further before we actually get a chance to talk alone, I change the subject. "So, Dad, you excited about the game tomorrow?" It's not a seamless segue, but I'm hoping it'll do the trick.

This seems to change his demeanor, and I feel like I can finally relax. "It should be fun…assuming my interrogating the two of you hasn't gotten my invite revoked."

"Don't be silly," I say, poking at the bananas on my crepe before taking a bite.

Everybody else follows my lead and digs into their brunch before Dad starts asking Greyston about what he was doing in Houston.

"I was there signing a young baseball player who's fresh out of college," Greyston explains. "He was being scouted by a few teams but had no representation, and the Diamondbacks are very interested in him. We had him signed by Thursday, and have begun the process of getting him a contract for next season."

This then starts a debate of the Phillies versus the Diamondbacks between my Pennsylvania-born father and an Arizona-raised Greyston while Mom and I talk about school and her job.

"I'll be happy when winter break gets here," I tell Mom.

"I feel like I'm running on fumes."

"I tried to warn you, sweetheart," Mom tells me, her tone indicating that she's sympathetic to my plight, but not quite saying, *I told you so.*

As brunch wears on, I begin feeling full a lot sooner than I was expecting. While I'm sure my hangover has something to do with my diminished appetite, I refuse to let more than half of my meal go to waste. After eating my entire crepe and about a third of everything else, I finally admit defeat and place my napkin on my plate. We don't leave right after our meal, instead choosing to stay for a few more cups of coffee and catch up.

"You know," Greyston says when my mom starts talking about having us over for dinner in a week or two. "I was thinking of inviting my folks over for dinner next Sunday. Why don't the two of you join us?"

It's ridiculous how happy something as small as Greyston inviting my parents to meet his parents makes me.

Wait... His parents? I'm going to meet his parents? In a *week?*

"That sounds lovely," Mom says to Greyston. "Just let us know what time, and we'll be there."

With our plans for next Sunday finalized, we decide it's time to go. Dad and Greyston have a mild debate over who will pay the bill. Ultimately, Dad wins, saying it was him and Mom who invited us out.

It must be hotter outside than I was anticipating when we left the house, because I begin to feel slightly uncomfortable as we walk through the parking lot—almost flushed—and there's a faint prickle running along my arms and neck. Once I'm buckled in and Dad's started the car, I roll my window down in hopes that the fresh air will help.

It does a little, but my skin still feels like it's crawling.

"Juliette?" I turn to look at Greyston. "Are you okay? You've been scratching at your neck since the restaurant."

Mom turns around in her seat, and Dad looks back at us through the rear-view mirror. "Oh? I hadn't realized. Yeah, I'm fine. I must still be a little hung over." I move to scratch my neck again, but Greyston grabs my hand and stops me.

He unbuckles his seatbelt with his other hand, scoots across the seat until he's sitting right next to me, and uses the backs of his fingers to sweep my hair behind my shoulder so he can look. The tips of his fingers trail across my skin, and I smile, remembering how his fingers felt trailing down my neck in the kitchen earlier.

"You look a little red," he tells me softly. "Like you're breaking out in a rash."

"It's probably from the heat," I assure him, bringing my hand up and laying it on his. "I'm sure it's nothing."

He shakes his head and holds my gaze. "It's not that hot outside, Juliette."

Curious to see if he's right, I look at the digital temperature display mounted above the rear-view mirror and see that it's actually a little on the cool side. Then I realize what probably happened. "My crepe." Greyston looks at me curiously before he, too, draws the same conclusion as me. "I'll bet they accidentally put strawberries on it and Mel corrected them. They probably didn't even replace the crepe, just the bananas."

"Do we need to stop somewhere, kiddo?" Dad asks.

I shake my head, pulling Greyston's warm hand away from my neck and threading my fingers through his; it's not that I don't enjoy his touch, but the warmth of his hand only makes the itching worse. "No, I've got some antihistamines and some hydrocortisone cream in my washroom." I look out the window, feeling the breeze on my face and neck. "God, this is so embarrassing," I whisper to myself.

Greyston pulls his hand free and places it on my thigh, giving me a gentle squeeze and redrawing my focus to him. "Hey, don't worry about it."

"Oh, I'm worried," I tell him softly, hoping my parents aren't eavesdropping. "You think this is how I wanted the afternoon to go?"

"We have all the time in the world," he assures me, running his hand back and forth over my thigh.

The gesture reawakens my desire for him, sending my pulse racing and my mind whirling. Before I let my growing craving for him take control, I lay my hand over his and stop it from moving before laying my head on his shoulder. "I'm going to need you to stop doing that," I whisper, tilting my head up and meeting his gaze. "It's making it hard to concentrate."

"My apologies." He doesn't really *look* apologetic, what with his sly smirk and mischievous eyes.

I settle back against him and look toward the front of the vehicle. When I catch my dad's eyes in the rearview mirror once more, he winks at me, and I give Greyston's hand one more squeeze before turning back to look out the window.

We arrive home a short time later and say goodbye to my parents before heading inside. I have to laugh when Greyston makes a point of locking the door before pulling me into his arms and kissing me softly.

I want nothing more than to pick up where we left off this morning, but the irritating itch that's covering my arms and neck is far too distracting. "Hey," I whisper, leaning my head back and looking him in the eye. "I really need to hop in the shower and put my lotion on. I'm sorry."

His eyes roam down, and he gently pushes my hair away from my neck again. His fingertips tickle the skin below my ear, and I shiver slightly. I desperately want this to be one of those moments between us where I get all weak-kneed and light-headed…

Oh, who am I kidding? Rash or not, Greyston still has that effect on me.

Leaning in, he places a gentle kiss on my jaw, just below my ear, before running his finger faintly along the length of my neck. "It's really not so bad," he tells me, reaching for my right arm and pushing the sleeve of my shirt up to my elbow. "See?"

It takes a minute, but I'm finally able to tear my eyes away from the line of his jaw—where I'd been intently focused since the minute he started checking out my neck. I'm pleasantly surprised to see that he's right; the rash isn't *too* bad. It's still worse than I'd prefer—because I'd prefer *no* rash—but it's not quite as inflamed as it has been in the past.

"Go take care of yourself. I'll be down here when you finish up." He stands up straight, after giving me one final peck on the lips, and turns me toward the stairs.

"Okay. I'll be down in a bit."

Once upstairs, I close myself in my washroom and start the shower. I pull my shirt off and lean in toward the mirror to get a closer look at my neck. Thankfully, it's barely noticeable, which means I'll be able to walk around with it barely covered in order to help clear it up. If it had been any worse, there would have been little to no chance I'd leave my room for as long as it took.

As I strip down, I notice that the rash is mainly on my arms and neck with just a few very faint pink splotches on my chest. It's so minimal that I'm confident I should be able to clear it up within a few days.

I test the water to make sure it's not too hot, because the last thing I want to do is exacerbate the problem, and step inside, closing the glass door behind me. The cool water feels even better on my skin, so I pull my hair off my neck and let the water wash over it for a few minutes before I lather up.

After my shower, I pull on a tank top and my jean shorts before I take a couple of antihistamines and apply some cream to my arms and neck. I'm just finishing up and putting my lotion away when I realize that this day has done a total one-eighty since I woke up this morning.

Even though I had felt pretty miserable that I had potentially ruined my relationship with Greyston, it was like we had actually opened a door to an entire world of possibilities. Then, when we stepped through that door together, everything else just fell into place. Sure, it took a minute to step around all of the crazy misconceptions we'd both formed about each other, but we eventually found our way.

And then I ate strawberry-tainted crepes.

"Stupid allergies," I mutter, turning off my bathroom light and heading downstairs. The minute my bare feet hit the cool tile at the foot of the stairs, I call out for Greyston.

"I'm in the living room, Juliette."

The TV's not on as I wander into the living room, and there's no music playing, either. It isn't until I enter the room completely and look down from behind the couch that I see he's laying on it. "What are you doing?"

"Contemplating a nap, actually," he replies, looking up at me with that crooked smirk.

"Oh yeah?" I inquire, leaning on the couch back and staring down at him.

He nods, raising his arm and offering me his hand. "Care to join me?"

I don't have to think about it long before I'm completely on board, because I'm still feeling pretty exhausted. "Now," I say, placing my hand in his, "by *nap*, do you actually mean sleep?"

Catching me completely off-guard, Greyston sits up quickly and pulls me over the back of the couch until I'm lying on top of him, laughing. "How are you feeling?" he asks, running his hands over my upper arms soothingly.

"It's not so bad," I reply, pushing my wet hair back over my shoulder and overlapping my hands on his chest before resting my chin on them. "I'm just lucky it wasn't more than trace amounts. This should clear up in a couple of days."

"That's good." Greyston's hands move down my ribs, his thumbs grazing the sides of my breasts, before they glide over my back and come to a full stop on my ass. The right side of his mouth quirks up, as does his eyebrow. "I should probably tell you that these shorts are just plain cruel." His fingers do a familiar little dance along the frayed edge of the denim, making me quiver.

"Oh?" I inquire, and he simply nods, his fingers still trailing along the back of my thigh. "Well, I can go change if they're going to pose a problem." I'm only teasing, but Greyston reacts as though I might actually follow through.

His hands grip my ass firmly, trying to hold me in place, but only making me think about taking him on the couch right now. "Don't even think about it."

I place a soft kiss on his lips and sigh contentedly. "This is nice. Why didn't we see this for what it was earlier?"

Greyston chuckles and brings a hand up to play with the length of my damp hair. "I'm kind of surprised you didn't, actually. Especially when I came to your parents' place for dinner. I was an absolute mess." He pauses, looking contemplative for a moment before smirking. "God, when you licked that whipped cream off your finger, I thought I was done for."

Blushing, I give Greyston a little shrug. "Would it make you feel better if I admit that seeing you do the same thing almost made me pass out?" I pause briefly before continuing. "Why didn't you just say something?"

He sighs. "I wanted to—so many times—but you'd just gotten out of a relationship, and I didn't want to complicate our situation any more than I knew it would already be due to how I was starting to feel about you." He laughs lightly. "And then you kept talking about Toby, and I just assumed…well, you already know what I thought."

My body chooses that moment to remind me just how worn out it still is, and I yawn. "Oh, sorry," I mumble through it.

"Don't be. You're still exhausted, and I promised you a nap." He strokes my hair, and the sensation of his fingers on my scalp lulls my eyes shut. I feel his lips on my forehead before he rolls us both over so we're lying on our sides, facing each other.

Even though the couch is more than wide enough for the two of us, I intertwine my legs with his and drape my arm over his waist to anchor me to him while we sleep. With his strong arms wrapped solidly around my upper body, I fall into the deepest sleep I've ever had.

When I wake the next morning, I go to my ensuite to wash up before heading downstairs to start breakfast. I tie my hair back and inspect my rash, fortunately seeing that it's already clearing up. The bigger splotches are mostly gone, and some small, upraised pink spots remain. It's a relief.

I take a couple more antihistamines and rub more cream on my neck and arms before washing my hands and brushing my teeth. Ready to start my day, I put my toothbrush back in its holder and head down to the kitchen to start breakfast.

I dig through the fridge and pantry for a few minutes before ultimately deciding on pancakes. Once I've gathered all of the ingredients, I put a frying pan on the stovetop to warm while I start mixing the batter. I add a dash of cinnamon to them, because my mom always does, and pour the first two onto the pan.

The sliding door opens as I pour the next couple of pancakes into the pan, and I turn to see Greyston walking in, drying his hair in his big fluffy towel. I may get a little distracted by the beads of water that are dripping from the ends of his hair and onto his shoulders. Of course, then they roll down his toned body in thin rivulets until they meet that sexy v-shaped muscle and disappear with it behind his trunks.

"That smells amazing," he says, coming up behind me. "Cinnamon?"

"Yup. Mom makes them this way," I explain, turning back to the pancakes.

Greyston's left hand comes to rest on my hip while the other trails over my neck and shoulder. "I can't believe how much better this looks today." I shiver when his hand continues down my arm and ensnares the other hip, and my hand clenches the spatula when his lips touch down just below my ear. "How was your sleep?" he asks in a gravelly voice, his warm breath fanning over my neck.

I sigh, letting my head fall to the side to allow him better access. "Good. Yours?"

He kisses me again, just below the last spot. "Same," he admits, turning me around to face him. "Do you have any idea how difficult it is to fall asleep, knowing you are just across the hall?" His hands are now flat on my back, but his fingers are teasing the hemline of my shirt before they slip under.

My brain goes a bit foggy as his fingers stroke the skin of my lower back, and I clear my throat. "I think I have a basic understanding about how hard it might have been." It doesn't dawn on me—what I've said, and moreover, how he took it—until Greyston smirks and his eyebrow arches suggestively. This is all it takes for me to push through the lusty haze. "You're filthy," I tease, poking his wet, naked chest. "That's *not* what I meant." With a laugh, I turn to flip the pancakes.

Greyston chuckles, resting his chin on my shoulder so he can watch me. "How long do I have until breakfast, beautiful?"

It's the first time he's called me by anything other than my name, and I have to admit, it makes me a little weak-kneed. "About fifteen minutes."

"Okay, I'm going to go and hop in the shower," he informs me, kissing my shoulder softly before heading toward the door. "I'll be right down."

"Sounds good."

True to his word, Greyston returns fresh from his shower within the fifteen-minute timeframe I gave him, dressed in dark jeans and a Cardinals jersey. He looks pretty damn delicious, and I almost forget about breakfast entirely.

Snapping out of it as Greyston opens the fridge and reaches for the OJ and maple syrup, I pull the last two pancakes from the pan and plate them while he takes his seat. Smiling, I place his food in front of him and sit down. "What time is the game today?" I ask, laying my napkin on my lap.

"One," he replies, pouring syrup on his pancakes. "Your parents will meet us there between twelve and twelve-thirty."

I laugh. "I bet my dad's been up for hours. He's probably stoked for today."

Greyston takes his first bite, and I wait to see what he thinks. His eyes close, and he moans while he chews. It probably shouldn't, but his reaction to my cooking has a very visceral effect on me, and I'm right back to wading through a fog of lust. "This is amazing."

"Thanks," I reply softly, turning to my own breakfast and trying to think of a topic of conversation that can help distract me. I decide to ask about Xander's trip. It turns out that Greyston wants to show Xander the area, maybe invite him over for dinner.

"That could be fun," I tell him. Then I remember how Daphne was drooling over his picture the other day, and I smile. "Daphne will be excited to hear he might be moving to the area if he signs with the Diamondbacks."

Greyston laughs. "Well, let's not overwhelm the poor guy. And if you have any ideas on some fun things we could do, feel free to suggest them."

"Fun?" I question, looking at him with an arched eyebrow. "You know who you're talking to, right? I'm the polar opposite of fun, remember?"

"Juliette, please," he scoffs. "I may have only just met you, but I can tell you know how to have fun."

Smiling, I reach over and pat his jean-clad knee. "You're so adorable when you think you're right." He chuckles. "I'll try to think of something. Maybe tell me a bit about him."

"Well, he's fresh out of college—but you already knew that. His dad served in the army, and up until about two years ago, he thought he wanted to enlist." Greyston goes on to tell me what he knows about Xander, and I try to think of what we could do before it suddenly comes to me.

"Paintballing," I tell him. "You should go paintballing."

"You want me to take my baseball-playing client *paintballing*?" he asks.

I nod excitedly; it's been forever since I've been, and I kind of hope he'll invite me. "Yeah. It'll be fun! My dad knows a great place. We used to go all the time when I was younger."

"You," Greyston starts, "used to go paintballing with your dad?"

"Sure," I tell him. "Come on, you said you wanted to do something fun."

Greyston thinks about my suggestion for a moment before finally nodding. "All right. I'll talk to Toby and see what he thinks, but something tells me he'll be all over it." He pauses briefly. "You'll join us, right?"

"Wouldn't miss it," I tell him, standing up and grabbing our empty plates. "Who knows, maybe I can teach you a thing or two."

"Oh, I bet you can," Greyston replies cheekily from his seat.

Placing the plates in the sink and turning it on, I look back over my shoulder. "Behave yourself."

Greyston leans forward on the counter and shrugs. "Doubtful."

Once the dishes are done, and the kitchen is clean, I excuse myself to go and get dressed so we can head out for the game soon. I'm actually pretty psyched; it's the first football game I've ever been to.

"Dress a little warmer," Greyston calls after me. "It's not an open stadium, but you might still get a little chilly since it's supposed to be a bit cooler today."

"Thanks." Knowing this, I decide on a pair of light blue jeans, a white long-sleeved t-shirt, and my black Chucks.

The drive to the stadium isn't very long, and we're early enough that we find decent parking right away. As I unbuckle my seatbelt, Greyston rushes around to open my door for me, making me smile. I place my hand in his outstretched one and let him help me out. "Thanks."

"Juliette!"

I turn around to see Mom and Dad walking across the lot toward us, and wave. "Hey! How was your morning?" I hug them both before we walk together toward the entrance.

"Your dad's been pretty excited all morning. He was up before dawn," Mom teases, nudging my dad with her elbow.

"Give a guy a break," Dad grumbles good-naturedly. "You'd be just as excited if this was Cirque du Soleil, Anne."

Mom loops her arm through my dad's and leans in to kiss his cheek. They talk amongst themselves, nuzzling noses and whatnot while we walk, so I stop paying attention. Instead, I take Greyston's hand and lace our fingers together, leaning on his shoulder as we pass through the doors.

"They sure are passionate," Greyston says, reaching into his back pocket for the tickets before handing them over to be scanned.

"Yup," I agree, trying not to think about their...*passion*. "It's great, because I know they're incredibly happy, but you have to be careful because they go from zero to kinky in seconds." Greyston laughs loudly. "You laugh now, but you can't un-see the things I've been subjected to."

"Should we grab a bite to eat before we find our seats?" Dad suggests.

We all decide that's a good idea and head toward the concession. My parents stand in front of us, Mom's arm still looped through Dad's, and wait their turn. I'm looking up at the menu, trying to decide what I feel like having, when I feel Greyston's body press up against my back. His arms wrap around my body, and he rests his chin on my shoulder, kissing my cheek before reading the menu boards too.

"I don't know what I want," I confess. "What's good?"

"I'm a fan of the hotdogs," he responds.

"Yeah?" He nods against my shoulder. "Okay then."

Mom and Dad step away from the concession with their food; Mom opted for a slice of pizza, and Dad got a hamburger. When they turn around and see Greyston's arms wrapped around me as we wait in line, they smile—yes, even Dad.

Greyston must notice too, because he gives me a gentle squeeze and kisses my cheek again before we step up to the cashier and order. We each get a hotdog and decide to share a soft drink. I flinch when I see the price of our food, but Greyston doesn't, paying for it all with a smile before picking up our cardboard tray and leading the way to our seats.

There are already tons of people in their seats, and Dad seems like he's losing his mind as we follow Greyston down the aisle. I can't understand why; everything he says makes absolutely no sense to me because I don't know a damn thing about football.

"You didn't say the tickets were on the fifty-yard line, Greyston," he says.

Chuckling, Greyston leads us down a row that's about thirty rows back from the front one. "I had to keep a little mystery between us, Cam."

While we finish eating, Dad and Greyston start talking football, and Mom and I try to keep up. I'm picking up bits and pieces—touchdowns, kickoffs, four downs—but I'm still feeling beyond lost. I mean, I understand some of it, but until I see it happening in front of me, I don't know that I'll fully grasp it. And even then I know I'll have questions.

The game is set to start in less than a half-hour, and the crowd is simply buzzing. Looking around, I'm kind of astounded by the number of football jerseys in the stadium. It makes me want one.

"Hey," I say, placing my hand on Greyston's knee. "I'll

be right back, okay?"

He looks confused, standing when I stand and placing a hand on my waist. "Where are you going? Do you want me to come with you?"

I laugh, pressing my palm to his chest. "No, That's okay. I'll be right back. If I get lost, I'll text you to come find me."

Nodding, he leans in to give me a kiss and then lets me pass. On my way, I let my parents know I'll be back and then head out of the seating area. I'm not sure where I have to go exactly, but there's enough people milling about the area that I should be able to get directions.

I stop the first couple I see, and they gladly point me in the right direction. Thankfully, it's not too far from where I came from, so I shouldn't have too much trouble finding my way back.

When I reach the front of the line, I see that they have two different styles: one that's mostly red, and another that's mostly white with red sleeves. I mull it over for a couple of minutes before deciding on the white one. I thank the sales-person for basically robbing me blind, and then take my new jersey to the washroom so I can put it on.

My phone buzzes in my pocket, and I pull it out to see that it's Greyston telling me kickoff is about to start.

I tap out a quick reply, telling him I'm on my way, and hit send. I quickly use the facilities, wash my hands, and then head back to my seat. I find the section easily enough and smile wide when Greyston's eyes pop open upon seeing me.

"Aw, Jules, really?" Dad groans, clearly not satisfied with where my loyalties have fallen.

"Sorry, Pop," I apologize, stepping around them to get to my seat and struggling with my balance along the way.

Greyston holds out his hand for me, and I take it to keep from falling into the row of people in front of us. Before letting me go, though, Greyston pulls me to him, his hand running over the fabric of my new shirt. "Are you trying to kill me?"

"You like?"

A familiar grumble escapes him, exciting me. "Let's just say I'm going to have a very difficult time concentrating on the game."

I step up onto my tiptoes and kiss him before we take our seats. Once we're settled, Greyston's hand finds a home on my thigh as we wait for everything to begin. We rise from our seats when it's time for the National Anthem, and I smile up at Greyston as everyone in the stadium sings along.

The game starts, and I have to admit, it's pretty exciting. While I don't get everything that's going on, Greyston does a really good job at explaining things to me in a way I can understand. Dad is trying to ruffle Greyston's feathers the entire game, especially when the Eagles score a touchdown that puts them ahead of the Cardinals.

The majority of the crowd is not happy about this, and I find myself momentarily worried. It's especially worrying when halftime rolls around and the Cardinals are still down by seven. Since there's nothing really going on, Mom and Dad excuse themselves, leaving Greyston and me alone for a bit.

"Are you having fun?" Greyston asks.

I nod emphatically. "I really am. It's a little confusing, but I think I understand the basics." I lean forward in my seat, taking Greyston's hand and lacing my fingers with his. "Thanks for inviting us. It's really great, and Dad's having a blast."

He pulls my hand to his lips and presses a kiss to my knuckles. "I couldn't imagine being here with anyone else, Juliette."

I lean closer to him. "Well, that's good, because I wouldn't go to a football game with just anyone."

Mom and Dad return from wherever they snuck off to—honestly, it's best if I don't even ask—and it looks like the game is about to get back underway. The second half of the game is interesting. The teams both seem to be doing well, but, much to Greyston's dismay, the Eagles win the game. He's a good sport, though, listening to Daddy relay the winning touchdown as we walk through the parking lot.

We stop at my mom's SUV, and my dad turns to us. "Thanks for inviting us along, Greyston."

"Anytime, Cam. I'm glad the two of you had a good

time." He shakes Dad's hand and then turns to my mom to do the same.

Mom pushes his hand away and pulls him in for a hug instead. "You two have a good night, okay?"

"We will, Mom," I tell her, hugging her and my dad next before telling them I'd talk to them later in the week. They climb into their vehicle, and Greyston and I head for his car so we can go home after what I can only describe as one of my top five favorite days.

So far.

chapter 17

After a spectacular weekend with Greyston and my parents, waking up on Monday morning seems kind of depressing. It's almost like the weekend was a wonderful dream, and now I'm being thrust back into reality.

Feeling less than enthused to start my day, I turn my alarm clock off, crawl out of bed, and head to my bathroom to get ready. As I finish up and head back into my room, I pull the hem of my oversized sweater down to cover my shorts, and the neckline slips, exposing my shoulder. I expect to smell breakfast cooking as I hit the hall, but I'm shocked to see that Greyston is still in bed. Fast asleep.

Not sure yet if I enjoy this view more than him swimming, I lean against his door frame, cross my arms, and watch him for a minute. He appears deep in sleep still as I let my eyes roam over his peaceful face. His hair is even more messy than usual, but instead of wanting to run my fingers through it to tame it, I want to make it worse.

The minute I notice his breathing pattern change when he shifts to roll over, I back away from his room and proceed downstairs to make coffee and start breakfast. I find the kitchen a little quiet, so I flip the radio on before digging through the fridge for the ingredients to make omelets.

Dancing to the music, I crack the eggs into the bowl and whisk them before pouring them into my oiled frying pan. When I notice the top is cooked, I sprinkle some shredded cheddar on it and fold it over.

"Now this is a sight I could get used to in the mornings," Greyston says from behind me, making me jump. He chuckles. "Sorry, I didn't mean to alarm you."

Laughing at myself, I remove the first omelet and pour the second one into the pan. "No, that's okay. I either need to learn to not be so jumpy, or tie a bell around your neck."

Greyston smiles, crosses the room until he's standing right next to me, and tugs at the hem of my sweater. "You know, I'm starting to think you're running around here in next to nothing just to drive me crazy," he says, grazing my bare thigh with the backs of his long fingers.

"And I'm starting to think you do *that*"—I nod my head in the direction of his hand on my leg—"to drive *me* crazy."

His hand moves up a little farther, above the fabric of my shorts until he's fingering the waistline of them. My abdomen quivers when his knuckle grazes the ticklish skin there as he dips a finger in and pulls me to him. My chest is pressed so firmly to him that he can probably feel my heart beating. He holds my gaze, eyes blazing, and I sigh when our lips barely touch.

"Greyston, our breakfast," I whisper, raising my free hand and teasing the hairs at the nape of his neck. Though, if I'm being entirely honest, the longer we stay like this, the more focused I am on how his body feels when it's pressed so close to mine than the stupid eggs.

Breakfast be damned.

He briefly presses his lips to mine before releasing my shorts. "You're right."

Regretting saying anything at all, I toss the spatula on the counter and grab his arms before he's out of reach. "Nonononono," I tell him, tugging him back to me and shaking my head. "I'm wrong. So wrong."

Laughing, Greyston kisses my forehead and moves around me to pour a cup of coffee. "No, you're not. I'd hate for you to be late for school because I wouldn't let you leave the house."

I pick up the discarded spatula, add cheese to the omelet, and fold it over. "I think you're just being a bit of a tease," I accuse playfully. "Building the anticipation between us." I turn and point the spatula at him. "I'm on to you, Masters."

He quirks a brow and gives me that devilish half-smirk. "Not yet."

I suddenly feel like my legs might give out beneath me, but I refuse to let him see this. "Funny." After dishing up the second omelet, I pick up both plates and head for the island. "Breakfast is ready."

Over breakfast, I ask Greyston if he's got a busy day. Apparently he doesn't have to go into the office until this afternoon, so after I leave, he plans to go for his swim. "I'd have preferred to have gone while you were still home." I eye him curiously. "It's just I hate that I've robbed you of your little routine."

My jaw drops. I'm stunned. "I…uh…I have no idea what you're talking about," I stammer, poking my eggs with my fork, refusing to meet his smug stare.

"Yeah, that almost sounded believable."

I set my fork down and turn to him. I'm not going to try and deny that I've been watching him, because he knows just as well as I do that I'm guilty, but his accusation has me curious about something. "So, you've seen me up there, and yet you still thought I was into Toby?"

"I wasn't certain what you were doing up there, to be honest…you very well could have been enjoying the desert view and fresh morning air," he admits, smirking crookedly at me. "It wasn't until we finally got everything out in the open that I finally put two and two together."

Laughing, I shake my head. "If only the two of us could have mastered basic math a week ago before jumping to all of the wrong conclusions."

Before I know what's happening, Greyston pulls my chair toward him, the feet scraping loudly against the tile. His warm hands are on my thighs, moving down to my knees where he curls his fingers and lifts my legs, resting them on his own. It's kind of awkward, but I don't really mind since I'm only inches away from straddling him—which must be his newest form of torture.

"Oh, I don't know." A tingle begins to work its way up my legs as his hands move up and down my thighs, his fingers occasionally dipping *just* beneath the hem of my shorts before resurfacing. There's a really good chance that my heart is going to give out at the rate it's beating. "I think things might be better this way," he says, his voice low and seductive, increasing my desire for him exponentially. "All of those nights spent wondering kind of…intensified everything. Don't you think?"

I nod once. It's not the most fluid movement given my brain is more focused on the fact that Greyston's hands are still running up and down my legs. Warmth spreads through my body, starting where his hands are touching me and moving all throughout until it settles in the pit of my belly, igniting a flourish of butterfly activity. No one has ever made me feel half as alive as Greyston, and if he's able to elicit this kind of response from me with only his hands…well, imagine the possibilities.

I lean in to press my lips to his, but when they're a hairsbreadth away, he whispers, "You're going to be late."

I move my head back and forth, allowing my lips to lightly brush his. "You're doing it again," I tell him softly. "Being a tease."

He refuses to acknowledge my accusation with anything more than a smirk. "You should go get dressed; I'll clean up."

"All right. But this isn't finished," I warn, leaning in and pecking his lips before hopping off my chair.

After quickly dressing, I grab my car keys off of my dresser and my book bag off the floor as I make my way out of my room. By the time I reach the bottom of the stairs, Greyston is there, holding a travel mug out for me.

"For you, beautiful," he says. "Have a good day."

I hum, brushing my nose over his. "You too."

Inhaling deeply, Greyston groans. "Okay, you should go before I force you to play hooky with me all day."

"I don't know," I whisper, my eyes moving back and forth between his and watching conflict spark in them. "That actually sounds like a lot more fun."

"Go on," he says, his eyes showing just how much he's struggling with letting me go. "I'll see you when you get home from work."

"'Kay." Walking out the door isn't easy; it's almost like it's the last step to accepting that my fantastic weekend really is over.

With a depressing sigh, I climb up into my car and buckle up. When I slip the key into the ignition and turn it, the engine clicks a few times, so I pump the clutch repeatedly to force it to turn over. Nothing. "Come on," I grumble, turning the key again. "Don't do this to me." I repeat this process several times, only to get the same results. Abso-freakin-lutely nothing.

Now I'm not just sad that my weekend is over, I'm pissed off that my week is starting off so crappy. I unbuckle my seatbelt, angrily flinging it back against the window, grab my bag as I throw my door open, and storm back into the house.

Greyston is just coming down the stairs in his trunks, and for a brief moment I forget all about my stupid car. Because he's half-naked and halfway between our bedrooms and me.

Then he has to ask the question that reminds me why I was upset. "What's wrong?"

"My stupid engine won't turn over." I grab my phone and start flipping through my contacts to find a cab company.

"Who are you phoning?"

"A cab. I don't have time to take a bus. I'm going to be late as it is now."

I've just found the number I need when Greyston's hand appears over mine, blocking the screen to my phone. "I'll give you a ride."

It's sweet of him to offer, but I feel guilty that I'm robbing him of his morning off. "No, it's fine. I don't want you to have to give up your morning," I tell him. "I've got some cash. It's fine."

"Juliette, I'm not going to make you take a taxi when I can go get dressed and give you a ride." He sounds resolute, so I just nod. A smile spreads across his face as he lets go of my hand, and he rushes back upstairs, re-emerging about two minutes later, fully dressed.

"Thanks," I say as he holds the door open for me, closing

and locking it once we're outside. "For the ride."

"Anytime, Juliette." He opens my car door for me and shuts it once my legs are safely inside, then runs around and climbs in next to me. "I'll have someone come over and take a look at your car this afternoon."

We arrive on campus a little while later, and Greyston parks near the doors. He hops out while I struggle to untangle the straps of my bag from around my ankles. How it happened, I have no idea; I'm just glad I noticed it *before* trying to get out of the car.

My door opens as I free my right ankle, and Greyston is holding out his hand for me. One look around at the students who've stopped to see what's going on forces my cheeks to warm. But it doesn't stop me from taking his hand. Nothing ever would.

"Thanks again for the ride." Greyston closes my door and pulls me closer, the warmth of his body making every inch of me hum. "I'll, uh, find a ride to work, and I bet Katie can drive me home afterward."

It's like he doesn't hear me. "What time is your last class over?"

"Three. But, Greyston—"

"I'll be here at three and drive you to work," he says, not letting me finish.

I shake my head. "No, Greyston. It's out of your way."

"Not really. I've got meetings nearby this afternoon. I'll see you at three." He leans down to give me a chaste kiss and then straightens up. "Have a good day."

"You, too."

I'm just walking away, my fingers sliding along the palm of his hand until only our fingertips are touching. Before we lose connection, his hand reclaims mine, and he pulls me back to him. Our chests collide, expelling all the air between our bodies and my book bag falls heavily to my side while he's still got a hold of my other hand behind my back, our fingers now woven together. There's a familiar spark in his eyes, and this excites me, making me forget all about the people milling around us.

"You forgot something," he tells me in that low, gravelly

voice that makes all of my senses numb to anything but him. His other hand comes up to cradle my face, and he lowers his lips to mine.

I don't mean to, but the minute he kisses me, I whimper, drop my bag the last few inches to the ground, and bring that hand up to lie on his chest right above his pounding heart. His thumb moves slowly over my cheekbone, and the fine hairs all over my body stand on end. Pushing up on the tips of my toes, I curl my fingers into the fabric of his shirt, holding him close as he takes my bottom lip between his and traces it with his tongue.

There's nothing in this world I enjoy more than being kissed by Greyston. At least, not yet, anyway.

Apparently I'm no longer in control of anything I do whenever Greyston's lips are on mine, because it's Greyston who ends our kiss, pressing his forehead to mine and smiling.

Panting breathlessly, I try to calm my racing heart. "Not that I'm complaining, but what was that for?"

"Just proving a point," is all he says.

My eyes snap open, and I shake my head. "And what point is that?"

Instead of answering me right away, Greyston's head lifts away from mine and his eyes drift off to focus on something behind me. Slowly, I turn my head to follow his gaze and find Ben standing several yards away. "Oh, I see." I smile. "He looks a little upset."

"Good," Greyston responds, tightening his hand around mine gently and drawing my eyes back to his. "Juliette, I'd like to take you out on a date tomorrow night."

I nod, a smile slowly spreading across my face. "I'd like that."

Greyston's smile rivals my own before he kisses my nose. "Okay, you should head to class. I'll see you in a few hours, beautiful."

My heart flutters each and every time he calls me that. Greyston releases my hand and bends down to pick my discarded bag up for me. I don't head right inside, choosing to wait until his car is out of sight. When it is, I turn around and come face to face with Ben.

Nothing he might have to say interests me, and I sure as hell don't want him to sour my once-again good mood, so I side-step around him and proceed toward the building. He's clearly dense, because he doesn't seem to take the glaringly obvious hint, instead taking it as an invitation to follow me.

"You know, Ben, I could have you charged with stalking," I threaten. "I'm pretty sure my father wouldn't even bat an eye."

He laughs, apparently mistaking what I've said for a joke. Greyston's right; he's a twit. "You know, you have a lot of nerve, Juliette," he tells me. "You get mad at me for screwing Delilah, when you were stepping out on your sugar daddy with Erik on Friday night."

His accusation stops me dead in my tracks, right in the middle of the hall. I turn to face him, glaring daggers that I hope to hell will maim him beyond recognition. When it doesn't work, I contemplate thrusting my knee into his groin and dropping him like a sack of potatoes.

"You don't know what you're talking about," I tell him venomously. "And even if you did, what you have to say means exactly jack-shit to me anymore, Ben."

"So, you didn't leave the party the other night with Erik all over you?" he demands, sounding somewhat jealous. "Because that's what a few people have been saying. I bet your sugar daddy—"

"Would you grow the hell up and stop calling him that?" I demand, growing more and more annoyed the longer I stick around to listen to his inane prattling.

Not wanting to hear another word, I turn on my heel and begin to walk away when Ben calls after me. "I don't get it; what does he have that I don't have?"

I refuse to stop, instead turning and walking a few slow steps backward as I shrug. "You mean, besides basic respect for our relationship?" Ben remains quiet, and I smirk cheekily. "Me."

At the end of the day, Daphne meets me by the front entrance and walks with me outside. She's rambling on excitedly about her psych class while we make our way to the lot. It isn't until Greyston comes into view that she clams up—or maybe I just can't hear her because he's smiling crookedly at me. It's more likely that, because Daphne isn't known for going mute for anything.

He's parked his car right at the end of the sidewalk and is leaning against the passenger side of his car, smiling wide when our eyes meet. As if that's not enough to make every single bone in my body turn into pudding, he's wearing a suit and tie. He pushes himself off his car, and I pick up the pace until we meet halfway. His arms encircle my waist, mine his neck, and he pushes his face into the crook of my neck, his breath tickling me.

"Hey," I whisper, teasing his soft hair with my fingertips. "I want to introduce you to someone." I turn around to see Daphne smiling wide. One of Greyston's hands remains on my waist, always keeping a physical connection between us. "Greyston, this is my friend, Daphne. Daphne, this is Greyston."

Greyston outstretches his free arm. "It's a pleasure, Daphne. Juliette's told me so much about you."

Smiling even wider, Daphne takes Greyston's hand and begins to shake it enthusiastically. "I've heard so many things."

This makes Greyston laugh, and I blush when he looks down at me with a cocky grin and an arched brow. "I'll bet you have. Though, I'm not sure how much of it was based on fact. Am I right?"

"There may be a possibility that I confided in Daphne about a thing or two," I tell him, reaching for his wrist and glancing at his watch. "Shoot, we should get going. I'll talk to you later, Daphne?"

"Sounds good! Nice meeting you, Greyston."

Greyston takes my bag and opens my door. I'm just about to step into the car when he grabs my upper arm and stops me, smiling as he leans down and gently presses his lips to mine.

"I never realized just how much I could miss that," I whisper, bringing my hand up to grip his tie. "By the way, this suit? It's like you're trying to kill me."

Chuckling, Greyston nods toward the car. "Come on, let's get you to work, shall we?"

I sigh. "If we have to."

"What time do you get off tonight?" Greyston asks as he pulls out of the lot. He realizes what he's said before I can say or do anything, and he starts laughing. "Get off *work*." He shakes his head at himself. "I'm sorry."

Honestly, I find it comforting to know that I'm not the only one who says ridiculously inappropriate things at the worst possible times. Smiling, I place my hand on his arm and give it a reassuring squeeze. "Nine-thirty." I glance over at him. "I'm closing tonight, so I'll grab a cab home."

"Not a chance." I'm about to protest again, but before I can, Greyston continues. "I told you I'd help you out until your car was fixed, and that's what I'm going to do."

"No," I protest, turning my upper body to him as much as possible in my seatbelt. "Greyston, it's too much. I'll figure something else out."

"It's really not a problem, Juliette. I don't understand why you won't let me help you." He seems almost disappointed that I'm so quick to refuse his help.

Dropping my eyes to my hands, I shrug. "I just don't want you to have to rearrange your entire life because my car is a piece of crap."

His warm hand moves from the gearshift to my thigh, making me inhale shakily. "It's really not a problem. I don't mind rearranging a few things to make this work."

"Fine," I concede, placing my hand over his. "But don't do anything that might jeopardize your work. If you can't drive me or pick me up for whatever reason, please let me know so I can figure something else out. Promise me?"

"Okay. I promise."

When we arrive at the café, I unbuckle my seatbelt and lean across the console to give Greyston a kiss. "Okay, I'll see you later, then. Thanks again for the ride."

The minute I open the door, I see Katie is alone behind

the counter and there's a lineup that almost reaches the door. I decide not to wait the additional twenty minutes before my shift is supposed to start. Instead, I rush behind the counter without changing into my uniform so I can make Katie's orders as she rings them in.

Within fifteen minutes, we're caught up.

"Thanks for starting early," Katie says, wiping the counter down.

"Yeah, no problem. Where's Paul?" I ask, pulling my uniform out so I can go change.

Huffing, Katie tosses her rag onto the counter and crosses her arms. "He called in sick, and no one could cover."

"Sorry. If I wasn't in class all afternoon, I'd have come in sooner. You know, if it's not busy later, you should go home early and I'll close up," I offer.

"Yeah? Cool." Katie picks up her cloth again and puts it in the sink before restocking the shelves. "Oh, by the way, was that your hunky landlord that dropped you off?"

I hum affirmatively, turning to give her a sly smile. "My car wouldn't start this morning, and he's kind of designated himself my personal chauffeur."

She must hear the happy lilt in my voice, because her eyes widen and her jaw drops. "Oh my god! Are you two together?"

"Yeah, we kind of are. We had the best weekend, and he wants to take me out on our first official date tomorrow," I tell her excitedly.

"Fun! Where's he taking you?"

I shrug. "No idea. I didn't ask."

"Well, whatever he's got planned, I bet it'll be amazing. He seems like the romantic type." Katie seems almost mesmerized as she talks.

As the hours go by, we don't see too many customers. We have our busy periods, but for the most part, it's pretty dead. By eight o'clock, I tell Katie to head home, because with only an hour left, I can probably handle things.

"Only if you're sure," she tells me. "I'd hate for you to get busy after I leave."

"It's nothing I can't handle," I assure her. "Go home."

Once I'm alone, I begin the pre-closing duties. I wipe down all the tables, sweep and mop, clean all of the coffee machines, and make sure that everything is stocked for the next morning. I have maybe three customers come in over the last forty-five minutes. After the last one leaves, I have nothing left to do, so I grab myself a double chocolate chip cookie and hop up on the counter with my back to the door to eat it.

"Busy night?" The silky voice both alarms and excites me, and instead of hopping down and going the long way around, I bend my legs and turn on the countertop until I'm facing him. Before I can dismount the stainless steel surface, Greyston has approached me.

"It's been all right," I tell him. "Better now that you're here." He's still wearing his suit, which either means he's been working all this time, or he left it on for me. His reasoning doesn't matter, really, because I really love this look.

He places his hands on either side of my thighs, his thumbs grazing the skin below the hem of my pleated uniform skirt, and he pushes his way between my legs. I'm beginning to compare our position to Saturday morning in the kitchen, and I feel a tingle building between my legs. I want him so badly, but know that we can't do anything here. It would be wrong.

Oh god, but so much fun.

"At the risk of sounding incredibly cliché," Greyston says in his low, sexy voice, "I really missed you today. Before this weekend, being without you wasn't easy—especially when I was in Houston—but now that we're finally on the same page, I found it hard to concentrate on anything all day."

"Well," I say, setting my half-eaten cookie down on the counter and wrapping my hand around his tie to tug him closer. "I'm here, and you're here."

Greyston lowers his face until his lips are within an inch of my own. I can feel the warmth of his breath on my face. My pulse begins to race, my skin prickles with anticipation, and my stomach knots with desire for him. Then, just as I feel his soft lower lip brushing my own, there's an annoying vibration against my thigh that distracts me. I assume it's a text and try to get back into the moment when it buzzes once more.

"What is that?" Greyston asks, dropping his eyes between us to the apron pocket I stowed my phone in earlier.

"My stupid phone," I grumble, reaching into the pocket and pulling it out to see who it is. My nose scrunches and my upper lip pulls back in a silent snarl when I see Ben's name glaring across the top of the screen. I hit ignore and set the phone down next to me. "Sorry, where were we?"

When that sexy half-smirk appears again, I pull him closer by his tie and am just about to kiss him when my phone vibrates again. This time it sounds a lot more annoying, rattling against the steel countertop.

Greyston's eyes drop to where it sits, and they narrow angrily. When it buzzes again, he pulls away from me and snatches my phone up.

Before I can even think about protesting—not that I'm going to—Greyston answers the phone in a hostile tone. "Hello?" There's a pause where I can barely make out Ben's voice. "She's busy, and last I checked, she wanted nothing to do with you." Greyston's anger is escalating, as is my desire for him as I watch this all unfold before me. I pull him closer with my legs. "So, unless you want a repeat of the first time we met, I suggest you back the hell off." He hangs up the phone and sets it back on the counter roughly.

I swallow thickly when my eyes fall upon the muscles in his clenched jaw. My gaze continues north until I see his forehead is furrowed in anger, before finally settling on his blazing blue eyes. Slowly, I run my fingers over the lines in his forehead, softening them slightly, then down to his jaw, and I pull him to me.

We kiss hard and fast, our lips pressed so tightly together they throb, and his hands ensnare my hips, pulling me to the very edge of the counter until he's pressed firmly between my legs. His slacks do little to hide his growing arousal, and my short skirt allows me to feel all of it. I've never loved my uniform more.

I moan against his ravenous lips when he thrusts his hips into me. When I pull away, I'm breathless and feeling a little light-headed. "I'm going to cash out, and then you're going to take me home before things get out of hand here."

After agreeing, he doesn't hesitate to let me down from the counter. My legs feel a little weak as I make my way for the door to lock it and flip the sign over. I eventually find my bearings and head back behind the counter for the register. Greyston snatches up my abandoned cookie, and I glare playfully as I watch him take a huge bite.

It takes a little longer than it should to cash out, but only because as I'm counting the coin, Greyston starts calling out random numbers to throw me off. It works time and time again, and it isn't until I threaten to pick up a shift and postpone our date that he stops. There's no way I would actually do it, but he doesn't need to know that.

After I've made the deposit and locked the money away in the safe for the night, Greyston and I leave the café together, locking the door behind me.

The air between us during the car ride home is charged with pent-up sexual frustration. Greyston's hand is clutching the gearshift so tightly that his knuckles are white. I yearn to lay my hand over it, to relax him a little, but I'm afraid that it will only make things worse.

We arrive home a short while later, and once we're inside, Greyston closes and locks the door before pulling me to him and pressing my back against the door. His hot lips trail over my jaw and down my neck while his hands grip and pull my hips to his again and again. My body grows hot, like fire licks the surface of my skin, and his hands move from my hips and up to palm both of my breasts over my shirt.

"God, you taste like coffee and sex," he murmurs, placing open-mouthed kisses on my neck.

I moan like some kind of porn star. Suddenly desperate for his lips to be on mine, I bring my hands to his face and draw him to me. We kiss, and it's not sweet and gentle, but aggressive and rough. His tongue sweeps over my lower lip before I open my mouth and meet it with my own.

With one hand continuing to massage my breast, the other travels down, pulling my shirt from the waist of my skirt until he's stroking the flesh of my belly. My skin quivers beneath his touch, and I whimper into our kiss when his hand travels down over the pleats, lifting the hem and stroking the apex between my thighs and teasing the edge of my panties. My lower half tingles and reacts to each and every languid stroke he makes, and the muscles in my stomach begin to tighten.

My hands tremble as I bring them to his tie and pull it apart, sliding it from his collar and letting it hit the floor before I set to work blindly unbuttoning his shirt. The minute I reach the bottom of his shirt and pull it from his pants, he stops kissing me, and I can see some kind of conflict in his expression.

"Juliette, I don't think we should rush into sex." My smile fades, so he tacks on. "I just…I want to do things right with you. After everything you've been through, you deserve to be treated right."

I admit, I'm a little sad. But at the same time, it thrills me that he's so considerate of *me*. "Okay," I mumble with a small nod.

The right side of his mouth twists up into a devilish little smirk, and a tremor of anticipation shoots down my spine, settling right where his hand was only moments before.

Why do I feel like this could be torture?

chapter 18

This has to be the most nervous I've ever been in my entire life. I feel more like a twelve-year-old girl about to talk to her big crush, and less like a twenty-year-old woman going on her first date with a guy she's known for a few weeks. This has the potential to go toe-up in the worst way, but that's probably just my pessimism kicking in.

When my last class of the day finally lets out, I rush from the building, already telling Daphne that I wouldn't have time to look for her. She was very understanding once she sensed my growing anxiety about the date tonight.

Greyston is parked in the same spot as the day before, just stepping out of his car as I walk briskly toward him. It's like he times his arrival to the second, and I smile brightly when he greets me. "Hey, gorgeous," he says, meeting me halfway and pulling me into his arms. I wrap my arms around his neck, and he lifts me off the ground slightly. "How was your day?"

"Too long," I sigh against his neck. "I was far too excited about tonight."

"You and me both." He sets me back on my feet and kisses my lips softly. "What do you say we head home?" I nod once in response, and he takes my bag and leads me by the hand back to the car.

"So, what exactly are we going to do tonight?" I inquire as we pull out of the parking lot. He's silent, staring a little more intently than usual, and it begins to worry me. Does he have to postpone our date for a work-related issue? "Greyston?"

"Sorry." He smiles and places a hand on my thigh. "I had a couple of ideas, but I'd be interested to hear a few of yours, as well."

"Oh." He's caught me off-guard, but in a good way, because this means he isn't postponing our first date. "Um, I don't know. Dinner and a movie?" He laughs, making me nervous again. Was I showing my age with my suggestion? Did he want to do something a little more...grown up? "What? No good?"

"Quite the opposite," he says, giving my thigh a gentle squeeze. "That was precisely what I was going to suggest."

"Oh yeah? Cool. So, what movie do you want to see?" I ask, placing my hand over his.

"You pick," he tells me.

I shake my head. "No way. I got to pick our movie last week. It's your turn."

With a chuckle, he turns a corner. "Well, I guess we'll have to check movie listings when we get home. How about dinner? What are you in the mood for?"

I contemplate this before humming. "I'm not sure. I'd be okay with theater popcorn, actually."

"Not a chance," he disagrees with a smirk.

"Why not? It costs just as much as any meal at a restaurant." He knows I'm right—I can see it in the way he presses his lips together and narrows his eyes, but I get the impression he's still not going to allow us eat *popcorn* for dinner...especially on our first date.

"That's beside the point," he retorts lightly. "What kind of guy buys a girl popcorn for dinner on their first date?"

"Uh, an awesome one."

"Why don't we go to Different Pointe of View? I hear it's amazing," he suggests, turning to look at me.

"Don't you need reservations?" I'm stunned by his choice of restaurant, and don't know what else to say.

He only shrugs. "Probably, but the owner is actually a friend of my mother's. I'll give him a call and see what he can do."

When we arrive home, I head up to my room to put my things away, and Greyston goes into the study to power up his computer to check the movie listings. He's just pulled up the theater's site when I enter the room.

"Find anything?" I ask, crossing the room and leaning on the desk next to him as he navigates his way to the listings.

Without warning, Greyston grabs me around the waist and pulls me down until I'm sitting sideways on his lap. I squeal in delight and shock, and wrap my arms around his neck.

"That's better," he says, one of his hands resting just above the curve of my ass and the other on my upper thigh. It's terribly distracting.

I shoot him a sly half-smirk and cock an eyebrow. "I'm sure it is. Now, what's playing?"

Together, Greyston and I scan the movie listings, and I'm totally cool when he chooses the latest superhero movie that has just come out.

With the tickets for our movie bought and printing, Greyston calls the owner of the restaurant directly and asks if there's anything he can do to get us in for dinner before our movie. He's more than accommodating, even being sure to offer us the best seat in the house, when Greyston offers up a couple tickets to a football game.

"Our reservations are for six," he tells me, setting my phone down on the desk.

"Sounds good. I'll just go shower and get ready then."

He smiles and kisses me lightly. "All right. I'll see you shortly."

Greyston and I part ways for the next little bit, and while I shower, he remains in the study and buries himself with work. Probably contracts or planning future trips or something.

By five o'clock, I haven't heard anything from Greyston. I'm almost ready and about to go off in search of him when I hear him call my name.

"In here!" I reply from my closet.

"You almost ready?" he asks from the hall just outside my room.

I pop my head out of the closet, hands by my ears as I put in a pair of silver hoops. "I'm dressed. You can come in, you know."

"I actually have to go and change, too," he tells me, his eyes roaming my body appreciatively.

I smile, knowing that I made the right choice when I grabbed these jeans. They make my ass look phenomenal, and I paired them with a deep purple satin top. To dress my outfit up further, I added a long silver chain around my neck, and it falls between my boobs. Greyston's eyes follow the chain, and he swallows thickly with appreciation.

"I just wanted to be sure you were almost ready."

"Oh, okay," I reply, letting my hands fall to my sides when I finish with my earrings. I run my fingers through my long brown hair, allowing it to flow over my shoulders and frame my face.

I see him still standing there, staring at me like he wants to devour me, and my brain starts coming up with excuses to stay in for the night. It's trying to sabotage me, plain and simple.

I cut it off at the pass, and head back into my closet. "I just have to grab a pair of shoes, and I'll meet you downstairs?"

"Perfect," he replies, his voice sounding a little thick. "Give me ten minutes."

I smirk from inside my closet, perusing the shoes and boots I own for the right pair, and wonder what exactly he might do in those ten minutes based on how he was just ogling my chest. "Take all the time you need."

After finding the perfect pair of heels, I head downstairs, shoes in hand. I stand by the front door and slip them on when I hear Greyston descending the stairs. I nearly choke on my breath when I see him in the same well-fitted jeans as before, but he exchanged his sweater for a white button up shirt and a black tie. On his feet is a pair of matte black dress shoes, and his dark hair is finger combed back. My knees threaten to buckle, and I wonder if I'm going to be able to walk in these shoes now.

He's in front of me in seconds, and I reach for him, grabbing his tie and thinking about pulling him in for a kiss that I'm sure will get out of hand. He's stronger than I am, though. "We should go, or we'll miss our reservation."

I nod once, reaching behind me for the doorknob and turning it. "Later, then."

Greyston exhales heavily and presses his forehead to mine, holding my gaze with his stormy blue eyes. "You can count on it."

The drive to the resort that houses the restaurant isn't a short one, but the view once we arrive at the top of North Mountain takes my breath away.

"This is incredible," I whisper as we head into the main entrance and toward the restaurant.

Greyston's hand clasps mine, tucking it into the crook of his elbow as he escorts me through the restaurant doors and toward the hostess podium. "Better than popcorn?" he teases.

I can't help but laugh. "We'll see."

The hostess looks up at us, smiling brightly. "Good evening. How can I help the two of you tonight?"

"We've got a reservation under Masters," Greyston informs her with a kind smile.

She glances down at her reservation book, nods, and grabs a couple of menus. "Perfect. Right this way."

After hugging the menus to her chest, the hostess leads us to a table next to the floor-to-ceiling windows, and Greyston pulls my chair out for me before taking his seat across from me. I look out the window, my eyes going wide as I take in every last detail of the view from the mountaintop. Below us, I can see the Valley's desert landscape and the bright lights of the city while the sun sets on the horizon.

"Your server tonight will be Emma," our hostess tells us. "Can I take your drink order? Perhaps some wine for the lovely couple?"

"Oh," I say, peeling my eyes from the amazing view. "Um, no thanks. I'll just have water for now, please."

"I'll have the same," Greyston replies, looking toward me with a smile.

I reach across the table, squeezing his hand. While I'm grateful that he's willing to forego drinking if I can't, I also can't approve of the sacrifice. If I was twenty-one, I would absolutely indulge in a glass or two of wine. "Please, have a glass of wine. Just because I can't, doesn't mean you shouldn't be able to indulge."

He raises his eyebrows, looking at me in a way that makes me wonder if he thinks I'm testing him. I laugh softly. "You're sure?"

"Yes. I'd feel guilty if you didn't."

Greyston looks back to the hostess and orders a glass of red wine. When the hostess leaves, I open the menu and gasp, looking up at Greyston with wide eyes.

"What is it?"

My eyes move between his and the menu a few times. "Have you seen these prices?" I demand softly so as not to offend anyone within earshot. "Maybe the popcorn would've been a more reasonably priced meal."

All he does is laugh. He *laughs*. Like this is no big deal.

"Enough with the popcorn. There's no way in hell I am going to let that happen." He glances back at his menu and shrugs. "Besides, these prices aren't so bad considering the restaurant and the beautiful scenery.

I lean forward until my chest is pressed against the menu. "Greyston, I *barely* make minimum wage. This is crazy. I mean, thirty-five dollars for *fish*?"

Then he *winks* before offering me a smile I'm sure is meant to be reassuring. It's not...at first. "True, but I'm willing to bet it's amazing and worth every penny."

My cheeks warm, and I scrunch my nose. "You're right. I'm being kind of a downer, huh?"

"I never said that."

"It was implied," I quip, dropping my eyes back to the menu.

There's a brief moment of silence before Greyston speaks up again. "I almost forgot to tell you that Callie's mechanic was able to figure out what was wrong with your car. Apparently your alternator needs to be replaced."

That sounds expensive. I worry about the food prices again.

"He's ordered the new one and thinks your car will be

ready in a couple days."

"That's great," I say, because it is, but I'm also mentally figuring out how much money I have in the bank.

"Hi there," our server greets happily, setting our drinks on the table. "I'm Emma, and I'll be your server tonight. Have you decided on what to have yet?"

I look up to Greyston and close my menu. "I have, if you have."

He nods. "I have. Go ahead."

I shift my gaze back to Emma and place my order. "I'll have the lemon roasted garlic chicken, please."

Emma jots it down on her notepad and then turns to Greyston. He reaches across and takes my menu, handing them back to our server. "And I'll have the filet mignon, please."

Offering us another smile, Emma heads off to put our orders in, leaving Greyston and me alone with the beautiful view. "This is amazing," I repeat. "I know the night's only started, but you should know that no one's ever taken me anywhere like this before."

He doesn't seem too surprised by my confession, but he inquires further, anyway. "So Ben never…?"

My laugh fills the restaurant, gaining a little attention from the neighboring tables. "No. Ben never did anything unless there was some kind of direct payoff for him in the end. And taking me out for a thirty-dollar dinner would mean he was spending his precious money on someone other than himself." I pause, feeling my blush deepen.

"So, uh, how was your day?" I ask, sitting back and trying to change the subject.

Greyston takes a drink of his wine before answering. "Good. Callie came over and we talked about Xander flying in next week." The expression on his face changes instantly. He almost looks guilty and apologetic. "Actually, I needed to talk to you about something that Callie mentioned today."

"Oh?" There's no denying how nervous I am based on his expression and tone.

"I have to fly out to Chicago."

While I'm a little sad by this news, I have to wonder if

he's expecting a more extreme reaction. All he'll get is my support. "When?"

"Not until next Wednesday," he rushes to explain. "I'll only be gone a couple of days." He pauses, waiting for my spirits to lift, most likely. "Actually, while I'm away, why don't you see about getting us in for paintballing that weekend?"

I don't know if he thought this would cheer me up, but it definitely did. "Yeah?" I am definitely excited. "For how many?"

"Let me talk to Callie and see if that's something she would be open to."

"Okay," I reply, feeling my sadness fading. "So that would give us an uneven number—you, Toby, Callie, Xander, and then me…" I pause for a moment, hesitant as an idea comes to mind. "Would you be opposed to me inviting Daphne along if that's the case? To make the teams fair, of course."

"Sure, why not? I don't see that being a problem."

My mood lifts, excited for this outing together. Soon our conversation slowly segues to dinner with our parents this Sunday. I'm definitely nervous about meeting Greyston's folks, but I know it can't be avoided forever.

"What if they don't like me?" I inquire nervously.

Smiling, Greyston takes my hand across the table. Like always, the feeling of his thumb running over the back of it relaxes me. "They're going to love you."

"And if they don't? Then what?"

He laughs. "Well, then I suppose my relationship with them is over." I know he's joking, so I force a light laugh.

"I'm serious."

"They'll love you because—" He stops suddenly. "Because you're amazing and funny and bright."

I can't stop myself from blushing when he says the things he says. I can only shake my head and smile through it. "You've really got flattery down pat, huh?"

With a shrug, he says, "I like to think of it as one of my stronger traits."

"I bet it works on all the girls."

"Only one that matters," he quickly adds.

"I rest my case," I say with another laugh. I love how happy he makes me. It's definitely not something I'm used to experiencing so regularly in a relationship, which I suppose is a good sign for us. "How is it you're not taken?"

Greyston smirks. "Oh, I'm quite taken with one girl in particular."

"I'm serious," I retort with a playful giggle. "How were you single when we met?"

The air shifts to one a little more serious—but only a little. "I'm a very busy man," he explains. "Some women can't handle how often my job takes me away. While it's been less lately, it's still more than most women sign up for when they get involved with me.

"My last relationship ended about a year ago," he continues. "We'd been together almost twice as long. Over the course of the first year, she started to show signs of being overly clingy. She took to picking fights with me every time I had to go out of town, and she told me I had to make a choice: my job or her. I loved my job, so the choice was easy." I'm shocked to hear that Greyston had been with someone so selfish.

"Because she wasn't the first to tell me my job was a problem, I just decided I wasn't going to date anyone seriously for a while." He pauses, his eyes locked on mine, probably trying to glean my reaction from my expression. "I hope you understand that how I feel about you—even after only a short amount of time—far surpasses anything I ever felt for her, and I'd like to think that if you ever gave me the same ultimatum, I might choose differently."

I shake my head, touched by his admission. "That's sweet, but I would never make you choose. I'd like to believe I'm not that selfish in nature. It's your job, and while I might not relish the idea of you going away, I'm a big girl and can take care of myself."

Our food arriving puts our conversation on hold for the moment as Emma offers us some fresh-ground pepper. I accept, and we begin eating. "Oh, god," I say, adding a little moan to it. "Okay, this is definitely better than popcorn."

When I open my eyes, I notice Greyston shift in his seat, and I smile. His laugh sounds a little nervous at first, but soon it's genuine and hearty. "I'm glad to hear it."

During dinner, we talk about the movie Greyston chose. I admit, I don't know much about the comic books or the characters, but I have enjoyed all of the other movies in the franchise that I've seen already. After I polish off the last of my chicken, Greyston asks if I want dessert. I look at him a little sheepishly. "Um, I'm kind of saving room for that popcorn still."

"No problem," he replies with a grin. "I'd be okay with that, too."

Emma drops the bill on the table, and Greyston snatches it up before I have a chance to reach for it. Truthfully, it's probably best I don't look, because I'm pretty sure I'd pass out if I saw just how much our meal came to. I do reach into my purse for my wallet so I can pay for my share, though.

"What do you think you're doing?" he demands.

"Paying for my dinner?"

He shakes his head and pulls out enough cash to cover dinner and probably a pretty decent tip. "No, you're not. I don't know how that last asshat you dated did things, but *I* asked *you* out. Tonight is on me."

I don't put up a fight; instead I embrace this new relationship dynamic with open arms. Having doors opened for me, chairs pulled out, dates paid for…a girl could get used to this. "Okay. Thank you."

By the time we leave the restaurant we've got about an hour until the movie. This is plenty of time, so Greyston doesn't rush, instead allowing us both to enjoy the leisurely drive.

We luck out, finding a decent parking space in the middle of the lot, and we head inside. It isn't a surprise that the line for our movie is huge as everyone waits for the last show to let out.

Greyston places a hand on my lower back, drawing my attention to him. "Why don't you wait in line, and I'll go get the popcorn?" he suggests.

I agree, requesting extra butter on the popcorn—I hate

the dry pieces. Before I leave him, I pop up onto my toes and kiss him on the lips, taking my ticket and heading toward the auditorium while he stands in the concession line.

He joins me in the massive lineup ten minutes later, struggling to balance the large popcorn and two drinks. He's also grumbling about how it all cost close to half of what our dinner did. Stepping over the thin rope separating the line from the rest of the common area, Greyston hands me my drink.

"Thanks." I take a sip. "What time is it?"

He checks his watch. "Almost eight. Has the other show let out yet?"

"Yeah, I think they're just cleaning the theater now." Just as soon as I speak, a few staff members emerge to let everyone in. We manage to find seats in the middle of the row and near the top. It isn't long before the entire theater is packed and the lights dim.

As the previews play, I reach over and help myself to the popcorn in Greyston's lap. We both point out which upcoming movies we'd like to see, and it surprises me—though it shouldn't—to find we have pretty similar tastes in films.

I'm caught by surprise when Greyston leans in and places a finger beneath my chin, turning my face to his and kissing me softly. I release a sigh, my desire erupting and pushing through my veins. I can taste the salt from the popcorn on his lips, and I kiss him a little more firmly. It only takes a second to remember where we are and that we're surrounded by hundreds of other people, and we pull apart, breathless and frustrated. Even though we'd both like to carry on like a couple of horny teenagers, I settle for sidling up to him instead. I slide my arm beneath his and rest my head on his shoulder as we watch the movie.

We don't move (except to eat popcorn) for the first half of the film. Eventually, my ass starts to fall asleep, so I move to shift my weight, pulling my legs onto my seat and tilting my knees toward Greyston. He sees this as an invitation to rest his hand on my thigh—not that I'm complaining. As his thumb moves back and forth over the denim, I drop the hand I was tickling his arm with to his leg. I'm aware of just how close it is to the zipper of his jeans, but he doesn't react one way or another, so I figure he's just really into the movie.

I don't know what comes over me, but I feel the need to see just how far I can take this.

While I know it's highly inappropriate, I adjust my body again, this time brushing the side of my breast against his arm. No reaction. He just looks at the screen. With my head still on his shoulder, I continue to watch him through my upper lashes. I flatten my hand on his thigh, my pinky finger grazing the bulge in his jeans. He swallows thickly, and I smile triumphantly, victory swelling in my chest and making my body tingle.

I tilt my head slightly, wanting to feel his lips on mine—to hell with a full theater. He looks down to find me smiling, my hand moving up his thigh until I'm almost palming his crotch.

"Juliette," he warns under his breath.

I return my eyes to the movie, but my hand remains on his thigh, still moving and feeling his body react to my touch. It's…empowering. I'm almost drunk on the feeling.

Finally, his hand slides from the outside of my one thigh to between them. He moves it up, the tips of his fingers tracing the heavy seam of my jeans. Excitement zips through my veins as I take a shuddering breath. It doesn't take long before his hand rests at the juncture between my legs, and I react by curling my fingers into his thigh and bicep, unable to fully process what's happening.

His hand continues to move, this time back and forth against the seam of my jeans. I want more—need more—but I know it can't happen here. I'm still aware of our surroundings, even if my vision is starting to darken around the edges. My breaths become shallow, and I dig my nails into his upper arm. My other hand continues to move over what I can only now imagine is a full-blown erection.

We're seriously like a couple of teenagers.

The movie finally ends, and I'm so worked up from the last forty-five minutes or so—we both are—that I can't wait to be home and see where all this might lead. I move to stand, but Greyston's hand presses down on my thigh, stopping me.

I'm confused, until I look at the expression on his face.

"Just...give me a minute," he pleads, his voice gravelly. He leans over and places a kiss below my ear. "You've worked me into quite a state."

A few minutes go by before Greyston and I deem it safe to leave. He lets me walk in front, his hands on my hips as we maneuver through the thick crowd. His thumbs slip beneath the hem of my shirt and tease the bare skin of my back, making my body hum with desire all over again.

It feels like forever before we reach the car, and just as I grab the handle, Greyston flips me around and presses his body to mine, sandwiching me between him and the car. His hands grip my ass firmly, inviting a sharp gasp from me as he lifts me until we're face-to-face. I lean in to kiss him, but he pulls back before I connect. I whimper when he changes course, letting his lips ghost along the shell of my ear. I twist my fingers into his hair tightly when he lowers me back to the ground.

"You have no idea what it is you do to me."

"I think I might." My voice cracks.

Without another word, Greyston unlocks the doors and opens mine for me. I ease into the car, my legs trembling, and he rushes around to the driver's side. He definitely drives above the speed limit—something my dad would have his head for, but we'll just keep it a secret between us; I happen to like Greyston's head right where it is.

When we arrive home, I'm just about to open the front door when Greyston stops me, turning me toward him and pulling me close under the porch light. I look up at him, smiling, yet confused.

"I just wanted to say I had a really great time tonight," he says.

I wind my arms up around his neck and look up at him through my lashes. "Me too." I bite my lower lip gently, my fingers curling into the back of his shirt as the sexual tension between us mounts. "It doesn't have to end, you know."

A smirk tugs the left side of Greyston's mouth upward, and he leans down, his lips brushing mine softly. "I want nothing more than to take you up on that offer," he says, his words rolling over me like silk. "But I don't want us to rush into anything. That's just not how I was brought up, and it's not what you deserve."

His confession causes me to tremble in his arms, and he finally presses his lips to mine in the sweetest goodnight kiss I've ever experienced. It's firm, but gentle, passionate, but not too insistent. It leaves me wanting more.

He pulls away after a couple seconds and smiles down at me, opening the door behind me and walking us through. We lock up and head up the stairs together, stopping in between our bedrooms where he drops his hold on my hand.

"Goodnight, Juliette." He kisses me sweetly on the cheek before taking a backward step to his room.

"Goodnight, Greyston," I reply softly, retreating to my room and flopping down on my bed, blissfully content as I play our first date on loop in my head before falling asleep.

chapter 19

The sun slowly creeps across my bedroom floor on Sunday morning. I'm still tired, but when I hear a splash outside, I sit up excitedly. Not only am I excited because Greyston is half-naked outside in the pool, but also because I don't have to work at all today. After a lot of pleading, I convinced Katie to pick up my shift so I could take at least one day off after a busy week at school and an exhausting day at work yesterday. Sure, I had to take a couple of extra shifts next week to make up the hours, but knowing that Greyston was going to be out of town those nights anyway made my decision much easier. This way I wouldn't have to be home alone more than necessary.

Instead of stepping out onto the balcony to watch Greyston swim his lengths, I decide to join him in the pool instead. The last time I was in the pool wasn't entirely voluntary, and I figure this could be a good way to start our day off together.

I finish my morning bathroom routine, I go to my dresser and rifle through my top drawer until I find a light green two-piece swimsuit. I quickly tie the straps of the tiny triangle top and then tighten the ties on my hips before exiting my room. On my way down the hall, I grab a fluffy towel from the linen closet and hop down the stairs excitedly.

Wanting to surprise him, I peek through the window above the kitchen sink to find him still cutting through the water gracefully, none-the-wiser to my even being out of bed yet.

Quietly, I slide the patio door open and step out onto the cool stone, padding softly toward the pool. It's definitely a little chillier now that we're into December; we've honestly been lucky to have the warm weather as long as we have. I toss my towel next to Greyston's on the lounge chair and head to the edge of the pool deck. While I would love to dive into the pool, the truth is, I'm just not that graceful and would probably hit the water with a painful *slap*. To avoid this, I to sit on the edge of the cement deck, slip silently into the water, and wait for him.

It doesn't take him long, noticing me when he lifts his head to take a breath. He looks a little shocked to see me, but his shock is quickly replaced with pure delight as he swims forward until he's able to stand on the pool floor. Our eyes lock as he walks forward, placing his hands on either side of me and effectively pinning me to the wall of the pool.

"What a pleasant surprise," he says, leaning in to kiss me softly. "Sleep well?"

"Well, I didn't fall asleep on my books, so that was a nice change from the rest of the week," I tell him, only half-joking. "You?"

He shakes his head. "I've missed you."

"I'm here," I whisper, pushing his wet hair off his forehead before wrapping my arms around his neck. "I've always been here, I've just been busy."

Between studying for mid-terms and work, not to mention Greyston's job, our schedules just didn't line up. We were lucky if we got a half hour together before I disappeared to my room for the night to hit the books.

Greyston sighs, one of his hands disappearing beneath the water and securing itself to my hip, his pinky twirling the tie that holds my bottoms together. "Me, too. If we didn't live under the same roof, I'd be afraid you'd think I was avoiding you or flaking out on you after our date. It's been torture not spending more time together." He leans in and kisses my neck. "Not being able to kiss you as much as I'd like..." His fingers curl into the soft flesh on my hip. "Not being able to touch you as much as I'd like..."

There's no holding back the moan that slips past my lips

as I pull his face to mine and kiss him deeply. His hand releases my hip before slipping down my thigh slowly until he reaches my knee and pulls it up to his waist. I whimper against his lips when he pushes between my legs, and I tilt my hips forward, craving more.

Moments like this are why I feel waiting is an insane notion. It's not that I don't understand why we *should*. I get it. I do. But when he says the things he says and does the things he does...well, it's really hard to stick to.

With a groan, Greyston stops kissing me and presses his forehead to mine. "While I would love to keep doing this, don't we have to get you to work?"

Smirking, I shake my head and bring my other leg up around his waist, hooking my ankles behind his back. In this position, there's no hiding just how turned on he's become. "Nope." I tighten my arms around his neck, displacing what little water is between us until our chests are pressed against each other. "I swapped my shift with Katie so we could spend the day together."

His eyes brighten, the outer corners creasing when his smile reaches them. "Really?"

I shrug. "I figured we deserved an entire day to ourselves after our schedules kept us apart for the last few."

Greyston exhales and tucks my hair behind my ear. "Always so considerate." His fingers move through the length of my hair and back beneath the water, trailing down my arm and making me shiver. "So, what *are* we going to do today?"

Arching an eyebrow, I glance up toward the sky and hum. "Mmmm. I think what we're doing right now is a good start."

"You know," Greyston says with a faint chuckle, "I'm starting to think you're not nearly as innocent as you've led me to believe..." I regard him with confusion, and he continues. "You're somewhat of a vixen."

This makes me laugh, because I know that to be the farthest thing from the truth. "You have no one but yourself to blame," I tell him, tightening my legs around him.

Something mischievous flashes in his eyes, and I shudder. "Is that a fact?"

Resolute, I nod. "Absolutely. If you weren't so good at what you do, then I'd probably be able to stop thinking about wanting you all the time."

His hands grip my ass, pulling me against him firmly until my eyes close, and I stifle a loud moan. "You know," he says, his voice low and gravelly with lust, "I've imagined doing unspeakable things to you in this pool since the day I met you."

I sigh. "Just one more thing we have in common, then," I admit quietly, wiggling my hips against him in an effort to entice him to act on his fantasies. I'm shameless, I know.

"Unfortunately..." Disappointment floods my veins as I wait for him to continue, but he doesn't have to.

"Hey!" Toby calls out, his feet slapping loudly across the stone tiles of the patio.

"Doesn't anybody knock anymore?" I mutter under my breath.

Chuckling, Greyston rubs my upper arm. "Easy, tiger."

I look behind me to see Toby and Callie walking toward the pool, and then back at Greyston, who looks a little uncomfortable. "I'm sorry," I whisper, feeling incredibly guilty that he's going to have to suffer.

Greyston smiles reassuringly and shakes his head before turning his attention to Toby. "I thought you were coming by at eleven?"

I turn around to see Toby arch an eyebrow at him before looking down at his watch. "It's eleven-thirty."

"It is?" Greyston inquires, looking at me, seemingly shocked. "Damn. Okay, why don't you give me a few minutes to finish up out here and get changed?" Greyston asks Toby, who nods in response before heading back inside with Callie.

"Sorry," Greyston apologizes. "I didn't realize what time it was. I thought you had to work, so Toby and Callie were going to come over to go over a few things for my trip to Chicago."

"Oh." I nod. "Okay."

"It shouldn't take long," he's quick to assure me, pulling

me back into his arms. "And then maybe we could pick up where we left off?"

"Perhaps," I contemplate playfully before remembering something. "Oh… Our parents are coming for dinner today, remember?"

Greyston nods. "We've got plenty of time. Though, I will have to run into the store to pick up a few things. Care to tag along?"

"As if you even have to ask," I tell him.

Greyston kisses me softly before we exit the pool. We grab our towels off the lounge chair, wrap them around our waists after drying our upper bodies, and head for the patio door hand-in-hand.

"I'm going to go and get dressed," I announce.

Greyston leans forward and kisses the tip of my nose. It's a small, innocent gesture, but it always serves to take my breath away while making me feel special and adored.

Leaning in, I ghost my lips over his. "But you better make good on your promise to make it up to me, Masters."

His eyelids drop slightly, and he groans. It pleases me to know I have a very similar effect to the one he has on me. "I assure you, I will."

"You two gonna spend all day making googly eyes and kissy faces at each other?" Toby says, closing the fridge behind me.

"Thought about it," I joke, shooting a friendly wink Toby's way.

Greyston looks to Callie, and then shakes his head at Toby. "I'm going to go and get dressed. I'll be right down, and we can go over Mills's contract."

Once we're in the hall between our rooms, I turn to Greyston. "I'm going to go and shower. You should head downstairs and do what it is you have to so I can have you all to myself for a bit before dinner." Before tearing myself from his warm embrace, I pop up on my toes and kiss him softly.

He groans as I step away, and I can feel Greyston's eyes on me as I make my way to my room. My newfound confidence stirs, and I reach for the bikini tie around my neck and tug it free. It falls slack around my neck. I clutch it to my chest before it falls and then turn to find Greyston gawking.

Smiling, I reach behind me and untie the other string. "You know, for every minute you stand there staring, you could be doing your work." Feeling emboldened, I tear the top from my body and toss it at him, closing my door before he can get a good look.

I lean my back against the door and stifle a giggle when I hear him start to grumble. "That's just mean," he says loud enough for me to hear. "Thanks for the souvenir, though. I'll be sure to keep it somewhere safe."

His bedroom door closes across the hall, and I push myself off the door to hop in the shower quickly. Dressed in jeans and a fitted tee, I head downstairs to find Greyston, Toby, and Callie still at the kitchen table going over the folder splayed before them. "Hey," I greet. "I'm kind of hungry, do you guys want lunch?"

Greyston's the first to look up, smiling wide. "Sounds great, babe."

It's the first time he's referred to me as anything but my name in front of others, and my breath catches slightly. My cheeks warm, and I avert my eyes when Callie and Toby exchange a glance between them. "Anything in particular?" I inquire, opening the fridge and rifling through it. "I could make soup and sandwiches?"

No one objects, so I set out making lunch. By the time it's ready, they're just finishing up with work, and we all sit around the kitchen table. I take a seat next to Greyston, Toby sits on his other side, and Callie next to him.

"So, about Xander's trip next week..." Greyston interjects. "Juliette suggested paintballing. Are the two of you up for it?"

Toby's the first to agree, not even pausing to think about it. "Hells yeah! Come on, Cal, it'll be a lot of fun." It takes a minute, but she decides to join in, and we begin to figure out what day might work best for everyone. I make a mental note to text Daphne later to find out her availability. She'll be so excited when she finds out that the ball player she was drooling over will be there.

After lunch, Callie and Toby head home. Greyston walks

them to the door while I clean up our dishes. I've just finished loading the dishwasher when I feel strong hands on my hips and warm lips on my neck. It's hard to focus on washing the pot in my hands with Greyston's fingers teasing the sliver of skin between my shirt and jeans, so I give up trying.

"Thanks for lunch," he whispers, his warm breath tickling the skin of my neck.

"If this is how you're going to thank me for cooking, I might just have to do it more," I tell him, turning in his arms. When my eyes catch the time on the stove, I groan. "I guess we should probably go to the store for whatever it is you need for dinner."

Greyston tucks a strand of my damp hair behind my ear, his eyes showing remorse. "I'm sorry."

His apology confuses me. "What for?"

"This can't be what you expected when you took the day off to spend with me," he explains with a shrug.

"Don't be ridiculous. You didn't know I took the day off," I remind him. "And besides, it doesn't really matter to me what we do with our time together."

"I suppose you're right. Okay, let's go. We'll have plenty of alone time after dinner tonight." He leans in and kisses me softly before whispering, "And I promise to make this morning up to you."

Giggling, I meet his intense gaze. "Come on. If we don't go now, then we won't get this done."

That mischievous gleam has returned to his eyes, and he reaches for me again. "Oh, I think we could."

Laughing, I place my palm flat against his chest, holding him at arm's length. "Down, boy."

Thankfully, it doesn't take much convincing to get Greyston out the door, and soon we're at the store, wandering the aisles, filling our basket with fresh produce for a salad. We continue through the store, grabbing fresh buns from the bakery and cheese from the deli before paying and heading home. Greyston and I each take a bag to carry, and when we arrive home, we set to work in the kitchen prepping dinner.

Greyston is apparently against buying pre-formed hamburgers and makes his own. After the burgers are formed, he covers the plate and puts them in the fridge before moving onto the salad. Just as he begins washing the vegetables, there's a knock at the front door. I inhale sharply, my nerves taking hold, knowing that it could be Greyston's parents at the door.

Sensing my apprehension, Greyston kisses my temple. "Relax. You stay here, and I'll go get the door. Keep yourself busy by starting the salad," he suggests, handing me the very large kitchen knife.

I laugh. "You really think it's a good idea to be giving me a sharp knife? I'm shaking like a leaf."

Shaking his head, Greyston sets the knife on the counter. "I'm sure you'll be fine. I'll be right back, okay?"

"Sure. Take your time. Don't rush." Once he's out of the room, I carefully pick up the knife and begin slicing the tomatoes for the salad. I'm just finishing up when I hear voices approaching—all three familiar to me.

Looking up, I see Greyston enter the kitchen first. My parents are flanking him, and I breathe a sigh of relief. Mom's carrying a bowl of pasta salad, and Greyston promptly takes it from her and puts it in the fridge.

"Hey, Mom. Dad." They both smile my way before their eyes briefly drift down to the counter I'm chopping vegetables on...the very one they saw Greyston and I on last weekend.

"How's your weekend been?" I quickly ask, diverting their attention. "Good? I hope it's been good."

"She been drinking?" my dad asks, nudging Greyston.

I roll my eyes. "Har har," I deadpan. "You're a real comedian, Pop."

"Why don't I give both of you the tour while Juliette sobers up," Greyston teases, shooting me a wink.

"Oh, good. Side with him," I tell him. "We'll see how that works to your advantage."

"Why don't you guys go on ahead? I'll stay with Juliette," Mom suggests with a laugh, moving behind me and placing her hands on my shoulders in a show of support.

Before Greyston and Dad leave us alone, Greyston grabs

Dad a beer and Mom a glass of wine.

Mom perches herself on one of the stools. "How've you been, sweetheart?"

I smile wide, focusing on the cucumber I'm cutting so I don't slice my finger. "Good…really good, actually."

"You and Greyston seem to be getting closer." My cheeks warm, filling with a deep blush, and this only invites her to dig a little deeper. "Oh, my. Just how *close* have you gotten, Juliette?" she prods playfully.

"What?" I ask, surprised, even though I really shouldn't be; we'd had a very similar conversation when Ben and I were dating.

"Oh, don't play innocent with me, Juliette. I'm your mother. We talk about these things." She pauses, gauging my reaction, and when she deems it safe to continue, she smirks. "So, have the two of you had sex?"

"Oh my god!" I hiss. "Could you at least *try* to keep your voice down? As if Dad needs to know we're having this discussion!" Mom only rolls her eyes and waves her hand in front of her, silently urging me to continue.

I sigh. "Okay, fine. But before I tell you anything else, let me preface this by saying that if the words 'your father and I' leave your mouth at any point, this conversation—or any future ones regarding this matter—will not happen. We clear?" She contemplates my terms for a moment before acquiescing with a nod. "Good."

"So…?"

"No, actually we haven't taken that step yet," I confess, sounding *mostly* proud about it. The sexually frustrated lower half of my body isn't super happy about it.

It's Mom's turn to be surprised—only hers is genuine. "Really?"

I press my index finger to my lips, reminding her to be quiet. "We've decided to wait, and Greyston has proven to be quite the gentleman; we're moving forward at a good pace."

Just then, Dad and Greyston come back into the kitchen, laughing. However, when Greyston's eyes find mine, his laughter dies immediately. He looks from me to my mom, and then back to me, his concern growing by the second.

I force a smile, grab the dishtowel, and wipe my hands. "Hey. How was the tour?"

"Fine," Greyston replies, crossing the room and standing next to me. "You okay?"

Mom heads back to her seat, and I nod. "Yeah. I'm good."

The doorbell rings, but instead of acknowledging it, Greyston's gaze is still trained only on me. I offer him another smile and place my hand on his chest before excusing myself to answer the door.

"You know what?" Mom speaks up. "Why don't Cam and I get it? You two work on that salad."

"You sure you're all right?" he inquires, his eyes searching mine for some kind of indication.

Heat flares beneath my skin, and I try to laugh his concern off. "Yeah. We were talking about some things I didn't think my dad should hear when you showed up." He arches an eyebrow knowingly, and I shove him lightly. "You have a salad to prep," I instruct playfully.

With a nod, Greyston turns back to the counter when he hears our parents approaching. We stand in wait, watching the entrance as our guests all come into view. His mother is a petite thing, slender and not much taller than me, with ivory skin and caramel-colored hair, while his dad is about as tall as mine, only fairer skinned and dark blond hair. In her hands, I see that Greyston's mom is carrying what looks like a freshly-baked apple pie. This makes me smile and blush, remembering dinner at my parents' and how Greyston and I had shared similar feelings about whipped cream. Even if we didn't know it at the time.

"Mom," Greyston greets, abandoning his salad again and taking the dessert from his mother and placing it on the counter before he pulls her into a firm embrace. "I trust you've been well?" She nods, and then her eyes find mine, Greyston's gaze following. "Juliette, I'd like to introduce you to my mother, Jocelyn, and my father, Daniel. Mom, Dad, this is Juliette. She lives here now."

Jocelyn's smile widens and she moves past Greyston, taking my hands in hers. "Oh, Juliette. It's a pleasure to finally meet you."

"It's nice to meet you, too," I tell her. "Greyston's told me so much about you both."

Daniel laughs warmly, eyeing Greyston. "And yet, we've heard very little of you."

"I've been busy with work," Greyston reminds them. "Actually, since I've got you both here, now might be a good time to tell you that Juliette and I are…involved."

I suck in a deep breath and hold it, suddenly terrified for some kind of backlash. While they both seem great, their perception of me could vastly change now that they know their son is seeing his much younger, college-attending tenant. What if they start to see me as some kind of gold-digger, using their son for a free place to live while I get my degree?

The minute Jocelyn pulls me into her arms, I relax…a little; the fact remains that I'm being hugged by a woman I've only just met. "Then you must be the reason our boy has been in good spirits the few times we've talked to him."

I laugh as she loosens her hold on me. "Yes, I suppose I could be."

Greyston clears his throat, and I turn to him with a smirk, only to find him nervously running his hand through his dark hair. "Mom, can I offer you a glass of wine?"

"Well, I wish you would," she teases with a light laugh. Greyston pours one for her, and as she takes it, she turns to me. "Juliette, won't you have a glass of wine with your mother and me?"

"Oh," I say, looking at Greyston and then my father. "I would, but I'm not quite old enough yet. I'll take a rain check, though? Perhaps I can cash it in in February?"

"I'll hold you to that," Jocelyn promises before turning to the guys. "Why don't the three of you leave us women to chat?"

I'm suddenly nervous about this idea, and Greyston can tell. Problem is, the smile on his face tells me he doesn't really think I'm in any real danger.

"Well, gentlemen," Greyston says. "What do you say we grab a couple of beers and go throw the burgers on the grill?"

With the guys outside, I go about finishing up the salad

while Mom and Jocelyn talk and share a little about themselves. When my mom mentions her bakery, I swear Jocelyn almost falls off her stool. "Oh, I absolutely love your carrot cake! I don't know what you do to it, but I've never tasted better!"

Mom laughs modestly. "Why, thank you. I'd be happy to give you the recipe." This news excites Jocelyn beyond belief.

When I finish the salad, I place it in the fridge and go to the sink to wash my hands. As I lather the soap, I glance up through the window at the exact moment Greyston does, and we lock eyes. Even without saying anything verbally, he speaks volumes with his eyes. Offering me a half-smirk, he arches a brow and tilts his head, almost as though he wants to know if I'm all right.

Offering him a curt nod, I smile and mouth, "We're fine. You?"

He only shrugs in response before something gleams in his eyes, and he smirks almost wickedly. "I want to vacuum," he mouths, and my eyebrows knit together in confusion. *Vacuum?* He looks like he's fighting to contain his laughter, which only serves to make things worse.

Needing him to clarify, I move only my lips, over-annunciating each syllable. "You want to vacuum?"

Looking down at his burgers and laughing, he shakes his head and says, "No".

Even more perplexed, I move my lips over and over again, trying to figure out what he means. *Vacuum…vacuum… No, not* vacuum… *I want to f…* "Oh!" I cry out loud, slapping my hands over my mouth and turning around to see that I've startled our mothers. "Sorry. The, uh, water was hot."

They go back to their conversation about cheesecake or brisket or whatever, and I narrow my eyes, turning back toward Greyston. "You're bad," I tell him silently, making him laugh again as he flips the burgers.

"You want to bring me the cheese?" he asks, and I stand there for a minute, trying to decipher if he's *actually* saying something else. When I'm sure he's really asking for cheese, I grab it from the fridge and take it out to him.

Dad and Daniel are sitting at the patio table talking while Greyston grills our dinner. I sidle up to him, setting the cheese on the ledge next to the grill. "You're terrible," I tell him. "Who knew you had such a dirty mouth?"

He laughs again. "I'm sorry. I just couldn't help myself. If it's any consolation, I really did say vacuum." Leaning in, he brushes my hair off my neck and presses a kiss just below my ear before whispering, "And while I often wonder what it might be like to..." He pauses for a minute, exhaling a single laugh against my neck and making me shudder "...*fuck* you, know that I plan to worship every inch of you—for hours if at all possible—when we do finally take that step."

Desire shoots through every cell in my body, igniting a spark that spreads warmth through my veins and over my skin. Before we get ourselves too worked up, I clear my throat and take a step back. "How much longer until dinner?"

"Not much. Why don't you start bringing everything out to the table?"

When I head back inside and let our mothers know that dinner should be ready soon, they help me carry the food and flatware. We've just finished setting the table when Greyston brings the plate of burgers over, and we all take our seats.

Dinner looks and smells amazing, and it tastes even better. After everyone has had their fill, the men having decided on seconds, Greyston and I work together to clear the table while Jocelyn warms dessert in the oven and rejoins the others, leaving Greyston and I alone in the kitchen to do dishes.

"Your parents are great," I tell him, putting a plate in the dishwasher.

Greyston laughs softly. "I told you they'd love you."

"Yeah, yeah, yeah. You were right... Wait a minute, you're not one of those men who feel the need to flaunt the rare occasions that this happens, are you?" I tease.

His laughter grows as he closes the dishwasher and wraps his arms around me. "I assure you that it's rare I'm *wrong*," he quips, kissing the tip of my nose.

Just then, the oven timer chimes, so I reluctantly pull free of his arms. "Well, that was before you met me," I remind him with a playful smirk. "Come on, let's grab dessert and head back outside."

I pull on the oven mitts and grab the pie, carrying it toward the patio door while Greyston opens the fridge. Curious, I turn to look, only to see him hold up a can of whipped cream, waggling his eyebrows devilishly.

Laughing, I shake my head and mumble, "Just terrible."

He follows me out onto the patio. "Yeah, you've said that once or twice today."

"And I'm sure it won't be the last."

After dishing up, I grab the can of whipped cream and accidentally-on-purpose get some on my finger while applying it to my apple pie. The minute I lick it off, Greyston arches an eyebrow at me and brings his left hand under the table and settles it on my thigh—not in an inappropriate way; our parents are seated around us, remember. We're not animals.

Usually.

He decides to keep his hand on my thigh while we eat, his thumb moving back and forth slowly, and I don't mind the constant connection to him—even if it invites feelings that I'm going to have to force down until later.

"So, Juliette, what is it you're studying?" Daniel asks.

I swallow the bite I'd just taken and smile. "Oh, I'd like to get a job in publishing, so right now I'm kind of majoring in a little bit of everything—primarily focusing on English and marketing."

Daniel seems genuinely impressed, and we continue to talk about my schooling for a bit. Mom and Dad listen to me talk about school and my plans for the future, beaming proudly.

After dessert, we stay out on the patio and continue to get to know each other. It isn't until my dad notices that it's already nine o'clock that we decide to call it a night; we'd all been having such a good time that I hadn't even realized how late it'd gotten.

Greyston and I walk our guests to the door and say goodnight, promising another dinner soon. Once they've climbed into their vehicles, Greyston closes the door and sets the alarm, and I head upstairs to change into my pajamas.

I've already traded my jeans for a pair of grey shorts, and

am just removing my shirt to pull on a blue tank top when there's a knock on my half-opened door. I turn around to see Greyston's face through the opening, and I invite him in with a nod. He glances over my almost-naked torso appreciatively before perching himself on the edge of my bed. He pats the spot next to him, and I pull the top on before joining him, folding my right leg up under me.

He places a hand on my bare thigh, and a deep tingle starts in my belly and moves down to settle not too far from where it rests. I want to urge him to shift his hand inward, but I also like the idea of taking things slow. Plus, I'm nervous. "Greyston," I whisper, my eyes dancing back and forth between his.

He exhales forcefully, his warm breath fanning across my cheek and neck. "I know. I said we should wait, but it's just so difficult to keep my hands off of you," he admits, leaning in and pressing his lips to mine. He doesn't let the kiss get out of hand, though, pulling away just as my lips begin to part.

"So," I say hoarsely, licking my lips. "What should we do for the rest of tonight?"

With a confident smirk, Greyston says, "Why don't we play a video game?"

"Um, I'm not very good at video games," I confess sheepishly.

Greyston laughs, taking me by the hand and leading me upstairs. "Works for me. I'm tired of losing."

"Oh, good," I tease. "I see we're going to keep this fair."

Greyston opens the door to the game room, and we step inside. I flop down on the leather couch and watch as Greyston opens the cabinet below the wall-mounted TV and starts reciting the names of his video games. I decide on the sports one because Greyston seems the most excited about it.

As he puts the game in the console, I cross my legs in front of me and settle back against the couch. Greyston sees this and eyes me curiously. "What are you doing?"

"Getting ready to game," I tell him, holding out my hands. "Controller, please."

Greyston shakes his head, slaps his hands against mine,

and clasps them before pulling me to my feet. "This game doesn't use controllers."

I'm not so in the dark that I don't know what this means, and I suddenly feel nervous. "I don't know about this."

"Come on," Greyston says, waving his hand at the TV, and I stifle a giggle at the sight. He moves through a variety of screens until we get to one where we select the game we want to play. "You pick."

"Oh, um…" I look at all of my options, finally settling on tennis. It's been years since I've played, but I feel I'm probably better at that than, say, skiing.

I have to admit, it's a lot of fun—even if I feel a little silly at first. Naturally, Greyston wins the first several games, but I'd like to think it has more to do with him trying to make me laugh on purpose with his over-exaggerated arm movements whenever he hits the ball.

An hour later, I'm feeling pretty worn out from both the game and the non-stop laughter. "Okay," I tell Greyston. "While you kicking my ass repeatedly has been wonderful, I'm wiped. What do you say we head to bed…that is, if you want to?"

Greyston smiles. "Of course I want to. I'll just tidy up in here, and I'll come say goodnight."

I pause in the doorway, biting my lower lip. "Or, you could join me?" I sound uncertain, and I know it's because I'm not used to initiating stuff like this.

"Perfect," he quickly agrees, putting my mind at ease.

Back in my room, I turn down my comforter and crawl in to wait for Greyston. It's not long before he joins me, wearing flannel pants and a t-shirt and crawling into bed behind me. He wraps his arm around me and holds me close, his fingers working the hem of my shirt up so he can lightly trail them over the exposed flesh of my abdomen.

"So, Christmas is coming up," he reminds me. "What do you want?"

I sigh when his finger tips tickle my ribs. "Honestly, I just want to hibernate. I want to relax and not have to worry about work or school."

"That sounds nice. Does your family have any big traditions?"

"Not really. We fly my gran out and have an intimate family dinner. How about you?"

Greyston nods. "Yeah. Mom usually cooks, and we sit down, just the three of us. When I was younger, we used to vacation in the Canadian Rockies for a couple weeks. We've been too busy for that lately." He sounds sad about this, so I snuggle in closer.

I yawn. "I wonder if our moms would agree to having a big Christmas here. That could be fun."

"That would be pretty great," he agrees. "Maybe we should invite them over to suggest it."

Even though I'd been fighting it, another yawn breaks loose.

Greyston laughs, kissing the back of my neck, and he pulls my body closer to his as he whispers, "Sweet dreams, beautiful."

I hum contentedly. "Goodnight, Greyston."

The way his strong arms are wrapped around me, holding me close, makes me feel safe and secure, and it's not long before I finally fall fast asleep.

chapter 20

My phone buzzes from the counter while I finish sweeping up the kitchen floor. I rush to it, knowing that Greyston planned to let me know when his plane landed after a long three days away. It was scheduled to land about ten minutes ago, so I had a pretty good feeling this was him.

Hey, beautiful. Plane landed safely. I'm back in the city.

Excited, I tap out a quick message. Thanks to a surge of adrenaline, my hands are shaking so hard that I have to keep retyping a few words in order for the message to be legible. My thumbs are so damn uncooperative.

I'm so happy to hear that! Do you want me to come get you?

Thanks, but I've got a town car for when Xander lands. That way I can take him to his hotel. I should be home around noon, though.

I'll be counting down the minutes ;)

I sit on one of the stools at the island and pull my feet onto the seat, wrapping my arms around my legs and resting my chin on my knees as Greyston and I text back and forth for the next hour. I'm so freaking excited for him to be home. I only wish we had the day to ourselves; our paintball game was scheduled for this afternoon, so we wouldn't be alone until dinner.

Thankfully, I took the night off so we can spend that time together doing whatever we want.

A positively wicked idea strikes me unexpectedly, so I spring off the chair and fly up the stairs to my room. I quickly shed my shirt and pull the blanket of my freshly made bed back before climbing under the sheet. I run my fingers through my hair, and then I hold my camera up, holding the edge of the sheet in a way that barely covers my naked chest and shows a lot of my upper leg.

Happy with the photo, I attach it to a message:

tick tock ;)

Giddy with excitement, I cross my legs and watch my phone for his response. I wait, growing impatient with every second that ticks by, anticipating that damn ellipsis bubble that shows me he's responding. It doesn't come, so I decide to call him instead.

The call connects on the first ring, but I don't wait for him to say anything. "Did you get my picture?"

He laughs softly. "Indeed I did. Kind of unfair to send me something like that when I'm still well over an hour from seeing you, don't you think?"

Stifling a giggle, I hum, trying to sound sultry. "Nah. I don't think so. I was just giving you a tiny preview of what awaits when you get here."

I think I hear him groan. "Please don't let that be a joke."

This time I can't hold back my laugh. "Well, yeah, it was, but now…"

"I think it's official. I've corrupted you."

"Not at all. You've just liberated a part of me that's been suppressed." I sigh softly. "And I don't know about you, but I kind of like it."

"Oh, I definitely like it," he explains. There's a pause, and then Greyston comes back on the line, the mood shifting from playful to business. "Xander just showed up. I'll be home within the hour, though. You get everything set up?"

"I did. I was able to reserve the court for two." Excitement zips through my veins; I haven't been paintballing in ages, and I can't wait to get in the arena and have fun with Greyston and our friends.

"Perfect."

I'd be lying if I said I wasn't good, and I don't think he really realizes the situation he could find himself in. "When I was asking Dad for the number, I think he was a little sad he couldn't come. But he's got to go to work."

Greyston laughs. "Well, I think that having one trained marksman in the game is more than enough, thank you very much." I can tell he's only joking, but I smile, knowing he's not too far off the mark.

I don't tell him this, though, not wanting to worry him; it has been ages since I've been, so there's a good chance I'm a little rusty. "Ha ha. It's not like he trained me to be some kind of sleeper agent. He only wanted me to be able to take care of myself."

"I'm just saying, if we had him along, none of us would stand a chance against the two of you."

I decide to amp up the playful banter, maybe even stir up a little of Greyston's competitive spirit. "And you think you stand a chance with just me?" It's only a flash, but I sense his apprehension over the phone. "Well," I continue, "I guess we'll find out later."

He's trying to mask it, but I hear the uncertainty in his voice. "You don't scare me."

The right corner of my mouth twists up into a smirk as I hum. "You probably shouldn't have said that."

He laughs again. "I'll see you soon, okay?"

Happy to hear this, I release a sigh. "All right. I lo—" I stop myself, having almost dropped a bomb on him without even realizing I might feel this way. I try to laugh it off. "See you soon."

With the countdown officially on, I hop out of bed, get dressed, fix the blankets, and then try to decide what to do. Daphne will be here around one, so I've definitely got some time to kill. Remembering I have a little bit of homework I could get a head start on, I sweep my hair up onto the top of my head haphazardly, and then grab my books from my room. I don't feel like being cooped up in the house for the next hour, so I take my books out to the pool, and sit in one of the lounge chairs that's bathed in sunlight.

It's difficult to focus at first, but soon I'm wrapped up in my report, and time flies by. I get stuck toward the end of the assignment, tapping the eraser of my pencil against my textbook in hopes of knocking loose my block. I let my eyes drift out to the desert, and then I get the distinct feeling that I'm being watched.

Slowly, I turn around, almost certain I know whom it is. He's still in the house, just behind the sliding patio window. I want to act cool, but my attempt is futile; I drop my books on the ground, my assignment momentarily forgotten, and I rush toward him. He opens the door and steps through, meeting me on the patio and pulling me into his arms. He peppers my cheek, jaw, and eventually lips with kisses, and I laugh.

"Why didn't you call?" I inquire, his lips moving down my neck.

I feel his lips curl into a smile against my shoulder. "I think a better question is why aren't *you* waiting for me upstairs?"

Feigning innocence, I glance up to the sky. "I didn't want you to think I've become predictable."

My response makes him laugh. "Juliette, you're far from predictable. In fact, you've done nothing but surprise me from the day we met."

"Again with the flattery," I tease, my fingers lightly grazing the back of his neck and making him shiver. I giggle. "Ticklish?"

"Is this really a game you wish to instigate?" he challenges, his right eyebrow arching.

I smirk, feeling the air between us shift. "Maybe... Unless there's something a little more...*gratifying* that you can think of."

His expression seems contemplative, his right hand drifting down my body and over my ass until he grips my thigh and pulls it up around his hip. Feeling unbalanced, I lift the other leg, hooking my ankles together behind his back. "I think a *little* might be undershooting just how gratified you're about to be," he tells me.

"Careful. You don't want to oversell yourself or anything," I shoot back, my voice low and airy.

"Sultry *and* funny...a dangerous combination, Miss Foster." His hands squeeze my ass, pulling me against him. I release a whimper, but it's short-lived when a throat clears behind Greyston. My cheeks burn when I remember we aren't alone, and I glance up. There, in the doorway to the kitchen, is Xander.

Smiling, Greyston turns around, taking my hand and leading me toward the house. "Juliette, I'd like to introduce you to Xander Richland. Xander, this is my..." He pauses, looking toward me with a perplexed expression. "Girlfriend?"

I bite my lower lip, trying to keep my smile from growing so wide it hurts; it doesn't work. I nod, a giddy laugh building in my chest. That, I manage to maintain control over, thankfully. "Juliette," I offer up, holding my right hand out, and Xander takes it in his. "It's nice to meet you."

When he smiles, I notice the shallow dimple in his left cheek. He's about five inches taller than me, slender and athletic. His curly dark hair is long, hanging just above his chin, and his dark brown eyes are soulful. He looks trustworthy, and his energy reads the same.

Before Xander can say anything, the doorbell rings. "That's probably Daphne," I announce. "I'll be right back."

When I open the door, Daphne is fussing with her hair. Her eyes snap to mine, and she smiles. "Hey!"

I step aside to let her in, and we make our way toward the kitchen. "Come on, you can help with lunch before we have to meet Toby and Callie."

"Cool."

We enter the kitchen to find Greyston rifling through the fridge while Xander looks through a folder—contract negotiations, most likely. Both their heads lift in our direction, and Xander stands up straight, clearing his throat and running his hands through his curly hair.

"Ladies," Greyston greets, shooting me a wink as I round the island. He closes the fridge and kisses my temple. "Daphne, Xander. Xander, Daphne." He holds his hand out.

Xander nods his head curtly, the left side of his mouth turning up as he looks down at Daphne. "It's a pleasure." He reaches out for her hand, and I have to bite my lip to keep from giggling when I see Daphne blush as he kisses her knuckles. She's not a blusher—not ever—so this is huge.

"So, um…" Daphne stumbles for words—another first. "You play baseball, right?"

Xander's smile widens, and he nods. "I do."

"And do you like it?" she asks before cringing and shaking her head. "That was stupid. Of course you do."

"It wasn't stupid."

"Hey, Daph?" She slowly looks back over to me. "You mind giving me a hand?"

Looking beyond grateful, she nods. "For sure."

Greyston sets a few things out for lunch, so Daphne and I start preparing a light lunch. While I put together a platter of sandwiches, Daphne cuts the vegetables and arranges them on another plate while Greyston heats some soup. Once everything is ready, I offer to take the food out to the patio. I'm just setting the plate of sandwiches down next to the vegetables when Greyston appears beside me, placing the soup down and kissing my cheek.

"Thanks," I whisper just as Daphne and Xander join us.

We all take our seats and have a pleasant lunch with delightful conversation, and every so often, Greyston's hand finds its place on my upper thigh. This does little to help the desire I feel for him. I sense he knows this, but the masochist in me refuses to break our connection for even a second of reprieve.

"So, Xander, how was your flight in?" Daphne asks, reaching for a sandwich.

"Pretty good, thank you." Xander turns to Greyston. "And the hotel is incredible. Thank you and Toby again for taking care of everything. Y'all have officially gone above and beyond."

"We're just trying to show you everything Phoenix has to offer," Greyston tells him.

The food disappears quickly, and soon the four of us are working together to tidy up so we can get ready for our afternoon of fun. Greyston can sense my excitement and reaches over and places his hand on my lower back while I dry the last few dishes and put them away. This of course only invites back a different kind of excitement, even if he doesn't really mean for it to—or maybe he does—and I find myself thinking about what we might do once we're alone again. Even just remembering the intensity of his stare when he first arrived home sends shockwaves through my veins.

The sexual tension between us continues to mount with each day that we wait, and while I know his intentions are good, I feel like I'm going to burst at the seams if we wait any longer. Glancing over at him, I bite the inside of my cheek and wonder if maybe he's thinking the same thing…

"You've been awfully quiet," he points out. "Plotting out your war strategies?"

"Something like that," I say with a sly little shrug. "You scared?"

Turning his head, he arches a brow and gives me that crooked smirk that I love. "You gonna take it easy on me?"

"Aw," I coo, reaching out and placing my hand on his cheek. "Not a chance."

Greyston laughs. "Didn't think so. Thought it was worth asking, though." Even though I can sense he's a little nervous, I know he's excited about our afternoon.

Behind Greyston, Daphne starts laughing as she saunters in from the patio. "She is going to destroy you."

"Thanks for the vote of confidence," Greyston grumbles, shaking his head and rolling his eyes, all while smiling. "Come on, then. Let's head out before we're late."

chapter 21

We're about ten minutes late from when we said we wanted to meet, but Greyston insisted we stop by the store so he could grab an energy drink. When we finally arrive, we find a parking spot in the lot, right next to Toby and Callie's luxury SUV.

My excitement continues to escalate with every step, and I'm practically pulling Greyston behind me. The minute we walk through the doors, I can hear a game in progress, and a rush of adrenaline surges through me. I'm shaking.

"Hi," I enthusiastically greet the man at the counter. "I have a reservation for six at two."

He checks his computer and nods. "Juliette Foster?"

"That's me."

"All right, well the last group is just wrapping up, so we'll just go over everything you'll need to know while we wait. Do any of you have your own equipment?" he asks, looking at each of us. "No? Well then, full equipment rental is nine ninety-five per person, and that gets you everything you'll need for the afternoon, including one hundred rounds of ammo. Should you find you need more ammunition, we have price packages for them."

After he gives us the low down, I reach into my vest for my wallet when Greyston stops me, placing a hand over mine. "I've got this," he says.

"No, it's okay," I assure him. "I want to."

"Maybe next time?" he offers gently. "I was going to expense it to the agency."

Smiling, I push my wallet back into my pocket. "Oh, right. Of course."

Greyston gets everything squared away, and we all collect our equipment. Once we're suited up, I begin to explain how to use the guns. It's not a surprise for me to learn that all three guys have done this before while Daphne and Callie haven't. So, as we make our way to the field, I walk ahead with the girls and tell them how everything works.

"So, you can shoot one paintball at a time," I begin to explain, showing them how the trigger mechanism works on my unloaded gun. "Or, you can use the double trigger for rapid-fire shooting. You go through more rounds, but I find it a little more fun."

"Of course you do," Greyston quips from behind me.

I turn my head to look back at him, narrow my eyes, and smirk. "You want to be my guinea pig?"

"Nope," he says quickly, holding his hands up in surrender. "Sorry. Please, continue."

"I have a question," Callie pipes up. "How bad, exactly, is this going to hurt?"

"Well, if you get hit—and you will—you'll be sporting a pretty sizable bruise tomorrow." Thinking back to the last time I went, I try to figure out how to explain the feeling. "The initial impact stings like crazy, but you'll be so hopped up on adrenaline that you'll barely even notice.

"Now," I continue, stopping and turning around to face everyone as I load my paintballs into the chamber atop the gun, "do we want to play as individuals? Or in teams?"

"Teams!" Callie and Daphne cry out simultaneously, and I snicker.

It isn't shocking that they would want to team up, especially considering they've never played. Truthfully, it would be pretty cruel to set them loose when the rest of us have. I'm sure the guys would go easy on them, but I can't just send them off alone their first time out.

We continue talking about how we should split up, deciding to switch up the teams every round to keep it fair. Once we arrive at the field, we discuss the first set of teams.

Callie and Daphne seem to be more than willing to play guys versus girls when I suggest it.

The guys all seem confident that they can win. Even Xander gets in on the testosterone-fuelled comments they fling our way as they affix their masks to their faces and walk backward away from me and the girls.

"Good luck, sweetheart," Greyston says confidently, giving me one more wink and a brief glimpse of that crooked smirk before lowering his mask completely and joining his teammates.

Maybe it's that I've allied myself with two paintball virgins that's boosted his confidence enough to think I *need* luck, or maybe he's just trying to rattle me; whatever it is, this only awakens my instinct to play as hard as I can…and win. Thinking back to all the times my dad brought me here, I remember everything he ever taught me about strategy. Sometimes we'd play against each other, others it would be him and me against a few of his deputies. He and I were pretty evenly matched, but it was rare that we'd lose against his men.

I may not have had much time to hit the range with him in the last two years, but I'm still fairly confident in my abilities.

I lower my mask, Daphne and Callie following suit, and we march onto the field. The minute the game begins, the three of us duck behind one of the bigger obstacles, several paintballs firing in our direction and barely missing us. Behind me, I hear gunfire and realize that Daphne is firing on the guys as they split up and take cover; she's a natural, proving I chose my teammates well.

Splitting up is a smart move, I'll give them that, but I'm not going to abandon Callie and Daphne until I've had a chance to go over some kind of plan. We move along, crouched low behind the obstacle, and when I hear the turf being disrupted several yards away, I hold up a fist to stop them so I can listen. The footsteps stop for a minute but then pick up again before fading, so I signal for us to move again, pumping my arm up and down to indicate we speed up—well, the hand signal is clear to me, anyway.

"What does that mean?" Daphne asks.

"I don't know," is Callie's reply. "Juliette, what does that mean?"

I can't help but feel slightly exasperated—mainly because they're talking loud enough to get us noticed—so I turn around and lift my mask. "It means talk really loud so that they find us," I snap, immediately regretting it, because it's not like they knew what I was trying to say; my competitive nature often tends to manifest less than desirable bursts of anger. "Sorry. Just, come on. We need to be quick."

My words come a little too late, though, as Toby launches himself over the barricade we're hiding behind like some kind of super ninja and starts shooting. We all return fire, but are too late to save Daphne—thankfully we each hit him with one or two rounds ourselves.

"Son of a BITCH!" she cries out, clutching her thigh where Toby hit her with three paintballs. "Okay, I knew it was going to hurt, but I didn't think it was going to feel *that* bad!"

"Damn," Toby exclaims, sounding surprisingly enthused. "I just got nailed by three chicks!"

Callie lifts her mask and tries to fight a smile, failing when she starts to laugh. "Oh, grow up."

Toby's smile widens. "What? That's totally how I'm going to tell this story."

We all laugh before I remember we're still in the middle of a game. "Okay, you two, get out of here. This'll be over soon."

Toby slings his rifle over his shoulder and slaps his hands together. "Oh, man. I can't wait to see this."

The minute Toby and Daphne are off the field, I turn to Callie. "You okay if we split up? If we stay together, we're sitting ducks."

The look in her eyes is slightly unsure, but there's also a glimmer of excitement in them—likely from the adrenaline of taking Toby out of the game. "You bet."

"Okay," I tell her with a nod. "I don't know how good Greyston is, but I suspect Xander's probably got target practice of some sort under his belt. Keep your eyes peeled and your hearing tuned. Stay low and stay hidden."

We part ways, and as I move quickly, looking all over for any sign of Greyston or Xander, I hear Callie cry out; she's been hit, and now I'm on my own. I turn in the direction I heard her, and I see Xander retreating about thirty yards away. He's not quick enough to duck behind the huge column, and I fire three shots, hitting his lower leg once and his upper body twice.

I take a minute to listen to my surroundings. Hearing nothing, I move to peek around the corner. A paintball whips by, missing my shoulder by a fraction of an inch, and I throw myself back against the wall. *Where the hell is he hiding?* Adrenaline pumps through my veins, my heart beating faster and faster, and my breathing increasing.

I take a couple of deep breaths in an effort to calm down so I can hear more than just the blood pumping through my body, and also so I can move to a new location without my heavy breathing giving me away.

I take another glance around the corner, not finding any sign of him anywhere, and I bolt out into the open, throwing myself behind another obstacle and scanning the area. I see movement several yards away, and I open fire, splattering five orange paintballs against the far wall.

"He's fast," I mutter under my breath.

As soon as he's found cover, I see a flash of dark hair above his mask, and then hear the rapid firing of several paintballs in my direction. I feel the sting of the first one as it grazes my arm, but it doesn't explode until it connects with the obstacle behind me. It's a close call; one that fuels my desire to win.

The game goes on for a while longer, each of us escaping the other's attack by a fraction of an inch time and time again, and I'm beginning to wonder if Greyston hasn't been faking his nervousness over the last couple of days. I wouldn't put it past him. Strategic bastard.

Out of breath from my latest sprint, I hide behind a pillar and duck down before moving along out of sight. He's over by the entrance to the arena, and I make my way toward him silently in hopes of a sneak attack.

And that's when I feel it: something inside me stirs and I know he's close. I only wonder if he can sense me the way I can sense him. It would be wise to assume he can, so I keep moving, listening carefully for his following movements. I hear the shuffle of his feet on the other side of the obstacle, and I spring up like a jack-in-the-box, firing two rounds into his chest before he can react.

I'm feeling pretty good about winning the first round, and I can hear everyone making their way over, congratulating me on my victory. There's something in Greyston's eyes as he raises his mask that tells me this isn't over. He never really struck me as the type to be a sore loser. Competitive, yes; sore loser, definitely not.

I decide that I'm probably reading too much into it and try to put it behind me. "You were good," I tell him, taking my own mask off. "Really made me work for it."

Greyston smirks, and my fear of him being upset dissolves completely. "Won't be the first time today," he assures me, and I feel like there's a double meaning to his words. He leans in close, his lips brushing my ear. "Let's go again."

"Wanna be on my team?" I ask, stepping forward, gripping the waist of his pants and pulling him to me. Locking eyes with him, I pop up onto my toes and let my nose brush his, our mouths so close, yet so far from each other. "I'll protect you." My voice is barely a whisper, and I feel Greyston's lips curl up when mine finally graze them.

"It's a tempting offer, sweetheart, but I'd like a rematch." His hands rest on my hips, his fingers curling and holding me firmly in place, and my heart flutters. He's doing this on purpose—dazzling me the way he does in order to throw me off my game.

I hum, licking my lips and pulling back. "It's your funeral, Masters."

After being congratulated, we reset the teams. This time, Callie and Toby are with me, and Xander and Daphne have sided with Greyston. Four minutes in, Xander has taken out Callie, and Toby gets Daphne. It's two on two, but Toby is proving to be a good ally.

"Greyston is mine," I tell him with a smirk as we duck

behind a barricade to avoid being hit.

"Careful there, Juliette, Greyston's mighty competitive. He's been known to not take too kindly to losing sometimes," he warns me.

I smile and arch an eyebrow. "Well, I'm not just going to roll over and play dead. I think I'll take my chances."

We split up shortly after our conversation, and I'm just making my way across the field when I feel the sharp sting in my upper arm first and then my ass where Greyston's red paint has marked me. "Ow! Damn it!" I shout, skidding to a stop and turning to see my assailant.

He's just standing there, holding his gun and looking pretty damn smug.

Making himself known isn't his best move, because Toby avenges me, shooting Greyston. We leave the field, and Greyston seems pleased at having shown me up. And also a little disgruntled at having his victory so short-lived.

"Good game," I say, sidling up to him as we walk to where Daphne and Callie are watching the game. "We even now?"

Smirking, he looks down at me, mischief shining bright in his eyes. "Not even close."

It's interesting to watch Toby and Xander play against each other. Xander is stealthy and very tactical, while Toby has clearly been influenced by one too many TV shows and movies—not that it isn't hilarious.

Xander is the winner of the second round, and after he and Toby make their way back over to us, we split up into different teams. Greyston and I remain on opposite teams, his own competitive spirit fuelling mine further.

We play three more games over the next couple hours, and I am the last person standing for two of them, having taken Greyston out to reign champion. While I should feel pretty good about it, I can't help but sense *something* is off about him as we make our way to the front counter to drop off all of our equipment.

He seems incredibly tense, and I can't help but wonder if maybe Toby was right; maybe I should have just let him think he was better than me—even if it goes against everything I know.

We say goodbye to everyone, and even then, Greyston barely cracks a smile, asking Toby if he would mind taking Xander back to his hotel. Tentatively, Greyston presses his hand into my lower back to lead me to the car, and as we go, I notice Daphne and Xander exchange phone numbers.

Even though he's acting a bit odd, Greyston still opens my door for me and waits for me and Daphne to get in before closing it and running around to the driver's side. I'm unsure how to broach the subject of his behavior, especially in front of someone else. I mean, clearly calling him a spoilsport will result in a fight—and this isn't something I want our first fight to be about.

"You okay?" I ask, hesitant.

"Fine."

Ah, a one-word answer that all women are familiar with. Something is definitely bothering him, and I'm not sure I'm ready to unearth it, so I leave it alone.

He remains silent, his hands on the wheel at ten and two—except when he has to shift. The fact that he doesn't reach out and place a hand on my thigh is a little disheartening, but I'm not going to plead for his affection if he's upset. I know we need to talk about this, but I don't want to do it in the car, because if he is upset, and we do indeed fight about this, it's probably not safe. No, I'll wait until we're home.

The air in the car seems thick and suffocating with our unspoken issues—even Daphne is quiet—and I silently beg for us to arrive home soon so we can begin to wade through it. I glance over at him several times, taking in the paint speckled on his face and neck, and the streaks of blue and orange in his dark hair, and notice that his eyes remain glued to the road. His hands clench the steering wheel so tight that his knuckles are white, and his breathing is deep, making his chest heave.

We arrive home, and I throw the door open. I say goodbye to Daphne, putting on a smile and telling her I was glad she could make it. We hug before she heads to her car, saying goodbye to Greyston, and then I head to the house before Greyston even shuts his car door. Once I'm in the house, I remove my shoes and head for the stairs; I need a minute to myself before I talk to Greyston, so I'll have a shower and try to figure out how to bring it up.

I think what upsets me most is that this afternoon was supposed to be fun, and while I had a good time initially, now I'm pissed off that Greyston's acting like a big baby. Was I just supposed to let him win? That's not how I'm wired.

"Juliette," Greyston says from behind me, closing and locking the door. I turn from the middle step and look down at him. He looks confused. "Where are you going?"

"To have a shower," I reply sharply. "I'm covered in paint—it's all in my hair, and you don't seem too keen on talking to me right now, anyway. When you're ready to talk, you know where to find me." With that, I turn and head up to my room.

After undressing, I stand before the mirror on my closet door in my bra and panties and inspect my soon-to-be war wounds. In total, I took seven shots today: the ones to my upper arm and ass that I received first, I got two on the back of my left thigh, two on my stomach, and one just above my left breast. The welts are dark red, and the bruises have already begun to form in the center; by morning, they should be huge and painful—but totally worth it.

Well, up until Greyston started acting like a crab.

My hair is streaked with red, yellow, and blue paint, there are splatters on my face and neck where my mask didn't cover, and my hands are painted with a rainbow of colors from every hit and the backsplash of paintballs that hit the wall next to me.

With a sigh, I reach behind me and begin to unclasp my bra when my bedroom door opens suddenly. It startles me at first, but when my eyes lock on Greyston's for the briefest of seconds, I don't see anger or hurt in them; I see desire.

He's across the room in a flash, pulling me into his arms and kissing me hard. I moan when his tongue runs along my bottom lip, and my toes curl as he lifts me until our faces are level.

I pull back slightly, and my eyes dance between his, confused. "What are you doing?"

He smirks. "Kissing you," is his quick reply.

"But...why?"

His eyebrows pull together. "Do I need a reason?"

The minute his lips brush the bare skin of my neck, I temporarily forget about what had been upsetting me. His lips kiss, spreading warmth through my entire body. His teeth nip, and goosebumps arise. His hand moves down and grips my ass, lifting me and pressing me against the nearest wall. He pushes his way between my legs and hitches them up high around his hips, making me whimper. Even though he's still got his jeans on, I can feel his erection pressing against me, and I pull him closer by digging my heels into his ass.

His lips, teeth—and now tongue—continue to explore my neck while my mind races with how quickly his mood has turned around. I know I shouldn't question it, but I just have to know...

"Wh—" I pant and moan, unable to form a conscious thought when his tongue licks the hollow of my throat. "What's gotten into you?"

I can feel his lips curl up into a sly smirk against my skin. "I think a better question would be: what's about to get into you?"

As usual, his dirty talk makes me moan and thrust my hips against him, seeking out some kind of friction to appease the pulse of arousal between my legs. It's hard to focus as his lips resume their mission. "We...we can't. I th-thought... Oh god, don't stop." Rational thought is fleeting...and then it returns again. "Wait."

"For what?" he rasps against my neck, slowly working his way down over my collarbone.

With all the willpower I can muster, I press my hand flat against his chest and push him back a little. "Don't you think we should...I don't know...talk?"

He no longer looks at me with confusion, but concern. "About what?"

I arch an eyebrow, unsure if he's serious. "Your behavior after paintballing," I tell him.

This only makes him smile, and his hands move up the

outside of my thighs, his fingers hooking into the sides of my panties. "Mmm hmm."

"It was kind of upsetting." My confession forces him to pause, and he stares at me in shock. "I just... I thought we were having fun." I exhale loudly. "And then you barely spoke to me until we got home."

Soft fingers touch my jaw as Greyston cradles my face in his large hands, my body still firmly pinned between him and the cool wall. "You think I was upset about losing to you?" I shrug despondently. "Baby," he croons, his soft voice rolling over me like warm water. He runs his fingers through his hair and sighs. "Watching you today was...well, it was the sexiest thing I've ever seen."

My eyes snap open, and my jaw falls slack in his hands. Did I really just hear him right?

He shifts his hips between my legs once more, and his hands drift back to my thighs. "You were so confident out there today—proving it time and time again with every shot you made—and you were so focused and in control." Pausing, he chuckles lightly. "It's no wonder I lost so many damn times."

"Well," I say, feeling relieved and a little stupid for misreading him—again, "that, or you just suck."

Greyston's chuckle turns into a deep laugh. "It took every shred of self-control I had to keep my hands off of you, because I knew that even the slightest touch would result in me taking you wherever we were." Slowly, his hands travel up my outer thighs to my ass, pulling me against him. I wince when his fingers press into one of my bruises, and he pulls his hand back, looking remorseful.

"Comes with the territory," I assure him as he lets me slide to the floor, leaning over to inspect it. He's got to move my panties slightly in order to see the area entirely, and I sigh when he ghosts his finger over the tender flesh.

He abandons the area when he notices the ones on my stomach and chest. "Jesus," he mutters, tracing around them with his thumb. "Where else?"

"The, uh, back of my thigh." I bite my lip and reach out to tug his shirt up his body. "Really, I'm fine. I'd be willing to bet I left my own marks on you." He raises his arms as I remove his shirt, and I take in the two deep purpley-red marks on his left pectoral. I let my fingers glide over them, the pads of them barely making contact with his skin, but his body reacts, the light hairs on his chest prickling into goosebumps.

I lean forward and press a gentle kiss against the reddened flesh, and Greyston groans, his body pushing against me and making me whimper. My hands move up his chest, feeling his hard muscles, and then up around his neck until I'm fisting his hair.

"I don't know how much longer I can wait," I admit softly, looking up into his stormy eyes.

He smiles, moving his hand between us and into my panties. My eyes begin to roll back into my head as his fingers glide back and forth. "Greyston," I breathe, letting my head fall back.

The hand that's not busy pushing me closer to climax moves up my back and undoes my bra, letting it fall slack around me. I release my hold around his neck and toss the bra to the floor as Greyston takes one of my erect nipples into his mouth. His warm tongue flattens against my breast before he grazes his teeth over the pebbled flesh, driving me absolutely crazy.

"More," I pant, and Greyston eases his fingers into me. But it's not enough. "I need you."

Before he can protest, I undo his jeans and let them pool around his ankles before working his underwear over his erection to join them. He removes his hand from between us and looks at me, his eyes not showing any sign of objection before he hooks his fingers back into the sides of my underwear and tugs them down my legs.

This is happening. My palms begin to sweat, and my heart is beating rapidly as I look over his paint-splattered face. Without warning, he scoops me up and whisks me over to my bed, pushing me back until I'm lying before him, and then he joins me. I can feel the tip of him resting against my heated flesh. Slowly, I push my hips forward, forcing his length to slide through my arousal, and we both release a satisfied moan.

And it's still not enough.

"Greyston," I whisper again. Unable to take even the smallest space between us, I wrap my legs around him. I grab his face and pull him down to me, kissing him hard while digging my heels into his backside and forcing him to rock against me again and again.

His hips continue to move, his erection gliding back and forth between my lower folds, and it has me teetering on the edge of pure bliss, while still craving more. Whimpering, I thrust my hips against him in hopes he'll take the hint and take me.

He doesn't, though. His lips pepper a trail over my jaw, down my neck, and then he stops at my breasts. I arch my back up off the bed when he wraps his mouth around one of my nipples, and when his tongue traces circles around it, I thread my fingers into his hair to hold him against me and moan loudly.

Disappointment pours over me when he releases my breast and continues down the length of my body. I can't stop my hips from undulating beneath him as he presses soft and firm kisses to my abdomen, trailing his tongue from one hip-bone to the other. The passion builds, making it hard to breathe, and Greyston's lips are hot against my skin. I look down nervously when his hands slip back up my thighs and freeze.

His blue eyes burn into mine, and then he lowers his face, his lips—then tongue—grazing the skin of my inner thigh and slowly moving north. I gasp the second I realize his intention, his tongue barely touching the juncture between my thighs, and I press my foot against his chest roughly, pushing him away.

"W-wait." I prop myself up on my elbows and look at him, panic rising until it eclipses my pleasure. "I don't… That's… *No.*"

He looks perplexed. "No? Why Not?"

When he makes no indication of moving, I drop my foot, averting my gaze. "I-I guess it kind of…I don't know. I don't really like it."

He sits back on his heels, staring. "What the hell do you

mean you don't *like* it?"

I only shrug. "I just don't. It felt...weird and rushed in the past, I guess."

His hand moves down over his face, maybe trying to wipe the shock from his expression. "Good god, Juliette. While I realize now's probably not the best time to have this discussion, I have to wonder what the hell was going through that jackass's head."

The somber tone in the room shifts again, inviting levity. I glance up at him, feeling a little more relaxed. His hands are on my thighs again, pulling me closer to the edge of the bed. I sit up and look at him, using my fingers to push his hair off his forehead.

"Do you trust me?" He kisses me lightly and gives my thighs a squeeze.

"Implicitly." His hand drifts toward my inner thigh, and I inhale a shaky breath when his fingers slide home.

"I don't want to do anything that makes you uncomfortable." I smile. "So if this is absolutely something you don't want to do, I won't press the matter." A finger slips inside, and I moan, digging my fingers into his shoulders. "But if you'll let me, I promise to make it an experience you'll never forget."

My eyebrows pull together as I push my unease aside and nod my acquiescence. "Okay," I whisper. "But if I don't enjoy it—"

He interjects quickly. "Just tell me to stop, and I will." He kisses me softly, then eases me back down onto the bed with his free hand while the other continues to move between my legs.

Nervous, I clutch the blankets as pleasure consumes me again, my body tingling. Greyston kisses the inside of each thigh before slowly removing his hand, and I whimper at the loss. He adjusts our position until my legs rest on his shoulders, and then he lowers his head. My gut reaction is to push him away the second his tongue makes contact, but instead I tighten my grip on the blanket and instill all the trust I have in him.

I don't know why, but I lift my head off the mattress and

watch him. It's strange at first, but then his tongue slides over a sensitive spot that turns me into a simpering mess, and I gasp, my hips pushing into his face out of instinct, seeking out even more. His eyes snap up to find me staring down at him. Like a gentleman, Greyston waits for me to give him the okay to continue, and I nod—I think. I'm honestly a little disoriented.

He proceeds slowly, and my breathing becomes heavy—labored. My legs tighten around him, pulling him closer and encouraging him to keep going. Greyston increases his efforts, using a little more pressure, and I fall back onto the bed with a moan, unable to keep my body upright anymore. He was right; this is incredible.

"Oh, god." Pressure continues to build like a storm in my belly. Everything gathers in the middle, swirling around, and it's only a matter of time before all hell breaks loose. I'm no longer in charge of my body, succumbing to pleasure, and my hips rock against Greyston's face.

My legs tremble, and I think my moans of approval are growing louder—honestly, it all sounds so far away as I get lost in the fog of ecstasy. One of my legs shifts, my foot pressing against Greyston's shoulder, and I feel him pull back slightly before I weave my fingers into his hair and hold him in place.

"Don't stop," I plead. "Please, god, don't stop." It takes my brain a minute to register what Greyston does next. It's so many different sensations at once as he guides me closer and closer to the edge. My body is in that zero-gravity stage as an orgasm prepares to push me. I've been here before; I've just never been given the chance to fall.

"Juliette." His voice sounds far away, but I find my way back to it, focusing on it and using it to ground myself. "Look at me, baby."

I prop myself up onto my elbows again and look down at him. I watch as his right hand and tongue work simultaneously, and it's almost too much. My senses are completely overloaded as I watch him, feel him, hear him… And that's all it takes before I'm free-falling.

I collapse back onto the bed, wave after wave of bliss

washing over me. The bed shifts, and Greyston is making his way up my body, a confident smile on his face. "That was..." I can't even find the words to describe just how incredible it was.

Thankfully Greyston seems to still have his wits about him. "Amazing." He leans in to kiss me, and I balk, my eyes widening and darting between his and his lips.

The thought of kissing him after he'd just... It gives me pause. But then it makes me curious. Bringing a hand up, I place it along his jaw, my thumb moving across his full lower lip. It's soft, still a little wet, though from his tongue or going down on me, I can't be sure. My curiosity continues to climb, and I can see he really wants to kiss me, so I curl my fingers, drawing him forward. I'm still hesitant, but I finally press my lips to his.

The kiss is quick, pulling back just as Greyston's lips part and his tongue slides along my lower lip. I gaze into his excited blue eyes and lick my lips, tasting myself as he had for the first time. It's...different, but not awful. Greyston watches me as I appraise the situation, and his eyes darken with desire. I pull him back to me without warning, and kiss him, plunging my tongue between his lips and moaning as I slip my hand between us and around his stiff length.

He groans into our kiss, his hips moving into my hand before I pull it free. Our lips part, and I scoot back on the bed, making room for Greyston to be a little more comfortable. I am ready to take this final step with him. We both are.

Instead of joining me, he pulls away and bends down. Confused and breathless, I watch as he picks his pants up and rifles through the pocket. On his way back over to me, he drops his pants back to the floor, but my eyes remain locked on the foil packet he's holding between his fore and middle fingers.

He's barely rejoined me on the bed before I grab the back of his neck, roughly pulling him toward me. Our lips unite in a kiss so firm it almost comes across as needy, and his hard dick slips easily between legs. I begin to move my hips, forcing him back and forth between my thighs, but never letting him enter me—even though that's what I want more than anything right now. I can tell he's being careful to keep this from happening, and the minute I hear that foil packet tear between us, I silently rejoice.

"God I love how wet you are," he announces, and I moan again, unabashedly grinding myself against him.

"And I love..." I momentarily consider not finishing the sentence because I don't speak this way—ever—but some kind of switch flips in my brain, and I just go with it "...how your hard cock feels against my pussy."

This does something to Greyston—something fierce and primal—and before I know it, he's entering me.

Sans condom.

It feels... Oh. My. GOD. It feels fucking amazing. I didn't fully realize just how different sex without that thin latex barrier could be; it isn't just that we're joined even more intimately— skin against skin—but that he's the first man to ever gain my trust enough to let this happen.

I never would have imagined that I'd ever partake in dirty talk, mostly because I was afraid that whoever was on the receiving end of it would laugh at me, essentially killing the moment.

Not Greyston, though. There hasn't been one time that I can recall where he's ever intentionally made me feel like what I've said or done has been ridiculous, and he's never laughed at me—not even when I thought he was gay.

Before things can get too far, we stop kissing, and my body trembles as my orgasm threatens to retreat. He looks almost tortured, like he's struggling with something before he pulls out and slips the condom on, and I'm not ashamed to admit that I fully enjoy watching him roll it over his length. Once it's in place, he wraps his arms around me, pulling me closer to him until I can feel him again.

Our eyes lock, and all I can see is how much he cares for me, and with a whimper, I pull his face back to mine and kiss him. With our bodies pressed together, Greyston slowly pushes his hips forward. The sensation unparalleled to anything I've ever experienced. Greyston moans into my mouth the minute his hips rest flat against my thighs, his entire length sheathed within me. It's amazing; my whole body feels like it's on fire—like millions of electric shocks are crackling and sparking beneath the surface of my skin.

I tighten my legs around Greyston's waist, holding him close as I shift my hips against him, and he slowly pulls out and then sinks back in, repeating this satisfying, yet completely torturous motion over and over and over again.

I'm close to my release, and Greyston knows it. His eyes lock on mine, and he resumes his careful pace. The tempo of his hips increases, gaining not only speed, but also depth, and hitting me at angles I've never even dreamed of before.

And, for some reason, it's *still* not enough.

Greyston's hand grips my wrist, and he raises it over my head, holding it against the mattress while he brings the other up to join it. My hips meet his, making our combined thrusts a little deeper, a little more intense, and *a lot* more satisfying. I whimper at the loss of his lips on mine, but the sound turns to a sigh as he kisses down my jaw and over my neck.

"Oh god, Juliette," Greyston growls, pressing his forehead to my neck, dampened by sweat. "You feel so fucking good." His voice is raspy, and his words punctuated with every push.

"Yes." I sigh, my hands clenching against the bed while his free hand travels over my body—groping, pushing, pulling. Every muscle in my body begins to tighten, and my heart pounds heavily against my ribs until it and our labored breaths are all I hear. "S'good," I murmur.

The minute Greyston's hand releases mine, he ensnares my hips and pulls me roughly against him, causing another orgasm to crash through me, shattering the flimsy barrier that struggled to keep it contained. He cries out against my neck as my hands fall to his muscular shoulders, and his fingers curl into my skin. His hips move in short, determined movements, and I can feel him pulse and release inside me.

My legs tremble around him as I let the final waves of euphoria wash over me, and Greyston's head remains against my skin as our breathing steadies once more. The entire time we stay like this, I start to feel emotional—I'm not going to cry, or anything, but...it's the first time I've ever gotten anything out of sex. And I'm not just talking about the orgasms;

the emotional connection between Greyston and me makes things even more intense.

As I try to catch my breath, Greyston plants soft kisses across my chest and up my neck until he's kissing me softly. My legs tremble beneath me, so he wraps his arms around my waist to steady me.

"That was..." I say breathlessly as Greyston kisses the side of my mouth and then makes a trail down along my jaw. "That was just...I can't even...*Wow*."

He stops kissing me, raising his head to me. There's something in his eyes that I can't quite decipher because I'm still trying to wrap my head around how completely blissed out I feel right now. "Juliette, was that..." He pauses, almost like he's not sure what it is he wants to say. "That wasn't your first orgasm, was it?"

I can feel myself blushing furiously. "What? No, of course not. I've had...I think."

Greyston pushes my hair back from my face with a light chuckle. "If you think you have, then it's been my experience you haven't." Slowly, he lifts his face, his eyes hooded and relaxed. "You're amazing," he says softly, kissing me once.

"Thank you," I tell him, instantly feeling stupid, because I'm not actually thanking him for his recent statement. "I mean...for being you. I didn't know that sex could be that..." I pause, unable to think of a word that accurately describes how I feel about what just happened between us "...fucking epic." That'll have to do.

Slowly, I loosen my legs from around him, and Greyston withdraws from between them. My legs dangle off the edge of the bed, and I'm a little shaky. I find my bearings soon enough and reach up to run my hand along Greyston's jaw, smearing the small paint spots across his skin from where the sweat had loosened it. "What do you say we clean up and then curl up on the couch with something to eat?"

Greyston waggles his eyebrows suggestively, and I giggle. "Maybe we should worry about feeding our bodies to keep our energy up," I counter as Greyston offers me a hand while I climb off the bed. We walk toward the bathroom together where he starts the shower and ushers me inside first.

The warm water washes the paint splatters from my skin, causing it to trickle down my body and toward the drain when he finally joins me. He pulls me to him again, and I feel his length stir against my hip.

I arch an eyebrow at him. "We can think about that after we've eaten."

"Oh," Greyston quips, "I assure you I'll be thinking about it the entire time."

chapter 22

It only takes a few minutes after our shower to fix my hair while Greyston goes downstairs to make us a light snack. After wiping up the water droplets on the counter, I enter my closet and throw on a pair of grey shorts and a black t-shirt before skipping down the stairs to find Greyston slicing some fruit.

"Hey." I pop up on my toes and kiss him lightly before taking my seat.

Greyston grabs us a couple glasses of water and then joins me. I thank him before picking a slice of peach up off the plate and taking a bite. Greyston clears his throat, drawing my eyes to him, and it isn't until I see the reddened tips of his ears that I realize he's flustered about something. It's adorable.

"So," he says, "I have to admit, today's probably the best 'welcome home' I've ever received… Even if we had to postpone it a couple hours."

"Well, I guess I should be flattered, huh?" Pausing, I look down at the plate of fruit again. "And it was totally worth the wait."

"I couldn't agree more," he interjects before dropping his eyes and clearing his throat. I can tell he's nervous, but I can't figure out why. It isn't long before he enlightens me. With a nervous laugh, he swivels his chair until his body faces mine. "Today was…unbelievable, but I think we should talk about your comfort levels. It's probably a talk we should've had before now, if I'm being entirely honest."

My stomach does about fifty backflips and a flying half twist. Not sure how I should reply, all I can come up with is, "Oh?"

"After you confessed to not being particularly fond of oral sex—even though I'd like to think I changed your mind..."He winks, and naturally, my cheeks blaze. "Well, I'd hate to do something that could make you uncomfortable or push you past what you're ready for."

I both appreciate and understand his acceptance of my inexperience. While I know that an almost-twenty-one-year-old woman with my sexual rap sheet is definitely a rarity, he has been so gracious and patient with me as we entered this relationship.

"Okay." I take a drink of water.

Through my periphery, I notice Greyston clasp his hands. "I realize this is an awkward conversation for us to be having, but given everything you've told me about your past with Ben, I think it would be best to put it all out there."

I smirk. "Are you saying there are things you're not comfortable with sexually?"

Silent for a moment before he laughs, he says, "I suppose there are, but probably not as many as you'd think."

My mouth falls open, and my eyes widen. I can't stop the images of Greyston in every sexual situation imaginable from running through my head—it's not just whips and chains, either. "Like what?" I ask, unable to keep the question from coming out.

"We'll get to that. But first, I'd like to know where you're at."

I pick my jaw up off the floor and shake the filthy slideshow from my head. "So, what? You want to know positions and stuff that I like?"

"For starters." He shrugs. "But also other things... Like role playing, light bondage, and other taboo things."

My eyes widen again, this time more than before. "You mean like S and M?"

"Oh, *god,* no... Of course, I'm not saying I would be opposed to tying you to my bedframe with one of my ties—or you tying me to the bed, for that matter—if that's something you're eventually comfortable with. But, you know, stuff like that."

Knowing he's not into the darker side of sexual gratification—hey, I might not engage in it, but I've read about it—I relax. "Um, I don't know. I guess I hadn't really given much thought to it before. It might be fun, I suppose. But not right away, right?"

He places a hand over one of mine, smiling reassuringly. "Of course not. I just thought it might be a good idea to lay it all out on the table so I don't do something in the heat of the moment that might freak you out."

I know it shouldn't be, because Greyston has never judged me for my choices or lack of experience, but having this conversation is a little awkward. I hate bringing Ben up in any capacity around him. Maybe it's because I'm embarrassed that I could be so blind for so long about what kind of person he was or that he was robbing me of actually enjoying sex for the better part of our relationship. Whatever the reason, this conversation isn't exactly easy, but I cooperate, because it is important.

"Well, I guess I'm not sure if anything makes me *overly* nervous. I mean, it's not like Ben was too concerned with making sex about me." I pause, suddenly remembering something Ben had been pushing for more recently. I reach for some honeydew and stare at it for a second. "One thing Ben seemed to want to try that I wasn't so sure about was…um…" I don't need a mirror to tell me how red my face is; I can feel the flames of hell beneath my skin, reaching all the way to my ears this time.

"Tell me," he gently urges.

I'm nervous, because what I'm about to confess is quite crass. "Um, anal sex." My voice is so quiet, even I can barely hear it.

Nodding, Greyston reaches for his glass. "So, you'd like to take that off the table?"

My eyebrows pull together as I watch him take a drink. "You'd like anal on the table?" Greyston chokes and sputters on his water, and I'm horrified when my question actually registers in my brain. "OH, GOD!" I slap my hand to my mouth. "I'm sorry...that's not what I meant! I just..." I can't even explain this away. I'm horrified.

Greyston waves his hand and clears his throat. "No need to apologize. It's my fault. I knew what you meant, but—being a guy—I may have taken it a little too literally."

Things are awkward between us for a moment—how the hell can they not be? I can't bring myself to take a breath big enough to fill my lungs, and I'm feeling lightheaded. Greyston turns my chair to face him, and he places his hands along my jaw. "Consider it a non-issue," he says softly.

I can't explain it, but just like every time he puts his hands on me, confidence surges through me. I'm not a meek person, by nature, but this—sex—is such a foreign area for me. Greyston never makes me feel inadequate, though. Quite the opposite. He makes me feel sexy and beautiful...like I can do anything.

I take a bite of my honeydew. It's juicier than I'd anticipated, and just as I'm about to lick the drops from my lips, Greyston pulls me to him, kissing me. His tongue sweeps over my lower lip and takes care of the problem for me. Content, I hum as Greyston sits back in his chair, swiping my honeydew from my fingers and eating it.

I narrow my eyes playfully, picking up some cantaloupe and having a bite. Then I smile and hold the remaining half out to him. Instead of taking it from me, he wraps his lips around the orange fruit, his tongue lapping at the juice dripping down my fingers. I try really hard to keep from blacking out and attempt to change the subject. Instead, I yawn. It's not even that late, and yet I'm completely wiped out.

"I'm sorry," I mumble, covering my mouth.

Smiling his understanding, Greyston holds out the plate, silently offering me the last slice of Honeydew. I decline with the shake of my head, and he slips it into his mouth before putting the plate in the dishwasher. "We should get some sleep."

"Greyston, it's barely even eight," I argue half-heartedly.

"I know, but it's been a long day. I'm beat from my flight and paintball, and I'm pretty sure my ability to bestow multiple orgasms on you has exhausted you." He smirks, and I laugh. Loudly. "Besides, I have to be up early to go over Xander's contracts with him at the office."

I'm too tired to argue, especially since the thought of falling into a nice warm bed sounds heavenly. Greyston takes my hand and pulls me from my chair and out of the kitchen. Soon we're in the hall between our rooms, and Greyston turns to me. "Any preference?"

I shake my head. "Not really. As long as there's a bed."

Kissing me once, Greyston leads me to his room and ushers me into bed before joining me. Warmth surrounds me as he presses his body to mine, draping his arm over me and holding me close. He presses a soft kiss to the back of my neck before we say our goodnights, and soon we're both fast asleep.

Greyston leaves before eight in the morning, waking me only long enough to kiss me and tell me he'll call when he's on his way home. I promptly fall back asleep, waking a couple hours later refreshed and ready to face the day.

After brushing my teeth and hair, I do a bit of house cleaning. Okay…so it's not the house, per say, that needs to be cleaned so much as my bedroom. Who knew that two people being reunited after only a couple of days could wreak such havoc? At first, I think it's just our scattered clothes that are the issue, but when I pick up my pants, I find that the lamp on one of the bedside tables had been knocked over and broken.

"Whoops," I whisper, not really feeling remorse for the fallen accessory. I grab my phone from the back pocket of my jeans and take a picture to send to Greyston. After setting my phone down, I begin carefully picking up shards of glass and ceramic and toss them in my wastebasket.

I abandon the lamp pieces when my phone buzzes on the table, and I literally laugh out loud as I read Greyston's response.

I thought I heard something fall over last night. Can't say I feel bad. It died for a very good cause. ;)

Falling back onto my heels, I reply, smiling wide the entire time.

I couldn't agree more...but what about the matching one? Will you be able to replace it?

Setting my phone on the floor next to me, I pick up a few more pieces before Greyston responds.

No need. We'll break that one later ;)

I laugh again—really loud and extremely unladylike; it's probably a good thing I'm completely alone in the house.

You're terrible. Get your work done; I'll see you in a bit.

I make the bed next, remembering as I smooth the blanket how my hands clutched at it, drawing it toward my body as pleasure vibrated all the way down to my bones. A warm tingle spreads through me, making me shiver. Thinking about how his tongue felt against my heated flesh leaves me somewhat breathless, and I have to shift on my knees to ease the pulsing between my legs that seems to increase with each passing second.

The more I think about the events of yesterday, the more I begin to wonder if Greyston will expect a little reciprocity in that department. It's not that I'm necessarily *against* the idea, but I've never done it—not for lack of Ben trying, mind you. He tried. And he tried. And he *tried*. He even threatened to stop doing me this "favor," and I had to contain the urge to laugh in his face and tell him I was more than okay with that. Much to my dismay, he didn't remain true to his word—which actually doesn't surprise me now; he was probably still holding out hope I'd eventually cave. I still held firm in my decision not to return the "favor," though, and just wished for our time between the sheets to be over.

But Greyston? Yeah, I could probably give it a shot for him.

Resolute with my plan, I finish cleaning up the bedroom, discarding the shards of glass and ceramic in the outside trash bin before running back up to my room and firing up my computer. I know I don't have a lot of time before Greyston returns home. I can only imagine that the level of humiliation for being caught looking up how to give my boyfriend a proper blow-job would easily trump my parents walking in on Greyston and me two weeks ago.

Without a doubt.

My computer doesn't turn on right away, so I try again. Nothing. The light for the power button doesn't even come on, so I check to make sure the AC adaptor cord is plugged in to both the computer and the wall. It is. However, when I wiggle it a little, the battery light flickers on and off several times, which means the wiring is ruined and I'll need to replace it.

"So much for that idea," I huff, slamming my laptop closed and crossing my arms like an angry toddler.

Then I remember that Greyston has a computer. Would it be wrong for me to look up questionable material on my boyfriend's computer? What if he found out somehow? I would be humiliated. Though, if I made sure to clear the history, no one would be the wiser…

Realizing I don't have much time, I rush to Greyston's office and turn on his iMac. I open Safari, and my fingers hover over the keyboard; it almost feels wrong to even be contemplating this. Taking a deep breath, I enter words I've never spoken, much less typed, into the search browser and hit enter with closed eyes.

While I know the Internet is positively swarming with porn, it still surprises me a little to see just how many hits I come up with. The first few are…terrifying, and I close them almost immediately… Yeah, *almost*—I'll admit I linger a little longer than I probably should.

There are a few videos I find…informative, and they also serve to be quite titillating. The longer I watch, the more excited I find I'm becoming about trying this with Greyston—I just hope I don't mess it up. That's my biggest fear: what if I'm no good?

As I continue to research, I feel the deep tingle that's been moving through my body intensify between my thighs, forcing me to cross my legs. I'm suddenly regretting this idea, because I've grown quite aroused, and Greyston's not around to lend a hand, so to speak.

I've become engrossed in one video in particular, resting my elbows on the desk and propping my head in my hands as I watch this couple. Suddenly, keys in the deadbolt of the front door startles me, and I frantically close the window before running down to find Greyston walking in.

"Hey," he greets with a bright smile as I descend the stairs. He pulls me to him and kisses me firmly. "How was your morning?"

My cheeks warm, remembering what I was just doing, and I shrug. "F-fine. I just finished tidying our rooms after making your bed." He looks ready to say something, but my nerves force me to cut him off. "I was just going to go make some lunch. You hungry?"

His expression changes minutely, and I briefly wonder if he can see how anxious I am. It doesn't last long, though. "Actually, I have to run upstairs and check an email. My phone didn't open the file properly when Callie sent it to me."

"Sure."

"I won't be long," Greyston promises, kissing me sweetly before heading upstairs.

In the kitchen, I search the fridge for something to make. I pull out sandwich ingredients and am just starting to organize everything when anxiety slowly starts creeping its way along my spine. I shake it off, because I really have no reason to worry that I can think of, and I begin washing the few dishes I've dirtied.

Then it hits me like a wrecking ball. "Oh, shit," I mutter, dropping the knife back into the sink and running out of the kitchen. I launch myself up the stairs, taking them two at a time—even though this has proven in the past to be hazardous. When I barge into Greyston's office, out of breath and probably looking completely insane, he slowly raises his wide eyes to mine.

The entire time I was running up here, I hoped that I was only imagining the worst…but as I read the expression on his face, it's confirmed: I didn't actually *close* the Internet window in my hurry to greet Greyston, but only *minimized* it. It figures this would happen to me.

And just when I'd started to think my humiliation streak had ended.

chapter 23

I'm breathing heavily, trying to figure out how to explain the massive amount of porn I'd Googled, and my face is burning hotter than ever. Before I can say anything to get myself out of this mess, though, Greyston stands up and crosses the room to me. He wraps his hand around my wrist and pulls me into the room, closing the door and pressing me against it. The look in his eyes eliminates any embarrassment I feel, replacing it with the familiar warmth of arousal and lust for him, and he presses his hands to the door on either side of me, effectively pinning me in place.

"I think you'd better explain your Internet usage, Miss Foster," he commands in a firm voice that makes my stomach flip and my heart flutter. I suddenly imagine myself in a schoolgirl outfit while he's in a suit and tie, and I've just been called to the principal's office.

Only, in reality, my old high school principal was a balding man with a beer belly and chronic halitosis. Gross.

When his nose brushes the skin of my cheek, his lips moving closer to my ear, I bite my bottom lip and fight back a whimper. At an agonizingly slow pace, his lips ghost over the skin below my ear, and goosebumps prickle up all over my body, making me sigh.

"I don't..." I begin, my brain losing temporary connection with my mouth when his teeth graze the tender skin of my neck. "Can't..."

Suddenly, one of his hands has moved from beside me

and is quickly unbuttoning my jeans. It takes him no time at all, and I gasp when he slips the hand inside and begins sliding his fingers back and forth between my legs, teasing me.

"Can't?" he inquires before nipping at my neck again and inducing a shudder through my frame. "Why not?"

"It's..." I pant as he presses his fingertip against my clit, making me thrust my hips into his touch. My body temperature rises, my heart beats so loud and fast it's almost hard to hear anything else. My fingers curl against the wood of the door behind me as he continues his sensual massage. "It's embarrassing."

He groans, the vibration of the deep, throaty sound sending a jolt straight through me. I throw my arms around his neck and thrust my fingers into his hair. "There's nothing *embarrassing* about me fucking your mouth. And based on how wet you are, I'd say you quite liked it."

I never in a million years thought that hearing such words would make my body react so positively. I always figured that if I'd heard anything so crass, I'd either laugh maniacally or be completely repulsed. But there's something about Greyston talking dirty in the heat of the moment that turns me on even more. Maybe it's because he's usually so chivalrous and proper.

Whatever the reason, my entire body hums with anticipation of the next filthy thing to come out of his mouth.

"Did you have something special planned for later?" he asks, his hand moving back as he sinks his fingers into me, making me bite back another loud moan.

"I wanted...wanted..." I'm having trouble speaking as his fingers move in and out of me slowly, curling and pressing, pushing and sliding. "Repay...last night..." My ability to speak is apparently on the fritz, but I think he understands—at least, I hope to hell he does.

"Sweetheart," he whispers, sounding a little stunned. He removes his hand from between my legs—much to my dismay—and pulls his face away from my neck, smiling. "You don't have to repay me. I didn't do it so you'd feel obligated to reciprocate. I got just as much pleasure from going down on you as you did."

My cheeks warm, and I look up at him through my lashes. "Somehow I doubt that to be entirely accurate," I tease, thankful that I'm once again able to form a coherent sentence—even if that means Greyston's not feeling me up. I shrug. "I wanted to…try. The problem is, I've never…" He's silent, so I continue. "So I thought I'd research a little. I don't want to suck."

"Well," Greyston says with a cocky smirk, making me regret the last bit of my confession. "Technically—"

While I'll always be grateful for the way he's able to lighten an embarrassing moment, I can't help but stare at him wide-eyed and slack-jawed. "You know what I mean!" I cry, swatting his chest playfully.

"I do," he assures me with a chuckle. "But I want you to know that I don't expect oral sex in return every time I go down on you—you'd get pretty exhausted if that were the case." While I know he's kind of-sort of kidding, hearing that he intends to spend a lot of time with his face between my legs makes me a little weak-kneed—and even more turned on.

I pull his face back to mine, kissing him deeply and coaxing a groan from him as his hands fall to my hips. Snaking an arm between us, I undo his pants and slip a hand into them, gripping his hardening length and working it from base to tip. He moans his approval against my lips, bringing his hands up and threading his fingers into my hair. Needing him right here and now, I release my hold on his erection.

"Don't," he orders gruffly, eyes soft—pleading. "Please, don't stop, baby." I listen to him, squeezing a little harder and watching his eyes fall shut as his groan fills the room. "God damn…best fucking way to come home."

I look up at him, the lusty expression on his face making my body burn for him. "I'm going to need you to take your pants off now."

He's quick to push his pants over his hips, letting them fall around his ankles. There's a brief moment where he struggles to kick them off before giving up in favor of pushing my shirt up and palming my breasts.

His approval spurs me on, so I pump my hand faster

over his length, and his hips rock into my touch, seeking more. I'm feeling a little bolder—confident, even—so I smirk up at him and ask, "What do you want me to do?"

He opens his eyes, the lids heavily hooded as they search mine before falling so he can watch me stroke him. When my palm moves over the tip and then back to the base, his legs stiffen and he moans. "Take...*oh, fuck*...take me in your hot little mouth," he pleads.

It's kind of fun to watch him unravel under my touch for once—to know that it's *me* that makes him feel this way gives me another boost of confidence, and I slip to my knees between him and the door, eye-level with his erection. He mutters a long string of expletives as I lick my lips. Glancing up at him through my lashes, I see he's watching me raptly, his eyes wide and his chest heaving, and he cradles my face affectionately.

I'm so nervous—but not enough to back down from this if it's going to make him feel good—so I take a deep breath and wrap my lips around him. The salty taste of him fills my mouth, and I have to admit that I'm not repulsed by it. I don't know why I thought I would be, but I'm pleasantly surprised to find that I'm not, and it encourages me to keep going.

"Jesus...*fuck*," he hisses as he leans forward, and I hear the soft sound of his nails curling into the heavy wood door behind me. Of course, I can only assume this to be the case since I don't think I'm talented enough to multi-task my first time out.

It's strange—not in a bad way, though. Greyston's erection is bigger than the last one I'd been exposed to, so I'm not comfortable enough to take him into my mouth entirely...not just yet, anyway. I'll work my way up to it, because based on the videos I watched earlier, the men really seemed to enjoy that. To make up for it, I place my hand below my lips to act as some kind of extension and move slowly up his length. I'm careful to keep my lips firm against him, and when I reach the top, I swirl my tongue around it before plunging back down. Greyston seems to respond positively to this, his hips thrusting forward.

As my head continues to bob slowly—carefully—I'm beginning to understand what Greyston said about him getting as much pleasure out of going down on me; my lower half *aches* to be tended to; it's almost enough to make me throw in the towel, pull him to the floor, and straddle him. *Almost.*

"Fuck, baby," Greyston pants above me. "You're a fucking natural at this." My ego swells, and I pick up the pace a little, even feeling confident enough now to look up at him as I continue.

His lips part, and he's breathing hard while staring deep into my eyes. The intensity of his stare forces me to shift and wriggle in an effort to quell my own growing desire.

I'm so turned on that I can't even suppress the moan that's been building deep in my belly since I wrapped my mouth around him. This elicits a similar—albeit a more guttural—sound from Greyston as he threads his fingers into my hair. He pushes it away from my face and holds it behind my head while he guides me a little faster...then a little deeper—but not too much because he's more than aware of my comfort level. His hips begin to move in time with my head, and I'm slowly losing my mind.

Greyston's body tenses, holding my head still midway down his length. I try to keep going, but he pulls me off and urges me up his body. While I would love more than anything to bring him to climax and taste him entirely—a surprising thought for me, to be sure—I'm ready to have my needs met, too.

He roughly pulls back up his body, pressing his lips to mine, pushing his tongue between them and deepening our kiss. I moan at his forcefulness, my tongue caressing his firmly—insistently. I start to remove his shirt, breaking our kiss for only a moment to pull it up his body before he removes mine as well. His hands find my breasts, and I arch into his touch before he growls and spins me around.

My entire body shakes when he tugs my shorts down and lets his hands slowly move up my outer thighs before slipping around the front and slipping between them. I thrust my pelvis back, feeling his erection against my ass, and I do it again without thinking.

"Greyston," I plead as his lips travel down my neck and

over my shoulder. His body leaves mine, and I'm about to protest when I hear the rustle of his pants and foil tearing. Soon, he's gripping my hips again, adjusting them slightly before easing into me.

"Greyston..." I pant, reveling in the way he fills me completely every time he plunges into me.

"That's it, beautiful," he whispers breathlessly, thrusting harder and harder. "Let me hear you."

"Oh god, Greyston!" I cry out when he thrusts so hard he hits that sensitive spot inside of me that makes my toes and fingers curl. I desperately claw at the door.

He pulls his hips back and steps away from my body, leaving me dangerously on the edge. Before I can ask him what he's doing, he takes my hand and leads toward his desk chair. I step out of my shorts while walking, and as soon as he's seated, I move to straddle him while he holds his erection, using his other hand to guide me down slowly; it's the sweetest kind of torture one can imagine, and this new position makes every muscle in my body tense as it fights off my release for a few more minutes.

Once I'm resting against his thighs, he ensnares my hips again and begins guiding my movements. I get the hang of it soon enough, and place my hands on his chest while my hips move with his guidance. He never releases his hold on me, and he starts pulling me a little rougher, my clit rubbing the spot just above the base of his cock. All at once, my body reacts; every muscle tenses, my fingers curl against his strong shoulders, the nails biting in and leaving little half-moon mark in his skin, and I cry out as Greyston's hips thrust up into me in short, precise jolts.

His mouth falls open in a silent cry, so I release my catlike grip on him with one hand and lay it along his jaw, drawing him into my eyes. "I want to hear you," I tell him, my words punctuated by my panting breaths.

His fingers tighten around my hips, tingles of pain quickly morphing into a warm rush of pleasure as the sensation shoots through my body, and my toes curl. He pulls me against him, faster and rougher, as he races toward his own release.

"Oh, Juliette," he grunts.

"Yes..." I whimper as I feel the swell of another orgasm rolling in. "Oh, god."

"Baby...I'm going...holy fuck...I'm gonna come." Then, with a loud, almost roar-like cry, Greyston thrusts his hips up into me one final time, pulling me against him as our orgasms crash down around us.

Breathing hard, I collapse against him, our chests, sweat-slickened and heaving, pressed together. We sit in the almost-silence of his office, the mid-day sun filtering in through his window and spreading across the hardwood floors, and bask in post-orgasmic bliss.

Our first time had been amazing, and I honestly didn't think that anything would ever top it—until right now. The way Greyston reacted when I gave him a blow job will be forever burned into my mind, not to mention how uninhibited I've become since we finally gave in to our urges.

"That was incredible," I pant, combing my fingers through his hair.

With a satisfied hum, Greyston nods. "I can't stop thinking about that damn blow job." I bite my lip and scrunch my nose, readying myself to hear what he thought now that the moment has passed. "It was mind-blowing."

"Yeah?" I'm relieved that I haven't misread him again.

Closing his eyes, he sighs and nods. "Mmm. It's hard to believe it was your first time. You really did your homework."

Reminding me of all the porn I looked up makes me blush, but I wouldn't take it back even if I could. Instead of clamming up like the old Juliette would have done when reminded of something borderline-humiliating, I shrug. "You know me...I take my studies very seriously."

My body shakes when Greyston laughs, and sooner than I'd like, he's ushering me off his lap. "What do you say we clean up and go grab a bite to eat? I don't know about you, but I'm fucking starved."

Nodding in agreement, I follow him to his room and excuse myself to use the bathroom. When I return, Greyston takes his turn while I throw on one of his T-shirts and head downstairs to finish preparing something to eat.

I'm just putting the finishing touches on a couple of sandwiches when I feel warm arms around my waist and a head on my shoulder. His lips touch down on my neck briefly, and I smile, bringing my hand up and placing it on his cheek as I turn to give him a quick kiss.

We decide to eat in the living room so that Greyston can watch ESPN—for work, he claims, and since he's a sports agent, who am I to argue his reasoning?

"Did you talk to your mom about dinner tomorrow?"

"Damn. I knew I was forgetting something," I tell him, remembering how we both wanted to talk to our families about the holidays. "I'll text her and remind her. Do you think our mothers will be okay with us hosting Christmas?"

Greyston smiles. "I think if we spin it right, they will agree to almost anything."

The thought of both of our families under one roof for the holidays excites me, and what has me even more keyed up is for my Gran to meet Greyston. Even though she's pretty traditional, she's always been able to keep an open mind about a lot of modern customs. Now, I'm not entirely sure how she'll feel about the fact that Greyston and I are living together having only been together a short time, but I think if it gets explained that we were roommates first and a couple second, she might be a little easier to appease. Of course, Greyston is a total charmer, and I know that he'll be able to win her over within the first few minutes of meeting her.

Yeah, Christmas with both of our families is going to be pretty spectacular if we can make it work.

chapter 24

"Baby, can you get the door?" I shout from the kitchen as I check on the lasagna.

I've been in the kitchen almost all day preparing the food while Greyston has been on a cleaning spree in light of the family dinner we're throwing tonight. While I'm sure we're going overboard, I really want to butter them up before we suggest sharing Christmas together.

"Sure," he says from right behind me, startling me. With a laugh, he kisses my cheek and grabs my ass—because he can—and then returns the cleaning products to their place beneath the sink. "How's dinner coming along?"

"Good." I close the oven and stand up straight. "It should be ready right away."

The doorbell rings again, and I nod him away. "Go let them in before they think we're up to no good in here... *again*."

Greyston rushes off to answer the door, and I start grabbing plates and cutlery. I've just begun to set the table when I hear Greyston and our guests returning. "Can I grab you each a glass of wine?" he inquires, and when I turn around, I see that my parents are the first to arrive.

"Mom, Dad." I abandon the table settings for a moment to greet them both. "Thanks for coming."

Mom pulls me into a bone-crushing hug and kisses my cheek. "Wouldn't miss it. Dinner smells amazing, Jules."

"Thanks. It's, uh, one of Gran's recipes." Knowing just

how much my parents enjoy my grandmother's cooking, I felt this was an appropriate choice if I was going to try and get them to agree to Christmas here.

"Oh!" Mom exclaims. "Speaking of Gran, her flight will be in at three on the twenty-third. Your father and I will be working, so would you mind picking her up?"

"Not at all. I'd love to." I turn back to the table and finish setting it. "Did you want me to bring her to the house? I could cook dinner and have it ready for when you and Dad got home."

"That sounds great," Dad interjects.

When Greyston clears his throat, we all turn to look at him. "While I trust the mechanic did an exceptional job on your car, I don't know that you should take it to the airport. Why don't I arrange a town car?"

"It's really not a big deal," I try to tell him, but he just smiles, his eyes pleading with me.

"Please? I'd really rather know you and your grandmother are safe." Understanding his reasoning, I concede without arguing, and Greyston smiles victoriously.

When the doorbell rings a second time, I excuse myself to answer it while Greyston pours the wine. Bright smiles greet me as I throw the door open, and before I can welcome Greyston's parents, Jocelyn pulls me into a tight hug.

"Juliette, darling, how've you been?" she inquires. "It feels like ages since we've seen each other."

I squeeze her a little tighter, realizing just how much I care for her and Daniel already; it still amazes me just how readily our parents accepted our relationship—especially given how quickly everything had happened between us.

"I've been good," I respond as we end our embrace. "How about the two of you? Greyston says work is keeping you both busy?"

Jocelyn nods. "It is. I'll be thankful for the few days off around Christmas to properly plan a holiday feast."

Forcing a smile that I hope doesn't look too nervous, I nod toward the kitchen. "Shall we?"

I lead them into the kitchen, and we find my parents sitting at the table while Greyston is tossing the Caesar salad.

"Wine?"

Nodding, they join my parents and begin talking. After grabbing two glasses from the cupboard, I open the wine and have just touched the neck of the bottle to the rim of one glass when I overhear my mother and Jocelyn's conversation.

The usual pleasantries are there, and they talk as though they've been friends for years. It eases my anxiety over asking a little, because the fact that they get along so well is promising for an unforgettable first Christmas with Greyston.

"Thank you, Juliette," Daniel says, taking his glass.

"Dinner should be ready soon," I announce, heading over to the oven and taking the lasagna out to sit for ten minutes before I serve it. "In the meantime, Greyston's got the salad ready." I look to Greyston.

Smiling, he picks up the bowl. "Right. Here you go," he says, setting the bowl in the middle of the table.

After refilling Greyston's wine, and pouring a glass for myself, I join them at the table and we dish up. Daddy eyes me, his eyebrow raised, and I laugh. "It's my first—and will be my only—glass, Dad."

As we all dish out and begin eating the salad, we talk about work—or in my case, school—and then the conversation shifts to the upcoming holidays. Mom and Jocelyn exchange stories from years past and then talk about what they've each got planned this year.

"Juliette," Jocelyn speaks up, and I look over at her. "I know you'll be spending the holidays with your family, but we'd just love if you could stop by our place for a little bit, as well." The look on her face suddenly changes, almost like she's afraid she's overstepped some kind of boundary, and she glances toward my parents. "If that's all right, of course. I certainly don't want to step on anybody's toes."

Before my mom can object to Jocelyn's invitation, I push my chair back and clear everyone's salad dishes away, smiling as I wander toward the sink. "Actually, this is kind of why Greyston and I invited you all here tonight." Grabbing the glass lasagna pan, I bring it back to the table and sit down to see all eyes are on me.

My hands begin to sweat, so I wipe them on my jeans

and take a deep breath. I'm so nervous that I'm sure they can probably hear how hard my heart is pounding, and I begin to fear that they might think this is a horrible idea. The words are on the tip of my tongue, but my apprehension practically chokes me, refusing to let me say anything.

Thankfully, Greyston comes to my rescue.

When he gently places his hand on my rapidly bouncing knee, I feel a bit of my unease lift, and my heart flutters and then calms minutely. "Juliette and I were thinking that maybe we'd offer up our home, and we could have both families join together for Christmas this year. This way, there would be less time travelling, and we could spend the entire day together."

We're met with blank stares, and I inhale a deep breath, gripping Greyston's hand in mine tightly and waiting. When they don't say anything right away, I finally find my voice. "It's just, we don't want to lose out on any time with either of you—or each other—and while I know we haven't been together that long, and we see each other every day, we just figured this was a simple solution." I feel winded, so I take a deep breath to replenish my lungs before I continue rambling. "Obviously, we don't expect an answer today. There's a lot to consider. We're not asking that you give up the usual traditions, we're simply offering our space and hoping we can maybe start a few new ones."

Mom and Dad exchange a glance, having one of their silent conversations, and Greyston's parents seem to be doing the same. Then they all look at each other before turning back to Greyston and me. Even though I doubt that even a minute has passed, I feel like it's been quiet for an eternity. I'm just about to say something—what, I don't really know—but the minute they all smile, I feel my entire body relax and the excited jitters kick in.

"Well, while I can't speak for Jocelyn and Daniel," Mom starts to say, "I can definitely say that your father and I would be delighted to come here for Christmas. As long as you let me help out in the kitchen so you're not running yourself ragged."

Jocelyn is quick to add on to what Mom said with a

bright smile. "We'd be delighted to have Christmas here with everyone. But I'm with Anne. I want to help with the cooking and the baking."

Squeezing Greyston's hand on my knee out of excitement, I nod emphatically. "Of course. We wouldn't have it any other way," I assure them. "I figured we could all contribute something."

My smile widens until my cheeks begin to hurt as Mom and Jocelyn begin talking a mile a minute about plans and favorite recipes for the holidays. Meanwhile, our fathers are the first to dish up their lasagna, sharing their thoughts on the latest hockey game. Watching them get along so well makes me even more excited for the holidays, just knowing that we'll all be under one roof for an entire day. Honestly, I'm so happy with the way this turned out—even though I know I really shouldn't have expected any less—and I can't wait for the next two and a half weeks to fly by.

chapter 25

The days leading up to Christmas have been jam-packed. Not only have I been busy with school and work, but I've been trying to help Greyston with the preparations for our shared Christmas with our parents. He's being pretty secretive, though, and I'm not sure what to make of it. I'm fairly certain it has something to do with whatever he's getting me for Christmas, which just adds a lot of pressure on me to make sure I find the perfect gift for him.

Did I mention I don't work well under pressure? No? Well, I don't.

The Sunday before Christmas, Greyston and I pick out our first Christmas tree as a couple. Yet another milestone I didn't realize would excite me this much, but it does.

We wander the lot together, my hand tucked in the crook of his elbow as I lean into his side. It's surprisingly warm out for December, but the smell of fresh pine needles sets the mood just fine. When Greyston first told me that it had been a year since he decorated his home, I could see how much he was looking forward to our joint celebration. Apparently he was travelling a lot at this time last year, coming home long enough to celebrate with his folks, and then he was off again.

Both of us are a little surprised when we find the perfect tree so soon into our search. I couldn't contain my excitement when we came across the seven-foot-tall Douglas fir. I imagined it in our living room, right in front of the large window that looked out onto the street.

Greyston tells the salesperson we'll take it and arranges for it to be delivered the next day. I'm off on winter break now, so Greyston and I will be able to decorate it together.

Cue another wave of excitement.

On our way home, Greyston suggests we stop to buy an obscene amount of Christmas décor. And I mean *obscene*. Apparently, even when he did decorate for Christmas, he did as much as most bachelors would. Which isn't much, statistically.

When we arrive home, I get start decorating the inside of the house, rearranging the living room so the tree will fit in the spot I envision it in. I hang the green garland and sprigs of holly on the mantle and place red and green candles atop it. Just outside the window, I see Greyston on the ladder, hanging the outdoor lights.

I move into the foyer, decorating the banister and doorframe with more garland, indoor lights, and holly, and I hang a beautiful full wreath on the outside of the door. The finishing touch, much to my delight, is a sprig of mistletoe in the center of the doorway between the foyer and living room. I hope to take advantage of it. A lot.

Pleased with my work so far, I carry the theme over into the kitchen, hanging more garland around the island, placing more candles, and even adding holly between and around them to make a festive centerpiece.

By sunset, the house is done, save for the missing tree. We settle in on the couch, a fire burning in the fireplace despite the warmer than average weather outside, and sipping on a glass or two of wine. Greyston is sitting with his back to the arm of the couch, and I've placed myself between his legs, my back to his chest as I run my free hand up and down his leg. We sit like this for a few hours after dinner, just talking about our day and trying to get gift ideas from one another. I continually get the feeling that Greyston is plotting something, but it only motivates me to find the perfect gift for him, too.

The rest of the week looks like this for us, except now our tree is set up, looking lush and glorious in its designated spot. It completes the room, and makes me deliriously excited for the impending holiday celebration.

The morning sun shines through the balcony window, stretching across the floor and bathing Greyston's room in light. Greyston is pressed against my back, kissing my shoulder and wrapping an arm around me to pull my body closer to his. All I can do is groan, not wanting to get up just yet.

"Baby." Greyston's voice is soft, the low tenor tickling my ear. "Sweetheart, it's time to wake up."

I groan, rolling over to find him smiling down at me, looking bright-eyed and bushy-tailed—whatever that actually means; I'm still too tired to try and figure it out. "Hi." He kisses the tip of my nose and runs his hand back and forth across my stomach as I stretch. "Merry Christmas, beautiful."

"Merry Christmas to you," I respond in my scratchy morning voice. The feel of his hard body pressed against me gives me an idea, so I check the time, groaning when I realize just how late it is and knowing we'll have to wait. "So much for asking for an early present," I pout, pushing my bottom lip out for effect.

"What did you have in mind?" he asks. I turn my body to him completely, slipping my hand beneath the sheet and running my fingers along his hard-on. He stops me, grabbing me around the wrist before I can show him my intentions. He looks conflicted, but he manages to stay strong. It's admirable—annoying, but admirable.

"How about a shower together? If we don't get out of bed soon, then I'm afraid I won't want to leave all day...and with everybody set to arrive in a couple hours, that wouldn't be very hospitable of us."

My previous disappointment over his rejection disappears, and I smirk wickedly. "Can we fool around in there?"

"When have we not?" he quips, yanking the sheet off our naked bodies and inviting a chill to nip at my skin.

With only thirty minutes, we manage to sneak in a quickie before getting cleaned up and dressed for the day. We have so much to do still, but we need to make sure the turkey gets in the oven first—as per our mothers' extremely precise instructions.

I head over to my room and pull on a pair of jeans and a

soft red sweater. I forego socks for now, and then I meet Greyston in the hall so we can get started on the morning preparations and have a bite to eat.

"You look nice," I tell him, appraising his faded jeans and gray sweater.

"Thanks." He takes my hand. "As usual, you look absolutely stunning." He pushes a strand of my damp hair back from my face, his fingers trailing down until it traces the neckline of my shirt. "This color against your skin…this neckline…" His eyes follow the trail his finger sets, stopping at the lowest point of my neckline. I begin to worry that maybe it's a little too immodest for Christmas with our families. His gaze only lingers for a second before he looks at me again.

"Is it too low? Should I change? I mean, our parents and my gran will be here… I don't want to offend anyone."

Smiling, Greyston shakes his head. "It's perfect. You have nothing to worry about." He presses his lips to mine and takes my hand. "Come on. We should go start in the kitchen before everyone arrives."

Greyston starts on breakfast while I begin prepping the turkey for the oven. Our families will be arriving around noon, and Greyston suggested we have a light breakfast since we'd probably be grazing all day before dinner was ready this evening. We're expecting our mothers to bring quite a bit of food, so we don't want to be too full.

Our breakfast is ready just as I'm putting the turkey in the oven, so we sit and have a private breakfast. I look at Greyston as he takes a bite, and I smile, spearing a few eggs on my fork. "So, are you going to give me a little hint about my present?" I ask.

"Sorry," he replies. "It's a surprise."

He's been saying the same damn thing for the past few days. It's starting to get old. I don't really expect him to tell me anything, but I'm naturally curious how he even managed to get me anything when I really gave him nothing to work with.

"I don't even understand how you found something for me. I mean, all I said was I wanted to sit around and relax over winter break. How does that equate to a present?"

All he does is shrug. "I guess you'll just have to wait until everyone gets here to find out."

The doorbell rings before I can try to find out anything else, and my eyes widen with excitement. "Looks like I won't be waiting that long to find out!" I cry out, kissing him quickly. I take my plate to the sink and then run through the house to answer the front door while Greyston starts to clean the kitchen.

"Merry Christmas!" I exclaim when I open the door to find my parents and grandmother. I hug them each before taking their coats and hanging them in the closet. I take Gran's hand and hook it into my arm as I lead them through the house to the kitchen. Greyston had wanted to meet Gran the other day when I picked her up, but wound up getting stuck at work. He was pretty disappointed about it, actually.

"Your father and I will just go put the gifts under the tree, sweetheart," Mom tells me before turning and heading the other direction.

"Sure, Mom." I shift my focus back to my grandmother. "I'll show Gran the kitchen."

We walk into the kitchen just as Greyston is finishing up with the dishes. I can tell he's a little nervous, and I can't help but feel it's my fault for telling him that Gran is a pretty traditional woman.

"Hello," Greyston speaks up, coming forward and holding out a hand to Gran. "I'm Greyston Masters. It's a pleasure to meet you, Mrs. Foster. Juliette's told me so much about you."

Gran looks to me briefly before accepting Greyston's outstretched hand. "And I've heard quite a bit about you, as well, Mr. Masters."

"Greyston, please," he suggests. "Can I offer you something to drink, Mrs. Foster? Something to eat, perhaps?"

"No, thank you, dear. Anne served up a rather large breakfast this morning." Gran smiles and squeezes Greyston's hand. "And you can call me Gran."

I watch as Greyston finally relaxes, and I step forward, popping up onto my toes to kiss him lightly. "See. I told you she'd like you," I whisper.

The doorbell rings again, and Greyston suggests we migrate to the living room for our gift exchange. I take Gran while he answers the door for his parents.

"Mom, I told you not to worry about gifts," I hear Greyston tell her as I help ease Gran onto the couch. "You've already done so much to help me out with Juliette's."

Interesting, I think to myself with a smirk.

"I know, but that was technically your gift to Juliette. We had to get her something, too. Don't worry, we were sure to coordinate."

These clues are no good. I still have no idea what's going on. It's like he's doing it on purpose at this point.

Greyston and his father join us in the living room, and I hear Jocelyn make her way toward the kitchen. After putting a stack of presents beneath the tree, Daniel sits on the couch next to my dad, and I introduce him to Gran. As they become acquainted, I sit on the floor next to the tree, leaning against the large armchair we moved from the corner of the room.

Soon, Jocelyn appears, passing by Greyston who is standing in the doorway still with a grin on his face. She sits next to Daniel on our gigantic couch and introduces herself to Gran. Greyston's parents ask me about school, and I ask them about work. We get caught up in a conversation that comes on so naturally, I find myself momentarily basking in the moment. Everything about this just feels...right. Like my life was meant to turn out this way. And all because of an ad in the paper. Who knew.

I sit back and listen, laughing when my mom tells everyone a story about her first Christmas with my dad after they got married and how she burned the turkey. This opens up a new discussion about everyone's first Christmases together, and I look up at Greyston, still standing in the doorway, arms crossed and leaning against the doorframe while he watches us all. Smiling when our eyes meet, I pat the seat of the empty chair, and he finally joins us, kissing the top of my head as he sits.

"Should we hand out presents?" Greyston asks, settling in behind me.

Nodding excitedly, I start organizing the gifts into piles

so I can hand them out. I'm quite perplexed to find quite a few of them are mine—and they're mostly massive.

I hand the gifts out to our parents and Gran, and then I resume my place in front of Greyston and watch while our family opens their gifts. Dad's up first, and the look in his eyes when he opens his Diamondback season tickets makes me extremely happy. Truth is, I had no idea what to get him, and it was Greyston's suggestion to go this route.

"This is…" He looks down at the booklet and then up at us. "Thank you both. It's amazing—and entirely too much."

"Nah," I say with a shrug. "Just promise you'll take me to a game."

"Really?"

"Yeah." I nod. "I had a great time at that football game, and I've recently decided to experience new things." I toss a quick sideways glance at Greyston, and he smirks. "Besides, it's so rare we spend any real father-daughter time together anymore. This would be perfect."

"You've got yourself a deal," he agrees quickly, turning to show Mom his tickets before she opens her gift.

Her mouth falls open when she opens the long, slender black velvet box that contains the necklace and spa gift card we got her. "Thanks, you two. This is absolutely perfect." She stops and looks at me with a wide smile and wet eyes. "This necklace is stunning, honey."

"I saw it and just couldn't resist," I tell her. "It has our birthstones in it."

Mom blinks away a few emotional tears and asks my dad to help her put the necklace on. "It's exquisite." I get the feeling that something might be on my mom's mind; I've never known her to be this emotional over a gift before—regardless of the sentiment behind it. Before I can ask her if she's okay, she hands a gift to Gran.

"Here, Mum. This is from Juliette and Greyston."

I shift in place, getting up onto my knees, eager for my gran's reaction. I'd spent so much time on the main part of her gift before Greyston and I went out and got her a set of personalized ceramic pie plates as well.

She's always been happy baking for her family, so the

pie dishes were a big hit, but when she got to the actual gift...

"Oh, Juliette," she says, flipping through the pages of the scrapbook I'd put together for her. "When did you find the time to do this?"

"Well, I've been working on it for the last year, but knowing I wanted to give it to you for Christmas, I really pushed myself to get it done these last two weeks." I pause, slightly nervous, even though the look on Gran's face tells me I shouldn't be. "Do you like it?"

The album contains all sorts of family photos, and when I first showed Greyston the finished product, he seemed completely captivated by the stories they told.

Behind me, he rests his hands on my shoulders and kisses the top of my head. I sigh, bringing my right hand up and placing it over his, and he gives my shoulder a gentle squeeze.

"I think she likes it," I tell him, shifting and lifting my left arm to rest on his lap. Greyston's hand moves up and down my forearm, making me sigh.

He laughs. "I told you she would."

Gran sets her scrapbook aside for later so Greyston's parents can open their gifts next. Like my dad, Daniel gets a set of season tickets. Apparently this isn't too much of a shock to him; he gets the same thing every year. Greyston even foresaw our dad's maybe wanting to go to games together, making sure the seats were close.

Jocelyn beams when she opens the envelope containing the donation that Greyston and I made to a children's charity. Greyston explained to me that his mom has always been heavily involved with a lot of charities in the area, ever since he was little.

"Thank you both," she says, her eyes

I'm about to let Greyston open his present, but before I can say anything, he hands me the present from the top of my pile. Not one to refuse the chance to open my gifts, I accept, tearing the paper from the box from Gran.

It's a beautiful present, but also a bit confusing considering I live in Phoenix. "These are lovely," I assure Gran as I pull the hand-knit scarf from the box and wrap it around my neck. There's a matching pair of elbow-length mittens that are made out of the softest wool I've ever felt. "Thanks, Gran.

"You're welcome, dear," Gran replies sweetly. "I was glad to have something to busy myself with for the last several weeks."

I pull the gloves off, but keep the scarf on, loving how warm and cozy it is, but I find myself worrying about Gran's possible senility. "Here's hoping Arizona experiences some kind of cold snap so I can make proper use of them," I joke.

I don't miss the strange look exchanged between everyone on the couch, but I don't know what to make of it either. I pick up the next box from the pile. It's from my parents.

Usually, my parents are really good about getting me something I desperately need—a new computer for school, clothes—but what lies in this box is even more bizarre than my gran's gift.

I pull the parka from the box, the tag catching my attention immediately. "Down-filled?" I look at Mom and Dad. "Is Arizona expecting sub-zero temperatures sometime soon?"

Mom grins, the sparkle in her eyes telling me she's keeping something form me. "Always best to be prepared."

I remove the snow pants from the box next. "Snow pants, Mom. You bought me snow pants." I run a hand through my hair, seriously confused about what's going on. "I've never even seen snow before.

"What?" Greyston chimes in from behind me. "*Never*?"

I shake my head, the confusion starting to clear after his reaction. Does he have something up his sleeve? "Well, not *really*. I mean, there was that one time years ago where it snowed here, but it melted before it even hit the ground."

Still confused and now questioning everyone's motives, I reach for the plain envelope that sits on the last box. Greyston snatches it up before me, confirming my suspicions. "This one is actually to be opened last, sweetheart."

I arch a brow suspiciously. "Okay." I grab the final box and open it. "Winter boots." I nod, pulling the gorgeous white boots on and loving how the fur cuff around my calf looks. They're really quite beautiful, even if extremely unnecessary.

I'm quiet for far too long, and everyone is staring at me, probably expecting me to say something, but all I can do is wonder where we might be going that I'll use all this stuff. Colorado? Montana?

"They're awesome, but I have to wonder if you're all insane or expecting some kind of ice-age apocalypse, or…?"

Laughing, Greyston hands me the envelope. "Here. This one's from me. Maybe it'll help clear everything up."

My excitement surges, and I tear open the envelope, pulling out a folded piece of paper and a photo of a log cabin nestled somewhere in a winter wonderland.

The final pieces of this strange puzzle click into place, and I look up to Greyston.

"A cabin? You bought me a cabin?"

Greyston shakes his head. "No, I didn't buy you a cabin. This one is only on loan." He nods toward the folded piece of paper. "Open it."

I do, and I find plane tickets to Whistler, British Columbia, Canada inside. He's taking me on a vacation? Suddenly my gift seems lame. "No. Greyston, this is too much," I try to tell him, even though I'm feeling pretty excited about it.

"You said you wanted a relaxing vacation." His smile widens. "And what's more relaxing than a cabin in the mountains of Canada?" I stare at him, completely perplexed. "Whistler is beautiful this time of year, and there's no better place to go skiing."

I almost choke on the breath I take. "Skiing? But I've never—"

"New experiences, right?" he says with a wink.

While I do feel he went above and beyond in the gift department, I can't help the smile and excitement from pushing my concerns aside. I jump to my feet and throw myself onto Greyston's lap. "Thank you! This is amazing." Now that I've opened Greyston's gift, all the others make sense. "Thank you all so much."

Mom looks at us, her expression reflecting just how happy she is. "We just want you to have a good time. And be sure to take a lot of pictures."

"I will," I tell her. "I promise."

It's Greyston's turn to open his gifts now, and while mine isn't nearly as extravagant as the one he gave me, I really hope he loves it. I slide off his lap and hand him the box. "In light of your gift to me, this seems…lame."

He's quick to tear the wrapping off and open the box, revealing the titanium Michael Kors watch I spent a pretty penny on. He immediately takes it out and puts it on his wrist. It's a little too big, but he doesn't let that stop him from wearing it. "This is amazing, Juliette."

"Yeah? You like it?"

"I love it." He leans forward and presses his lips to mine softly—any harder and we'd probably get carried away like we so often do. "Thank you."

Next, he opens his gift from his parents, extremely happy with the gift cards because he states that he's in need of new boarding equipment. Just mentioning snowboarding makes me nervous and excited all at the same time.

"Here," I say, handing him the last gift.

Inside is new winter gear—a jacket, ski pants, and gloves—and he seems pretty pumped about it. He's about to thank my parents when my mom speaks up.

"If you don't like them—or if you have a set already—the gift receipt is in the bottom of the box there."

Greyston is quick to dismiss her concerns on whether or not he likes his gift. "It's great, Anne. Really. My current set is more than a couple years old, so I was due for an upgrade. Thank you."

We sit around for the next hour, talking about and showing off our gifts. I am so excited about the trip, I keep asking Greyston questions and telling him I can't wait to go away with him—just the two of us, no interruptions. I do voice my concerns that maybe he spent a little too much.

"The cabin belongs to my parents, and they were more than happy to loan it to us for the week we'll be in the mountains. All I paid for were the tickets," he assures me, and this makes me feel a little better.

Our mothers and Gran head into the kitchen to check on the turkey and prepare some of the other dishes, while our fathers follow them to grab a beer. Finally alone, I crawl onto

Greyston's lap.

His eyes wander over my body, lingering on the slight view of my cleavage, and his hand moves from my knee and tugs on the fur cuff of my boot playfully. "You like your presents, baby?" His hand moves back up my leg until his hand is on my upper thigh, the tips of his fingers pressing against the inner seam of my jeans.

Afraid he might move his hand, I squeeze my thighs together, forcing his hand exactly where I want it. I stifle a moan and nod. "When do we leave?"

"The day after tomorrow," he whispers, pushing his face into my neck and kissing that ticklish spot beneath my ear.

"So, I have all day tomorrow to pack and prepare?" He nods. "Good. There's something I need to do tomorrow before we go."

He arches his eyebrows questioningly. It feels nice to keep him in the dark for once.

"Which would be?"

I smile, feeling a little devilish as I plan something I truly hope he'll love. "A surprise."

chapter 26

The look on Greyston's face when I refuse to tell him what it is I have to do tomorrow before we go on our trip is priceless. Even though I am super excited about this vacation, having never been anywhere outside the US before—especially not in the winter—I still feel like he's gone a little overboard. The cabin in the picture was beautiful, and I can't wait to go away with him for the week. Sure, we're not really disturbed much here, but going on a trip with my boyfriend, far away from even the slightest possibility of any kind of intrusion, is definitely appealing.

"You're really not going to tell me?"

Shaking my head, I run my hand over his arm, lifting his sleeve and looking at the watch I bought him. "Sorry. Can't."

"I think you mean *won't,*" he grumbles. Then, he leans forward and kisses my neck, his fingers curling into my inner thigh slightly. This makes my pulse race and my breath hitch, and he strokes the seam of my jeans. Tingles course through my body, settling between my legs, and I bite back a moan of desire. "Of course, I might have a few ways to extract information from you."

His teeth bite down gently, and I sigh, ready to tell him anything he needs to know. The sound of our fathers' voices returning from the kitchen draws my attention away from the way his hand feels wedged firmly between my thighs long enough to rise off his lap. Honestly, I'm glad they made themselves known, because I would have been horrified if they'd have found us like that. An innocent kiss—or even a not-so-innocent one—would have been a little easier to handle...but heavy petting? Yeah, pretty sure my dad wouldn't recover from that a second time around.

Suppressing my feelings of desire as much as I can, I place my hands on the armrests of Greyston's chair, leaning over to kiss him softly. "I'm going to go see if I can lend a hand in the kitchen. You boys behave."

Kicking off my insanely warm new winter boots, I pad barefoot to the kitchen, where Mom, Gran, and Jocelyn are busy working on a few things for dinner. I pass by Dad and Daniel, popping up on my toes to kiss my father's cheek, and continue on my way.

The closer I get to the kitchen, the stronger the inviting smell of the turkey is; I'm instantly transported back in time to happy memories of countless Thanksgivings and Christmases with my family. The holidays have always been my favorite time of year. There's just something about being together with my family, sitting around the table, our dinner plates full in front of us as we talk, laugh, and share stories of years past.

This Christmas is fast becoming my favorite of them all, having my family and Greyston's all together under one roof. Sure, I was a little afraid that neither of our mothers would relinquish their hosting duties, and we'd be forced to split the holidays between houses. It was such a relief when they agreed, and it was an even bigger relief when Gran showed up this morning and accepted Greyston right away—not that I should have been too surprised, I suppose; I talked about him enough the other day in the car as the driver took us to my parents' house.

Naturally, Gran asked all sorts of questions about my relationship. At first, she didn't seem too keen on the idea that we were living together already, but I was quick to explain that I was renting a room in his house before we even realized there was something between us. The expression on her face was proof enough that this wasn't what she wanted to hear. She wasn't upset about it, but she was concerned because the situation had the potential to become complicated. I understood where she was coming from, but after talking to her about him a little more, she started to understand and told me that she only mentioned it because she wants what's best for me.

I stand in the doorway to the kitchen, watching them all fuss over different things; Jocelyn is busy putting various kinds of tarts and squares on the festive platters Greyston and I had left out this morning, Gran is skinning carrots and potatoes, and Mom is basting the turkey. They work together like a cohesive unit, and it only further cements this as my favorite Christmas so far; I'd like to think they'll only get better as the years go by—though, I suppose this one might be hard to top since I got a trip to the mountains.

The minute my mother notices me hanging out in the doorway she closes the oven and motions for me to join them. "Come on in, honey. Lend a hand."

Not wanting to step on any toes, I smile and shake my head. "No, that's okay. Greyston and I said that you could carry on with your yearly traditions. I'm okay to just hang out."

"Don't be silly, Juliette," Gran admonishes as only Gran does—which is in a tone that should never be taken too seriously. "Get in here and make yourself useful."

I grab a paring knife from the knife block, stand next to Gran, and pick up a potato from the counter in front of her to peel. I've just made the first slice when Gran leans closer to me, speaking her next words in a low, hushed voice. "Besides, judging by the way that boy looks at you, you'll have to start building your own traditions."

My cheeks burn, and I can only imagine the shade of red they are as I laugh nervously. While I know how I feel about Greyston—and I'm pretty sure he feels the same way—it seems like I'd be tempting fate to think that far into the future so soon. It's too late, though; Gran's playful comment has me imagining Greyston and I sitting together on our couch as three smiling children tear open brightly wrapped gifts near the Christmas tree.

"What's got you grinning like a court jester?" Mom asks, bumping her hip against mine as she sidles up next to me.

Clearing my throat, I shake my head. "Nothing," I lie, my voice cracking slightly—a sure sign of my guilt. Thankfully, my mother doesn't press the issue, instead wrapping an arm around me and hugging me close.

"Thank you for suggesting we all celebrate together," Mom says, resting her head against mine as I continue peeling potatoes. "It's wonderful to have everyone here." When her voice quivers, my eyebrows pull together in concern, and I set the knife and potato down so I can focus on her.

"Mom?"

Quickly, she pulls her arm from around me and dabs at the inner corners of her eyes with the pads of her index fingers. "Sorry." She laughs. "The holidays always make me a little emotional."

While I know this to be true, I also know that she's never *this* emotional. First, she got more than a little choked up when she opened the necklace I got her, and now, she's crying… I get the feeling that something deeper is going on, and my stomach knots when I begin to fear the worst: that maybe she's sick.

I need to know, but I know that now is probably not the time to ask, so I try to push it to the back of my mind. It's completely unsuccessful. When I almost cut my thumb for the fifth time, I throw in the towel and excuse myself. "I'm going to step outside for a minute," I tell them, heading for the patio doors.

Once outside, I walk toward the pool and stand along the edge, looking out toward the desert. It's a little chilly, and the cool breeze bites through my light sweater, so I wrap my arms around myself in an effort to warm up a bit. My mind races, trying to find some other explanation for my mother's odd behavior. I'm unable to think of anything that could be taken in a positive light—especially since her mother died of cancer ten years ago. That alone brings me right back to the absolute worst scenario possible.

My eyes begin to burn, and I blink back my tears, afraid of anyone seeing how upset I am. Logically, I know I shouldn't be this upset without confirming my fears, but I'm finding it hard to remain rational.

"Here you are." Greyston's soft voice rolls over me, granting me a momentary reprieve from my distress. He drapes the jacket he keeps by the patio door over my shoulders and wraps his arms around me, resting his chin on my shoulder and kissing my neck. "What are you doing out here?"

I think about telling him what's bothering me, but I don't want to sully his mood as well until I know for sure. So, instead of unloading my thoughts on him, I smile and turn in his arms. "Just…taking it all in," I tell him breathily, wrapping my arms around his waist and snuggling into his chest. When he doesn't say anything, I wonder if he suspects I'm keeping something from him. If he does, though, he doesn't allude to it; instead he presses his lips into the top of my head and runs his hands up and down my back, causing a current of heat to move within my body.

"It's a little cold out here," he whispers against the top of my head. "Why don't we go back inside?" I look up to find him smirking. "I'd hate for you to catch a cold before we go on our vacation."

Attempting my most genuine smile, I nod. "Yeah, that probably wouldn't be good."

Taking me by the hand, Greyston leads me into the kitchen. I hang up his jacket and smile at our mothers and Gran as Greyston continues to lead me through the house. Confused, because I should probably help out with dinner a little more, I look up at Greyston. "Where are you taking me?"

Without answering, Greyston turns down the hall before the foyer—out of sight from both the kitchen and the living room—and presses me against the wall. His hard body is hot against mine, and his lips find mine, firm and insistent. It doesn't take long before my troubles are mostly forgotten, and I pull his hips closer by his belt loops, my body softening in his arms. His tongue sweeps across my lower lip once, and just as I'm about to deepen our kiss, he pulls away, smiling.

"There you are," he whispers, kissing the tip of my nose lightly and pushing a loose strand of hair away from my face, the tips of his fingers ghosting down the side of my cheek.

"What's bothering you?"

I knew it was silly to think he didn't pick up on my anxiousness; he's always been so perceptive of any sudden changes in my moods. "It's probably nothing," I tell him quietly, and when he doesn't say anything, I know he's waiting for me to continue. "It's just...my mom's been acting a little...*strange*." I take a deep breath, feeling my tears threaten again, but I hold them back. "She was more emotional than I thought she'd be when she saw the necklace, and just now in the kitchen, she thanked me for suggesting we all share Christmas together, and then cried."

Instead of feeding my fears, Greyston smiles and runs his hands up and down my arms in an attempt to comfort me. "Sweetheart, I'm sure she's just happy to be here with everyone."

"I know," I tell him, letting his voice of reason stand in for mine. Dropping my eyes to his chest, I nod and repeat his words in my head a few times, letting them sink in until I believe them myself. "You're right. I'm probably being ridiculous... It just seems odd, is all."

"Well, there's no sense getting yourself upset until you find out, right?" he reasons, and I give him a little shrug in response. "And *if* your mother has anything to tell you, she'll tell you when she's ready. You can't force it."

He's right, of course, so my head bobs in agreement once more. "Okay."

Taking me by the hand, Greyston and I head back to the living room. Our fathers are talking about football as Greyston takes his seat in the chair, and instead of letting me sit on the floor, he pulls me down onto his lap. Dad glances up at us, and I expect his gaze to be disapproving, but instead he smiles and returns to his conversation with Daniel, allowing me to relax into Greyston's embrace. His left hand rests on my thigh, and I glance at his watch again, sitting a little loose around his wrist.

"We should take this in to get properly sized," I suggest, tugging at the loose links.

"Maybe I'll do that tomorrow while you're out doing...whatever it is you're doing." His tone is playfully pouty, making me giggle.

"Sure. I actually just have to go to the mall, so maybe we could ride together and split up for a bit before meeting for lunch," I suggest.

Having just secured our afternoon plans for tomorrow, our mothers and Gran return, taking their seats on the couch. The next few hours are filled with stories from my and Greyston's childhoods—both adorable and embarrassing—until the timer for the oven can be heard throughout the house.

Mom and Jocelyn jump up, and I turn, kissing Greyston softly. "I'm going to go and lend a hand in the kitchen."

I've barely made it out of the living room when my father speaks, stopping me dead in my tracks. "Greyston, why don't you go and carve the turkey?" My head snaps toward the couch, and Dad looks up at me like I'm watching him grow two extra heads. "What?"

"But *you* usually carve the turkey." I look to Daniel, assuming that he is usually the one to carve the turkey in their home, too, and he only smiles.

"True," Dad says, pulling my attention back to him. "But this is your house, and maybe Greyston wants to start his own traditions."

I look to Greyston again, and the corners of his lips are slowly turning upward as he stands from his chair. "Sure."

Greyston and I make our way to the kitchen, and just as we enter, Mom's placing the turkey onto the island counter. "Juliette, honey, would you tell your father the turkey is ready to be carved?" she asks without looking up at me.

"Um, actually, Greyston's going to carve it this year. Dad and Daniel seem cool with it," I inform her. Now, I'm honestly not sure how I expected her to react, but glistening eyes wasn't it. Wanting him to understand why I've been thinking the way I have, I nudge Greyston, and he gives my hand a reassuring squeeze.

"Well, come in, you two!" Jocelyn exclaims. "Let's get dinner on the table before your fathers get grouchy."

While Greyston carves and plates the turkey, I take my place beside him and begin mashing the potatoes, and Mom and Jocelyn are at the stove working on the gravy and vegetables. When all is said and done, Greyston and I extend the kitchen table so we can put the food on it while Mom goes to the living room to tell everyone else that dinner is served.

"Dinner smells amazing," Dad praises, finding his seat.

Nodding, Daniel is quick to agree. "I'll say. You ladies outdid yourselves."

With everyone at the table dishing up, I grab the wine from the counter and bring it over to fill everyone's glasses. I start with Greyston's and work my way clockwise around the table. After filling Dad's glass, I reach between him and Mom for hers, but before I can grab the stem, she holds her hand out and stops me.

"Oh, none for me, honey. Thank you," she says softly, glancing up at me.

While her turning down a glass of wine isn't exactly unheard of, I still find myself a little stunned; family dinners are the only time she really ever drinks.

"What?" I ask, momentarily thinking I misheard her. "Sorry, did you want white? We have white."

Something flashes in her eyes, and it takes me a second to recognize it as apprehension. She shakes her head, dropping her gaze from me, and turns back to the table. "No. No wine for me today, thank you."

My confusion grows, and I look around the room. Dad's eyes are on his plate, his posture rigid and his hands flat on the table. Jocelyn and Daniel look at me, their expressions telling me they don't know anything. Gran avoids my gaze also, and Greyston's eyes are wide with what looks like realization.

Every thought that something might be wrong with her suddenly dissipates, and all the pieces come together in my mind like a jigsaw puzzle: getting teary-eyed over my gift to her, being emotional about us having everybody together for Christmas, and now her refusal to drink.

"Holy shit," I blurt out, not thinking clearly enough to harness the profanity in front of my parents or Gran. "You're pregnant."

Mom's silence is answer enough. Nobody else in the

room says a word, instead choosing to look at anything but me as I absorb this news. While I'm relieved that she doesn't have some terminal illness, the fact remains that my forty-four-year-old mother is pregnant. I may not be a doctor, but even I know that she's no longer in her prime child-bearing years, and that this pregnancy might very-well be more difficult than when she was in her twenties. But, on the flip side, I'm going to have a little brother or sister.

"Sweetheart?" Greyston's voice breaks through to me, and I turn to look at him, my lips slowly twisting up into a smile.

"You're right," Mom confesses, pushing her chair away from the table. "We wanted to wait to tell you until you came back from your vacation and we'd had our first ultrasound done, but yes, Dr. Lundstrum confirmed that we're expecting." Pausing, she gauges my reaction to hearing this. "Are you…okay?"

Nodding, I hand the wine bottle to Greyston and pull my mom into my arms. "Of course! I mean, I'm still a little shocked, but if you're happy, then I'm happy."

Congratulations fill the room as I hug both of my parents. I feel silly thinking that anything was wrong with my mom, and I feel much more relaxed now that I know the truth behind her odd behavior.

We all take our seats around the table and begin dishing up, and Mom leans over and kisses my dad. It's the first time I'm not even a little repulsed by their PDA. In fact, it's comforting to see just how in love they are after all these years. It's something I never really thought about before, but I aspire for it in my own relationship. Almost as though he can read my mind, Greyston's hand finds mine beneath the table, and he squeezes it lightly, shooting me a brilliant smile when I bring my eyes to his.

After dinner, everyone lends a hand in the clean up, and once the kitchen is clean, they decide to call it a night. Greyston and I walk them to the door, hugging each of them as they prepare to leave.

"You make sure you call me the minute your plane lands," Mom whispers into my ear as she hugs me tightly.

"Yes, Mom," I assure her. "Congratulations again, and you take care of yourself, okay?"

"I'll make sure of it, kiddo," Dad assures me.

After hugging Mom, I prepare to say goodbye to Gran. She pulls me into her tightest embrace, and I feel a little emotional; saying goodbye to her is always difficult given how close we've always been. "Thanks for being so awesome about everything, Gran," I tell her. "It was so good to see you again."

Jocelyn and Daniel step forward to say goodnight next, hugging both Greyston and me and wishing us a Merry Christmas and a safe trip to Whistler.

"Thanks again for everything," I say. "The use of your cabin, the amazing gifts…"

"Of course, dear," Jocelyn replies. "You two have a good time, and we'll do dinner when you return."

"Sounds perfect, Mom," Greyston tells her.

With everyone gone, Greyston closes and locks the door before turning to me. "So…did you have a good Christmas?"

"The best." Sighing contentedly, I wrap my arms around his waist and snuggle into his warmth.

He kisses the top of my head, then turns us for the living room. "And your mom…" We reach the couch and he sits, pulling me down onto his lap, waiting for my reaction before he continues.

I smile. "I'm still a little shocked, but she seems happy."

"Are you?"

I think about his question for a minute before I decide to just be honest. "Yes and no." Cocking his head, he regards me with curiosity. "No, because she's forty-four, so I worry that she's at risk for more complications given her age." Greyston nods along in understanding. "But, at the same time, they've both said that they wanted more kids…it just never happened for them, so I'm excited that they've been given the chance." Slowly, my lips curl up into a smile. "Plus, I get a new baby brother or sister out of this, so that's pretty cool."

"Good," Greyston says. "I'm glad you're okay with it, because I think they're pretty excited."

Then, out of nowhere, the day catches up with me,

waves of exhaustion rolling over me and making me yawn. Greyston chuckles into my hair as I cuddle up to his chest. "What do you say we head up to bed? I'm feeling pretty wiped out, too. Plus, we should rest up if we're going to brave the mall tomorrow."

Nodding slowly, I push myself up and stand. "Sounds good."

After changing into my pajamas, Greyston and I crawl into bed, and it isn't long before we both fall right asleep.

chapter 27

Greyston and I are sure to be up and at the mall early so we don't have to fight the crowds. After giving him a quick kiss, we part ways, and I head off to a few different lingerie shops. The only things I've ever purchased in them before have been bras and underwear. Up until recently, I've never really been interested in this sort of thing—I mean, what was the point if a) the man (Ben) wasn't going to appreciate it, or b) it was just going to get taken off? But now? Well, now I want to look nice for Greyston. I want to feel sexy and desired. I want to see the look on his face when I come into the room in a tiny, lacy outfit. I want his eyes to go wide and his jaw to drop as I make my way across the room to him... Yes, that is exactly what I want.

I leave Frederick's of Hollywood $250 poorer, but I don't think twice about it since I've got quite a bit of money saved up anyway due to my kickass rental price. I've purchased a couple new bras—sexier ones—and matching panties as well as three pieces of lingerie in varying degrees of naughty.

Naturally, I bought a much more innocent piece, a sheer white negligee, to use the first night—kind of as a way to test the waters—and then I bought another that's a little more risqué, all black lace and short with a matching thong and garter... I even bought some thigh-high stockings and am going to stop for a pair of sleek black heels to go with it; Greyston is sure to lose his mind. Last in my bag of new sex-clothes is a red and black corset that pushes my breasts up and together, making my cleavage look…well, it looks amazing. For someone with such small boobs, I never knew they could look that good. To go with the corset, I bought a sexy pair of lace panties…of course, there's something more to them than that—or, should I say *less*? In an act of pure impulse, brought on by Bad Juliette on my left shoulder reminding me that trying new things was fun, I forewent the regular lace panties and snatched up a pair of the crotchless kind. Yup, I, Juliette Foster, now own a pair of crotchless panties.

After stopping in a shoe store and grabbing a pair of the highest heels I've ever owned, I grab my phone and am about to call Greyston to see if he's ready to meet for lunch. However, just as I'm about to hit *send*, I stop in my tracks and stare at the storefront sign before me for a minute. Excitement pounds through my veins, and Bad Juliette appears again, telling me to do it because it'll be so worth it. The more I think about it, the more I realize she's right, so I gather up my courage and step inside.

If the crotchless panties don't make Greyston lose his mind, you better fucking believe that this will.

"You're going to freeze your ass off," Greyston warns from his spot on my bed as I step out of my walk-in closet in a white long-sleeved sweater and a skirt. "I know you've never seen snow before, but you realize just how far north Canada is, right? Not to mention, we're going to the mountains."

I smile sweetly and saunter across my room to where he sits; I am fully aware that a skirt probably isn't what most sane people would choose to wear, but I have a method to my madness—one that Greyston isn't quite aware of…yet.

"I've got jeans in my carry-on, just in case," I assure him, pushing my way between his thighs and wrapping my arms around his neck. He welcomes me by placing his hands on my hips, his fingers curling into the denim of my skirt just above the swell of my ass.

Raising his eyes to mine, he smirks. "Just in case?" He

laughs, slowly moving his hands down toward my thighs. The second the tips of his fingers touch the flesh of my leg just below my skirt, a shiver runs through me. While the most innocent touch from him always excites me, I'm definitely a bit more sensitive; it's probably due to the two of us not having sex in two days—not for lack of my wanting to or his trying, I just...didn't want to spoil my latest surprise before our vacation started.

"God, you smell fantastic," Greyston groans, hooking his fingers beneath the hem of my skirt and lifting it slowly. He kisses the column of my neck, and I sigh when his thumbs press against my thighs and move in...and up—

I snap out of my lust-induced haze when he grazes my panties, and I place my hands firmly on his shoulders and take a very difficult step away. Naturally, he is undeterred and removes his hands from beneath my skirt, grabbing my hips and pulling me back to him quickly with a low, disapproving growl.

"I wasn't quite done," he tells me gruffly, lifting the hem of my shirt and trailing his fingers along the waist of my skirt until he reaches the button. Slowly, he begins to release it, his warm breath wafting over the skin of my stomach and causing goosebumps. He chuckles once and frees the button. "I love watching your body react to my every touch..." he cements his point by flattening his hand over my abdomen and moving it up under my shirt to my right breast "...my every kiss..." my eyes fall closed the moment he presses his lips to my now-exposed hipbone and then licks the skin "...my every breath." When he blows on the newly-wet surface, a fresh wave of goosebumps flourishes across my skin, and I momentarily forget that a big part of my plan is for *me* to be driving *him* wild with desire. He's turning the tables on me, and I can't have that.

Even though I would give anything to let him continue on like this, I open my eyes and look down at him. Grabbing his wrists, I stop him from taking this any further because I want to reveal his big surprise once we're officially on vacation.

"That's the second time you've stopped me from making

love to you, Juliette," he admonishes playfully, his tone low and dripping with desire. It surprises me when the pulse between my legs intensifies. "You realize we haven't had sex since Christmas morning in the shower, right?"

"I do." Smiling, I release one of his wrists and run my fingers through his hair. "But if I let you continue, then we're going to be late getting to the airport, and you don't want us to miss our flight, do you?" Even I know he can't argue with reason.

Smirking, he tugs me toward him again by the open waist of my skirt. "I'll be quick."

With a loud laugh, I fall onto his lap, and he begins kissing my neck again—probably because he knows it renders me completely powerless against him. "As romantic as that sounds," I tell him softly, "I'd really rather wait until our vacation begins." Pausing, I bite my lip and shrug. "I've kind of got this whole thing planned…"

"And I'll get the surprise you promised me?" he inquires, lifting his head and arching his eyebrow.

"Definitely."

Appeased for the time being, Greyston lets me get up and finish packing my things. After we double-check our bags to make sure we haven't forgotten anything, we head out to the town car that's just arrived. Greyston's regular driver opens the door for me and takes our bags to the trunk while we climb in. Once our luggage is put away, the driver climbs in and pulls away from the curb.

Knowing that this marks the beginning of our first time away together, my excitement skyrockets. Beside me, Greyston throws an arm over my shoulder and pulls me close, kissing my temple. "I'm looking forward to this vacation with you," he whispers.

"Me too," I tell him, relaxing into his embrace. "There's so much I'm looking forward to."

Using his other hand, Greyston grabs my legs and swings them over his thighs, turning my body toward his. "Like?"

His fingers trail up and down my outer thigh, making me shiver and lose focus momentarily. "Being alone, for starters," I quip quietly, nodding my head in the driver's direction.

Greyston chuckles, leaning us forward a bit to push a button on the roof console. A privacy screen rises from behind the driver's seat, and I shake my head in mock-disapproval. "What else?" he asks, slipping his hand up under my skirt and palming my ass.

"Seeing the mountains," I reply breathily as his hand continues to knead my ass cheek. I bite back a moan when his long fingers graze my inner thigh, and I try to keep myself from fucking him in the backseat of the town car; somehow having his driver as an audience doesn't really appeal to me. "And skiing. Absolutely everything about this trip is going to be great."

For the rest of the ride to the airport, Greyston and I canoodle in the backseat. We don't get any farther than a little over-the-clothes groping, which can only bode well for what I hope to happen soon enough. When we arrive at the airport, Greyston quickly adjusts himself before we step out and collect our bags from the driver. Inside, we print our tickets and check our suitcases before heading to security.

The entire time we wait to go through the metal detectors, I'm worried about those random searches where they pull you into a private room. I know it's just a precaution, but I still don't want it to happen to me.

"Next!"

I breathe a sigh of relief when I realize I'm being called forward through the metal detector…and in the opposite direction of that private room. I remove my shoes and put them in the bin with my carry-on before stepping through. Silence is heard as I make it to the other side, and I collect my things as Greyston is called next. With both of us clear, we head for our gate, grabbing a coffee along the way. By the time we arrive, we've still got a thirty-minute wait. I'm growing terribly anxious, but only because I'm just so excited.

"How long is the flight?" I ask, sipping my coffee.

"Three hours."

I nod once. "That's pretty good. What are we doing when we get there?"

"Well, we'll pick up the car and then drive to the cabin to unload our luggage. After that...well, we can go skiing, check out downtown Whistler...whatever you want."

Smirking, I turn to him. "Anything?"

He leans forward and brushes his nose over mine, his lips barely touching down on mine. "Absolutely anything."

"Good," I whisper. "Because I have big plans for this week."

Even though we're in the middle of the airport, Greyston closes the gap between us and presses his lips to mine. It's definitely not the most passionate kiss we've ever shared, but it's enough to get my libido going.

My phone buzzes in my pocket, and I groan, ending the kiss. "Sorry," I grumble, reaching for it and looking at the screen. I smile again before answering. "Hey, Mom."

"Hi, sweetheart. I just wanted to call and wish you both a safe flight."

"Thanks. I'll be sure to call you when we get there, okay?"

"I'd appreciate that."

I can hear the worry in her voice, and I have to remind myself that this is the first time I've been so far from home without either of my parents. Up until recently, I was their only child, so it would only be normal that she'd be a little uneasy.

"Do me a favor while we're gone, though?" I implore.

"Sure."

"Take it easy, and try not to worry too much?" She laughs lightly, probably in an attempt to throw me off.

There's a brief pause between us as I wait for her response, but she finally speaks up. "Okay," she says. "I promise."

"Thanks." Suddenly, there's an announcement coming over the intercom for pre-boarding passengers. "Our plane's about to board now, Mom, so I'll talk to you in a few hours, okay? I love you. Tell Dad the same?"

"Of course. I love you, too, honey."

After hanging up, Greyston and I start to grab our belongings and head for the gate while the few pre-boarders disappear behind the doors past the attendants. My anticipation mounts with every step we take. I'm practically vibrating when I hand my ticket to the female attendant.

Greyston and I find our seats easily, and he's kind enough to take my carry-on and put it in the overhead compartment for me. I stand back and wait for him to slide in next to the window, but he shakes his head. "Actually," he begins, "you can take the window. I tend to get slight vertigo if I catch a glimpse at how high we are."

Learning this about him shocks me. "Really?"

He runs his fingers through his hair, his expression adorably nervous. "Yeah. It's ridiculous considering how much I fly every year. I only booked the window seat because I figured you might enjoy the view of the mountains as we fly over them."

"That's so sweet," I assure him, popping up on my toes and kissing him lightly. "Thank you."

We take our seats and fasten our seatbelts as we wait for everyone else to get situated. Out of respect for Greyston, I close the window for now, and he smiles in response before kissing my temple and placing his hand on my thigh, just below the hemline of my skirt. His thumb moves back and forth over the skin above my knee, and I loop my arm through his and rest my head on his shoulder. His scent surrounds me, and I sigh in contentment.

Soon enough, after everyone has found their seats and the flight attendants have delivered their safety spiel, the plane pulls away from the gate and taxis down the runway. As we ascend, I think quietly to myself, and I realize that, while I thought I loved Ben, I was never truly content with him the way I am with Greyston. Ben and I had good times, don't get me wrong—this observation isn't based on our final weeks, mind you—but even with all the good in our relationship, nothing ever felt like it was *right*. I never once envisioned a future with him. I didn't imagine what it would be like to live together, to get engaged and married—to have *kids*—and while I haven't really thought about Greyston and I getting married—until now, anyway—I have thought about a future with him.

"You're awfully quiet, sweetheart," Greyston murmurs against the top of my head. "Penny for your thoughts?"

"Keep your money," I quip, tilting my head up to meet his gaze. "I was just taking a trip down memory lane, realizing for the first time that I've never been this happy before." I pause as he presses his lips to my forehead. "I used to complain for the longest time that my parents were more than a little inappropriate, but, now that *I'm* happy, I see now just how in love they still are—and that's rare to find nowadays. I want us to have what they have."

Greyston's eyebrows rise. "A baby?"

I laugh, unable to control the volume. "No," I assure him, and then I shrug a little. "At least…not any time soon." This doesn't seem to cause him further panic, so I relax.

"I want to be as happy as I am right now, but twenty years from now…and longer."

He still seems a little stunned…but not afraid. No, definitely not afraid. "Y-you think about that kind of thing? With me?"

Now it's my turn to be both a little freaked out and stunned, and when I speak, it comes out a strangled whisper. "You don't?"

Immediately, his features soften, and he turns in his seat as much as possible. "Oh, no, I *do*, I just didn't think you did because…well, you're so young. While I'd hoped you would—" He stops himself, shaking his head. "It's just, I wasn't sure you wanted…*shit*. No, that's not right, either." I smirk, trying really hard to keep it from becoming a huge smile. It's nice to see him flustered for a change, but I don't let him suffer too long before I rescue him.

"Well, I think about it…actually, I've *been* thinking about it a lot more since Christmas, if I'm being entirely honest. I may be young, but I know what I want, and I want you. Always."

His eyes reflect his happiness as well as his desire, and he leans in, pressing our foreheads together. "You just had to say all of this on the airplane, didn't you? I can't even begin to tell you what hearing all of that is doing to me."

Smiling, I decide that now is as good a time as any to officially start our vacation. "I know this is only slightly off topic," I begin quietly, "but I was wondering if you could help me out with something." Greyston regards me with quiet curiosity, and I continue. "I've been looking to acquire a membership into a very exclusive club."

"You're pledging a sorority?" he asks, clearly not picking up on my suggestive undertones. "I don't understand how I'm going to be able to help you with that."

Slowly, and without breaking eye contact, I unbuckle my seatbelt—now that it's safe, of course—and lean closer, letting my lips brush his. "Not that kind of club." His eyes widen with realization, and I smile triumphantly. "You interested?"

He looks around the cabin of the plane; it's not overly crowded, but it is over half-full. "I don't know…"

"Wait a minute." I pause and watch as he turns back to look at me. "Are you telling me you've never…?"

"It's an *airplane,* Juliette," he says as if that's reason enough to not have sex on it.

"Yeah, and?" I counter, feeling pretty satisfied in myself for suggesting something even *he's* never done. Suddenly empowered, I stand up and begin to exit our row, facing him and putting his face directly in line with my lower half. "New experiences, remember?"

Before heading to the washroom, I lean down and kiss his cheek, lingering long enough to whisper in his ear. "I'll wait five minutes. If you don't show up, that's fine. We can wait until we're in Whistler. I just thought this could be fun."

I head to the washroom and close the door before checking my watch. My heart pounds as I attempt to pace around the tiny space, and the longer I wait—even though it's only been less than a minute, I begin to wonder if I should abort this mission before Greyston has a chance to decide. It's pretty risky, after all, and as I take a look around, I can tell that this will probably be pretty diff—

A light knock on the door jars me from my apprehension, and before I can open it a crack to see who it is, the door quickly opens and Greyston joins me in the tight space. The look in his eyes is absolutely wild with desire. He doesn't allow me the opportunity to say anything before he flips the lock on the door and pulls me into his arms, crushing his lips to mine as he backs me against the countertop.

Any thoughts I previously had about this maybe being one of my worst ideas I've ever had immediately dissipate when he palms my ass and lifts me onto the counter. My hands work furiously to unbutton his shirt as his tongue sweeps over my lower lip, and I moan softly, pushing the shirt down his shoulders a little because I know that we don't have the luxury—or the time—to get completely naked here. I let my hands roam freely over his muscular chest before moving down to his belt. As I undo it and his jeans, he slides his hands up my thighs and grips the thin sides of my thong. Slowly, he slides it as far down as he can before he has to take a step back to remove them entirely, and I open my eyes just in time to see him slip the scrap of fabric into his pocket.

He smirks devilishly. "Figured I needed some kind of souvenir to mark our initiation."

"Smart man," I tell him, reaching out and grabbing his open belt. "Now get back here."

Not wasting another minute, Greyston steps forward, and my legs part, forcing my skirt a few inches up my thighs. I can feel the bulge of his erection behind his jeans when he presses against me, and I work quickly to undo his pants.

Warmth rolls over me as his strong hands move up the outside of my thighs, and I release a soft moan when he curls his fingers and drags his nails back down them lightly. I'm just about to beg him to fuck me when, out of nowhere, the plane rocks. My hands fly out to support myself against either wall, while Greyston's hands clamp down on my legs. We both laugh nervously. Thankfully, it passes soon enough, and we quickly resume our heated make-out session.

He struggles a minute to push my skirt a little farther up, so I lift myself up to assist him, and his hands take the opportunity to roam over my ass, freezing the instant he grazes the naked flesh between my legs. I hold my breath and wait for his reaction; I had been so caught up in the sensation of his hands on me—and just how delightfully *bad* we were being—that I forgot about my last minute decision at the mall yesterday. He drops his eyes and takes a very small step away, his back hitting the wall as his right hand moves up over my thigh and between my legs to explore the newly bare flesh there.

"What did you *do*?"

Based on his question alone, I suddenly find myself a little nervous that he doesn't like it, but as his hand continues to move back and forth, his fingers slipping between my folds and gliding with ease over my sensitive flesh, I'm reassured. "Do you like it?" I ask him, breathing heavily as he eases his fingers into me with a guttural groan and lowers his lips to my neck. I throw my arms around his shoulders, holding him in place, and rock my hips against his hand. "I'll take that as a yes."

His free hand comes up and lifts my shirt, tugging the cup of my bra aside so he can palm my breast. "Greyston," I gasp when he curls his fingers inside of me and finds that hidden spot that pushes me closer to the edge of release. Needing more, I slip my hands between us again and push his pants down over his ass, carefully working them over his erection. I dig the condom from the pocket of my skirt and hand it to him.

Understanding, Greyston raises his head from my neck and removes his fingers from between my thighs. He rolls the latex over his length, then pulls me to the very edge of the counter and lifts my right leg until my foot is flat against the wall behind him. Once I'm positioned, eases me back until my shoulders rest against the mirror behind me. Then he grips my hips firmly before slowly entering me as I bite back a groan, trying not to alert the flight attendants of our indiscretion.

"Jesus, Juliette, you're so fucking beautiful," he tells me, his eyes trained on the site of his cock disappearing inside of me.

Curious, I shift my weight and look down, wanting to see what he sees, and when I do, I cannot bring myself to look away. Watching him thrust in and out of me is the most erotic thing I've ever seen in my life, and I can feel my entire body tense in preparation of my climax.

"I'm...not..." Greyston growls between thrusts. "*Fuck!* I'm not going to last much longer."

A deep tingle begins to emanate throughout my entire body, and I fall back to the mirror, unable to hold myself upright anymore as I creep closer and closer to pure bliss. Greyston's right hand leaves my hip, moving up to grope my tit roughly before moving down my arm until he ensnares my wrist and lifts it above my head, holding it against the mirror. Then, his other hand leaves my body, going straight for my other wrist, and he guides it between us.

"Touch yourself," he commands, his hips moving a little less rhythmically as he watches.

Nodding, I let my index and middle fingers glide over my swollen clit; it's so sensitive that I have to bite my lip hard to keep from crying out. I watch Greyston's face as I pleasure myself, and he is focused raptly on our joining bodies, picking up the pace and racing toward his orgasm. His grunts and groans fill the small space, and I'm sure we can be heard, but I don't really give a shit as my fingers press harder and swirl faster over my tender flesh. Occasionally, they'll graze his length as he pulls out, and he's quick to slam back into me over and over again until his eyebrows pull together. His jaw clenches, and his hold on my wrist tightens as his hips stutter and jerk against me. It takes me a couple more passes over my clit before I'm coming, too, every muscle in my body contracting around him.

Smiling lazily, Greyston peppers kisses across my sternum before pressing them firmly against my lips. "Fuck that was hot," he growls, biting my lip. "Best fucking club I've ever been a part of."

Quicker than I should be in my post-orgasmic daze, I decide to play with his choice of words a little. "Been a part of many *fucking* clubs, Mr. Masters?"

He chuckles, pushing himself up and releasing my wrist from above my head so we can right our clothes. "Behave yourself."

Smiling mischievously as I tuck my breasts back into my bra and pull my shirt down, I shrug. "Little late for that, don't you think?"

He laughs quietly, helping me down from the counter and pushing my skirt back down my thighs. He quickly washes his hands while I clean myself up, and then I do the same. He listens at the door for a moment before opening it a crack and slipping out. I immediately lock the door to keep anyone else from coming in while I wait a few minutes before emerging as well. When I feel enough time has sufficiently passed, I open the door and head back to my seat. I try to ignore the way the flight attendant stares at me, but I feel like she knows what we were up to. I begin to panic, my heart racing and my breathing speeding up. I pass by her, and she doesn't say anything, so I breathe a sigh of relief and find Greyston in his seat.

As I pass in front of him, it doesn't escape my notice that his eyes linger in the general area of my zipper, and I can only imagine he's thinking about what I'm *not* wearing underneath.

Once I'm securely buckled next to him, I lean in. "Am I going to get them back?" I whisper, and he laughs.

"I told you they're a souvenir of my initiation."

"And where's mine?" I demand playfully.

He only smirks, leaning forward and grabbing the magazine from the seat back in front of him. "You check your neck?"

My eyes fly open, and I reach for my phone, turning camera on and flipping the view so I can see myself. When I do, I see the lovely quarter-sized hickey he left on me. "What are you, fifteen?" I ask with a laugh, trying to tug the low neckline of my shirt up to cover it. "Who does that?"

"Men who are in the moment and trying not to alert the staff that they're getting lucky in the washroom."

I think about this for a moment and decide his reasoning is solid. "Fair enough."

Two hours later, the announcement is made that we're flying over the mountains, and that our expected arrival in Vancouver will be within the hour. Greyston tells me to open the window, and when I do, I see the most breathtaking view of snow-capped mountaintops and the greenest trees I've ever seen.

"Wow," I breathe, fogging up the window. I watch for as long as possible, and when the view passes, I close the shade and relax back into my seat and anticipate our descent into British Columbia.

As promised, the plane is touching down on the tarmac within the hour, and we're making our way toward our gate. When the seatbelt light turns off, a chorus of *clicks* can be heard as everyone unfastens them and begins to gather their things. Greyston grabs our carry-on bags from the overhead compartment and we make our way for the front of the plane. As everyone before us exits, the attendants wish them a pleasant stay in Vancouver—or wherever their final destination may be—but when we reach them, they both smirk knowingly.

"On behalf of the airline, we hope that the two of you enjoyed your flight." My cheeks blaze hot, and I force a smile to my face, nodding nervously. "Enjoy your stay in B.C. Stay warm, you two."

The instant we're off the plane, Greyston and I burst into a fit of laughter and make our way to collect our luggage. If the rest of our vacation promises to be as great as the three-hour flight was, then I am more than ready for it to officially begin.

Plus, I still have a few special surprises up my sleeve for Greyston.

chapter 28

"So, what are we going to do first?" I ask, excitement zipping through my entire body.

Greyston glances outside, his forehead furrowing. "Well, first I'm going to suggest you change out of that skirt while I wait for the bags. I won't have you catching a cold on our vacation.

"Always so bossy," I quip, taking my carry-on from him and kissing his cheek. I scan the area we're in and quickly find the restrooms. "I'll be right out."

Once inside one of the stalls, I hang my bag on the hook on the inside of the door and remove my jeans. I drape them over the bag and remove my shoes, standing on top of them versus the germ-riddled washroom floor.

I slip my skirt off, remembering that I'm down a pair of underwear and didn't think to pack a backup. How was I to anticipate Greyston would keep them? Going commando in a pair of jeans isn't something I particularly want to do, but that's okay. Less to take off later, right?

I balance precariously on my shoes while I put my jeans on, trying not to think about what's on the floor just in case I might step on it. When I manage to get my pants on without any mishaps, I put my shoes back on and toss my skirt in my bag. I stop at the sink to wash my hands and fix my hair a little, then I'm on my way out to the luggage carousel where Greyston waits for our bags. He's just pulling them off the conveyor belt when I reach him.

Before he leads me out into the cold, I stop him so I can grab my jacket and boots out of my suitcase. We head over to a nearby bench where I exchange my Chucks for my new winter boots and pull on my winter jacket.

We step outside, and I stand on the edge of the sidewalk for a minute, looking at the ground and feeling a little cheated when I don't see any snow.

"I thought you said there'd be snow," I remark as Greyston places a hand on my back and urges me forward with a laugh.

"There will be when we get to Whistler," he assures me as we dodge a few puddles. "It rarely snows in Vancouver, actually. Don't worry. There'll be more than enough as we drive farther east."

I'm not sure where we're going at first until Greyston waves at a man across the street, standing next to a newer gold Lexus SUV.

"Mr. Masters," the man says, handing the keys to Greyston.

"Thanks for bringing the car, Jack," Greyston says, shaking the man's hand.

"Any time, Sir. Have a good stay, and let me know when to pick the car up after you drop it back off here."

"Will do. Drive safe, and say hi to Martha for me." Greyston raises a hand again to the car behind the Lexus. In the passenger seat is a kindly older woman who waves back. I'm probably right in assuming this is Martha.

Jack leaves as we load our bags into the back of the SUV. I'm still a bit perplexed, and Greyston must sense this.

"Mom and Dad own the Lexus. They called their year-round caretakers to drop it off here for our arrival," he explains, closing the back and wrapping an arm around me.

He'd said when we first met that his parents were comfortable financially, and I had seen evidence of this over the last few weeks as I'd gotten to know them. But this? A cabin in the Canadian Mountains? A luxury SUV that they only use when at the cabin? This seems to go beyond simply "comfortable." I'm starting to think they're filthy rich.

A cold wind picks up, and I grab onto Greyston's arm a

little tighter, sidling up to him to shield me from the wind as it cuts through my jeans. "Wow! Even though there's no snow, it's still unbelievably cold. I'm glad you suggested I change."

With a laugh, Greyston unlocks the SUV. "I wasn't joking. Though, if you find Vancouver cold, I'm a little afraid to take you to Whistler." I laugh nervously, half-hoping he's just kidding. Truthfully, I suspect he's not. "But don't worry, the car should warm up soon, and we'll be at the cabin before you know it... Actually, it's probably going to be quite a bit colder this evening, so we can just light a fire and stay in all night, if you'd prefer?"

Curious about what else he might have planned, I quirk an eyebrow. "As opposed to?"

Greyston shrugs non-committedly. "I hadn't really made plans for tonight. I figured we'd play it by ear."

I slip into the passenger seat and rub my hands together. "Staying in and lighting a fire sounds wonderfully warm," I tell him, trying not to let my teeth chatter too loudly.

Once he's behind the wheel, Greyston starts the car and turns on the heated leather seats. Within minutes, a blast of warmth moves through me, starting at my ass. It's both odd and amazing at the same time. I laugh in response, and Greyston turns to me, right eyebrow arched.

"It's stupid," I try to tell him, but he insists on knowing what I'm thinking. "I've never, um, *experienced* heated leather seats before." The warmth travels to my cheeks—then again, that could very well just be me blushing. "It's a strange feeling."

In an effort to pass the time on our drive to Whistler, I ask about the cabin and the resort we'll be skiing at, and then I ask what all he has planned while we're there. I'm about to argue with his plan of taking me out for a few drinks when he tells me that the legal age here is nineteen—*nineteen*.

I look at the clock on the dashboard and notice that an hour has passed since we left Vancouver. The gloomy clouds have cleared, a bluer sky and the sun having taken its place. Soon, there are heaps of snow along the side of the road, and I'm completely awestruck by the passing scenery as we draw near the mountains.

Another thirty minutes pass before I remember to call my mother to let her know our plane landed safely. She's happy to hear we're on our way to the cabin and reminds me to check in again in a few days and take tons of pictures. Before our conversation goes on too long, I promise to call Mom when we get to the cabin so my cell bill isn't hit with all sorts of roaming charges.

Greyston turns to me as I slip my phone back into my pocket. "Would you mind if we stopped at the grocery store before the cabin? We can always go out to a nice restaurant, if you'd rather we wait for tomorrow."

"Nah," I reply, looking out the window at the approaching mountains; they're breath-taking. "That's fine… It's so beautiful here. Cold, but beautiful. How long have you been coming out here?"

Greyston navigates the streets with ease, which makes sense since he's vacationed here since he was little. "I was ten when they bought the cabin," he answers my question. "They could see how much I loved it here over the first few years we'd vacation."

"When's the last time you came here as a family?" I ask, peeling my eyes away form the view and looking at him.

"It's been a while. I've been busy building the agency, so we haven't been able to coordinate our schedules." His smile falters, and his eyebrows pull together. "They're actually thinking of selling. It's one of the reasons I wanted to bring you before that happened."

His sadness fills the car, and I lay a hand on his lap. "I'm sorry."

Greyston shakes it off, smiling again. "It's just a part of life, I suppose."

We arrive at the store a little while later, and I cuddle up to Greyston as we walk through the lot. I clench my teeth to try to keep them from chattering, but it's no use, and now my jaw hurts.

Greyston wraps an arm around me, hugging me closer. "You'll adjust to the colder climate soon, sweetheart.

"I'm not too worried. Besides, you promised me a cozy

night by the fire, so…"

We walk through the market, aisle by aisle, filling our cart with the necessities we'll need for our week-long stay at the cabin. We grab plenty of fruits and vegetables, meats, and then a few extra things we don't *need,* but figure we may want if the mood strikes—chocolate, ice cream, and a few other various salty and sugary snacks. As we approach the checkout, I realize we've forgotten the milk. Naturally, Greyston offers to go get it while I begin to unload the cart, but I go instead.

I'm gone less than two minutes, and when I return, I find Greyston standing at the checkout…with his arms wrapped around another woman.

This isn't exactly how I imagined us kicking off our time away. What it *does* is reawaken the hurt and betrayal I felt when I found Ben exiting my dorm room after banging my roommate—amplified exponentially, given it's Greyston in some other woman's arms.

I feel like I've been punched in the gut, the heavy feeling spreading throughout my belly and then moving outward. I grip the milk jug tightly, my right hand shaking, and my eyes stinging. My chest tightens, making it hard for me to breathe, and I force myself to move forward, needing to know what the hell is going on, and I only just catch the tail end of whatever they're talking about.

"Well, I couldn't wait around for you my whole life, now could I?" she says, her voice soft and airy, almost melodic.

I blink back the burn in my eyes, clearing my throat to force them to acknowledge my presence. Greyston sees me first, smiling as though I didn't just catch him with his arms around another woman, and when she turns around, her bright green eyes catch mine.

She's gorgeous. Her light brown hair is filled with fine highlights and cut down to her shoulders, framing her slender face. She's about my height, and her smile is wide, showcasing a row of perfectly straight and white teeth.

Greyston reaches for my hand, pulling me to his side. I'm reluctant, my feet heavy like they've been cemented to the ground. He wraps an arm around me, easing the feeling of betrayal that continues to fester and build inside me, and he kisses my temple, taking down the first of several bricks from the wall I'm building to guard my heart from breaking into a million pieces. I can tell he's trying to assuage my fears that he isn't attracted to this woman. I feel pretty stupid for even thinking that he would look at another woman in that way—especially since he's always said how much he despises Ben for doing what he did to me.

"Juliette, this is Gemma."

"Hi." It's all I can say as I offer her a slight nod.

Gemma flashes that million-dollar smile again, reaching out and taking my hand in hers; even her nails are perfectly manicured, making me self-conscious. "Hi!" She turns toward Greyston, the look on her face almost admonishing. "I had no idea you were seeing someone!"

"It's still pretty new," I answer, no inflection whatsoever to my voice. "So, uh, how do the two of you know each other?"

"Greyston's my agent," Gemma offers up, and I feel my body relax slightly. I'm still a little tense due to feeling like an ass for assuming there was something deeper going on.

"Oh." I offer her the first genuine smile I can muster. "And what is it you do?"

"I snowboard." Gemma looks at Greyston again, green eyes sparkling. "In fact, if you guys want, I could hook you up with passes to the resort while you're in town." She reaches into her purse—designer, naturally—and pulls out a business card, handing it to Greyston. "I assume you're staying at the cabin while you're here?"

She's been to the cabin?

"We are," he responds without pause, voice remaining steady. I can't get a read on whether or not this is strictly a personal relationship, and I'm starting to wonder if my past with Ben hasn't made me a little suspicious. Okay, *a lot* suspicious. He hands the card to me, and I look at it: Gemma MacKay.

"Perfect. Give me a call, and maybe Dom and I can take you to dinner while you're in town." Gemma checks her watch, then holds her hand up. "Well, I have to get going, but

I'll hear from you guys soon?"

Greyston looks down at me for my input, and I don't want to seem like a fuddy-duddy when I don't really know what may or may not have happened between them years ago. I give him a nod, and Greyston smiles before responding. "Definitely."

Gemma saunters away, and Greyston and I pay for our food before heading back out to our vehicle. The more I think about it, the more stupid I feel. I only saw them hug. That doesn't mean anything, and I'm growing more and more sure that I've unknowingly let what Ben did affect the way I view all relationships now. While I didn't love Ben, what he did made it hard for me to trust certain situations.

Greyston suggests we head over to the liquor store for a few different kinds of wine, and I remain lost in thought, not sure if I should say anything or just let it go. Unfortunately, Greyston is more perceptive than I'd like, because once we're back in the vehicle and headed for the cabin, he places a hand on my lap, drawing my focus to him.

"I feel stupid," I tell him, dropping my eyes again. "I saw you with her—with Gemma—hugging her, and I jumped to the conclusion that the two of you had a romantic history. Especially when she made that comment about not being able to wait for you."

My fears are validated when Greyston doesn't say anything right away. "Oh." My thoughts start to get away from me again, wondering if this was the ex who made him choose between her and his job. If that's the case, then I don't have anything to worry about...but what if she's someone else entirely?

Greyston's hand slips over mine, his eyes remaining on the icy roads. "Juliette, it was so long ago, and we were both single and had been drinking." His thumb moves over the back of my hand, soothing away a small portion of my anxiety. But not all of it. "And it was only that one time. Gemma and I...we're *friends*. That's it."

Knowing that he and Gemma had some kind of a past—even if it was a one-time thing, fuelled solely by loneliness and alcohol—stung. I know he's got a past—so do I—but that doesn't mean I want to hear about it or meet his exes. The last thing I need is to picture them together and wonder if maybe seeing each other again will reignite the spark between them, leaving me in the lurch. While I want to believe Greyston would never do that to me, I can't help but let my thoughts wander in that direction, given my track record.

I nod, but I am still unable to say anything. It isn't long before Greyston pulls the SUV to a stop and puts it into park, turning to me. "Look, I'm twenty-seven—I have a history. While I'm sure you don't want to hear that I've been with other women, you know that I have been. The only thing you need to know is that my past is exactly that: my past." He reaches out and takes my other hand now and places his forefinger under my chin, drawing my eyes up to his. "I want *you*. Got it?"

I believe him when he tells me this. It's hard not to believe him when he speaks with an ironclad conviction that makes my knees tremble and my pulse race. And I do—believe him, that is. I care about him far more than I ever thought was possible, and, while I realize that we haven't known each other that long, I now understand what my mom meant about knowing the instant you meet "the one." Greyston is that for me. This isn't to say I'm ready to settle down and get married just yet—I'm still only twenty and beginning my life—but I see a future with Greyston if he's patient enough to wait for me to finish school and start my career.

I can't help the corners of my lips from curling upward slightly, and soon I'm smiling. "Yeah. I do."

I sense his relief as he leans in and kisses me. I can't stop myself from affirming my feelings for him by placing a hand on the back of his neck and holding him close. Greyston pulls back with a smile.

Laughing lightly, I rest my forehead to his. "Sorry for acting like a jealous freak. I don't want to be that girl, but after—"

He doesn't let me finish, shushing me and shaking his head. He places a hand along my jaw, his thumb stroking my cheek. "I know. I get it. Just believe that I would never do what he did to you, okay?"

"Okay." I sound a little more confident than before, even sitting up a little straighter. "So, uh, I guess we should keep heading to the cabin, huh?"

Greyston smirks and cuts the engine. "We're already here." He slips out of the car and rushes over to my side of the vehicle. I don't expect him to slip on the icy terrain in front of the SUV, especially considering he's no stranger to the ice and snow. I have to bite back a laugh, and I suddenly feel leery, because if *he* slips on it, then I'm basically screwed. I can barely walk on a good day; adding unfamiliar elements into the mix isn't going to bode well for my tailbone. Ice plus the uncoordinated is an equation for disaster.

He doesn't fall, thankfully, reaching my door a couple seconds later.

"Smooth," I tease when he pulls my door open, offering me a hand.

When my feet touch the ground, Greyston nudges my side and tickles me. "Let's just remember who's never skied before, shall we? This won't be a repeat of our paintball game a few weeks ago."

"We'll see," I add with a little giggle, trailing behind Greyston as we go to grab our bags.

As I step out of the car, I look up the small hill that the log cabin sits on and smile. It's even more amazing than the picture Greyston gave me. Stairs lead us up to a covered front deck where two sets of bay windows face east. While I have yet to see the inside, I can only imagine what it will be like to watch the sunrise in the mornings with a warm cup of coffee. The outer walls of the house are those of a traditional log cabin, and I instantly fall in love with the beauty of the home surrounded by fluffy white snow.

I sling my carry-on bag over my shoulder while Greyston carries both of our suitcases, and then he nods me toward the snowy path that leads to the front deck. The snow crunches beneath our feet as we approach the stairs. He sets his suitcase down and grabs the key from his pocket to unlock the door.

If the outside of the cabin impressed me, it really

shouldn't come as a surprise when I am rendered breathless upon stepping inside. I drop my bag suddenly, stepping farther into the room and looking around. The main construct of the building remains intact, with large solid wood beams supporting the upper floor, and a staircase to my left that leads upstairs, where I assume the bedrooms are located.

The main floor is completely open-concept, with the living room off to the right, well-lit by the two front windows that sit on either side of a large fireplace. The furniture is modern and plush, and I can tell that Greyston's mother has decorated it; she's got a certain style that seems to have carried over into her work on Greyston's place back in Phoenix as well. Just past the living room, beyond the couch and the table that sits behind it, is the kitchen and dining area. They are both awash in the light of the setting sun behind the house that streams in through the wall-to-wall windows there.

"Oh, wow. Greyston..." I begin to say, my voice soft and barely above a whisper.

The door closes softly behind me, and I hear the quiet *click* of the lock sliding into place before Greyston's arms wind around my waist and his lips touch down on the exposed skin of my neck. "Welcome to Whistler, sweetheart."

chapter 29

"This is..." I try to find the words to describe how I feel, but anything I think of seems lacking. "Well, it's incredible."

With his lips moving up and down my neck, he chuckles, sending a shiver through my body as he removes his arms from my waist and picks our luggage back up. "Come," he says. "Let me show you upstairs."

I grab my carry-on again and follow him up the stairs, my eyes still taking in the simplistic beauty of his home-away-from-home. Upstairs is no different: everything about the house structurally remains original with its visible wood beams supporting the roof and the older wooden window casings. There are two bedrooms toward the back of the house, a large bathroom along the north wall, and a third, slightly larger bedroom along the entire east wall. Upon further investigation, I can tell that the bathroom has been remodeled with a more modern vanity and tub, and the bedrooms have this cozy feel to all of them, made even more inviting by the large beds and thick, fluffy duvets.

Naturally, I assume the larger room is Greyston's parents', so when I begin to exit it with my bag, he stops me. "Where are you going?"

"Across the hall?" I reply questioningly.

"This is our room," he tells me, setting our bags down at the foot of the bed. "My parents let me have first pick when I was a kid, and naturally, I wanted the biggest room in the house," he explains, lifting his bag onto the bed and opening it to unpack. "Since they had the master suite back home, and we really only stayed here a few weeks a year, they let me keep it."

Greyston and I work on unpacking our bags quickly before retrieving the groceries from the already chilly SUV and putting them away. By the time everything is done, the sky has darkened a little more, and my stomach is growling. Smiling, Greyston hands me the telephone and leads me back to the living room.

"Why don't you call your parents, let them know we made it to the cabin, and I'll start on dinner?" he suggests, motioning for me to sit on the couch while he starts a fire in the fireplace and then lights a few candles on the coffee table in front of me. When he shoots me one of his sexy smirks, pairing it with an equally panty-wetting wink, I know he's got his own agenda for tonight.

After he's finished, he leans down and kisses me softly. "I'll bring you a glass of wine and then start on dinner. You just sit back and relax."

Greyston leaves me alone in the living room, the smell and crackle of the fire relaxing me even more than I already was, and I dial my parents' number. It rings twice before Dad answers.

"Hey, Dad," I say happily. "How's it going?"

"Pretty good, kiddo. How was your flight?"

I pause for a quick second, thinking about just how "good" the flight really was, and I smile. "It was great. Over before we knew it."

"And the drive to the cabin?" he asks, sounding excited to hear about my trip. "Greyston drove safely, I gather?"

Once a cop, always a cop. I laugh. "Yes, Daddy. We drove very carefully."

I talk to Dad a few minutes more before Greyston reappears with my wine and then retreats to the kitchen again to start dinner. I tell Dad all about the cabin and the weather before he tells me he has to let me go so he can get ready for work.

"Okay. Love you, Dad."

"Love you, too, Jules. Here's your mother," he says,

handing the phone off.

Mom and I talk for a bit while the air around me is infused with the smell of dinner. My stomach rumbles several times before I tell my mom that I should go help Geyston. After saying our goodbyes, I hang up the phone and set it on the end table, grabbing my half-full glass of wine and joining Greyston in the kitchen.

Making my way for the stove where Greyston is hard at work, I set the glass down on the counter next to his and wind my arms around his waist. I stretch up onto my tiptoes to peer over his shoulder at what he's cooking, but it's futile; he's too darn tall, so I settle for kissing the skin above the neckline of his sweater. He seems to appreciate this, because he groans and reaches behind him with one hand to run it over my hip and ass.

"Careful," he warns playfully. "Wouldn't want me to burn dinner because you've distracted me, now would you?" He turns his head to look at me, and I push my bottom lip out into a mock-pout. This makes him laugh as he pats my backside lightly and returns his attention to dinner.

When he declares the meal done, I help add the finishing touches before we plate the chicken, steamed vegetables, and potatoes and sit next to each other at the dining room table. Greyston lights a couple of tall pillared candles and refills our wine glasses before pulling the shades back from the window so we can watch the fresh snow falling from the sky. Once again, I'm rendered speechless as I watch the already-thick blanket of snow growing, and a big part of me can't wait to get outside tomorrow.

"I know I'm going to start sounding like a broken record," I say, reaching over and placing my hand over his, "but this is so amazing. Thank you again for such a wonderful gift. You really are perfect."

Greyston chuckles, giving my hand a squeeze. "While I appreciate that you think so, I'm far from perfect," he tries to tell me, even though I have yet to see one thing that would tell me otherwise.

"If you say so," I reply with an over-exaggerated eyeroll.

Dinner is phenomenal—which is no real surprise—and when we're finished eating and cleaning up the kitchen together, Greyston suggests we relax in front of the fire. Now, I had snuggling on the couch in mind, but Greyston's idea was, admittedly, much more romantic: he suggested we sit on the white faux-fur rug right in front of the fire with our wine while he showed me photos from past vacations. Originally, I thought it odd that there'd be pictures in their vacation home, but Greyston tells me that one of his favorite things to do as a kid before bed was to sit in front of the fire with his parents and a mug of hot cocoa and go through them. I've painted a sweet image in my head of a pint-sized, and very dark-haired, Greyston in his plaid flannel jammies, a hot chocolate moustache staining his upper lip, and a photo album nestled in his lap.

The temperature in the living room is rising, and I know that part of it is from being so close to the fireplace, but another factor is the proximity of my body to Greyston's. I'm sitting facing the fire, with my right leg bent out to the side and my left bent in front of me, my foot flat on the ground, and Greyston is sidled up to my left side, running his fingers through the lengths of my hair. I shiver every time his fingers ghost through the strands, and he leans forward to kiss the spot below my ear.

Smiling, I take another sip of my wine; I've had a few glasses now, and am beginning to feel the effects of it as it makes my limbs tingle and feel weightless. "You're distracting me," I tell him, flipping another page in the album that rests on the floor in front of me. "Tell me about this one."

Greyston laughs softly, rubbing his hand up and down my back as he peers at the picture I'm pointing at. In it, Greyston looks about ten, and he's outside, covered in snow, with the biggest smile I've ever seen plastered on his face. His brown hair peeks out from beneath his winter hat, and his eyes are alight with happiness and excitement.

"That would be from…oh, about eighteen years ago," he explains, scooting a little closer until his chest is pressed against my side. "We'd just gotten back from the resort, Mom was inside making some hot apple cider, and my dad and I were making a snowman out in the front yard." Greyston reaches behind him and grabs the bottle of wine, filling both of our glasses again. "One thing led to another, and before I knew it, a snowball fight had broken out." He laughs again as he recalls this memory. "Naturally, I excelled in sports at an early age."

"So modest," I tease, interrupting and nudging him lightly.

Laughing, Greyston shakes his head. "He didn't stand a chance."

I glance down at the picture again and smirk, tapping my finger on it and pointing out all the snow that covers him. "Looks like you might have gotten hit a few times, too."

Greyston scoffs, reaching over my leg and flipping to the next page. "I had to let him think he at least stood a chance."

"Oh, okay," I say, prodding him a little. "You tell yourself whatever you have to to help you sleep at night."

We go through the rest of the album, and Greyston tells me stories of his youth. Every story he tells me has me feeling closer to him than I ever thought possible, but it also makes me wish we'd met sooner. Of course, then I begin to think a bit more logically, and I realize that when he was nine, I'd have been two, and when he'd had his first real girlfriend at fifteen, I'd have been eight. This is not the recipe for romance, so I quickly derail that train of thought and thank the heavens that we met at this point in our lives—you know, when the age difference isn't quite so...well, gross.

"What about your childhood?" Greyston asks, setting the finished album aside.

"What about it?" I quip, finishing the last of my wine.

Smirking, Greyston slips one of his arms beneath my left leg, wraps the other around my waist, and pulls me onto his lap. "Well, where did you and your family go on vacations? What was your favorite thing to do?"

"Well," I begin, pushing a few strands of Greyston's slightly disheveled hair back off his forehead, "we used to spend a few weeks every summer in Florida. My mom loves the ocean, and we'd rent a house on the beach every year."

"Used to? Why don't you anymore?"

I shrug. "Time, I suppose. It's hard to coordinate our schedules during the summer."

"So what were your favorite things to do while in Florida?"

"Dad was pretty into boating, and while I wasn't particularly skilled at it, I enjoyed water skiing," I tell him, gaining a big smile from Greyston.

"Water skiing," he repeats. "So you are a little more adventurous than you've led me to believe."

I snicker. "I don't know about *adventurous,* but—"

Greyston's barking laughter interrupts me. "Oh, I think that the flight attendants would probably agree with me that you're a thrill-seeker."

Feeling the need to remind him that our initiation into the mile high club was just as much his adventurous side as it was mine, I open my mouth to speak, but he cuts me off, pressing his forehead to mine and curling his fingers into my lower back. "Honestly, it's one of the things I admire most about you. You're not easy to read like most other girls."

"You say that like you know what every other girl on the planet is thinking," I reply cockily.

"Most are terribly transparent." He sighs before ghosting his lips over mine, teasing me and making my longing for him swell. "But you…you're always keeping me on my toes, Juliette."

Greyston's hands continue to move over my back, slowly lifting my shirt and setting the entire surface of my skin ablaze. I hum, brushing my nose over his and teasing his lips with mine. "Well, I think I'd much rather have you on your back than on your toes right now."

"See," he says with a breathy chuckle as he slips his hands beneath my sweater and removes it, "always surprising me."

I make quick work of the buttons on his shirt, push it off his shoulders, and throw it behind me—careful to avoid the fireplace. Our lips crash together in a frenzy of lust and need as Greyston's hands move down my body and come to rest between my legs. He strokes the inner seam of my jeans, making me whimper and writhe against him, before popping the button and slipping his hand behind the denim.

He hisses when he comes into contact with my bare skin, pulling his lips from mine and looking deep into my eyes. "I can't believe I almost forgot about this," he says, his voice low and raspy with desire as he moves his fingers back and forth over the smooth skin. When he moves his hand again, my eyes close, and I moan in appreciation. "We were so rushed earlier that I think I need to take things a little slower—appreciate your little surprise for me properly."

"Yes," I pant, "*please.*"

Seeming a little reluctant at first, Greyston removes his hand from my jeans and lays me down on the floor. He positions himself between my legs and hooks his fingers into the waist of my pants, working them down my thighs. Once he reaches my knees, I lift my legs straight in the air, and he pulls my jeans off the rest of the way, taking my socks with them as he sets them off to the side with our shirts. The warmth of the fire washes over my naked body as Greyston slips his own jeans off and kneels before me in his boxers, running his hands up the smooth flesh of my calves.

My fingers twitch with the urge to grab his wrists, pull him down onto me, and wrap my legs around him...but before I can follow through, he leans forward and kisses my abdomen, making my stomach flutter as he slowly works his way south.

"Oh, god," I breathe, lifting my head to watch as he kisses and nips at my hip bones before focusing solely on the warm, needy flesh between my legs. My pulse begins to race, my hands curling into the soft rug beneath me, and I'm no longer able to keep my head up the second he flicks his tongue over my clit. Instinctively, my hips rise up off the floor, seeking even more pleasure, and Greyston grips the tops of my thighs, holding me as still as possible while driving me completely insane with want.

The pressure of his tongue alternates between soft and firm, fast and slow, and I continue to shift my hips beneath him as much as possible as my orgasm builds. The rough stubble that's scattered along his chiseled jaw brushes against the sensitive skin of my inner thighs, sending a rush of arousal through my veins like electricity. My mind becomes muddled with every languid stroke of his tongue, and I'm seconds away from begging for him to take me. He crawls up my body and I feel his stiff erection—still hidden behind his boxers—against my very needy flesh.

His mouth meets mine in a searing kiss that renders me unable to think of anything other than how his lips feel, how I can taste nothing but wine and sex on his tongue, and how his hard cock keeps hitting me in almost all the right ways. Unable to take the waiting any more, I bring my legs up his body and attempt to work his boxers down with my toes; I'm unsuccessful, but he gets the hint, grabbing a condom. He breaks our kiss to roughly push his pants down his hips before putting the condom on and thrusting into me.

The sensation of him inside me makes us both cry out with fulfillment, and soon our hips are undulating in tandem as we both work toward our mutual release. Every time he thrusts his hips, the muscles in my body tense a little bit more, the coil tightens in the depths of my stomach, threatening to spring free at any moment.

"Jesus, Juliette," Greyston breathes against my lips, moving one of his hands down my body and gripping my ass hard, pulling me against him.

Soon enough, I'm lost in the moment, reveling in the way he feels moving above me, and how he holds my gaze. My climax quickly builds back up to where it was only moments before, and just as the first ripple of pleasure passes through me, Greyston's hand ventures further until he's very gently massaging the area just below our joined bodies.

"Oh, god!" I cry out, my back arching up off the ground when my orgasm rips through me. I claw at Greyston's back, his hips jerking through his own release, and my vision goes slightly dark and cloudy as every muscle in my body tenses and then relaxes. My arms and legs tremble as they fall back to the floor, and Greyston rolls off of me and onto his back, but pulls me against him while we try to catch our breath.

chapter 30

It isn't surprising that I fell asleep so easily the night before. Sure, the flight wasn't overly long, but I was just so relaxed after dinner and a few glasses of wine—not to mention having worn ourselves out having sex in front of the fire. It was the perfect first night here.

There's a bit of a chill in the air when I first wake up, but instead of getting out of bed to turn up the heat, I scoot back on the bed until I feel the warmth of Greyston's body against my own. When my feet touch his, he groans and jerks them back.

"Your feet are freezing," he croaks, draping his arm over me and pulling me closer while avoiding my feet. He gives it a few seconds before tucking his flannel-clad legs and bare feet against mine. "I can go turn up the heat, if you want."

I hum contemplatively. "I think you're doing a bang-up job of that right now."

Greyston chuckles, kissing my neck and tugging the blanket up over our shoulders. "Why, Miss Foster, are you trying to seduce me?"

"No," I say with a laugh. "I'm trying not to freeze to death."

Greyston sees my playfulness as a reason to retaliate, and soon, he's tickling me relentlessly until I'm thrashing beneath the thick comforter and howling with laughter. Moments later, the blanket is down by our feet, completely defeating its purpose, and I roll off the bed and away from

Greyston.

Unlike in Phoenix, I'm dressed in flannel pajamas. I contemplated wearing one of my new pieces of lingerie for Greyston last night, but it was quite a bit chillier in our room than it was in front of the fire, so I decided to save it for tonight.

"So, what's the plan?" I ask, picking out a pair of jeans and a white turtleneck sweater.

Greyston makes the bed while I get dressed, but his focus isn't solely on the bed. I don't fail to notice that his eyes are on me the entire time I'm changing. If the look in his eyes didn't turn me on so damn much, I'd probably find it a little creepy. Okay, no I wouldn't.

"Well," he begins, "we'll go to the ski resort today and get in some time on the slopes and then maybe go for dinner tonight."

I pull my sweater on and nod. "Cool." It suddenly occurs to me that I'll likely be on the beginner hill for the entire day while I learn. "You're not going to waste your mad skills babysitting me on the kiddie hill, are you?" Greyston regards me curiously. "I just don't want you to feel obligated to stay with me all day. You shouldn't have to miss out because I've never done this before."

Laughing, Greyston tosses our pillows into place and walks over to me. "I won't be missing out," he assures me. "We've got all week, and I'm confident you'll do just fine and will be itching to hit the more advanced trails soon enough. I'd prefer to make sure you're comfortable on them before allowing that to happen."

After Greyston dresses in jeans and a blue sweater, we head downstairs for breakfast. While I start cooking, Greyston calls Gemma to see if she can still get us passes to the resort. It still stings to know that the two of them have a history, but I believe wholeheartedly that Greyston would never betray me the way Ben did. Of course, this doesn't stop me from eavesdropping on his end of the conversation.

"So you'll be there in an hour?" There's a pause while Gemma says something. "Cool… I've got my equipment stored here, so I won't need rentals… No. Mom's skis are here, too… Oh, right. Actually, let me ask her." I look up from the cooking bacon and turn toward the island where Greyston is sitting. "I forgot to ask, but do you want to ski or board?"

"Ummm…" I'd never really given it much thought, actually. I probably should have.

"My mom's skis are here, but if you wanted to board, Gemma's got an extra one you can borrow. You're about the same height, so it'd be fine."

I think about my options for a minute, trying to figure out what might be easier, and I'm honestly not sure. If either of them are anything like water-skiing or wake-boarding, I'd probably have to go with wake-boarding, because I had a nasty habit of getting my water skis crossed and wiping out. Yeah, it's probably a smarter choice.

"I think I want to snowboard?" I tell him, sounding a little unsure before I nod resolutely. "Yes. Definitely snowboard." Smiling, Greyston relays the information to Gemma and tells her we'll be heading to the resort after breakfast.

By the time he hangs up the phone, the bacon and eggs are done, and I take them to the small table in the kitchen where Greyston joins me. While we eat, I ask questions about snowboarding: how to distribute my weight, what to expect…you know, things that will help keep me off my ass. Greyston answers as many questions as he can, but he assures me that there's only so much that he can tell me that'll actually help me. Apparently being thrown right in is the best way to learn. Awesome. I'll be on my ass in half a second flat.

After cleaning the kitchen, Greyston grabs his gear and runs out to the car, starting it to warm it up. I'm just about to put my jacket and boots on when he stops me. "Before you put your boots on, we should determine your lead foot."

"My what?"

"The foot you'll lead with on the board," he clarifies.

I shrug. "Well, I'm right-handed, so…"

Greyston chuckles. "That doesn't always determine your dominant foot for boarding."

I nod. "Oh, okay. How do I do that?"

"It's going to sound a little strange, but one way is to run across the floor and slide. Whichever foot you put in front is usually your lead foot."

This sounds like it has the potential for injury. "What other ways are there?"

He smirks. "Well, that was really the best and nicest way." He tries to suppress a chuckle, but fails miserably. "I could do to you what I did to Toby…"

"Which was?" I inquire with an arched brow.

"I stood behind him and pushed him. He stepped out with his left foot, and that turned out to be his lead foot," he explains.

This sounds even more dangerous than the other way. My reflexes are usually a little slow, so I'd likely land on my face because my legs would fail to react in a situation like that. "Okay. First of all," I begin, smiling, "that's just mean. Second, I hope you've got video of that somewhere. And third, I'll take option one."

"I figured you might. Besides, I wouldn't be able to bring myself to push you anyway," he tells me with a wink.

Feeling a little nervous—because I'm sure I'm about to wipe out and make a total ass out of myself—I cross the room, telling myself that as long as I don't have to slide a long distance, I should be fine. Sadly, I know that what I want to do and what's actually going to happen are going to be two totally different things. This is going to be interesting.

I take a deep breath and hold it as I take a few quick strides across the hardwood floor and then turn to the side. My right foot taking the lead as I slide toward Greyston. I'm pleasantly surprised when I stay on my feet and don't stumble at all. A small victory—yet one still worthy of celebrating—for sure.

"Okay. Right foot it is," Greyston declares, holding my jacket open for me to put on. "I always knew you were a little goofy."

My jaw drops. I'm not sure what to think or how to defend myself, not that I'm given the chance, because Greyston leans forward and kisses my cheek. "It's a term used for those whose lead foot is their right."

"Well, it's a horrible term," I argue somewhat childishly,

zipping my jacket up. "What foot do you lead with?"

"My left."

"So, if I'm *goofy*, then what the hell are you?" I ask, truly curious.

Greyston shrugs. "Leading with your left is considered regular. But that's not to say that any one way is more normal than the other. It's no different than being right- or left-handed. They just have odd terminology for it."

Accepting Greyston's explanation, I slip my boots on before grabbing my ski pants, mittens, and knitted hat, and we head out to the car. The cold air shocks me, rendering me momentarily breathless when I inhale. I can't get to the car fast enough as the cool air cuts through my jeans and nips at my bare face. Greyston treats it as though it's no big deal, which makes me feel like a total wuss.

"You'll acclimate quickly," he assures me, opening my door for me. After I've settled in my seat, he closes it and gets behind the wheel.

My teeth are chattering slightly, and even though I'm already in the slightly warmer vehicle, I pull my hat and mittens on. "Are you telling me you're already used to this?"

Greyston laughs. "Not exactly, but I've experienced colder stays here when I was younger, so I know things could be worse." He reaches over and places a hand on my knee. "You'll warm up as soon as we get moving. Trust me."

We drive to the resort and park the car. Greyston and I grab our things and head into the main building to meet Gemma and Dom, only to find she's alone. She smiles widely upon spotting us.

"Oh, good, you're here." She hands me the board she's been holding. "Juliette, I brought this for you to use today. No sense shelling out money for a rental if you don't have to, right?"

"Definitely," I agree. "Thanks."

Greyston looks around. "Where's Dom? I thought he was joining us. I was looking forward to meeting him."

Gemma shrugs, rolling her eyes. "Oh, he had some stuff to do today around town. I'm hoping he'll be able to join us for dinner. I think you'll really like him." Something feels off, but the ring on her left finger tells me I'm being ridiculous.

After renting my boots and buying a pair of goggles, the three of us head outside. Gemma offers to come with Greyston and me to the beginner hill, but I decline. I don't need more witnesses to what's sure to go down on that hill—me, and not in the kinky sex way that I like. No. I imagine something straight out of a cartoon where I fall and roll so fast that I form a giant snowball. While I'm sure the chances of that are near impossible, there's a part of me that feels confident that if it's going to happen to anyone, it'll be me.

Gemma tells us to have fun, then heads off to the lift while Greyston and I put our ski pants and boarding boots on. Once we're ready, we head for the beginner hill, but before we hit the lift to take us up, Greyston kneels before me, taking my board and flipping it the right way around before asking me to step onto it. Turns out Gemma is "goofy" too, which makes me feel a little more confidant. Once my right foot is in the binding, he attaches what he calls "the leash," and explains that it'll prevent a runaway board in the event of a wipeout.

I laugh. "In the event of?" I parrot. "You realize that there's no question about it, right? I'm *going* to wipe out. Several times, in fact."

Chuckling, Greyston stands up and steps onto his board with his left foot, attaching his own leash to his boot, and then he demonstrates how to push off as though we're on skateboards, and we head toward the lift. I'm a little nervous waiting for the lift to approach, and I jump slightly when I feel it, but Greyston helps me out, and soon we're on our way to the top of the beginner hill.

Once we're clear of the lift, I follow Greyston. We stop at the top of the hill and he instructs me to sit down with my board perpendicular to the hill. Once I'm seated, he helps me put my other boot into its binding, and then he shows me how to make sure they're tight enough. My feet don't move within the bindings, and they're secure in my boots, so Greyston deems me ready to go and helps me up. After securing his other foot into his binding, he shows me how to apply pressure to my planted foot. He decides to practice this a few times in a stationary position at the top of the hill before we attempt to go down. Which is fine by me.

"Okay," he says, standing next to me. "You want to bend your knees and keep your back straight so that you feel balanced, okay?"

"Uh huh," I reply nervously, slowly doing as he instructs and being sure not to go down the hill just yet. "Like this?"

"Good," he says, "but make sure you're not leaning your body when applying pressure." He must recognize my confusion, so he elaborates. "Pretend you're squashing a bug under your foot."

"Ew," I declare quietly, but do as he suggests.

"That's it. Just like that. Now lean back a little...but not too much, or you'll wind up on your ass." He watches me, smiling wide. I feel unsteady, but I'm able to right myself before I fall. "Good. Good," he praises. "Alternating from heel to toe is called carving. It's a little more advanced, so we should just stick to riding your heel until you're confident on your board."

Beaming, I look up at Greyston, and he smiles back. "Okay, so we're going to try the hill." I nod, my heart hammering nervously. "Remember, I want you to ride your heel edge first, okay? It'll act kind of like a snowplow and give you a feel for the board going slow so you can get used to it. Think you can do that?"

I visualize it in my head, and try leaning back on my board a little to see what it might feel like. "Yeah. Let's do this."

Greyston leads us forward a little, and then turns to me. "Steady and slow, all right?" I nod. "And, for whatever reason, if you feel like you're about to bite it, lean back—not forward. It feels a hell of a lot better to fall on your ass than it does your face."

Visions of the giant snowball replay in my mind, and I agree. "Got it."

Greyston urges me to push off, and I do, going as slow as possible while he follows. He stays close, watching as I struggle to keep my board from pointing straight down the hill. Sure, it's a small hill, but I still don't want to fly down it.

That's sure to end with me smacking into a tree, the wall of a building, or another human being.

I'd like to say that my first run is wipeout-free, but it isn't. I fall flat on my ass about thirty seconds in when I zig instead of zag. Greyston's right there to help me back up, and while I'm embarrassed, his constant assurance that I'm doing well helps to boost my confidence a little each time. I realize that wiping out is normal, but it bruises my pride as much as it does my tailbone.

Every run down the hill gets a little easier, and I find I wipe out less and less…until Greyston suggests I try carving. I start off slow, leaning back on my heel like before, and then I lean forward the way Greyston showed me before we went down the hill the first time. I make a mistake by leaning too far forward, and when I feel myself starting to fall forward, I over-correct, leaning too far back and toppling over so hard one of my boots comes loose from its binding.

Snow flies up next to me as Greyston stops abruptly, showing off a little. He helps me reattach my board and then offers me a hand up so we can keep going. He's smiling from ear-to-ear, and, even though I've wiped out far more than I'd hoped, I have to admit that I'm having a blast. Even the cold isn't bothering me much anymore.

We stay on the beginner hill for another hour—way more than Greyston probably ever bargained for—before I tell him I want to try a bigger hill. I'm sure if I'd asked him a half hour ago, he'd have been hesitant, but considering I've had less than a handful of wipeouts in that time, he's pretty open to the idea. He's sure to only take me to a trail I can handle, which isn't much longer than this one, but it's got a few more obstacles and rough patches that throw me off. I fall, but I'm not discouraged at all, and I even wave off Greyston's offer to help me up, wanting to get back on my own feet.

I feel kind of guilty for keeping Greyston away from the more advanced trails, but I can tell he's trying to make the most of it by doing a few fancy moves and turns every so often. I make myself a promise that by the end of our trip, I'll be good enough to take on one of the bigger hills with him.

Even though I've fallen more on the intermediate hill than I did on the beginner one, I want to keep going, even when Greyston suggests a little break. It isn't until I realize it's almost two in the afternoon that I agree to it—but only if he promises to bring me back out after we grab a bite to eat.

"So, what do you think?" Greyston asks as we store our boards and head for the chalet. I don't realize just how cold it is outside until a warm blast of air hits me in the face upon walking through the door.

"It's fun!" I exclaim. "I'm having a blast."

Greyston smiles, taking my jacket from me when we reach the restaurant. "Good. You're doing amazing."

Greyston and I both order a mug of hot chocolate and a chicken club with fries. We enjoy a private lunch, but the entire time, I'm thinking about getting back out there. While I had an inkling that I'd enjoy the sport, I never imagined being this taken by it. Normally, I'm not the biggest fan of cold weather, but I realize I've never really given it a fair chance. Honestly, I love the way the cool air feels on my face as I go down the hill, how crisp it smells, and how soft the snow is beneath me.

After lunch, Greyston suggests a walk around the grounds for a bit before we hit the slopes again. We put our jackets on, and Greyston takes my hand, leading me from the building and toward one of the walking trails. It's warmed up a bit since this morning, and the cold wind has died down a little. There aren't many people on the trails, making it even more romantic with the frosted branches overhead and the shimmery flakes of snow blowing in the gentle breeze. It's almost magical, and I snuggle into Greyston's side as I take it all in, not even caring that my face is cold and my nose is threatening to run. Sure, not my sexiest moment, but I can't find it in myself to really care about that right now.

Well, not *much*.

I'm so lost in the perfection of the moment that I'm caught off guard when Greyston wraps his arms around my waist and pulls me to the ground. My playful cry of surprise turns to laughter, and Greyston props himself up on one arm to look down at me. My first thought is to seek revenge, but seeing the flecks of snow in his dark hair and the creases in the outer corners of his eyes has me overcome with desire.

Despite the fact that snow has found its way up the back of my jacket and is melting against the skin between my ski pants and upraised sweater, I lift my head, bringing one mitten-clad hand up to cup Greyston's face as I draw him closer to me. Despite the winter chill, Greyston's lips are soft and warm against my own. Our big puffy jackets and ski pants keep us from getting too close, and they seem to trap in the heat that radiates from every pore of my body.

Because I know there's only so far we can go here, I open my eyes to see his are still closed and reach out with my free hand to grab a handful of snow. Greyston is none-the-wiser as I slowly raise my arm and press my snow-filled palm to the back of his neck. His eyes snap open in shock, and my lips curl up into a smile against his before I burst out laughing.

"I can't believe you just did that," he admonishes, his eyes glinting with a plan for revenge that I don't recognize until it's too late, and my moment of triumph is short-lived when he grabs his own handful of snow and shoves it down the top of my jacket. I'm lucky to have chosen a turtle neck, because, had I worn any other sweater, there would be a lot more melting snow between my boobs instead of the tiny droplets that are currently seeping through the fabric.

I jump to my feet before he can realize this and rectify it, but it's too late; a full-out snowball war has begun. It really isn't fair, because I've never been particularly good with throwing things and hitting my target. Give me a gun, and I can shoot circles around anything—as well as hit the target, time and time again—but give me a ball of any size and material, and I'm a lost cause.

As luck may have it, however, I manage to get a few shots in, and after about twenty minutes of this, Greyston and I are both covered in snow. I'm laughing so hard my stomach hurts, and Greyston leads us back toward the hill.

"You want to hit the slopes again?" Greyston asks, wrapping an arm around me and holding me close while he leans down to kiss the top of my head. I quickly agree, and we head over to where we left our boards, strapping them on and make our way to the lifts.

"Hey, you two!" Gemma greets us, having just come off her latest run. "How are you guys doing?"

I smile. "Good, actually. I think I'm getting the hang of it."

"She's a natural," Greyston brags, and I roll my eyes.

"Oh yeah, I'm a real pro."

Gemma laughs. "Well, I'm going to pack it in within the hour," she says. "Do you guys want to go somewhere for dinner afterward?"

I look to Greyston, who's waiting for me to answer, so I nod. "Yeah, sure. That would be great."

The three of us continue on toward the lifts, talking about meeting in the chalet in an hour, and then go our separate ways. Like earlier, I'm far from perfect, and I wipe out a few times, but the more I practice, the better I get. Carving is still a bit of a challenge, but I am able to manage it for a couple of minutes before falling on my ass. Not that it's surprising, but Greyston's amazing, and I hate that he's probably bored out of his mind on this stupid intermediate trail while I make a total fool out of myself. He swears that he doesn't want to be anywhere else and that he's having fun teaching me, but I can't help but feel like I'm holding him back.

"Look, there's about twenty minutes left before we have to meet Gemma," I tell him when we reach the foot of the hill. "Why don't you go to one of the more experienced trails? I feel bad for keeping you on the baby hills all day."

Greyston laughs. "Sweetheart, it's fine. I really don't mind."

"Maybe not," I counter, removing my board from my feet. "But I do. Go. Have fun."

"What about you?"

I shrug. "My legs are actually a little sore. I'll go inside and wait for you guys. Maybe grab a cup of hot chocolate or something."

"You're sure?" he asks, and I nod. "All right. I won't be long." And, with that, he kisses me on the cheek and heads back toward the lift while I head inside the chalet and order another mug of hot chocolate. I remove my ski pants and jacket, draping them over one of the plush chairs near the fire, and I sit down and let my drink and the fire warm me up a little.

By the time I'm done my hot chocolate, Greyston shows up with Gemma in tow. They've got their gear packed up and are laughing about something that happened on their last run. It makes me a little jealous that I wasn't there to experience it, but I get over it when I remember what a good sport Greyston has been all day while teaching me.

The muscles in my thighs are tight when I stand up, and I know that tomorrow isn't going to be good. Even though it didn't feel like it at all as the day went on, I know I've overworked them, and I'm going to be walking funny because of it. It sucks, because I really wanted to come back out here tomorrow—and every day of our stay here if possible—but now it might not even happen, unless I can find a way to get the muscles to relax.

Greyston picks up on it as I make my way toward them, and he eyes me curiously.

"My thighs are a little sore," I explain. "No big."

"You sure?"

I nod. "Yeah. So, where are we going for dinner?"

"Actually," Gemma says excitedly, "there's this great little restaurant in the heart of downtown. The food is to die for."

"Cool," I reply, trying to keep from letting my suspicious nature win. "We'll see you there, then. Is Dom meeting us there?" I inquire warmly.

Gemma offers a tight-lipped smile. "Mmm, probably not. He's still held up."

Gemma grabs all her gear, including the board she loaned me, and heads to her vehicle, while Greyston and I go to ours. We follow Gemma out of the resort parking lot and into town center where she pulls up to the quaint little restaurant, and then we meet her inside.

Our hostess seats us and tells us that our server will be with us in a minute. While we wait, we peruse the menus and talk about our day. Greyston goes on and on about how well I've done, and while I'm pretty proud of all that I'd learned, I think he might be over-exaggerating just a smidge.

Before I can tell him this, our server shows up to take our drink order. I'm just about to order an iced tea, when Greyston pipes up. "Can we get a bottle of cab sav and three glasses please?"

The server looks at Greyston, then Gemma, and finally me. Arching a brow, he says, "ID, please?"

My face heats up, and I look away, feeling embarrassed that Greyston tried to be sneaky and order me alcohol and we were caught anyway. "Oh, I actually don't think I have it on me," I lie. "Don't worry about i—"

Greyston places a hand on my thigh. "Sweetheart, the legal drinking age here is nineteen, remember?"

Relieved and somewhat excited, I reach into my pocket and grab my ID, handing it to the server. He looks it over, smiles at me, and hands it back. "All right. I'll be right back with that wine and give you all another minute or two with your menus."

The conversation between the three of us dies as we decide what to order, so by the time our server returns, we've all made up our minds. Gemma orders a steak dinner with a baked potato and seasonal vegetables, Greyston decides on a burger and fries, and I choose the rotisserie chicken with garlic-mashed potatoes and a side salad.

The ambiance of the restaurant is nice. It's a smaller place, probably family-owned, with dim overhead lighting and candles at every table. It's an intimate-looking place, and I feel like it should be weird that there are three of us at one table, but one look around tells me it's not that uncommon. There's a couple of families here, enjoying a night out with their kids, and several tables with what appears to be a couple groups of friends unwinding after a long day over a pitcher of beer.

"So, Juliette," Gemma speaks up, "how did you and Greyston meet?"

"Well, I was looking for a place to live after I left the dorms, and I happened across an ad in the paper," I explain.

Gemma looks a little confused, but Greyston interjects. "I'd placed it because I was looking for someone who'd rent the room and be there to watch the place whenever I'm out of town. You know how crazy my schedule can get," he tells her. "I'd never needed a roommate before because Kelli was always there when I wasn't."

"Ah, right," Gemma says, raising her wine glass to her lips and taking a small pull. "Almost forgot about her. You haven't had the pleasure, have you, Juliette?"

While I'd heard a little about Greyston's ex—mainly about her clinginess and ultimatums—I'd asked very little because I didn't want to know who came before me. Ignorance is bliss and all. I shake my head. "Um, no."

"Lucky girl. Let's hope it stays that way."

The conversation quickly steers away from Greyston's past girlfriends and back to how we wound up involved. Of course, Gemma finds our story hilarious—especially the part where I thought Greyston and Toby were a couple. The more I talk with Gemma, the more I like her. I feel silly for being jealous of Greyston's past with her, especially after hearing more about Dom. Curious, I ask about the wedding, and she tells me that they're only in the beginning stages of planning but that we should expect an invitation in the mail once they're ready to go out.

After dinner—which was absolutely amazing—Greyston and I say goodnight to Gemma and tell her we'll probably be at the resort again the next day. Gemma agrees to meet us there and offers to bring her board for me again, even saying I'm more than welcome to borrow it for the remainder of our trip.

As we walk out to our vehicle, I can tell that the wine has relaxed me just enough that my legs aren't as sore as they were earlier. They still feel pretty tight, and the muscles in my back and arms are starting to feel the same way. I'm not looking forward to what tomorrow is going to bring.

When we arrive back at the cabin, Greyston opens the front door and ushers me inside. After taking off our jackets and hanging them up, he turns up the heat and smiles. "Come on," he says, taking my hand and leading me for the stairs.

"Where are we going?" I ask.

"You're probably going to be sore tomorrow from boarding, so I thought a nice, warm bath and a massage might help relax your muscles enough that it won't be as bad," he explains.

Smiling, I follow him upstairs. "Just when I thought today couldn't get any better."

He leads me into the bathroom and starts the bath. As the room fills with warm fog, Greyston helps me out of my clothes, my back muscles protesting when I raise my arms to remove my shirt. Once I'm naked, Greyston follows suit and helps me into the tub first. I scoot forward so he can join me in the large tub, then he eases me back against him, rubbing my shoulders and then slipping a hand between us to massage the muscles in my lower back. I groan happily as some of the tension releases from my muscles, and Greyston kisses the back of my neck lightly.

"So, you had a good day?" he whispers against my skin, making it prickle.

"Mmm hmm," I hum, finding myself incapable of speaking due to how amazing the massage feels.

He continues to press soft kisses against my shoulder, his scruff tickling my skin while his hands knead my stiff muscles and relax me further. His hands wander around from my back, gripping my hips briefly before moving toward my legs. He's on a mission, and my body is responding accordingly—until the minute his hands make contact with my thighs. He doesn't even press very hard, but even the slightest touch has me wincing, and he recoils immediately, removing his lips from my shoulder at the same time.

Leaning forward, I bend my right leg slightly and try to work out the kink. "Sorry," I say, glancing back over my shoulder. "I guess I'm a little more sore than I thought."

"You have nothing to be sorry about," he assures me, rubbing the length of my back soothingly. "I should have had us pack it in earlier today."

"No." I shift my body so I'm almost fully facing him. "It was fun. I'm glad we stayed the entire day. I just guess we won't be going tomorrow like I'd hoped."

I'm scared he's going to be disappointed, but am pleasantly surprised to see nothing but understanding in his eyes. "It's fine. There's plenty more we can do while we wait for your muscles to recover."

I giggle, swatting his chest playfully. "While I would love nothing more than to participate in whatever naughty scenario your filthy little mind has conjured up," I begin, "would you be too broken up if I asked for a rain check?"

Smiling, he shakes his head. "You know, I don't *only* think about getting you naked." I give him a very pointed look that says *"yeah, right,"* and he chuckles, running his damp fingers through his hair. "Okay, so maybe ninety percent of my thought process revolves around your tits and ass, but for ten percent of my day, I'm thinking of other things."

"Like?" I challenge.

He pauses, giving this some serious thought. "Okay, so maybe it's slightly more than ninety percent of my thought process." My laugh echoes in the bathroom. "Seriously, though," he continues, slipping one hand around my back, the other tenderly beneath my legs, and pulling me back toward him. "The second I noticed your legs were bothering you, the only thought on my mind was taking care of you tonight. Sex was so far off my radar that it wasn't even registering."

"Really?"

He rests his forehead against mine. "Really."

Sighing, I bring my right hand up to cup his cheek. "Seriously, you're too good to be true. Most men would probably feel pretty put out by this. But not you. You're the perfect boyfriend."

Greyston exhales a nervous laugh. "Juliette, I've already told you I'm far from perfect."

"Well," I whisper, "I have yet to see the proof that you're not, so I find it hard to believe otherwise."

"You ready to get out?" he asks quietly, and I nod.

Greyston steps out of the tub first, wrapping a large towel around his waist before holding out his hands for mine and helping me out. He drapes a towel around my shoulders and runs his hands up and down my arms as he kisses me. "Come on." He nods toward the bedroom. "Let's go and get ready for bed."

On our way through the hall, I stop, suddenly remembering that I was going to surprise him with one of my new negligees tonight. He notices I'm not right behind him, and he turns around, eyeing me curiously. "Sweetheart? What's wrong?"

I scrunch my nose up, dissatisfied with this sucky turn of events. "I just realized that one of my surprises has been compromised by all of this."

Greyston's eyebrows lift, intrigued. "*Another* surprise? Do tell, Miss Foster," he urges. "Because if it's as good as the first..." His eyes travel down my towel-covered body, stopping at the shielded apex of my thighs before darting back up.

I shrug, a coy smile playing at my lips. "Can't. We still have a few more nights here. I'll just have to find a time to squeeze them in. Starting tomorrow, perhaps."

Snatching his pajama bottoms off the end of the bed, Greyston mock-pouts. "You're a tease."

Smirking, I grab my own pajamas, turn from him, and let my towel fall to the floor, giving him a full view of my backside. I can feel the heat of his stare on me, and I glance back at him. "Yeah, but you love it a little."

Laughing, Greyston flips the blankets back before rushing out of the room and adjusting the temperature once more while I finish changing. When he returns, we both crawl into bed, and Greyston draws me into his side, kissing the top of my head. "Goodnight, Juliette."

With a soft sigh, I curl my fingers into his t-shirt. "Goodnight."

While I'd had other things in mind regarding how to spend our evening, I have to admit that it really didn't turn out half bad. Greyston and I had a wonderful day full of firsts for me, and I couldn't wait to see what the rest of the vacation had in store for us.

chapter 31

Greyston lets me sleep in the next day, having decided the night before we were going to take it easy. I'm definitely warmer when I finally wake around noon, and it's not just because Greyston's body is wrapped around me, though it is a factor.

My thigh muscles are still pretty tight and sore, but the bath the night before helped. Greyston runs downstairs to grab me a glass of water and some ibuprofen before we hop in the shower. Now, normally, showering together usually leads to some pretty hot sex, but not today. My legs are too sore for that, unfortunately.

After we get dressed, we head down to the kitchen for lunch, and while we eat, Greyston suggests an afternoon stroll around the area. I'm told it's not too cold today, and he assures me the sun will help ease the bite of the winter air. It sounds like a wonderful afternoon, and after we're finished cleaning up, we put our jackets, boots, mittens, and hats on and head out. Greyston leads me down the trails around the cabin, and I'm, once again, left awestruck with the beauty of this winter wonderland. The way the frost-covered branches shimmer in the sunlight, the crunch of the crisp white snow, and the smell of the cool, Canadian air all add to the beauty. I understand why Greyston might be drawn here year after year—why anyone might be drawn here.

"I'm sorry I went overboard yesterday," I say, breaking the silence, my breath turning to fog in the cold air.

"It's fine. I should've been paying closer attention. Besides, we have another five nights to make up for it..." Greyston leans in, kissing me just below my ear. A shiver rushes through me, but it has nothing to do with the weather, and everything to do with Greyston. "And I plan to take full advantage of that fact."

I laugh. "I'm sure you do."

Greyston's attention is pulled from me as he reaches into his pocket and pulls out his phone. He glances at the call display before turning it off and placing it back in his pocket, ignoring whomever it is.

"Who was it?" I inquire, realizing after the fact that I'm being nosey.

"Gemma. She's probably just wondering if we're going to meet up at the resort today." He pauses, wrapping an arm around my shoulders, pulling me close, and pressing a kiss to the top of my head. "I'll call her when we get back home."

Inhaling deeply, I hug him around the waist as we walk, and I bask in the sound of him calling the cabin home. While it's not our home, it definitely feels like it could be.

We return to the cabin about an hour later, and I'm about to head into the house when Greyston stops me at the foot of the stairs. "Where are you going?"

"I thought we were going inside?" I said, pointing over my shoulder.

Greyston snickers, shaking his head. "It's snowman-building time, sweetheart. The snow is perfect for it today."

I hop off the bottom step, with a wide smile, excited because I've never made a snowman before. "Okay. Let's do this."

Greyston is adamant we attempt to build the biggest snowman we can, so while he rolls the bottom portion, I get started on the middle. We wind up using almost all of the snow in the front yard, brown pieces of dead grass peeking through what's left. It looks unappealing, but I'm assured it will be snowing by tonight, so the yard should be back to it's majestic winter wonderland by morning.

Placing the head on proves to be difficult since the first two pieces stand well over a foot or two taller than Greyston, but he finally succeeds before running inside to grab a few final touches—a hat, scarf, mittens, and a carrot—while I searched for rocks and sticks for the face and arms.

Once the arms are in place, I stand next to Greyston, wondering how we're going to apply the face and hat. I look over to find him crouching in the snow. "Hop on my shoulders. I'll give you a boost."

I'm nervous, but only because of my magnetism to disaster. Thankfully, Greyston is careful to keep me balanced while I affix the stones in place and put the hat on top of its head, then he lets me down, and we stand back to admire our creation.

"Hey." I turn to acknowledge Greyston. "Go stand by the snowman. I want a picture." I comply, skipping through the front yard and posing with our creation, and then we head inside for some hot apple cider.

"Have a seat," Greyston instructs, pulling an island stool out for me, then he rounds the island and gathers everything he'll need to make our cider. He puts the apple juice in a pot on the stove, and then comes over to the island to face me while he preps the rest. "How are your muscles?"

"Good, actually. There's still a little discomfort, but it's really not that bad." I lean on the counter to get a better look at him while he slices an orange and then cuts an apple in half, inserting cloves in a very precise manner through the skin. "Your mom teach you this?"

Nodding, he turns to add some brown sugar to the warming juice and giving it a stir. "Making apple cider with my mother as a child is one of my favorite memories. Her recipe is actually one of the best I've ever had.

"Smells good."

Greyston grabs the cutting board with all his fruit on it, and adds it to the pot, momentarily displacing the steam. He stands at the stove, stirring the cider, and the smell fills the air. Soon, he's pouring it into two mugs and nods toward the living room, mugs in-hand.

We settle onto the couch, and Greyston hands me my cider. I blow on it before taking a sip, and it's like tasting Heaven. "This is really good."

"Thank you," he replies humbly, taking a sip from his own mug. "So, I was thinking maybe we could go out and get you your own gear before going to the resort again." I raise an eyebrow, shocked and curious. "Or we can rent."

"But I thought…?"

"We shouldn't be spending our entire vacation with Gemma," he tells me.

I look down into my mug as it rests in my lap. "It's okay. I don't mind," I tell him softly, not even believing myself.

Greyston uses his forefinger beneath my chin to urge my eyes to his. "Yes you do. Even if just a little."

"Okay," I confess with a sigh. "Maybe I mind a little. It's not that she isn't lovely—she is—and I've been trying not to let things get awkward between us."

"I know. And I honestly never thought that we'd see her. Running into her was purely coincidental."

"I believe you," I assure him with a nod.

"This was supposed to be our time together, and I'm going to salvage the rest of our vacation starting right now. From this moment on, it's all about us."

Leaning forward, my smile widens, and I kiss Greyston gently. "Okay. As long as you realize it's not me making the demand." Knowing how his last relationship ended based on ultimatums, I want to make it clear that I will never do that to him.

He kisses me again. "Understood." Silence fills the room, and I watch as his lips curl up into a sly smirk. "So, you'll let me buy you new boarding equipment?"

"What?" I demand incredulously. "Oh no. I can't let you buy me equipment. This trip was more than enough."

Naturally, Greyston is prepared to negotiate. "You forget, all I had to pay for was the airfare, and it really wasn't that bad since I had some frequent flyer miles to cash in. But, if it makes you feel better, I'll let you pay me back. I just don't want to leave you without money to get by."

I feel like this is some kind of ploy, but I can't find the loophole, so I agree. "Okay. I'll let you pay for it now, but I'll pay you back." I meet his gaze and hold it. "Every penny."

If Greyston had a loophole in his deal for me to pay him

back, I'm hoping I've squashed it. It's doubtful, but I have to at least try. He takes a moment to contemplate this before he says, "You've got a deal. But take as long as you need. I really don't want you to be stressing about money, okay?"

I smile so wide my cheeks hurt. "You bet."

With it still being so early in the day, Greyston and I head into town to start looking at boarding gear. My legs are feeling better with every hour that passes, and I'm pretty excited about heading back to the resort the next day, and having my own gear would be awesome.

Greyston leads me straight toward the snowboarding equipment where he lets me pick through the various boards available. I take my time, trying to find a design I like, and while I do this, Greyston explains what I should be looking for.

"You need to take your ability level into account when choosing a board," he begins as I trail my fingers over a sleek black board with a bright blue design. "Because you'll want one more fitted to a beginner or intermediate skill level, this won't be your last board."

"Okay," I reply, moving onto the next one and taking everything he says into consideration; he is the more experienced boarder, after all.

"You'll want to look at the width of the board." I nod again. "Your board shouldn't be too much wider than your boots. If they extend over the edges too far, then you run the risk of them hitting the snow during hard turns, resulting in a wipeout."

"So I should pick boots first, right?" I shrug. "I mean, if sizing is anything like how regular shoe companies operate, then they could be different."

"You're exactly right."

Abandoning the boards for a moment, I try on several pairs of boots before I find a pair that fits comfortably, and then we revisit several boards I'm interested in. Upon further investigation, I notice that some of the boards have a slightly deeper curve to them, and that some curve up while others curve down or are flat. When I inquire about this, Greyston explains the different riding styles and how board length plays into that, too. He then tells me that I would be fine to look at any board suited to an All-Mountain style, and that it's what I borrowed from Gemma. Then he starts to explain the different board curves—or rockers, as they're apparently called.

"The ones that curve upward are *cambered* boards," he tells me, pulling a board out and showing me the upward bow. "It's the most traditional style of board, and is most popular because it will offer the most energy and pop. It has a smooth arch underfoot and touches near the tip and tail when unweighted. When the rider's weight is added, it will provide a long, evenly pressured running surface and edge."

He moves onto the next board. "This is a *rocker* board. These boards float well in powder and pivot more easily underfoot. They also tend to be less *hooky* at both the tip and tail, which makes them better for landing spin maneuvers when you can't get enough rotation."

My laugh travels through the store, drawing a few unexpected stares. "Well, I don't anticipate attempting any spin maneuvers, so we're probably safe to move on."

Grinning, Greyston grabs a flat board. "The flat board is pretty self-explanatory, being flat from tip to tail. This shape splits the difference between camber and rocker styles." I'm a little confused, but Greyston quickly clarifies. "Its turnability is more forgiving than a fully cambered board, and has more precise edging capabilities than a fully rockered one."

"Soooo…" I draw the word out longer than normal and laugh.

"You'll probably want to consider either a cambered board or a flat one," he gently suggests. "The cambered ones are the favored style."

I take everything Greyston has taught me into consideration before choosing the cambered style board. In the next hour or so, we go through the store so Greyston can help me locate the rest of the gear that I'll need, and then head to the checkout. I nearly choke on my tongue when the cashier tells Greyston the price. He hands her his credit card without hesitation, and she smiles at me as though who loves me so much. I balk at the thought, then begin to wonder if that might be true.

Sensing my shock, Greyston looks toward me. "No rush, sweetheart," he says, repeating his earlier words. "Take your time paying it back."

Outside, Greyston folds down the backseat of the rental to accommodate my new snowboard, and we head back to the cabin. My sticker-shock doesn't take long to fade as my excitement to try out my new gear takes its place.

"So, we're going back to the resort tomorrow, right?" I inquire hopefully.

Greyston doesn't take his eyes off the icy roads—and that's fine by me; I don't wish to be in an accident. "So long as you're feeling up to it. I don't want you to overdo it."

"I feel fine," I promise him.

He smiles. "Then I don't see why not."

When we return to the cabin, Greyston takes my board inside and stores it with his while I carry the rest of my gear. When our purchases are put away, we get a start on dinner, working together like a cohesive unit until our stew is put together and simmering in the pot.

Greyston's phone vibrates on the counter as a text comes in. One glance and I can see it's Gemma. Greyston looks before returning to our dinner prep instead of responding.

"Greyston, you can message her back. It's okay, really."

He just shakes his head. "It can wait." He grabs two wine glasses and fills them with a cab sav we tried the other night and enjoyed. "I want to spend tonight with just you. I'll get back to her in the morning."

"The fact that she's called a few times today suggests it could be urgent," I try to tell him, showing him how understanding I can be. His eyes meet mine, and I smile. "I get that you're trying to be the perfect boyfriend and not let anything interfere with our winter getaway, but you can take a phone call or two." I snatch his phone off the counter and hold it out to him. "In fact, I'm going to call Mom and Dad while dinner cooks, so why don't you take the opportunity to call Gemma back."

I take the phone and head to the living room to call my parents. There's no answer on the house phone, so I try my mom's cell after leaving a message, but it goes straight to voicemail, as does my dad's. I decide to call again in the morning, knowing full well they're probably...*too busy* to pick up, and I definitely don't want them to think this is an emergent situation.

Greyston joins me in the living room moments later, sitting next to me on the couch after setting the bottle of wine on the coffee table next to my almost-empty glass. "How are your parents?"

I shrug, snuggling into his side as he wraps his arm around me. "No answer. I didn't want to keep calling in case they were...busy." Greyston laughs. "Did you get a hold of Gemma?"

"I did." He takes a sip of his wine. "She wanted to know if we wanted to meet at the resort again tomorrow. I told her we were kind of hoping to spend some time alone."

A twinge of guilt seeps in, but at the same time, I'm happy. I don't like the idea that Greyston might feel obligated to avoid her just because I'm a little uncomfortable around her, knowing their past.

"I did, however, offer a compromise," he confesses nervously.

"Which was?"

"Dinner on our final night here." I turn my head to look up at him. "I'll make it an early dinner, and they'll only be here a couple hours."

"Okay," I respond. "As long as we'll still have plenty of alone time before we have to head back home." My stomach flops, knowing we won't be here much longer.

Greyston's lips touch down on the top of my head, and I feel them curve up into a smile. "Now," he mumbles into my hair. "Didn't you say something last night about a surprise for me?"

Biting my lip, I remember the lingerie still sitting, unused, in my suitcase, and I debate which one I should test out first.

chapter 32

As promised, Greyston takes me to the resort the next day. I'm extremely excited to use all of my new equipment—even if the price of it still shocks the hell out of me. If I hadn't fallen in love with the sport that first day, though, I'd think it was a bad investment, but I'm fairly certain that I'll get a lot of use out of it.

Well, only if Greyston and I come out here every year. Though, I suppose we'd have to rent a place, which sucks, because I've grown quite fond of this place.

Considering it's only my second day, I do better out on the slopes, and Greyston and I even hit a more intermediate trail. I fall down, of course, and I also hit a few sad excuses for jumps—they're really just tiny snowdrifts or packed down snow—that drop me flat on my ass when I can't land them. Given how small they are, it's humiliating, but all part of the learning curve. Unsurprisingly, Greyston makes it all look so effortless, and he assures me that I'm doing really well. I'm pretty sure he's just trying to make me feel better.

The next day, New Years Eve, Greyston has plans that he seems pretty excited about. Apparently there's a yearly celebration where families come out for music, crafts, food, dancing...and ice skating.

It shouldn't, but I'm a little surprised when I manage to do better with ice-skating than I did snowboarding. Now, I'm still not skating circles around him or anything—not many people are, to be honest—but I manage to hold my own, even though it's been well over ten years since I've been ice-skating in one of the indoor arenas that Phoenix has. While I'm obviously a little rusty, Greyston, naturally, excels at it. Jerk.

The chilly winter air only adds to the experience, and we're having a great time as the night wears on. Surprisingly, I've only almost fallen a couple of times—which my tailbone continuously thanks me for—and, after about thirty minutes, it starts to snow lightly. Everything about this night out—being with Greyston, the cool evening air, the snow falling almost whimsically, the music—is absolutely beautiful, and it's only made a little more perfect when the countdown begins and Greyston and I share our first kiss of the new year.

We're standing in the middle of the rink, surrounded by what feels like hundreds of people—some on the ice, others just off to the side—and everyone is counting down, waiting for the stroke of midnight. When the time comes, fireworks boom overhead, and Greyston turns me to face him, placing his gloved fingers beneath my chin and tilting my face up to his, but before capturing my lips, he smiles. "Happy New Year, sweetheart," he says as the fireworks continue to light up the night sky.

Stepping up onto the picks of my skates, I wrap my arms around his neck and smile. "Happy New Year," I reply. "I can't wait to see what the next year has in store for us."

He lowers his lips to mine. They're soft and warm, even with the winter chill in the air, and he kisses me with so much passion that it takes my breath away.

Breathing heavily as we break apart, I'm able to see our breath in the frigid night air. I lower back onto the blades of my skates, sliding back a little and losing my balance. Greyston's quick to steady me with a chuckle. "Come on," he says, tucking me into his side as we skate for the arena exit. "Let's head back to the cabin."

By the time we arrive, it's almost one in the morning, and Greyston suggests we head straight to bed since we have a lot to do tomorrow to prepare for our dinner with Gemma and her fiancé. Up in our room, I grab my pajamas and toss them on the end of the bed before I begin to undress. I've just grabbed the hem of my sweater when Greyston steps up behind me and covers my hands with his, taking over and pulling the soft fabric off my body.

I shiver when he pulls my hair from my neck, and I sigh when his lips touch down on the goosebump-riddled skin of my shoulder. Warmth blooms beneath my skin, pushing out any remnants of cold that remained only moments ago. Pleasure trickles through my body and down my limbs, making the tips of my fingers and toes tingle—at least, I hope it's the pleasure causing it and not the onset of frostbite. That would suck.

In the weeks that we've been together, we've had sex with wild abandon, opening my eyes to new experiences and the possibilities of our future together. We've also shared sweet, tender moments where I've never felt more special.

This is one of those times. We ring in the New Year with Greyston moving slowly above me. The way he looks at me is so intense that it moves me, his right hand trailing down my body, eyes following hungrily. He hooks his fingers behind my knee, hitching my leg up higher around his hips as he thrusts forward. His hand skims over the skin of my thigh, our hips slowly rolling in tandem as my release slowly builds. My eyes close, and my teeth tug on my bottom lip as I get completely lost in the passion that fills the room like fog.

I'm close…*so* close…

Then his hips slow, and when I open my eyes again, I see him staring at me once more. He cradles my face gently, urging my face toward his and molding his lips to mine. The kiss deepens quickly, our hips finding their previous rhythm, and my fingers curl into Greyston's back. My orgasm continues to coil, tightening in every part of my body with each forward thrust of Greyston's hips until it releases and I cry out against his lips. Any and all of my energy in my body shoots through the tips of my fingers and toes, my arms and legs trembling in the wake, and soon Greyston's body stiffens as he groans, his hands gripping me firmly through the final stages of his own climax.

He rests his head against my collarbone, his warm breath wafting over my damp skin, and sighs. A lazy smile spreads across my face, my hand trembling as I raise it from his back and run my tingling fingers through his soft hair. After a moment, our breathing regulates, and my legs stop shaking, making it easier to walk down the hall to the bathroom after getting off the bed.

It's late by the time Greyston and I are both back in bed, and he pulls me into his arms, my back resting against his chest. He holds me tight, pressing his lips to the base of my neck. "Goodnight, sweetheart," he whispers.

Sighing, I lace my fingers through his. "Goodnight," I reply softly.

I feel his lips curl up into a smile against my skin. "Let's get some sleep."

And, with that, I snuggle back into his embrace, close my eyes, and we fall asleep.

Everything is in order for our dinner party with Gemma and her fiancé. Greyston and I had spent the day cleaning the cabin while our roast cooked in the oven. By three in the afternoon, the smell that fills the air makes my stomach growl and my mouth water.

Because we'll be packing up and heading home the next day, we also worked to pack up most of the Christmas decorations so the caretaker wouldn't have to. I'm just reaching up to pull the mistletoe from the hook above the fireplace mantle when a pair of strong hand grabs me around the waist and spins me. I melt into Greyston with a moan of approval, letting his warm lips mold to mine.

I whimper when he pulls away, opening my eyes when the backs of his fingers stroke my cheek. "Leave it up," he suggests with a smirk.

Arching a brow, I stare up at him. "Because you need an excuse to kiss me?"

He ponders my teasing for a moment. "Well, no, but surprising you like that garnered me a very positive reaction from you."

I'm just about to respond when there's a knock on the

door. I pull free from Greyston's arms and cross the room, pulling the door open to find Gemma, hair perfectly straight and pulled over her right shoulder, and a man almost a foot taller than her. He's built like Toby, thick and muscular. It's obvious he works out—maybe even a little too much.

"Hi," I greet with a smile, holding my hand out toward him. "I'm Juliette. Greyston's girlfriend."

Dom returns my smile and takes my outstretched hand. "It's nice to meet you." He looks past me to Greyston and shakes his hand next. "Gem's told me so much about you."

A cold breeze slips past us, making me shiver. "Please, come in," I tell them, ushering them inside. "Let me take your jackets. Greyston, why don't you offer our guests some wine?"

While I hang the thick winter jackets in the main closet, Greyston shows them to the living room before he heads to the kitchen and pours the wine. I join him, helping him carry the glasses to our guests, and we sit on the loveseat across from them and engage in conversation while our dinner finishes up.

"So, Gem tells me this is your first time in the mountains?" Dom asks me.

I sip my wine and nod. "It is. It's pretty amazing, too. Cold, sure, but a truly wonderful experience." I look at Greyston as he settles his hand on my knee. "Unforgettable, really."

Greyston leans over and presses his lips to mine. When I glance back at our guests, I notice Gemma has looked away and is taking a large pull from her glass.

The timer on the oven goes off, so Greyston and I excuse ourselves to make the final preparations on dinner. While he carves the roast, I butter and season the vegetables and mash the potatoes. I make a quick gravy, and Greyston sets the table before calling Dom and Gemma to join us.

As we sit around the table, Dom talks about his job as a personal trainer. Turns out, he and Gemma met at the gym; he was her trainer during her off-season. They'd been seeing each other for just over a year when he proposed, and they tell us that the rest is history.

After dinner, Greyston offers up a chocolate cream pie and coffee with Bailey's for dessert, and we head back to the living room to enjoy it. About halfway through our dessert, Dom's cell phone rings, and he excuses himself to take the call, grabbing his jacket and stepping out onto the front porch for some privacy. The three of us carry on our conversation, Greyston telling Gemma how this might be his last time staying in the cabin because his parents are planning to sell. She seems sad to hear this, but is quick to offer up alternative solutions for him to keep vacationing out here.

Even with the fire roaring, I notice Gemma shiver when she sets her plate on the coffee table. "Cold?" I ask, confused, because I'm quite warm, and no one else has complained. Though, her shirt is a little on the lighter side while I'm wearing a sweater, so that could have something to do with it.

"Freezing."

Feeling generous, I set my coffee down and stand up. "I'll go grab you a sweater," I offer.

"Oh, Juliette, that's not necces—"

"Nonsense. I'll be right back."

As I ascend the stairs, I hear Gemma exclaim, "Oh my God! I remember this!"

Greyston's voice is barely audible, but I catch a few words and deduce they must be looking at one of the photos on the mantle. A flare of jealousy fills my belly again. I don't like that they have a history, regardless of how much he reassures me that it was just that: history.

Laughing at myself, I shake off the feeling, because Greyston isn't Ben. He'd never do anything to intentionally hurt me, and I know it's just my past insecurities that are making me question everything.

I grab a sweater from my suitcase and head back downstairs to rejoin the dinner party, but as I hit the bottom stair, I stop dead in my tracks and watch Gemma press her lips to Greyston's. I'm about to make my presence known when Greyston pushes Gemma away from him, eyes narrowed, cheeks flushed, and chest heaving.

"What the hell are you doing?" he demands.

It takes me a moment to fully realize what I just walked

in on, and it isn't until Greyston asks her what the hell she thinks she's doing that I fully comprehend.

Every fear I felt before came rushing back, slamming into me like a tidal wave and pulling me under. I struggled against the riptide of emotions, trying to see through it all clearly in order to act rationally.

"Juliette," Greyston says, his eyes wide with panic when he sees me standing there. I only glance at him for a second before I hone my icy glare on Gemma as she turns to face me.

"Oh, hey," she says innocently, as though she wasn't just making a move on *my* boyfriend while her fiancé is outside. She approaches me, eyes darting around nervously as she tucks her hair behind her ear. "Great sweater. I bet that blue looks killer on you and brings out your eyes." She reaches for it, but I yank it from her reach just as the front door opens.

"You need to leave," I tell her through gritted teeth. "Now."

"Gem?" Dom says from the doorway.

I ignore him as he enters the house after his phone call, instead holding Gemma's gaze and refusing to back down. Eventually, she laughs lightly, trying to brush off what I walked in on as nothing. "Juliette," she says in a light and airy voice. "We were just joking around. There was mistle-toe..."

Greyston moves around her and stands next to me. "Baby, let me explain."

I close my eyes and shake my head in response to him, then look at Gemma again. "I told you to get out. If you don't leave on your own, I have no problem removing you by whatever force necessary."

"What the hell happened in here?" Dom asks, finally making me aware of his presence.

"Maybe you should ask your fiancée," I tell him, crossing my arms.

He must not need an explanation, because the way he groans tells me he's figured it out on his own. "Jesus, Gem. *Again?* I can't keep doing this with you. I'm done."

This seems to sober Gemma, and she whips her face toward Dom before running to him. "Dom, babe. It's not what you think. I've had too much to drink." He shakes his head and opens the front door while she yanks on her jacket and boots and chases him into the cold, leaving Greyston and I alone.

Silence fills the room, the tension so thick not even a knife could cut through it. Greyston reaches for me, his fingers brushing my jawline as he tries to coax my eyes to his. There's so much going through my head right now, and I'm not even sure where to begin or how to process everything. Greyston looks at me, his eyes trying to gauge my reaction to everything. His eyebrows furrow in frustration before he opens his mouth to speak.

But I turn tail and head back upstairs, needing a moment to myself.

Greyston refuses to let this happen, and he runs up the stairs after me, following me into the bedroom. "Juliette, please. Let me explain."

I sigh heavily, shoving the sweater back in my suitcase, and I force a smile to my face. "There's nothing to explain, Greyston."

His fingers wrap around my upper arm, and he turns me to face him. "We need to talk about this."

Anger I didn't even know I was holding back surges forward, burning through my veins like lava.

The truth is, I'm hurt. In addition to being hurt, I'm also a little…confused. Oh, and pissed off. Let's not forget that one. I'm not necessarily pissed off at Greyston, because he did push her away from him. Have I not had to deal with enough in the last couple months? I mean, really. First, all that shit with Ben, and now this? What next?

Wait…scratch that. I don't think that tempting fate by asking that question is a good idea right now; I'll deal with one life problem at a time, thank you very much.

I hate her. No, really; I fucking *hate* Gemma.

I'm not a person who generally doles out a lot of hate because it just wastes too much energy, and, honestly, life is just too damn short for it. Sure, I dislike people—Ben and Delilah, for example—but I don't see the point in hating anyone. Or, I didn't until I saw Gemma make a move on Greyston.

I thought how I felt when I first learned of their tryst was the most jealous I would ever feel, but when I watched Gemma kiss my boyfriend…well, let's just say that was the twist that would keep the wound open for a while longer.

"What do you want me to say, Greyston? I told you so? I knew she was trouble from the minute I saw her with her arms around you?" I laugh, but it's dry and without humor. "I let it go because you told me it was all history."

"It is," he assures me, and I believe him—I do.

"Not for her."

"But it is for me, and that's all that should matter." He pushes his fingers roughly through his cropped hair. "She kissed me. I pushed her away the second her lips touched mine."

Bile and alcohol roll in my stomach from imagining Gemma with her lips on Greyston's. I close my eyes and count to ten.

"What are you thinking about?" Greyston asks, his voice nervous and unsteady.

I open my eyes to find him leaning against the dresser, eyes on me, brows pulled up and in. I can see how sorry he is, but my anger refuses to be appeased by that.

"I hate that I dismissed my gut feelings about her. But I told myself it was just my experience with Ben and Delilah that made me anxious about her hanging around so much."

Greyston sighs. "I know." He drops his gaze to his feet. "And you were right to not trust her. I should've seen it."

"Yes," I tell him harshly. "You should have. So why didn't you?"

I've barely finished asking my question before he reacts, his eyes blazing. "Because I'm so fucking in love with you, other women don't even register on my radar!" he shouts, startling me a little…until I fully register what he's told me.

chapter 33

"Wh-what?"

Greyston swallows thickly, pushing off the dresser and standing inches away from me. He's looking down at me, his eyes confirming what he just said. "I've known it for a while, but after everything you've been through, I didn't want to pressure you to have to say it back…unless you wanted to." Another pause. He rubs the back of his neck. "When we entered this relationship, you were a completely different person—nervous, and a little bit of a flight risk." I laugh, knowing he's absolutely right. "But in such a short amount of time, you've become this incredibly strong and confident woman, and watching this transformation made me fall hard and fast."

"You…love me?"

Greyston smiles, the corners of his eyes creasing. "I do. I love you more than I ever thought possible in such a short amount of time."

Everything that happened with Gemma instantly moves to the back burner; it's not gone, but it's no longer that important. Yes, we still need to talk about it, but first I need to acknowledge Greyston's confession with one of my own.

"I love you, too," I tell him, placing my hands on his chest. "Walking in on you tonight, and seeing you push her away from you felt like a kick to the gut. But you know what I realized?"

"What's that?"

"I didn't feel that when I caught Ben and Delilah. Sure, I was pissed, but more than anything? I was relieved." Greyston lifts one of my hands to his lips and kisses my knuckles. "I never loved him, even though I said I did. But you? You've been through more with me in the last few weeks than any boy has ever been, and it's brought us closer." Greyston moves to pull me closer, but I stop him. "This doesn't mean I'm not still angry, and we still have a lot to work through, but I believe you when you say you were blind to her intentions."

His hands cradle my face, and he rests his forehead to mine. "So blind. I only have eyes for you, baby."

This makes me smile, and my hands fall to his hips. "So, I guess this is our first fight, huh?"

Greyston nods, laughing lightly. "I would say so—though it's a pretty mild fight."

I bite my lower lip gently, looking up into his eyes and shrugging my right shoulder. "So does this mean I'm about to experience what make-up sex is like?"

In seconds, our fingers claw desperately at buttons and hems, our hands paw at newly exposed naked flesh, and Greyston pulls me into his arms and kisses me hard.

I accept, winding my arms around his neck and pulling him closer, my tongue tracing the line of Greyston's lips before deepening our kiss. His hands move down over my hips with purpose, slipping behind my jeans and grabbing my ass and lifting me up. He drops me onto the bed before joining me, and I snake my arm between us and into his pants, gripping his hard cock.

"Ah, *fuck*," he moans against my lips as I move my hand, tightening my grip slightly and repeating the action. Instinctively, he thrusts his hips into my palm while his hands move up under my shirt. It doesn't take long before we're scrambling to remove each other's clothes, and soon he's nudging himself between my legs and entering me. Without a condom.

The instant he's fully sheathed in me, he lowers himself until our bodies are completely pressed together, all air expelled from between us until we can feel one another's heartbeats, and he holds most of his weight off of me by balancing on his forearms.

As our hips roll together, seeking the pinnacle of ecstasy, Greyston attempts to slow our lovemaking. Maybe he's trying to show me how much he loves me, but I'm having none of it. Using all my strength, I roll us over, taking my place above him and setting our pace. I know that watching me ride him has always been Greyston's favorite, and I can tell he's already struggling to hold on. Desperate to chase the orgasm that's building rapidly, I move my hips up and down, back and forth, and around in sensual circles while my fingers curl against Greyston's chest, fingernails biting gently into his skin.

Every muscle in my body tenses, and the surface of my skin tingles from head to toe, my fingers going numb, as I teeter on the edge of losing control. Greyston's hands fly to my hips, curling around them and pulling me harder against him. Unable to hold back any longer, I cry out as my lower body tightens around Greyston, coaxing his own orgasm from him before collapsing on his chest, panting heavily.

We lay like this long enough that I get to feel his quickened heartbeat slow to its normal pace once more. His hand moves up and down my spine slowly as my eyes fall closed, contentedness blanketing the both of us.

"What are you thinking about?" I ask, shifting my head until my chin rests on my sternum.

He tilts his head to look at me and smirks. "Nothing really, just basking in the moment. You?"

"I'm going to miss Whistler," I confess. "I'm going to miss the cabin, and it makes me sad that we'll never get to come back here. We've built a few memories here, and I'm sad we won't be making more in the vacation home you grew up in." I pause, biting my lip lightly.

Greyston doesn't answer, but I feel his heart flutter briefly before it returns to normal. "What if we didn't have to say goodbye," he whispers, drawing curiosity from me.

"What do you mean?"

He smiles, lifting his hands to my face and pushing my hair back before cradling my jaw, his thumbs moving idly over my cheekbones. "What if I bought the cabin from my parents? For us."

I inhale sharply, stunned by this offer…but also a little insulted. It reminds me of how Ben used to approach a half-assed reconciliation.

Slowly, I slide off his body, sitting up and grabbing the blanket to cover my nakedness. Does he think that buying me an elaborate gift will make up for this? Does he think I'll just let it go?

"What?" He looks worried at my lack of reaction and he sits up, too.

"Are you trying to buy your way out of this entire thing? Like, you know how upset I am, and you figure that throwing a little bit of money at the problem will just make it go away?"

"That's what you think?" he asks, seeming quite stunned that this is how I've taken his offer. "Juliette, that's not what I meant at all. I'm sorry." He sounds sincere, and I appreciate it, because he must realize just how insulting something like that is. "I didn't even realize that's how you might take it."

Embarrassed, I shake my head. "It's fine. I should have known you better than that. Forget it…"

"Hey," he interjects. "*Never* feel like you can't talk to me about whatever's bothering you. Even if you think it might hurt my feelings. You mean everything to me, and I'm sorry if I made you question my motives. I'll do better."

With everything being aired out between the two of us, I'm starting to feel better—not a hundred percent, but I think in time I could be there.

"I'm still upset, and I don't know that it'll go away any time soon," I blurt out.

"Of course you are," he offers quietly. "That's completely understandable."

"I wish I could say that this will be easy for me, given I've been through something similar," I continue. "I want to trust you—no, I *do* trust you—but all I see whenever I close my eyes is her lips on yours… I don't know how to process it all." Greyston's hand reaches out to touch my arm, but he hesitates halfway before pulling it back and running it through his hair instead. "I know you're not Ben, and I believe you when you say you love me, but, after what happened with him?" I sigh heavily, trying to gather my thoughts enough to stop my rambling. "I'm scared, Greyston. Scared I'm just...not enough for you."

"Baby," he says softly, this time reaching out for me and taking my hand in his. I can't help it anymore; I turn to look at him, and his eyes are red-rimmed and glistening. "What are you talking about? How can you possibly think you're not enough for me? You're *everything* to me."

"I don't—I don't know..."

"Just tell me what to do to fix this," he pleads, sounding desperate, his hands moving up and down my arm like he's afraid I'm going to take off and this is the only way to stay tethered to me.

I shrug, my chin wavering, and I speak before really even realizing what it is I want to say to him. "I hate her." It doesn't have anything to do with his request, but now that it's out there, I don't regret feeling it or even saying it. "Gemma," I clarify, and Greyston nods as though he already knew that.

"I can understand that."

I shake my head and continue speaking, the words coming out faster than I expect. "No, I don't think you do. I don't *hate* people, Greyston. It's just not who I am. But Gemma? I fucking loathe her. I hate that she waltzed back into your life and disrupted it. I hate that she knows things about you that I have yet to learn. And most of all? I hate that I disregarded my suspicions so soon after meeting her."

An awkward pause fills the room as my last confession dangles in the air between us. My heart begins to pound, and I continue with my rambling. "I despise the idea that your agency represents her. You'll always be tied to her, going on the occasional business trip to do...whatever it is you do as her agent."

"Okay," he says, and I stop talking, confused and curious.

"Okay, what?"

"You're right," he replies. "It's not fair to you. Any of it."

He falls silent for a minute, locking eyes with me. "I'm done."

His offer shocks me, and my mouth opens and closes several times before I'm finally able to utter, "Wh-what do you mean you're *done*? Greyston, I didn't mean—"

"I'll hand her account off to Toby," he clarifies for me. "She's signed to the agency, not to me specifically. I don't want you to ever wonder…not that there'd be anything going on…" His words hang there for a minute while he takes a deep breath. "And besides, if the situation were reversed, I know damn well I wouldn't like the idea of you being alone with Ben for a school or business-related reason."

"Greyston, I can't ask you to do that," I argue, even though the second the offer is voiced, it's all I seem to want. I'm fully aware that I'm being unreasonable, yet I'm grateful he volunteered so quickly. It's all very confusing.

"You're not asking, sweetheart. I'm telling you I'm done with her. She crossed a line, and I wouldn't feel right representing her anymore, either." I continue to stare at him, bewildered, and he offers me a comforting smile.

"Greyston—"

"I know you didn't bank on any of this happening—neither of us did—and I'm sorry for that." He cradles my face in his left hand, eyes narrowing as he tries to read my expression. "What is it?"

"I sound like a self-entitled brat."

Greyston smiles. "No," he says, his thumb stroking my cheek once before pulling his hand away. "It makes you sound human, and I can't fault you for feeling this way."

A part of me wants to tell him that none of this is necessary, that I'm capable of acting like a mature adult while he continues to represent Gemma, but I can't. "Thank you," is my response instead, and I'm more than happy with it.

I'm letting the selfish twenty-year-old have her way this time, and I don't care what anyone thinks.

chapter 34

Greyston made good on his promise, telling Toby that he would have to handle all of Gemma's endorsement deals for the foreseeable future. Greyston said that they were both shocked to hear what Gemma had done, and I kind of developed a little girl crush on Callie when I learned that Toby had to restrain her before she could hop in her car and hunt Gemma down.

Okay, so it was more than just a little crush; had I been there, I probably would have kissed her.

The months seem to fly by. Maybe it's because I've been gearing up for finals and Greyston's been busy with work. However, even with all of the crazy in our lives, we still make time for each other. We'll always try to plan a quiet dinner together, and if we can't for some reason, we'll be sure to set aside a couple hours before bed where we turn off all phones, computers, and TVs so we can sit and enjoy each other's company before going to bed. Plus, we're still sure to keep a weekly date night ritual, which is always great.

This week's regular date has been postponed for Callie and Toby's wedding, and I am currently seated in one of the two hundred satin-draped chairs in the rented banquet hall. After arriving, Greyston left me with his parents, kissing me on the cheek and telling me he had to go uphold his best man duties. We find our seats, third row from the front as the first two rows were designated for family—turns out, both Callie and Toby come from pretty big families.

Smoothing the lines of my knee-length sapphire blue dress, I look around the room and take in all of the little details. Almost every chair in the room is filled, and I can feel the love that fills the air. Everything is tasteful from the paper lanterns and twinkle lights that hang from the ceiling, to the light blue and purple bows tied around the chairs, and the white rose buds nestled in them.

There's a string quartet up near the archway that Callie and Toby will be married under, and they've been playing since before Greyston and I even arrived. Everything about the wedding is absolutely beautiful, and has me wondering what my wedding—way *way* in the future—will be like. Will it be this big? Will we choose to elope? Vegas or somewhere in the Caribbean, perhaps? Maybe we'll go down to city hall with just our parents and have something super small and intimate.

Nah. We probably won't do that last one. That just feels wrong.

I laugh quietly to myself, because the fact that I've got this going through my head is a little silly. I mean, Greyston hasn't even proposed, and here I am, at someone else's wedding, wondering about my own, even though it's years away from happening. Is that normal?

As I'm looking around the room some more, trying to catch another glimpse of Greyston in his sexy tux, I spot Xander entering with a certain five-foot-tall, dark-haired co-ed on his arm. I wave at them from my aisle seat, and they make their way over, sitting in the two empty seats next to Daniel.

"Hey," I greet happily. "How've you guys been?"

Now that school is out, Daphne and I haven't seen too much of each other in the last two weeks. We talk and text all the time, but I'd been so busy trying to fit in as much quality time with my parents, Greyston's parents, and—of course—Greyston, that we'd been unable to coordinate a proper girls' day.

Not to mention, Daphne had been spending a lot of her spare time with Xander. A lot.

"Everything's good," Daphne replies in a chipper voice.

We sit and visit for a few more minutes before the music

changes, and a hush falls over the crowd. One look behind me tells me we're getting started as Toby starts to make his way down the aisle. Once he's in place, the white-curtained French doors behind the seated crowd opens, and each groomsman steps out with a stunning bridesmaid, dressed in a flowing lavender gown, on their arm.

The blonde on Greyston's arm momentarily brings out my inner green-eyed monster, but when I notice his eyes are locked on me, and he smiles *my* smile, I relax and wink at him. He chuckles lightly as he passes, and Josephine reaches across and pats my shoulder.

When the bridal party has reached their destination at the altar, Toby's adorable five-year-old twin cousins emerge. The little girl is dressed in an adorable knee-length white dress, a blue satin bow tied around her ribs, and the little boy is dressed in a smaller version of the guys' tuxes. They're so cute, and it makes me wonder about our wedding again—there must be something in the air. Will we wait that long to get married?

The music shifts into the traditional wedding march, and all of the guests stand up, turning toward the French doors where Callie enters, her parents on either side of her as they make their way down the aisle.

The ceremony is beautiful, and I find myself unexpectedly emotional when they exchange their vows. I never cry at weddings, and here I am, trying not to snot-sob all over my new dress. Apparently falling in love has turned me into a bit of a sap—not that I'm complaining.

After the ceremony, Callie and Toby have a photo session lined up while the staff and her wedding planner transform the room into a banquet hall for dinner. I hang out with Daphne, Xander, and Greyston's parents and watch as the wedding party is photographed. The minute he announces that the groomsmen and bridesmaids are free to go, Greyston finds his way to me, pulling me into his arms and kissing me softly.

"Hello, handsome," I greet, pretending to straighten his already-perfect blue tie.

He smiles. "Hello, yourself, gorgeous." His hands grip

my hips, his thumbs running over the smooth fabric of my dress, and he lowers his head, his lips brushing my ear. "I still can't get over how amazing you look in this dress. It's taking everything I have in me not to drag you back to the car and do ungodly things to your body."

A shiver rocks through my body and goosebumps race across my skin despite the dry, summer heat. "That sounds kind of hot," I whisper, trying to keep from laughing. "Especially with the weather the way it is. I can't imagine it would be too comfortable. It's going to be like an oven in there."

Laughing, Greyston kisses my neck once more and stands up straight, looking me in the eye. "All right, well if you have any better ideas…"

I smile coyly. "There's a pretty cozy-looking back room inside." The look on his face tells me he's seriously considering this, and while I would have absolutely no objections, given how unbelievable he looks in his tux, I shake my head. "Easy, stud. If we escape now, we're bound to get caught, and I doubt Callie would be too forgiving."

"You're right," he acquiesces. "Well, will you at least join me for a walk? We've got a bit of time to kill before the reception."

"I would love that."

For the next hour and a bit, Greyston and I walk hand-in-hand around the hall. There's a little park nearby where a few of the kids from the wedding are playing, and Greyston and I stop there. I flop down onto an available swing, and Greyston proceeds to push me. I'm pretty sure he's purposefully grabbing my ass every time he goes to push, but when I call him on it, he feigns innocence.

A squeal of delight catches my attention, and I see Toby's twin cousins come running over with their parents hot on their trails. The dark-haired boy heads straight for the jungle gym, his mother yelling after him to be careful to not get dirty, while the little girl stops a few feet from the swings, the look on her face falling when she realizes they're all full.

I drag my feet in the sand, stopping the swing and hopping off. When she sees me offering it to her, her smile returns, and she bolts toward me. "Thank you!" she exclaims, hopping onto the seat and holding on. "Will you push me?"

"Jilly," her mother says sternly.

"Please," Jilly amends apologetically. "Will you push me, *please*?"

I look to where her mother stands, and she smiles, nodding, and I grip the chains at Jilly's hips. "I would love to."

Greyston stays nearby while I push Jilly on the swings. She's absolutely loving it, laughing and squealing happily as her dark brown curls fly out behind her. "Higher! Higher!" she requests, and I oblige only too willingly.

When her mother tells her and her brother, Justin, that it's time to head back, she isn't shy about letting the world know she's disappointed. In an effort to save her mother the temper tantrum, I lean down to her level and say, "You know, I'm a friend of Toby and Callie's, too. Maybe you and I could play later. What do you say?"

This seems to make her happy, and she throws her arms around my neck unexpectedly before chasing after her parents and brother. When I stand up, Greyston takes my hand and he draws it up to his lips. "You were really sweet with her."

We head back to the hall, and when we walk in, the place is almost unrecognizable. The chairs now surround tables that weren't there before, and new lights and drapery adorn the tables and walls. It's so whimsical and romantic.

It's no surprise that the dinner is as elegant as it is delicious, and the wine is amazing—maybe even more-so since I'm very newly twenty-one and can legally drink it now. I raise my hand to the diamond necklace Greyston gave me that gorgeous day in February and smile fondly. He'd gone above and beyond to make my twenty-first birthday special.

We'd begun our day with a morning swim before getting ready for the birthday dinner he had planned. Our parents and friends had come over to enjoy a delicious meal and cake. Then came presents—even though I told everyone that they weren't necessary. Mom and Dad got me a new laptop for school after hearing that mine was out of commission—I chose to leave the rest of the story about how I found out it was broken out of the conversation, naturally. Daphne took me for lunch and shopping a few days later, and she helped me pick out the dress I'm wearing now. Greyston's parents bought Greyston and I tickets to Vegas. I know. It was extravagant and generous, and while I felt like it was too much, I admit, I'm excited for us to go in just a few weeks.

Then there was Greyston. He'd actually given me my necklace that morning. He said he just couldn't wait the rest of the day—he's not usually so impatient. The large square-cut stone is set in a white gold setting and hangs from a thin chain, falling delicately in the hollow of my throat. It's the most beautiful piece of jewelry I own, and I wear it every chance I get.

When dinner concludes, the dance begins. Callie and Toby look so undeniably in love as they dance around the floor, and it stuns me how light Toby is on his feet, because he just doesn't strike me as the ballroom dancing type.

Soon enough, the dance floor is full, and I think Greyston is about to ask me to dance when I feel a tiny hand wrap around my wrist. Looking over, I see the big brown eyes of one Miss Jilly. She's got the biggest smile on her face, and it's hard not to mirror her expression.

"Hi, there," I say, leaning over.

"Will you come dance with me?" she asks sweetly.

I look over at Greyston, who's grinning broadly, and he nods. "You don't mind?" I inquire.

I can tell by the gleam in his eyes that he doesn't, but I just want to be sure. In fact, not only does he seem to not mind, he seems amazed and full of admiration and wonder. Jilly leads me to the dance floor, and soon her brother and several other children join us. We're dancing away—and I use the term loosely, because none of us are really *dancing*. I don't know how long we're on the floor for, but several other kids and adults have joined us including Callie, Daphne, Toby, and Xander. I look around, wondering where Greyston is, when I feel his arms around my waist and his lips next to my ear.

"Mind if I steal you away for a minute?" he asks, and I nod.

I tell Jilly I'll see her later, but she's having so much fun that she doesn't seem to notice. I leave the group, Greyston taking my hand and pulling me from the dance floor and toward the main entry. It doesn't surprise me that he turns right instead of left, pulling me into the back room I mentioned earlier, because I sensed the heavy sexual undertones in his request a moment ago.

The second the door is closed, Greyston leans me against it, pressing his body to mine until not even a whisper of air can be found between us. The warmth of his lips as they kiss their way up the column of my throat makes me moan, and I twist my fingers into his recently-cut hair to draw his mouth to mine. Our kiss deepens quickly, the passion in the room thick, and his hands start to roam over the soft blue fabric of my dress until he's palming my breasts. His fingertips curl just over the plunging neckline until they brush my skin, and I arch into his touch.

Frantically, I begin to force his tux jacket over his shoulders, and he breaks contact with my chest only long enough to remove the jacket, tossing it on a nearby chair. His right hand finds my breast again, while his left one wanders down the length of my body and grabs my knee. He hitches it up over his hip until I can feel how aroused he is. Excitement shoots through my body, manifesting itself as a dull hum beneath my skin that seems to be most concentrated in my right thigh—the one that's currently wrapped around Greyston's body.

It isn't until the sensation stops and then starts again moments later that Greyston pulls his face from mine and chuckles. "I think you're thigh's vibrating," he teases, letting my leg fall back to the floor as he reaches for my hip and gently tugs on the pocket of my dress.

My phone. Of course.

Still breathing heavily, I grab my phone from my pocket—the biggest selling feature of the dress—and notice that it's my mom. Before she gets put through to my voicemail, I answer it. "Hello? Mom?"

"Oh, good!" she exclaims, sounding just as breathless as I am...which leads me to a horrifying conclusion that makes me shudder. "I didn't think I'd get you, what with the two of youuuuuu…" It startles me when she stops mid sentence, dragging the word "you" out and having it escalate into a cry of severe discomfort.

"Mom?" I demand, feeling my forehead pull up with worry. "What's going on?"

She takes several deep breaths, releasing them slowly, and in the background I can hear my father talking her through whatever's going on. Before I can inquire further, she says, "We're headed to the hospital, sweetheart. I was just going to leave a message since we knew you were at the wedding."

"Ohmygod!" I exclaim, looking at Greyston as my mouth turns up into a wide smile. When his own look of worry transforms into a knowing smile, he reaches for the doorknob behind me. "We're on our way."

"Oh, no," she says calmly. "Don't worry about that. We can see you tomorrow, honey."

"Don't be ridiculous! We'll be there as soon as we can." I hang up the phone just as Mom goes into another horrifically painful-sounding contraction, and Greyston and I head off to find Toby and Callie. They're with Greyston's parents, so we're able to them all at once before we leave the reception hall and drive to the hospital.

After finding a parking spot, Greyston and I rush into the hospital hand-in-hand. The woman at the main desk directs us to the maternity floor. Greyston and I wait a ridiculously long time for the elevator to arrive, and an even longer amount of time for it to reach the third floor. Okay, so it's probably a completely reasonable amount of time, but my excitement seems to be drawing everything out a little longer than normal.

As soon as we're off the elevator, we speed-walk down the hall toward the nurses' station, passing a few women walking around in hospital gowns, their significant others at their sides and rubbing their backs when they keel over in what looks like an excruciating contraction.

"I'm looking for Anne and Cam Foster," I announce to the nurse behind the desk, drawing her attention from the computer to me.

She offers me a bright smile. "You must be Juliette. Your parents are expecting you and asked me to send you both right in when you arrived. They're in room 305."

Not wanting to waste another second, Greyston and I scoot down the hall and open the door marked 305. It would figure the scene we walk in on isn't completely expected, especially considering I tend to have the worst timing on the planet when it comes to visiting my parents. Apparently having a baby doesn't change this.

"Oh, god!" I cry out, grinding to a halt just inside the door as I take in the scene in front of me: Mom is sitting on an incline on the bed with her legs up in the stirrups as the man I assume is her doctor and my father are investigating what's going on down in ladytown.

Greyston slams into my back, pushing me forward another step. When he registers what's going on, I immediately turn around, pushing on his chest and trying to cover his eyes. I know it's already too late, though. You can't unsee that shit. Trust me. I know.

"We'll, uh, be outside," I stammer, shutting the door behind us and pressing my forehead to the cool hospital wall. "That was…" I shudder before turning to look at Greyston, whose eyes are so wide he resembles a deer in headlights. I laugh, because it is kind of funny now—horrifying, yes, but still a little funny. "I'm so sorry."

He blinks a couple times, shaking his head, possibly in an attempt to shake the memory of my mother's vag from his brain. It won't be that easy, believe me. "It's…" He clears his throat and smooths his dress shirt, pretending to be unaffected. Yeah, right. "I'm fine. That was nothing."

I don't have the heart to call him on it. He has every right to try to repress that, so I nod in agreement. Before I can suggest we go to the waiting room, the door opens and the doctor steps out, smiling.

"Sorry about that," he apologizes. "Your mother is asking for you." He must sense our unease, because he laughs gently. "It's safe, I assure you."

Slowly, Greyston and I make our way to the door and push it open. As the doctor said, she's completely covered up.

Dad is next to her, holding her hand and talking to her, his forehead pressed to hers and their eyes closed. It's an innocently intimate moment, and it tugs at my heartstrings. One thing I've come to appreciate over the years is how undeniably in love my parents are after over two decades together. Sure, that comes with a few less than awesome memories of the two of them caught in the heat of the moment, but I'll gladly take the mental hit several times for witnessing just one moment like this.

The door clicks softly, drawing my parents' eyes to us, and they both smile infectiously. I cross the room and throw my arms around my mom, her tears of happiness dripping onto my bare shoulder. "Oh, I'm so glad you're both here!" she exclaims. "Sorry about what you walked in on."

I laugh, feeling my own tears of happiness stinging my eyes. "That's okay," I assure her, pushing her hair from her slightly damp forehead. "It's surprisingly not the worst thing I've walked in on the two of you doing."

Yeah, I can joke about it a little now. Just a little, though.

Dad snickers. "I didn't think this would be all that fascinating," he admits, confusing me. "Well, when you were born, it was rare that a father was in the room. I didn't know about half the stuff that goes on. Then there were the books…"

"Books?" I question, knowing my shock is plainly written all over my face. "You read pregnancy books?"

"It's all very fascinating," he says, flooring me further. "Makes me regret not forcing my way into the delivery room when you were born."

This conversation is both sweet and awkward, but I focus on the sweet.

Greyston and I stay with Mom and Dad a bit longer, long enough to witness several contractions. I ask my mom why she's chosen not to take the epidural, but she's a proud woman who "did this once before without drugs, and she'll do it again."

Personally, I'm getting the drugs when I'm in this position. You bet. No ifs, ands, or buts about it.

The doctor comes in, and Greyston and I step out again,

not needing to have a repeat moment of when we'd first arrived. This time, when he emerges, he directs us to the waiting room, telling us it's time for my mom to have a baby. I'm nervous, excited, and just a little bit scared. I'm once again reminded of her age and how there are more risks involved. It's all I can think about as I pace nervously in the waiting room.

Greyston must sense my distress, because he grabs my hand and pulls me onto his lap, holding me close and kissing my temple. I rest the side of my head against his forehead and let his whispers of reassurance wash through me as he runs his hand up and down my back. Soon, my apprehension begins to subside. When I look up at the clock, I see that almost two hours have gone by, and when I drop my eyes from the time, my father is walking into the waiting room with a tiny pink bundle cradled in his arms.

I pull myself off of Greyston's lap, my lips curling up into an exultant smile as I slowly cross the waiting room to my dad. There's a tiny movement beneath the pink blanket, and an even tinier squeak as I reach out and pull the blanket away from her cheek to have a better look. Greyston places a hand on my shoulder, and I look up at my dad expectantly.

"Juliette, meet your baby sister, Clara."

Carefully, he leans forward, and I instinctively hold my arms out to accept her. I'm nervous, sure, but more than that, I'm excited. I can't get over how small she is, and my emotions get the best of me. I don't cry, but I definitely swallow a lump in my throat. Completely awestruck by this itty-bitty human in my arms, I take in her features. From the dark tuft of hair that peeks out from beneath the knitted pink beanie on her head, to her long eyelashes and button nose, and right on down to her pouty lips that are moving in a suckling motion while she sleeps. She's absolutely precious.

I haven't stopped smiling since Dad arrived with her, and when Greyston leans in and kisses my cheek, wrapping his arms around my waist, I relax into his embrace.

Dad explains that Mom's doing great and that the doctor is just in there stitching her up—a very sobering comment that quickly disappears when Clara wriggles in my arms again. I sigh contentedly, and Greyston kisses the shell of my ear, his lips curling up into a smile against it before he whispers, "Seeing you holding a baby is probably one of the sexiest things I've ever seen."

Still grinning, I turn my face to him. "Just wait until it's our child." I can't believe my lack of filter, and I'm prepared to backpedal as Dad takes Clara from me and excuses himself to go see Mom, but Greyston surprises me.

"Marry me, Juliette."

epilogue

Announcing the celebration
of our love when we,
Juliette Foster
and
Greyston Masters
pledge our love as one
on Saturday, the 19th of November

A fresh new day, and it's ours.
A Day of happy beginnings.

The Camby Hotel
Phoenix, Arizona

I stare at the ad we placed in the paper for a few minutes. We both knew it was old-fashioned, but considering how we met, we also felt it was kind of perfect.

My hands shake with nervous anticipation as I set the paper down on the table. I can't believe the day is actually here. The last year and a half has been busy with wedding planning while I finished my final year of University and Greyston traveled more for work. His increase in work wasn't exactly ideal, but he still helped from afar, and he was so into making this day about the both of us.

That's not to say I didn't have a few bridezilla moments. I did. But he was super understanding and was always able to talk me off the ledge in his own special way. Our FaceTime chats were my favorite.

Music plays down the hall—the band that Greyston's parents insisted we hire for the processional. It was one of the many extravagant pieces to our wedding.

I look around the small room I'm in and smile. Daphne is in the corner with Callie, helping pin her blonde hair off to one side. Callie laughs at something Daphne said while rubbing her belly. Did I forget to mention Toby and Callie are having a baby? Well, they are, and it's so exciting. She's about five months along, and has the perfect little bump protruding from beneath the satin lilac-colored gown she's wearing.

Katie is sitting with them, sitting casually on the small couch along the wall and sipping champagne. All three of them laugh together, and I smile. Before I met Greyston, my friend pool was…limited. Most of my friends from high school had moved away for college, and we were so busy with school and our lives, that we simply fell out of touch. But these three? They were there for me through everything. Daphne and Katie were my rocks through my breakup with Ben, and I bonded with Callie instantly. It only made sense to include them on my special day.

"Oh, honey." I turn away from the girls just in time to see my parents and baby sister enter the room. "You look gorgeous," Mom says, pulling me into a one-armed hug while she holds Clara in the other.

When we part, Dad steps forward and wraps his arms around me in a tight hug. My fingers curl into the back of his tux jacket and I close my eyes. I can feel his reluctance to let me grow up in his embrace.

"You look so grown up," he murmurs into the top of my head. "I can't believe you're getting married today. Where's my sweet little girl?"

We loosen our grip on each other, and I take a step back. "I'm still here, Daddy," I assure him softly.

With tears in his eyes, he leans forward and kisses my forehead. "I didn't think I'd be this emotional."

"You and me both," I quip. Taking a deep breath, I run my hands down the front of my diamond white wedding gown. The strapless, sweetheart neckline fits me perfectly, emphasizing my smaller chest and making it look just a little more impressive. The bodice is tight, moving down over my hips and flaring out at the top of my thighs. The skirt is full, the fabric pulled together and pinned with hundreds of little Swarovski crystals to add a little personality.

"Think he'll like it?" I ask my mom, and she just laughs, setting Clara down. Her lilac dress is bunched up from being held, so Mom kneels down to fix the crinoline underlay, and then the dress. It falls to just below her knee, and is held with a darker purple bow around the waist. She looks so precious, toddling toward Daphne when she calls her over.

"He's going to be speechless," Mom assures me with another hug.

She sniffles over my shoulder and pulls back, wiping a tear from her cheek. Seeing her this emotional makes my own eyes sting, but I blink back the tears so I don't mess up my makeup.

Mom reaches up and fixes a wayward tendril of hair that has broken free of the pins holding it over my left shoulder. We share a moment of silence before there's a knock on the door, telling us everyone is ready.

Daphne walks over with Clara in her arms and Callie and Katie beside her. The three of them are beaming, and their happiness for me sets my mind at ease. The shaking in my limbs lessens.

"You guys look beautiful," I tell them.

"Well, it helps that you didn't follow tradition and choose ugly-ass bridesmaid dresses," Callie teases, and we all share a laugh.

I take Clara from Daphne and give her a kiss before handing her off to Mom. "I guess we'll see you out there," I tell her.

She kisses me on the cheek and slips out of the room while the rest of us prepare to move into the hall. When we arrive just outside the double doors, my chest tightens, and my hands begin to sweat. Callie walks through the door when the ushers open it from the inside, then Katie, and finally Daphne.

Now that it's just my dad and me, air seems hard to come by. I struggle to fill my lungs, and my stomach knots up as the room begins to spin. This is it.

Dad reaches out for me, noticing I'm in the middle of a panic attack, and the second he takes my left hand and loops it through his right arm, I feel a little better. Not completely, but I accept the slight reprieve.

"Just breathe, Jules," he whispers, placing his left hand over mine and patting it.

I do as he says, taking a deep breath in and then releasing it. I repeat this a few times, and then hold my breath when the doors swing wide and I'm met with almost two-hundred sets of eyes all on me.

"Breathe," Dad repeats.

Then my eyes find Greyston's, and my panic melts away when his smile stretches across his face. While he wasn't what I was looking for when I answered that ad two years ago, he has been there for me in more ways than I can count. He helped me find myself after being betrayed, and more importantly, he showed me what real love is supposed to be like.

A wave of calm rushes over me, and I step over the threshold anxiously, more than ready to start this next phase in our life together.

HORSE PLAY

a horse play novel ~ book one

I sank into the supple leather saddle, and with a sigh, I was home. We walked around the arena for fifteen minutes to warm her up, and I counted the perfectly spaced beats of her gait. *One. Two. Three. Four.* She wasn't favoring her leg, so I decided we would pick up into a trot. *One. Two. One. Two.* I rose on every other beat, and Hayley flipped her head slightly and snorted with delight. When I felt she was ready, I nudged her forward into a steady lope.

As we cantered around the arena, I kept my seat in the saddle, keeping her going by pushing forward. When we hit the corner, I turned her so we could change direction. She instantly flipped to the opposite lead, the change graceful and seamless. We moved smoothly around the low cross-rail that had been set up for last night's beginner jumper class and continued on.

We made a few more laps around the arena, and as we approached the entry I saw a man with a head of unruly brown hair watching us. I instantly recognized him as the man who had met with Dad this morning. His body was relaxed as he leaned over the top rail of the fence, and his right leg was bent so his foot could rest on the bottom one. He was wearing a pair of jeans and a sleeveless white tank that showed off his muscular physique.

As Hayley and I drew nearer, I took in the deep blue color of his eyes and the way they sparkled like sapphires in the sun. I was instantly mesmerized. We continued to lope around the arena, and when I caught the stranger's gaze again I got lost in his eyes once more. There was something in the way he was watching me that made me smile, and he returned that smile with one that caused a flurry of butterflies to erupt in my belly. Completely distracted by his smirk, I hadn't even realized that Hayley was headed for the small cross-rail just off the trail until we were nearly upon it.

On instinct, I leaned forward in preparation for her to take the jump, but as I did, Hayley stopped…and I kept on going. The ground came up to meet me far too fast, and all I felt was pressure in my head as I landed hard on my back.

ABOUT THE AUTHOR

A.D. Ryan resides in Edmonton, Alberta with her extremely supportive husband and children (two sons and a stepdaughter). Reading and writing have always been a big part of her life, and she hopes that her books will entertain countless others the way that other authors have done for her. Even as a small child, she enjoyed creating new and interesting characters and molding their worlds around them.

To learn more about the author and stay up-to-date on future publications, please look for her on Facebook and her blog.

https://www.facebook.com/pages/AD-Ryan-Author

http://adryanauthorblog.wordpress.com

Sign up for my NEWSLETTER to receive updates & exclusive content!

Made in the USA
Charleston, SC
26 February 2016